The Devouring

A. M. Shilling

Copyright © 2026 by A. M. Shilling

All rights reserved.

No generative artificial intelligence (AI) was used in the writing of this work. The author expressly prohibits any entity from using this publication for purposes of training AI technologies to generate text, including without limitation technologies that are capable of generating works in the same style or genre as this publication. The author reserves all rights to license use of this work for generative AI training and development of machine learning language models.

No part of this publication may be reproduced, distributed, or transmitted in any form or by any means, including photocopying, recording, or other electronic or mechanical methods, without the prior written permission of the publisher, except as permitted by U.S. copyright law. For permission requests, contact amshillingwrites@gmail.com.

The story, all names, characters, and incidents portrayed in this production are fictitious. No identification with actual persons (living or deceased), places, buildings, and products is intended or should be inferred.

Book Cover by A. M. Shilling

ISBN: 979-8-9941886-0-6 (ebook)
ISBN: 979-8-9941886-1-3 (paperback)

To Brendan Ha,
without whom this book would not exist.

This book contains mature content that may be disturbing to some readers. Discretion is advised.

Chapter One

Robert Panzieri opened his bedroom door and came face-to-face with death. Moonlight glinted off the sleek body of the Glock 19 pointed at his chest. Jason's black-gloved fist held the gun steady in the air.

A tense, uneasy silence settled between the men as they stared into the darkness obscuring each other's features. There was no mistaking Robert, however; thin wisps of gray hair crowned his head, and his clothes sloped a particular way across narrow shoulders. Even before he'd opened the door, Jason had recognized his gait as he approached, the weight and rhythm of his footsteps loud against the hardwood floor.

Robert raised his hands, palms facing forward. Light from the corridor behind him spilled around his gaunt frame and stretched toward the corner of a massive bed. "There's no use running, is there?"

"No."

"Is that you, Jason? No—I know it is. You're the only man I've met with the balls to accept a contract on my life. I suppose I should be honored. You were one of the best I ever hired."

Jason said nothing.

Robert twitched to his right.

Two silenced gunshots went off in quick succession. Robert hit the floor with a heavy thud. The sharp scent of gunpowder filled Jason's nose as he crossed the room and stepped around the bed. Robert lay on his stomach, one arm stretched toward the bedside table with the hidden pistol Jason had already removed. The wet, gurgling noise of Robert's death rattle filled the air. His body spasmed as blood oozed from the bullet wounds in his chest and spewed from his mouth.

Jason aimed at Robert's head and killed him with a third, final shot.

Moving with calm efficiency, Jason unscrewed the suppressor from his Glock, pocketed it, and tucked away the gun in the holster hidden at his waist. With his phone, he took several photographs of the corpse and sent them to his client with the encrypted text, *It's done.*

A moment later, he received a response: *Great work. I've transferred the rest of your payment to the account you specified. It's always a pleasure doing business with you, Mr. Ridley.*

Jason turned off the phone, removed the battery, and stowed both away, along with the empty bullet casings that had cooled on the floor. In Robert's massive, walk-in closet, Jason had stored a small, black duffel bag. Keeping his gloves on, he swapped the navy blue overshirt of his maintenance worker disguise for the plain brown bomber jacket in the bag. Then he put on a black, unmarked baseball cap for good measure. Though the penthouse's elevator lacked security cameras, several watched the apartment building's front lobby and the street outside.

With the bag slung over his shoulder, he left the bedroom and started down the hall.

A clear and pleasant chime from the foyer cut through the silence.

The elevator. Someone had arrived.

Without hesitating, Jason backtracked down the hallway and slipped into Robert's bedroom again. He kept the door open ajar, peeking through the crack and straining his ears to hear the newcomer over the wild beating of his own heart.

He'd spent weeks stalking Robert, learning the old man's routine with all its peculiarities. No one else was supposed to be there that night—a sweet spot of solitude in an otherwise packed schedule. An unexpected visitor was a problem, in more ways than one.

"Robert, are you home?" called a high-pitched voice. Melodious. A woman. Her heels clicked on the hardwood as she strode through the apartment. "Robert, this isn't funny. Where are you? Things are getting out of hand. We need to meet with the others and revisit our strategy."

Jason's professionalism demanded his escape. A witness stumbling upon Robert's corpse was less of an issue than them catching him at the scene of the crime. But the penthouse elevator was the only way out, and the woman's footsteps were growing louder. He could kill her, of course. It was a messy solution with unaccounted repercussions—at best, a hassle for both him and his broker, but at worst, a stain on his career.

And besides, there was his pride. He had a reputation to uphold. A man who murdered indiscriminately was no better than a serial killer, unable to control his urges.

That left one last option: threaten the woman into silence.

He drew his gun from its holster and cocked the hammer. Twelve bullets remained. Every muscle in his body tensed with anticipation. He glimpsed the sliver of her as she stepped into the space between the door and its jamb: a young woman with platinum blonde hair and dark business attire. She paused, her gaze falling upon the bedroom door.

"Robert?" she called again, uncertainty creeping into her voice. She moved toward Jason's hiding place.

He emerged from the room, smoothly shutting the door behind him, his Glock pointed at her chest. She jumped and screamed, eyes wide with terror.

"Quiet," he said.

She shut up immediately.

He swept his gaze over her from head to foot, memorizing her features. Tall and slender, she reminded him of a model; he guessed she was in her mid-twenties, the right age for one. Her button-up satin blouse, pencil skirt, and tights were much more conservative than what he expected from one of Robert's late-night visitors. Perhaps business roleplay was her specialty, especially considering her outburst upon entering.

"What's your name?" Jason asked after finishing his assessment.

"S-Sabrina." Instead of looking at him, she stared down the barrel of his gun, every part of her trembling.

"Full name."

"Kopanski. Sabrina Kopanski."

"Why did you come here?"

She didn't answer right away. "Just business."

"What kind of business?"

"Shipping. Robert—his family owns the harbor. The shipyard."

"And I'm supposed to believe that?"

She met his gaze for the first time. "Please. I'm not here for what you think. I swear. I—I shouldn't have come here at all."

"No. You shouldn't have." Jason stepped toward her, forcing her backward down the hall. "Robert's not here tonight, so this is what'll happen: you and I are going to leave here together. We'll exit the building, I'll hail you a cab, and you're going to go straight home. And if you so much as breathe a word of our encounter to anyone, I will find out, and I will kill you. Do I make myself clear?"

Sabrina swallowed. Nodded.

He motioned for her to lead the way. She turned and made a beeline for the elevator. He followed with his gun still drawn. In the close confines of the carriage, he pressed the Glock's muzzle against her back. She flinched at the contact but did not move away.

As they descended to the first floor, Jason expanded on his instructions. "When we leave the elevator, we're going to pretend we're friends who've just left a mutual friend's party because another guest insulted you. I'll be sympathetic to your hurt feelings. When you get into the cab, give the driver your address; I'll wait on the corner and wave goodbye. If you try to run, tell the driver the truth, go to the police, or anything besides what I've told you, I *will* find out."

Sabrina nodded again.

"What kind of comment would insult you?"

"I, um... I can't stand being talked down to."

"Then a man named Ron insulted your intelligence and tried explaining your own career to you, even though he knows nothing about it."

Her blurred reflection in the carriage's metal doors twisted with disgust.

"Perfect," Jason said, his flat tone at odds with his words of praise. "Keep that up."

The elevator slowed to a stop at the first floor. He tucked his gun back into its hidden holster moments before the doors slid open. As he and Sabrina stepped into the building's lobby, with its elegant dark wood walls and creamy marble floor, he donned a worried frown and soft voice. "You sure you don't want me talking to Ron? What he said wasn't cool."

Sabrina gaped at him.

Jason chuckled. "I know, I know—you can stand up for yourself. I just thought I'd offer."

"It's... fine. Thank you."

He suppressed a sigh of exasperation. At least she had the sense to reply instead of stare like a fish at the hand holding the rod. "I'd ask if you're sure, but honestly, I'd leave too. So I don't blame you."

"Yeah. I can't stand him."

Jason held the front door open for her as they exited. The city of Lancing sprawled out in all directions from where they stood, a behemoth of industry and urbanization. Skyscrapers stretched toward the starless night, their highest reaches obscured by blackness and clouds. Yellow lights scattered across countless windows like constellations amid a gridwork of darkness. At the street level, neon signs blinked and blazed, while streetlamps illuminated the sidewalks and roads. The persistent rumble of cars and chatter of pedestrians rose up in a cacophony on all sides; the ripe, pungent smell of piss, garbage, and weed blew by on a blustery wind. Shivering, Sabrina pulled her coat more tightly around her body. Jason kept her in his line of sight as he hailed an approaching cab. It pulled up along the sidewalk in front of them. He opened the door for her again.

"Have a good night, all right?" he said as she climbed

into the back seat.

"Thanks. You too," she said, avoiding eye contact, before sharing an address with the driver. Jason didn't recognize it as any place he knew. He committed it to memory.

He held his hand up in a reserved wave of farewell, a slight smile on his face, as the cab peeled away from the curb. Once it had blended in with the rest of the traffic, his smile faded into stoic neutrality. He started off in the opposite direction, pulling the brim of his cap lower over his face. No one on the street paid him any mind.

After walking for two blocks, he reinserted the battery of his phone and turned it back on. The home screen flashed at him. He opened the app that made encrypted voice calls and dialed a number he'd memorized.

"Grosmont Fish Market, Vince speaking," answered an older man after a couple of rings.

"I heard hornet tilapia are in season," Jason said, giving the passphrase.

"Oh, Jason, good evening." The curt professionalism in the broker's voice eased into familiarity. "What can I do for you?"

"I need you to keep tabs on someone for me."

"Who? Did something happen?"

Fighting the urge to lie, Jason said, "I finished a job half an hour ago, and a woman arrived on the scene before I could leave. I threatened her so I could get out of there." He gave Sabrina's full name, physical description, and the address she'd recited for the taxi driver. "Does any of that sound familiar?"

"No, not at all. I'll have my team look into her and send some runners to that address. Anything else I should know that might be useful?"

"She mentioned she did business with the target." Jason paused. People in his line of work were supposed to keep their clients' and targets' identities a secret, but without that information, Vince couldn't act. "Robert Panzieri."

Vince was silent for a long moment. "I see. Maybe your client was trying to set you up?"

"Doubtful. By the way he talked, he just wanted to eliminate some competition."

"And this girl claimed to be business partners with Robert?"

"Yeah, but I don't believe her. She was probably just a prostitute." Ahead of Jason was an alley with a dumpster. He ducked into its shadows and hurled the duffel bag containing his disguise into the trash.

"You're probably right," Vince said. "Still, lay low for a while. No contracts. Do your cover job. If this girl's smart, she'll put two and two together once she learns about Robert's death. I'll make sure she doesn't call the police—or do anything else stupid."

"Thanks, Vince. Update me if you learn anything."

"Of course. Goodnight, Jason."

After hanging up, Jason removed the SIM card from his phone and snapped it in half. He tossed the pieces into the dumpster and made to leave, but froze.

Every small hair on his body stood on end. Something was in the alley with him, watching. Not something harmless like an animal or a homeless person, but a predator. A threat.

He turned in a slow half-circle to face the black maw of the alley. It seemed to lengthen the longer he stared into it, stretching for miles into an endless abyss. He lurched from the sudden vertigo. A faint humming reached his ears, growing louder with every passing second. Hunger gnawed at him, but it did not come from within. It pressed against him from the darkness, a palpable sensation that filled the air with dreadful tension. The humming reached a distorted, droning crescendo. He pressed his palms against his ears instinctively, but the discordant, fluctuating noise was in his head, vibrating against his skull. When he squinted into the alley, he saw movement. Light. A ripple of nebulas, a collision of stars.

And at the very center, the suggestion of something colossal and all-consuming.

Chapter Two

Ayana looked up from her book at the sound of her front door opening. She grew still, listening to the movements from the floor below, conjuring the man and his actions in her mind's eye. Her husband was a creature of habit, always removing his shoes in the townhouse's entryway before hanging his coat and keys nearby. The latter clinked softly as they swayed on their key hook next to hers.

Finally, soft footsteps up the stairs signaled his approach. Smiling, Ayana slid a bookmark between the pages of her reading and set it aside. Jason ascended into their living room, dressed in a brown jacket she'd never seen before, a slim paper bag cradled in one arm. He looked like he'd gone for a walk to the store, but she knew better. He'd been working. If she stood close enough to him, she would smell the gunpowder.

He paused at the top step and stared at her, his expression inscrutable, though she thought she saw tension ease from his jaw.

"You're home early," she said, rising from the couch to cross the room and kiss his stubbled cheek. Warmth radiated from him, but she resisted the temptation to press herself into an embrace. The bag was in the way, anyway.

He kissed her cheek in return. "Work went off without a hitch. I even had time to stop by the liquor store."

Stroking his neck, she looked into his eyes, searching them for the truth. Beneath her touch, his muscles were tight with unspoken stress. Something unexpected had happened. But he'd returned home safely, in the end, and that was what mattered.

Ayana took the bag from Jason and reached inside. Lifting the black bottle of wine by its neck, she examined its glossy, golden label. "Château Pichon Baron," she read aloud before raising an eyebrow at him. They had visited one of its vineyards in the French countryside for a decadent wine and cheese tasting during their honeymoon. Tenderness bloomed in her chest at the nostalgic memory—and at his thoughtfulness. "The 2005 vintage, even. What's the occasion?"

He matched her smile with the slightest curl of his own mouth. "Can't I treat my wife to something nice every so often?"

Chuckling, she padded over to the open kitchen-dining area and set the bottle down on the island's granite countertop. He followed her there, circled strong arms around her from behind, and pressed his chest against her back. Her grin widened. She relaxed into him, tilting her head as his lips trailed kisses down her neck. Heat burned low in her abdomen, kindled to life by his attention.

"How much were you paid tonight?" she asked, her gaze lingering on the wine. Calculations ran through her head, weighing the price of the single bottle against their accounts. Was this the vintage that cost two hundred dollars, or two thousand? She couldn't remember, not with one of his hands sliding up the front of her silk nightgown.

"You can check tomorrow." The roughness of his voice in her ear sent a shiver down her spine.

Ayana turned in Jason's embrace and wrapped her arms around his neck. "Tell me, please," she said, injecting just enough force into the command to make him pause.

"Eighty thousand."

"Total?"

"Total."

She kissed him on the lips as a reward. A thrill swept through her when he reciprocated eagerly.

"Let's bring the wine upstairs," he murmured between kisses.

"We could," she said, slowing down as a new idea entered her head, an answer to a riddle she had yet to solve, "or we could save it."

"For?"

"Dinner at Connor's next week. I haven't purchased a host gift yet, and it would be perfect."

Jason's face darkened at once, and his hands dropped to his sides. He stepped out of her embrace, leaving her cold. "I bought the wine for us, not him."

Ayana held her husband's gaze. "I know, but bringing it means we can still drink it. We can use it to talk about our trip to France, which should impress his new girlfriend."

"I don't need to impress her or anyone."

"I *know*. But you *do* need to keep up appearances. We both do." She reached for his hand. When he did not pull away, she knew he understood. "You don't need me to remind you how important that is, especially if this girl is someone your brother will marry one day. Connor will tell her about your childhood sooner or later, and the earlier you charm her, the less trouble she'll be for us. She'll think his concerns are matters of the past, or at least less serious in the present."

The wrath in Jason's face only deepened. "He knows better than to talk about that."

Ayana sighed at his stubbornness and switched tactics. "Yes. At least, he should." Stepping closer, she cupped her husband's cheek with her other hand. "I promise this'll be the only time you have to play pretend for him. I'll make up excuses if they want to see us again. You know I'm an expert at that."

He frowned but didn't argue her point—a victory, no matter how small. Instead, he released his anger in a slow exhale. "Fine. Just this once."

"Thank you." Kissing his cheek again, she trailed her hand down the front of his body until it rested on the buckle of his belt. Her fingers worked the leather free. "Now, where were we?"

He stood without moving, and for a moment, she feared the topic of his brother had cooled his blood too much. Then he seized her with both hands, pulling her hard against him, and crushed her mouth in a bruising kiss.

· · · · ●·●·● · · · ·

On the day of dinner at Connor's, Ayana went to work with two cups of coffee from her favorite café instead of one. She spied her assistant already at his desk, unpacking his messenger bag. The bespectacled man looked up at her approach and smiled. "Good morning, Dr. Hudson," he said.

"Good morning, Rahul." She handed him one of the cardboard-sleeved paper cups. "Happy one-year anniversary with us. Sparrows Street Café does filter coffee and I thought you might like a taste of home."

His eyes lit up. "Oh, you didn't have to!"

"I wanted to. Consider it a 'thank you' for all your hard work this past year."

Ten clusters of desks occupied the spacious, open area that served as their office; her own was directly across from Rahul's. As she moved past him, she spotted a thin booklet on his desk she hadn't seen before. Its colorful cover depicted a menacing, tentacled shadow looming over a screaming man. Large, purple letters in a font that reminded her of cheesy Halloween advertisements spelled out the title, *The Void Between the Stars*.

She picked up the booklet. "What's this?"

Rahul rubbed the back of his neck, a shy gesture. "A vintage comic that came in the mail yesterday. I brought it to read during lunch."

"I didn't know you read comics."

"Never had a reason to mention it before."

Setting the book back down, Ayana considered ending the conversation there. She had zero interest in his personal life or hobbies, but discouraging idle conversation wasn't conducive to a good working relationship, either. At least he wasn't annoying and knew when to shut up. "Do you have a favorite comic?" she asked, finally sitting at her computer to begin the tedious process of logging in.

His eyes lit up. "Yeah! It's an earlier volume in this same series. They're episodic, you see. Anyway, there's a family living on a farm in rural America. The father and mother prefer life away from the city while the kids hate being in the middle of nowhere. One day, a meteor hits their property and starts killing off everything: the crops, the farm animals, and eventually the family."

"What happens at the end?"

"The alien goes back home to somewhere in space."

Ayana looked up at Rahul. "The… alien."

"Yeah. An alien arrives with the meteor."

Chuckling, she shook her head. "Okay then."

"You don't like sci-fi?"

She did not miss the flicker of uncertainty that entered his face. Ignoring it, she said, "This isn't science fiction. It's fantasy. A supernatural idea with no basis in reality, unlike sci-fi."

"Well... yeah, it's space horror."

"There's more than enough horror in the real world these days. I don't need to read stories about UFOs and cryptids if I want to be scared."

"What do you read, then?"

Ayana pulled a book from her tote bag and showed it to him. "Crime thrillers and mysteries."

Another man's booming voice cut through the quiet office. "Hudson! Goswami! What is this, a book club?"

Rahul yanked back his outstretched hand while Ayana turned to acknowledge their boss. What Harvey Blumenthal lacked in height, he possessed in girth, a considerable contribution to the force of his presence. He was also the only person on staff at Lancing Forensic Medical Center who bothered to wear a suit every day. That morning, he'd chosen to accessorize with a garish pink tie, which did nothing for him except accentuate the ruddiness of his own complexion.

"No, of course not." Forcing an apologetic smile, Ayana stowed her book into her purse. "We were just chatting while prepping for the day."

"You can chat at Goswami's happy hour celebration

tonight. You *are* going, right, Hudson?"

"No, sorry. I already have plans—dinner at my brother-in-law's."

Harvey harrumphed. "Always busy. You should make time for your colleagues. They held a one-year anniversary happy hour for *you*, after all."

Her smile remained plastered to her face until he'd shuffled over to harass another of his employees.

Rahul leaned in. "It's okay if you can't make it. I'd stay home with Oscar if I had a choice, but the party's for me, so…"

"And how is he?" Ayana asked, failing to remember which chronic illness plagued Rahul's husband.

"He's going through a flare right now, so it's kind of been a bad week. But my mother-in-law's visiting, so she can help him whenever he needs something while I'm at work."

"Well, I hope he feels better." Her computer chimed, signaling the completion of its startup procedure and saving her from further personal conversation. "Let's get to work."

Fifteen minutes later, she stood at one of four autopsy stations, dressed in scrubs, gown, surgical mask, face shield, gloves, and knee-high boots. A corpse lay on the table in front of her. The accompanying file named him a John Doe—identity unknown. His mop of long, unkempt hair and his ragged beard were streaked with silver and white; his skin was mottled from age and sun exposure.

Beginning her examination, Ayana commented on body rigidity and lividity. The information formed a clear image of the time of death and the stranger's position when he died: the middle of the night, while he was lying on his side. Rahul jotted down notes and took photos.

"Not much out of the ordinary on this one," he said after they finished the external inspection.

Humming a note of agreement, she picked up a scalpel and sliced into the torso, making a Y-shaped incision across the breastbone and down through the abdominal wall. She peeled back the flesh, exposing the rib cage and the organs underneath. Peering into the body cavity, she did a double take at the sight that greeted her. "What in the world?"

The dead organs of the corpse pulsed and quivered with clusters of black holes, none larger than a quarter, most of them much smaller. They reminded Ayana of black tapioca pearls or the honeycomb of beehives, except they swirled in a bizarre, hypnotic pattern. A sudden bout of vertigo seized her; she clutched the edge of the table until the dizziness passed.

Her assistant shot her a confused look, his face pale, sweat beading on his forehead. "Ever see anything like this before, Dr. Hudson?"

"No, never." She took a deep breath to steady herself. Her heart thundered in her ears. Carefully, she prodded one of the holes with her scalpel. The metal warped and twisted backward on itself, as if it were not steel at all but putty in unseen hands.

She dropped the tool and snatched her hand away. The scalpel slid across the intestines, hitting several more holes in its path. Within seconds, it was no longer recognizable. Its contorted form spiraled into the wells of inky blackness and disappeared.

Rahul took a step back. "It's just... *gone*?" he whispered, a tremble in his voice.

Ayana's mind scrambled for an answer, but she couldn't recall a single lecture, research paper, or textbook that mentioned such a phenomenon among the living *or* the dead. What she and Rahul witnessed defied all scientific logic as she knew it—but no, that was impossible. Dangerous thinking. There *had* to be a rational explanation.

She waited until her hands stopped shaking before picking up another scalpel. "I don't know what this is," she said at last, "but we're going to find out. Take photos. We'll try another way to remove the organs. Once we've finished the autopsy, we'll show everything to Harvey. He'll know what to do."

Chapter Three

Jason waited only a few seconds after knocking before his brother's front door swung open, revealing Connor. He acknowledged Jason first with a nervous smile, then turned it toward Ayana. "Hey! Good to see you! Come in."

"It's good seeing you too, Connor," she said, stepping into the apartment as he held the door open for them. Jason followed, his eyes sweeping the familiar interior. An open, central space combined kitchen, dining room, and living room, while a hallway at the other end led to a single bathroom and bedroom. The only exit besides the front door was the balcony, but they were on the fifth floor; no one could survive that jump. Connor had not rearranged any furniture or purchased new ones since Jason's last visit, which meant all the hiding places and ambush points were the same.

A woman stood up from the couch. Connor's girlfriend, Jason assumed—the one he and Ayana were there to meet. But as soon as he laid eyes on her pale skin, model's physique, and platinum blonde hair, he realized he already knew her.

Sabrina Kopanski.

She stared back at him with the same wide-eyed disbelief from before. He'd threatened her into silence, but a prey creature in flight mode often forgot all reason and logic in its effort to stay alive.

Summoning all the charisma he had honed over the years, he approached her with a disarming smile and outstretched hand. "You must be the girlfriend we've heard so much about."

She glanced at Connor, who was busy hanging Ayana's coat, before recovering and shaking Jason's hand. "Sabrina," she said, speaking as if she had to force the word out from around a stone in her throat.

When Ayana joined them, he introduced the women to each other. Observing their exchange of honeyed smiles and handshakes, he couldn't help but smirk at how much more beautiful his wife was. Ayana's mahogany skin glowed with warmth and vitality, her complexion flawless, her face made up just enough to enhance her features. The dress she'd chosen to wear that night—an elegant, dark gold number that made Jason's blood run hot whenever he looked at her—brought out the color in her umber eyes. Small, golden clips decorated box braids done up in an artful ponytail; they glinted in the light whenever she turned her head.

Gold-and-diamond stud earrings adorned her ears, while a line of diamonds on a delicate golden chain drew his gaze down her chest. Next to her, Sabrina was too dull and plain for his tastes.

"So, Connor, what's for dinner?" Jason asked, putting aside thoughts of undressing Ayana for later.

"Lu rou fan, dumplings, and stir-fried water lily, the way Grandma used to make them."

He grinned. "My favorites."

All four gathered at the kitchen table, where the meal awaited them, served family-style with white rice. Right away, he noticed the additional fork next to the chopsticks at Sabrina's seat. He watched as she picked the former over the latter, spearing several dumplings for herself while Connor poured the bottle of Château Pichon Baron into glasses.

"So how long have you two been dating?" Jason asked, putting food on Ayana's plate before his own.

"Only a few months," Connor said. He turned to Sabrina. "Four months?"

"Four months," she confirmed.

Jason pinned her with a curious look. "And how'd you meet?"

She addressed Ayana instead, as if his wife had asked the question. "At a fundraiser. My family's nonprofit does a lot of charity work for the unhoused and other vulnerable groups. In this case, for asylum seekers."

"I was conducting interviews for my most recent article and asked Sabrina some questions," Connor said, beaming. "We hit it off, so I asked her out."

"Do you work for your family's nonprofit, or were you just volunteering?" Jason asked.

"I work for them." Sabrina still wasn't looking at him. "It's called St. Julian's Foundation. Have you heard of it?"

Both he and Ayana shook their heads.

"That's all right. It's a newer organization. My grandfather founded it seventy years ago to help communities in need. Our headquarters are still in Boston, where my family's from, but we've expanded to other locations, like here. I'm on the marketing team—social media, community outreach kind of stuff."

Chewing his food, Jason considered how to word his next question. "Does your work also involve making deals with the big industries in Lancing? Banks, real estate... maybe even shipping?"

Alarm flashed in Sabrina's eyes, but Connor laughed and cut in, saving her from answering. "Nonprofits do sometimes get donations from those companies, but they usually focus on the little people. Did you ever read my article, by the way?"

Jason smiled at his brother. "Not yet, but I will."

"What about you two?" Sabrina asked. "What do you do for work?"

Ayana grinned over the rim of her wine glass. "Cut up dead bodies."

Jason's smile twisted into a smirk at Sabrina's open-mouthed stare. Once again, Connor interjected with an explanation. "She's a coroner."

"A forensic pathologist," Ayana corrected him. "The coroner is my boss, and he deals with much more than autopsies. Which is fine by me. I'd rather not have to talk with the police or testify at court." Her face pinched with sourness at the thought.

"Fun fact: a forensic pathologist is actually a licensed doctor of medicine, but a coroner is not," said Jason. "They're just elected officials."

"How does that make sense?" Sabrina asked.

"It doesn't."

Ayana shrugged. "If I really wanted to, I could find work as a medical examiner in another state. Be my own boss. But if I'm being honest, I like this arrangement. I can focus on the work I *want* to do, not on bureaucracy or politics."

Sabrina nodded slowly. "That's understandable. And admirable, too. Knowing what you want, that is."

"It took a while to get there. During medical school, I thought I wanted to be a surgeon. But then I had the rare opportunity to do an autopsy and I was hooked. Bodies are fascinating, but the way trauma affects them after death is very different than if they were still alive."

"I see." Finally wrenching her gaze away from Ayana, Sabrina peered at Jason. "Don't tell me you work with dead bodies too?" she asked, her tone carrying a note of accusation.

Jason forced an amused smile, not rising to her provocation. "No, thank God. I leave all that to Ayana.

I'm actually a freelance consultant for private security companies, helping them improve their operations, customer retention, and so on. I do a lot of work from home, but sometimes I travel to other parts of the country to meet with clients. I'm actually flying to Portland next week to meet a new one."

Even if Sabrina dared to call him a liar, she'd have no luck convincing the others. He'd carefully crafted his deception over the last decade so that even his brother was clueless about his real profession, and Connor knew better than to disbelieve him. As for Ayana—she was his accomplice, after all.

Right on cue, she chimed in. "It's tough sometimes. Jason might be gone for days at a time, leaving early in the morning and not coming back until late at night. But we manage." She squeezed his knee under the table; in return, he draped his arm around the back of her chair and stroked her shoulder. Glancing at each other, they exchanged fond smiles.

The display of affection was only long enough to plant seeds of doubt. Returning to his meal, Jason caught Sabrina staring at him, her brow furrowed in wariness or confusion—or both. Their eyes met and her expression cleared, melting into a pleasant smile. Beside her, Connor carried on with the conversation, oblivious. She didn't insinuate anything more about the encounter at Robert Panzieri's penthouse throughout the rest of dinner.

After the meal, the Ridley brothers stepped out onto

the balcony for a smoke. Jason gazed over the sleeping city, tobacco burning in his lungs and nostrils. In the blackness of that January night, he could only distinguish the skyscrapers by their lit windows. Far below, the siren of a distant ambulance screamed.

"This is my last pack," Connor said around the unlit cigarette held in his lips. His lighter clicked to life, casting an orange glow upon his face with its meager flame. "Sabrina wants me to quit smoking, and I figured better now than never."

Jason scowled. "Are you going to let her dictate everything in your life?"

"What? No, of course not. But she's right. It's not healthy. Doesn't Ayana nag you about it? She's a *doctor*."

"She doesn't care." She did, actually, but Connor didn't need to know that Jason tolerated her disagreement.

"Well, Sabrina does."

Jason said nothing. Leaning back against the railing, he watched the women through the sliding glass door that separated the balcony from the rest of the apartment. They had relocated to the couch. Sabrina was talking with animated energy, more than she'd exhibited during dinner. Ayana's expression and body language were open and friendly, but he knew she was parrying each prying question with practiced ease.

Connor followed the direction of Jason's stare, then looked back at him. "What was up with the interrogation earlier, by the way? You were more intense about it than usual."

Jason took a drag from his cigarette. "You need to break up with her."

Connor rolled his eyes. "Not this again. You always say that."

"I saw Sabrina last week in the company of an older man. Old enough to be her father."

Mild annoyance morphed into incredulous denial. "What?"

In contrast, Jason maintained a neutral, indifferent expression. "I'm serious."

"What exactly are you suggesting?"

"That you don't know your girlfriend like you think you do."

Connor shook his head vehemently. "That can't be true. Sabrina's a good person. She's loyal. She'd never do anything like that."

"Sure, because you definitely know everything about a person's character after four months."

"Oh, fuck you."

Jason stood up straight, eyes narrowing. "Excuse me?"

Connor hesitated. He shot a nervous glance at the door. "Sorry, I just... I like her a lot, okay? She's funny, smart, kind, super hot—"

"You think I give a shit about any of that?"

"No, no. But damn it, you never let me have this. I'm turning thirty-two this year and I've never been in a serious, committed relationship because you don't want me to be happy. I want to fall in love with someone, Jason."

Jason turned his entire body toward Connor, taking up more space on the narrow balcony. Connor's eyes darted to the door again as he shifted backward against the railing. Jason stepped into his brother's line of sight, forcing Connor to look at him.

Nowhere to go. Nowhere to run.

"Everything I've done has been for your happiness," Jason said, his voice low with warning. "If you'd stayed with any of those whores, you'd be begging me for cash just to pay rent because they'd have spent all your money on blow from their dealers."

"You don't know that." Connor's voice was small in comparison.

"And did you forget? I got your drug-addicted ass into rehab while you were still in college. I found you that part-time gig while you were finishing your degree. I let you live with me while you were looking for a job."

"I didn't forget."

"And you have the nerve to say 'fuck you' to *me*?"

"Look, I'm sorry!" Connor's eyes blazed with fury. "But I have a right to get married one day, like you! Except I actually know what love is!"

Jason's hand shot out and grabbed the front of Connor's coat. He dragged Connor closer until their faces were inches apart. "You have no rights. Not as long as you're *my* brother."

Connor shoved him away. "Fuck you. That's right—

fuck you! Ever since we were kids, you dictated everything in my life. Who I could play with, what I could or couldn't do, what toys or pets I could have. But I'm allowed to be my own person, not just *your brother*. Do you treat Ayana this way too because she's your wife?"

Jason shot Connor a sharp look. "Don't speak about things you don't understand."

"If you would just see a therapist—"

A red haze colored Jason's vision. Seizing Connor's coat again, Jason slammed him against the wall. He yelped as his head bounced on the brick.

"Your precious blonde chick has made you stupider than ever," Jason snarled. "You know better than to talk about that, yet here you are, being an idiotic little bitch. Now, I'm going to let you go with a warning; I don't want your girl to get any wrong ideas about me. But if you want to remain in my good graces, Connor, I better not hear those words out of your mouth ever again. Do I make myself clear?"

His brother nodded, whimpered.

"Good. If Sabrina asks about the shouting here, make something up. Something believable. Okay?"

"Okay."

Stepping back, Jason released his brother. Connor remained slumped against the wall, breathing hard. His eyes swam with unshed tears. Ignoring him, Jason picked up the cigarettes they'd dropped and put them out in the ashtray. Then he laid his hand on the sliding glass door.

"We're leaving. Don't call me."

Connor didn't look at him. "Okay," he whispered, voice breaking.

Chapter Four

Jason and Connor excused themselves to the balcony for a smoke, leaving Ayana to entertain Sabrina by herself—much to her chagrin. She had no interest in drawing out the social niceties, nor did she approve of her husband's filthy vice. Nevertheless, she suppressed the urge to shoot a frown at his retreating back; though she often scolded him in private for smoking, in front of a stranger, he was beyond reproach.

Sabrina, however, sighed with obvious exasperation as she sank into the couch. She gazed through the sliding door that separated the women from the outside world. "Connor told me he was quitting."

"Addiction isn't an easy thing to break." Ayana took a seat on the other end of the same couch. "All you can do is support him."

"You know, Connor and Jason are nothing alike. I had an inkling based on what Connor said whenever he talked about his brother, but they're way more different than I imagined."

From a distance, the Ridley brothers did look similar enough to be related. Both were tall men, with straight black hair and the same slant to their striking blue eyes. Physically, though, Jason cut a more impressive figure, his chiseled bulk a sign of robust, practical strength. Connor's lankier frame suited a runner. Jason's features were also more angular compared to Connor's rounder, more boyish face. Most obvious, however, was the difference in their demeanor. Connor had never given Ayana any reason to believe he was anything but honest and good-natured.

Jason, on the other hand...

Ayana regarded the men through the glass. They stood side-by-side, facing the city that lay beyond the balcony's railing. Light from the apartment spilled outside, but it only reached their legs. Darkness obscured their upper bodies.

And writhing within the shadows upon her husband's back were numerous, tiny black holes.

Panic flooded her in an instant, but before she could speak or act, her vision swam and a sudden, acute ache lanced through her skull. Wincing, she pressed a hand to her forehead.

Sabrina frowned at her. "Ayana? What's wrong?"

The pain and lightheadedness faded as abruptly as they arrived. Her heart hammering against her ribs, Ayana slowly raised her head and peered at Jason again.

The holes had vanished.

"I'm fine," she said, too quickly for her liking. "I just—I need some water."

In the kitchen, her thoughts returned to the morning's cadaver. Despite their efforts, she and Rahul hadn't been able to complete the autopsy. Their tools kept warping beyond repair whenever they neared the holes, making it impossible for them to remove and dissect the organs. She reported the oddity to Harvey after sewing the corpse back up, informing him of her intent to try again on Monday. Though he was skeptical, he reassured her he'd read the report and take necessary action.

When she had composed herself enough to resume small talk, Ayana padded back to the couch. Sabrina looked up from her phone and gave Ayana a once-over, smiling when she did. "Can I ask a personal question?" the younger woman asked.

For once, Ayana welcomed the distraction. "Of course."

"How long have you and Jason been together?"

"Three years. Married for two."

Most people reacted to that information with mild surprise, but Sabrina's shock was more akin to horror. "Really? You knew him for only a year before you got married?"

"Yes. We had a civil ceremony at the city clerk's office, so we didn't need time to plan anything extravagant. I didn't even bother with a wedding dress; I just picked out a white dress I already had in my closet."

The memory brought a tender smile to Ayana's face. Jason had been so handsome in his tailored black suit. She wasn't a romantic by any means, but the way he'd gazed at her when they said "I do" had made her heart flutter.

Sabrina's mouth opened and closed like a fish out of water. "What made you say 'yes'?"

"*I* proposed, actually, not the other way around. He and I are just very compatible. I don't think I'll meet another person quite like him."

She said nothing for a moment, then asked, "How exactly did you and Jason meet?"

"At a bar, believe it or not. Neither of us are heavy drinkers, but I was with some classmates from med school—we'd all just finished residency—and he'd completed a contract with a very prestigious client, so he and I happened to be celebrating at the same bar, at the same time. Our eyes met from across the room and he bought me a drink." Another fond, cherished memory.

"Sounds like a movie."

"It felt like one, yet here we are, three years later."

"And is married life everything you hoped it'd be?"

Ayana arched an eyebrow. Sabrina sounded like she was digging for dirt. What had Connor already told her about Jason's true personality? "Why? Are you hoping Connor's 'the one'?"

"Is there such a thing?"

Ayana chuckled. "No, of course not."

"Then maybe I just want advice. I'm twenty-six, but I've never had a relationship longer than a year, and that was back in undergrad."

"I don't think I'm the best person to give relationship advice."

"Why not?"

Before she could conjure a believable excuse, a muffled shout arose from the balcony. Her stomach twisting with sudden dread, she whipped her head toward the sound. Had the black holes returned? Was Jason hurt? But no, nothing was amiss. The men stood facing each other, speaking in muted voices, their exact words unclear. An argument? Tensing, Ayana glanced at Sabrina. All the blood had drained from the younger woman's face. She watched Jason and Connor with wide, round eyes, her body poised to spring from the couch at a moment's notice.

Ayana rested her fingers against Sabrina's wrist, drawing her attention from the altercation.

"What's your family's nonprofit called, again?" Ayana asked. Past experience had taught her that a person's desire to talk as much as possible about themselves often proved a sufficient distraction.

Sabrina looked taken aback—a good sign. "Oh, um… St. Julian's Foundation. After St. Julian the Hospitaller."

More shouts. Her nervous gaze drifted toward the balcony, so Ayana pressed the topic. "A religious organization?"

"More like it's guided by religious principles. My family's Roman Catholic, but St. Julian's isn't explicitly affiliated with the Church. But my father's a good friend of—"

Violent movement in the shadows, followed by a yelp of pain. Sabrina surged from the couch, but Ayana caught her wrist, holding her back. "Don't."

The women locked eyes. "Shouldn't we see if everything's okay?"

In the face of Sabrina's incredulity and concern, Ayana maintained a serene countenance and a light grip. "You want advice? They're grown adults, not children. We don't need to mother our men. So please, sit down."

Though Sabrina was slow to act, she did as she was bidden. Ayana released her wrist and offered a reassuring smile.

The glass door slid open and Jason walked through, seething and stinking of smoke. Ayana saw the look in his eye and stood in anticipation. "We're leaving," he said to her, his voice terse. As he passed the couch, he paused for a second in front of Sabrina. Though his rage lingered in the tightness of his smile, he managed to look apologetic. "Sorry to cut the night short so suddenly. It was nice meeting you."

He swept away without waiting for her response. Ayana moved to follow, but Sabrina stood abruptly, blocking her path.

"Wait." Sabrina pulled out her phone. "We should

get lunch sometime. I'd like to know you better, Ayana."

Ayana's smile faltered. "Oh, that's very flattering, but—" Jason called her name, beckoning her to his side. "Why not? Here's my number."

The women exchanged contact information, then Ayana said farewell. She cast a final glance at the balcony as Connor stepped through the door. Though she couldn't see any physical signs of a quarrel on his face, his pained expression told her enough. Before she could overhear him give an excuse to his worried girlfriend, she followed Jason out of the apartment. Her heels thudded dully against the thin, gray carpet as she caught up with her husband's long, impatient strides.

· · · · ●·●·· · ·

Ayana waited until they returned to the privacy of their home before broaching the topic of dinner. "What happened back there, Jason?"

The trip on the subway had cooled his temper enough that he no longer looked like he wanted to kill someone. Still, she spied the way his jaw tensed as he hung his coat next to hers. "Connor didn't like what I had to say about Sabrina."

"What did you say? She seemed perfectly normal. A little skittish, but normal."

He shook his head and stalked up the stairs. She proceeded after him, occupying her hands with removing her jewelry. When he continued into their bedroom on the third floor, she went, too. Pausing at her vanity, she put away her earrings and necklace, then crossed the room to where he'd begun unbuttoning his dress shirt. She rested her hands on his, stilling his movements.

"Let me," she said. She took her time undoing the rest of his buttons while he stood with his hands at his sides. The broad planes of his chest and abdomen revealed themselves. Sliding his shirt off his shoulders, she stepped even closer and pressed a soft kiss to his collarbone. "Tell me what happened, Jason."

He grunted, his hands rising to her hips. "It's nothing."

"It's not nothing. That woman was scared of you, though you gave her no reason to be scared. At least, until the end. After you and Connor went out, she asked me questions that felt... pointed. Like she knew something."

Jason sighed. He drew away from Ayana and sat on the edge of the bed. "She saw me at my last job, arriving on location after I'd killed my target."

Ayana grew still. Ice flooded her veins. "What?"

"I hadn't anticipated a late-night visitor. My target usually didn't entertain girls at his own home."

"Was this just last week?"

He nodded.

At any moment, the earth beneath her feet was going to crumble. She was sure of it. The house, the street—everything would collapse into rubble and dust. "You said it went off without a hitch!"

Jason took her hand. His touch was solid. Grounding. "And it did. The police haven't come for me. I silenced her, Ayana. I threatened to kill her if she ever spoke about seeing me that night, and I have people watching her every move. She hasn't acted since."

A dozen different scenarios raced through her head, each one ending with him behind bars. She didn't notice he had coaxed her onto the bed beside him until he was kissing the back of her hand. His other arm had encircled her waist. Pulling her hand from his, she turned toward him. "You should've told me."

He held her gaze. "When we got together, we agreed not to get involved in each other's lives, remember?"

"This is different. You could be outed. Now that she knows you're Connor's brother, what's stopping her from putting you in prison? She'll see it as saving him from you. I don't want to see you in court, Jason." Ayana's fingers curled around the covers of the bed.

Lifting her chin, he kissed her sweetly. "You won't. I don't make mistakes."

"But Sabrina—"

"Is a non-issue. Especially now that you have her phone number."

Ayana hesitated. "I thought you already have people watching her."

"I do, but she wanted to get to know you. We can use that to our advantage and keep tabs on her another way."

As much as she recoiled from having to socialize

with a stranger, the inconvenience paled in comparison to the nightmare that haunted her ever since she and Jason wed: their perfect life upended, her survival dependent on her rejection of him. "All right. I'll call Sabrina tomorrow and set up a lunch date."

"Thank you." Jason's hand drifted up Ayana's back and lightly massaged the base of her neck. With a soft sigh, she leaned into the touch. Her eyelids fluttered closed. "You were good tonight, by the way."

Warmth spread through her at the compliment. "Which part?"

"When you said being apart is tough sometimes."

She opened her eyes to find him staring at her with a familiar intensity. Her heartbeat quickened, and heat rose into her cheeks. "Every lie has some truth to it," she murmured. "I don't want to know the details of what you do or where you go, but I do miss you when you're not home."

He gave her the private, intimate smile she'd never seen him give anyone else. "You *do* love me."

"Was there ever any doubt?"

"Never." Dipping his head, he kissed her again. "I love you, too."

Chuckling, she lifted a hand and caressed his jaw. "No, you don't." Still, she pressed her body against his, hungry for the feeling of his bare skin upon hers. "But I won't stop you if you're going to pretend."

Chapter Five

Ayana sipped her cappuccino while she waited for her work computer to finish logging her in. Thoughts from the last few days swirled in her mind: the tense dinner at Connor's apartment, Jason's revelation afterward, Sabrina agreeing to a lunch date on Tuesday. Most prominent, though, was the situation with the John Doe. The memory of the anomaly had plagued her all weekend, lurking in the corners of her consciousness as she did housework and ran errands. At times, she thought she saw writhing clusters of black holes in the periphery of her vision, but when she looked closer, she found only tricks of shadow and light.

The strange phenomenon had loomed larger in her dreams. Twice, she'd woken up before dawn in a cold sweat, swirling nebulas and the dark shapes between them burned into her mind's eye. Both times, Jason's touch soothed her back to sleep, his kisses and caresses distracting her from the alien horrors. Three days after laying eyes on the cadaver, the memory of its secret affliction felt more like a fever dream than reality. Had she imagined it all?

No, impossible. Rahul had been with her. He'd seen the strange, pulsating holes, too.

As if on cue, he walked into the office, comic book in hand. "Good morning, Dr. Hudson."

"Good morning. How was your weekend?"

"Not bad, but... weird."

Somehow, she understood exactly what he meant. "Did you have strange dreams, too?"

He blinked. "Yes, actually... but not just that." He waved the comic book at her. "I read this over the weekend. It's about some archaeologists at a dig site. They discover a buried temple to an ancient god, and one by one, they get sick with the same symptoms as our decedent: holes all over their bodies, but outside instead of inside. Well, maybe inside, too, but the comic never shows it."

Ayana smiled, biting back a skeptical laugh. "Are you suggesting that the mysterious affliction in our John Doe is the result of an ancient curse?"

"I don't know about a *curse* but—"

"Rahul, religious superstitions aren't real. They're just stories people from the distant past told each other to explain things they didn't understand. What we found is a matter of science, not fantasy."

"But you saw what it did to the—"

She held up her hand, unwilling to entertain the possibility any further. "I'm sure there's a reasonable explanation. We just need to come up with a method to extract the deformed tissue safely and study it. Once we do that, we can understand whatever new disease or genetic mutation we're dealing with."

He lowered his gaze, his book clutched to his chest. "Of course. You're right. Sorry."

Sensing the need for a change in topic, Ayana asked, "How's Oscar doing?"

"He's out of bed again, at least. His doctor suggested a new trial drug to help with his pain, but our health insurance doesn't cover it, and we're not sure the risks will be worth the cost."

"That's tough." An empty platitude, but suitable for small talk.

At that moment, her computer's login process finished. She pulled up the John Doe's file and clicked on the tab for photographs. The first several showed the cadaver's external condition, including all the scars and tattoos the pair had noted as distinguishing features. The visual recording ended there, however. The photographs depicting the holes on the organs in the body cavity were gone. Ayana stared at her computer for several seconds, not registering the reality in front of her. When it finally hit her, she tabbed back to the detailed report and scanned the notes, her eyes darting back and forth in their urgent search.

All mention of the holes were gone, too.

"Rahul, did you update the report after I left on Friday?" she asked, her eyes glued to the impossible situation on the screen.

He'd disappeared behind his computer and was typing at his keyboard. "No. I went straight to happy hour with everyone else. Why?"

"Our notes are missing."

The clacking of plastic keys stopped. He stood and peered at her from over their computer monitors. "What?"

"I know."

"Did we forget to click 'Save' or something?"

"Not possible. He was our first decedent of the day, and I reviewed his report in the afternoon before doing lab analysis. I wanted to make sure it had all the details for Harvey's review." Her gaze snapped to meet Rahul's. "*Harvey*."

Her assistant shook his head. "Why would he tamper with the file, though? That makes no sense."

"I don't know, but at least we still have the body. The crematorium shouldn't be picking him up until tomorrow, so let's see if we can squeeze in an additional autopsy today." She pulled up the day's schedule and looked for her name. "Maybe this afternoon. The police brought in a possible homicide over the weekend and he's first on our list. Can you prep the station? I'm going to talk to Harvey."

"Sure."

Ayana locked her computer and left her desk. Down

a long corridor of dark blue linoleum and beige walls was Harvey's office; a brass plaque engraved with his name adorned the door. Standing in front of it, she took a deep, steadying breath, composing herself enough to knock without banging on the wood. His muffled voice ushered her inside. She seized the knob and threw open the door.

"Did you make changes to the report for Friday's John Doe?" she demanded before he could greet her. "The one I specifically asked you to look at?"

Her boss sat frozen behind his large, ornate wooden desk, one hand holding open a sleek leather notebook, the other outstretched toward a fountain pen in a brass holder. A deep blush reddened his face and ears. "Beg your pardon?" he asked, puffing himself up in a way that reminded her of an indignant bird.

"Rahul and I found *something* in a human body last week that defied everything we know about how people are supposed to work and look when dead. Why would you erase that from our files?"

"Hudson, I don't appreciate being accused of anything without proof."

"You're the only person besides us who even knew about it. Who else could've done it? Enlighten me, please."

"Perhaps it was Goswami."

She shot him an incredulous look. "Really? You think I wouldn't have asked him first? My assistant who was there with me?"

"Well, I can't read your mind—"

"We're going to do another autopsy on the decedent today. And while the body is open, I'm going to come right back and bring you into the suite with us. We need to work together to understand what's going on. This could be a new disease, Harvey. If we don't start studying it as soon as possible, it could be humanity's fate on our hands."

Clearing his throat, he tugged at the knot of his tie. That day, it was a sickly green color, the same as vomit or bile. "Hudson, I understand your commitment to science and medicine, which is very admirable, but—"

A knock at the door prompted Ayana to whirl around where she stood. Rahul leaned through the open doorway, apology written all over his face. "Sorry to interrupt, but..."

"Go on, Goswami," Harvey said. She thought he sounded relieved.

"The John Doe's gone. He's not in the lockers or the cooler."

She reeled as if slapped. Her face burned all over, and her jaw clenched hard enough to hurt. Spinning on her heel, she stalked across the room toward Harvey's desk. "You got rid of the body? A body with an as-of-yet unidentified condition that could potentially kill us all?"

"Hudson—"

"There's more," said Rahul. "The homicide case."

"What about it?" Ayana snapped.

He flinched but stood his ground. "He has the same surname as your husband."

Time stopped. In the resounding silence that followed, her heartbeat thundered in her ears. She swallowed and found her throat was dry. "There have to be a dozen Ridleys in Lancing."

"I know, but I thought I'd tell you. Just in case."

She glanced over her shoulder at Harvey. His expression was unreadable, which she didn't like one bit. "This isn't over," she warned him before hurrying after Rahul.

The ritual of donning her personal protective equipment restored some semblance of her composure, as if they were armor. Calmness radiated from her as she approached the stainless steel table and its cloth-covered corpse. Regardless of who lay beneath it, she planned to approach the examination with the professionalism required of her station. She checked the name on the file pulled up on the computer.

Connor Ridley.

The computer didn't lie, she thought. Except it had that morning. Notes and photographs she was sure she'd taken had vanished. Turning, she regarded the white sheet and the body beneath it. She had to be sure. She had to see it with her own eyes.

She yanked down the cloth to uncover the decedent's head. Connor's dull, lifeless eyes stared up at her from the table.

Ayana released the breath she hadn't realized she'd

been holding. "Fuck."

Rahul, who hovered on the cadaver's other side, looked up at her outburst. "Is it him?"

"It's him. My brother-in-law."

"Oh my God. I'm so sorry."

She shook her head. The appropriate words slipped out of her grasp—if there even were such a thing. Her career had inured her to the sight of death, but nothing had prepared her for seeing the corpse of a man she knew, whose home she'd been invited into. Who'd been alive and healthy just the other day.

"Do you need to step out? I can ask Harvey to reassign the case to another pathologist."

She considered the option. Another person in her position would have accepted the offer with grace; emotional attachment to relatives often interfered with the ability to perform examinations. The questions swirling through her head—the whats, the hows, and the whens of Connor's death—would be distracting for most people. Yet only autopsies provided those answers.

"No. I want to do it," Ayana said, steeling herself for what she might find. "Let's begin."

Chapter Six

Vince was waiting outside the Lancing Mixed Martial Arts Academy when Jason finished his usual morning practice. Despite being two decades older, age had not sunk its claws into Vince yet: a full head of graying brown hair crowned his head, and he stood straight-backed as he flipped through the newspaper. Jason walked past without so much as a word of greeting or sideways glance. Vince fell smoothly into step beside him, tucking the newspaper under one arm.

"Sorry I couldn't meet earlier," said Vince. "Busy weekend."

Jason saw no reason to respond to the apology. Skipping the small talk, he asked, "Any updates about the Kopanski girl?"

"Just that she does live at the address you gave me—an apartment in Bracknell—and works for a nonprofit company called St. Julian's Foundation. Their office is in Bracknell, too. She has a normal work schedule there: eight to five on weekdays. Besides that, she goes to a Pilates class and a Catholic church in her neighborhood."

"So she's not a prostitute."

"No, seems not."

"What's her connection with the Panzieris, then? Why was she at Robert's penthouse?"

"I'm not sure. I've been asking around, but no one in my circles has heard of her. What I *can* assure you about, though, is that she hasn't made contact with the police at all."

Jason wasn't satisfied. "Something's not right about her, Vince. I ran into her again on Friday at my brother's place. They're dating, apparently."

"Really? What are the odds. My boys did say she stayed at an apartment in Oldtown over the weekend, but I didn't think it was important." Frowning, Vince spun the thick, golden ring he always wore on his right pinkie finger. On its round, flat head was a European-style sword haloed by a sunburst. "All right, I'll have them tail her for another couple of weeks."

The men stopped at an intersection as the pedestrian signal turned red. A slew of cars rumbled past, but few pedestrians joined them on the sidewalk. Jason adjusted the strap of his gym bag to hang more comfortably from his shoulder, his eyes watching the traffic for an opening to jaywalk.

"Did she say anything to you on Friday?" Vince asked, still spinning his ring.

"She tried to insinuate my real career in front of Connor, but it didn't work. He still doesn't have a clue."

"Is there a chance she'll tell him?"

"If she does, he won't believe her. I'll make sure he doesn't." Connor's outburst on Friday meant nothing. Throughout their lives, he'd attempted little rebellions here and there, all of which Jason was quick to quash—with violence, if necessary.

Vince nodded, though his face remained creased with concern. "Good." He checked his watch. "If there's nothing else, I have to get back to the fish market."

Jason shook his head. With a final nod of farewell, Vince departed down the sidewalk, newspaper still tucked in the crook of his arm, hands stuffed into the pockets of his long coat. The traffic slowed to a halt and the pedestrian signal turned green. Jason strolled across to the other side.

At the opposite curb, his phone buzzed with a call from a number he didn't recognize.

"Hello?" he answered.

"Hello," replied an unfamiliar voice. Male, gruff, possibly middle-aged. "Am I speaking with Jason Ridley?"

"Yes."

"This is Detective Warren Fraser with Lerwick Square Police Station."

Jason maintained an easy pace and a neutral expression. If the police suspected him of a crime, they would not be calling him; they'd knock on his door with a warrant. Either this was a scam or they wanted something else. He committed Fraser's information to memory. "The police? Is something wrong?"

Fraser hesitated. "There's no good way to say this. I'm sorry. Your brother, Connor Ridley—he's dead."

· · · · ● · ● ● ● · ·

The Lancing Police Department's station in Lerwick Square loomed ahead of Jason, a two-story building of stone and concrete set between specialty shops and offices. As he neared it, his gaze swept along its exterior, noting adjacent alleys, the bars on the windows, and surrounding security cameras. The double doors of the main entrance faced the street, so, while he was still a block away, he ducked into a narrow lane to continue his approach from behind. From there, he walked a loop around the building, adding its side entrance to his mental file and taking care to avoid the cameras. Once he was satisfied, he doubled back to his original route and walked the rest of the way to the front doors without further detours.

Behind the thick glass of the front desk, a young officer looked up at Jason. "What can I do for you, sir?" she asked, offering a polite smile.

His own smile was thin and tight-lipped, his best approximation of nervous dread. "I got a phone call earlier from Detective Fraser about my brother, and, uh, I'm here for an interview."

"Your name?"

"Jason Ridley."

She dialed a desk phone and spoke with someone on the other line. After confirming Jason's presence was expected, she unlocked the door to the reception area for him using a button behind the glass. He thanked her and made his way into the other room.

Several long benches occupied the center of the spacious, well-lit chamber, while police memorabilia decorated the far wall. He scanned the interior for all possible exits and found only one: another door on the opposite end of the room. Though the openness of the chamber meant no ambush points, the benches were both tall and long enough to provide adequate cover. He chose a seat where he could observe both doors at once with only a slight turn of his head. While he waited, he ran through the different scenarios for breaking into the precinct.

Not that he believed he needed to. Not yet, anyway.

After a few minutes, a sandy-haired, middle-aged man walked through the second entrance, carrying a manila folder. Instead of a uniform, he wore plain clothes; the only indication he worked for the police was the badge around his neck. He made a beeline for Jason, extending his hand when he neared. Jason stood and shook it.

"Mr. Ridley, I'm Detective Fraser. I'm sorry the circumstances are what they are." Despite his sympathetic words, he looked Jason over with the same keenness as a predator assessing a potential threat.

Jason let his tense half-smile falter, then fall. "Is my brother really…"

"I'm afraid so. I met your wife at the forensic center after the autopsy, and she confirmed his identity for us."

Ayana had told him the same thing. She'd called him shortly after Fraser had, both to relay the news to Jason and share the answers she'd given the police during her interview. She warned of a second cop, too—Fraser's partner, a woman named Silva.

Fraser gestured to the door behind him. "Come with me, please. I just have a few questions for you."

He led Jason down a corridor with off-white walls and bland, tan carpet. As they passed plaques that read BRIEFING ROOM and EVIDENCE in silence, Jason stole quick, furtive glances at every door and branching path they did not take. With each glimpse, he expanded his mental map of the building, revising his hypothetical plans for forced entry and escape.

Eventually, the pair stopped in front of a room labeled INTERVIEW ROOM #1. Fraser held the door open with a look of expectation. Jason entered and sat on one side of the lone table, facing his reflection in the one-way glass. He peered at it, assuming the mild curiosity of an average man who'd watched plenty of cop shows and movies. In his case, though, he imagined the second detective, Silva, staring back at him from the observation room next door.

Fraser closed the door and sat across from Jason,

placing the folder on the table between them. He started the interview with standard questions, asking for Jason's full name for the record, occupation, and relationship to the deceased. Afterward, he leaned his elbows on the table and stared at Jason with the same assessing look from earlier.

"Were you and your brother close?" he asked.

"Yes, very close. We spent a lot of time together as children," Jason said without missing a beat. A half-truth. He didn't know what "being close" meant, but he knew normal people often felt that way about their siblings.

"And as adults?"

"Not as much, unfortunately. Our lives keep us busy." A beat, long enough for the distress to deepen on his face. "Kept, I guess," he corrected himself softly.

"When was the last time you saw him?"

Jason pretended to rally himself. "Friday. He'd invited Ayana and me to dinner to meet his new girlfriend. We arrived at around... oh... seven thirty? And left shortly after nine. Maybe nine fifteen."

"You were only there for an hour and a half? Is that right?"

"Yes, sir."

The corners of Fraser's mouth twisted into a contemplative frown. "Tell me more about what happened during dinner, if you could."

Alarm bells went off in Jason's head. Fraser wouldn't have asked the question if he didn't already know something had happened. Ayana had mentioned giving the cops a summary of the night but hadn't shared details. Vaguer was better, they'd agreed.

He hesitated. "I might've interrogated Connor's girlfriend a bit harshly. I couldn't help it, though. He's made some unfortunate romantic choices in the past, and I wanted to be sure she was good enough for him. But other than that, it was a pretty normal dinner. We got to know each other, Connor and I had a smoke after, and then Ayana and I left."

Fraser pinned him with a piercing stare. "Did you and your brother talk about anything in particular, either during dinner or afterward?"

Jason spread his hands. "No, not really."

"Is there any specific reason you left after only an hour and a half?"

"It'd been a long day, and my wife and I were both tired. We're also not much for socializing." His brow furrowed with his best imitation of regret and sorrow. "We should've stayed longer, though. If I'd known..."

Fraser deepened his forward lean, almost to a comical exaggeration. Perhaps he thought he looked imposing with his shoulders hunched and his arms crossed. Jason wasn't falling for it. "Did you and your brother ever argue?"

Once more, Jason's instincts screamed at him. Fight the intruder. Silence the meddlesome swine. "Sure. What siblings don't argue sometimes?"

"About anything in particular?"

He ran his hand over his face. "In the past, yeah. Connor had a drug addiction in college. We got into a lot of fights over it until I finally convinced him to go to rehab. Then there were his exes. Some were friends with his old dealers, while others *were* his old dealers. They weren't exactly the best partners, and I let him know that. I wasn't going to let them ruin his life. Needless to say, he didn't take my advice well. But that was a while ago. He'd been doing a lot better lately."

Fraser considered Jason for a long moment, then leaned back in his chair and uncrossed his arms. "Connor was found dead here in Lerwick Square, at Centerpoint Parking Garage. Forensics completed the examination earlier this morning and confirmed he died within minutes from gunshot wounds to his lungs. It happened on Saturday at approximately four twenty p.m."

That was new information. Jason memorized it all and remembered to look horrified. "Someone murdered him?"

"We're ruling it a homicide for now, but yes, someone killed him. Do you know of anyone who could've done this? Any enemies, for example?"

Jason searched his memories for anything Connor might've said, but he had a habit of not paying attention to his brother's interests. "No, sorry. I can't even imagine him with enemies, but... well, he *was* an investigative journalist for the *Lancing Daily*. If he ruffled some feathers, then maybe, but he never said anything about it to me."

"Did you receive any communication from him after you left his residence on Friday?"

"No, nothing."

"And what were you doing on Saturday?"

"I spent the day with Ayana. We baked egg tarts, watched a movie, and cooked dinner together."

Fraser's head bobbed in a slow, contemplative nod. He placed his hand on the manila folder. "These are photos of the body. You don't have to look at them if you don't want to, but I brought them just in case you want to see."

Jason had already made up his mind to look at the photographs, but he hesitated again, staring at the folder with a trepidation appropriate for a person who'd never seen a corpse in his life. He counted five seconds in his head, then nodded, swallowing hard. "Show me."

The folder slid across the table and into his hands. He opened it. The first photograph showed Connor sprawled out on dark concrete, a pool of dried blood framing his torso. Blood stained his white T-shirt and navy trucker jacket, too. The plain, mundane nature of Connor's clothing was a jarring contrast to all that crimson—or it would have been, if Jason hadn't created many similar crime scenes in the past. The image did, however, rip away the skepticism that had shrouded him since he received the news. Ayana had undone some of the seams, as she had no reason to lie, but photographic proof chased away the remaining doubts.

He took photos of his own victims for the same reason.

He flipped through the rest of the photographs, taking the time to examine the details of each one. White parallel lines painted at regular intervals on the concrete surrounding Connor confirmed the location of his death. No cars were visible, but that made sense; the police had cleared out the crime scene and taped it off to prevent unauthorized entry. Jason imagined how the murder might have happened: Connor walking past empty cars, minding his business, only to find himself at the wrong end of a gun. Had the killer been a thief looking for some quick cash? A coworker with a personal vendetta? A former college friend he'd once wronged?

Fraser's voice jolted Jason from his dark musings. "I think we can end the interview here. Thank you for coming today, Mr. Ridley. I'll keep you updated as the investigation progresses. Do you have any questions for me before you go?"

Jason was gripping the stack of photos so hard that he'd bent the thick, glossy paper. When he dropped them back onto the manila folder, they no longer lay flat. "Connor's things—where are they?"

Fraser took the folder back and gently bent the photos the other way to fix the crease. "With Officer Ballard at the front desk. Speak with her before you go. She'll hand over what personal effects were on your brother when we found him."

"Thank you, Detective."

When Jason went to collect Connor's possessions, the detention officer presented a worn leather wallet and a ring of keys, but no cell phone. She repeated Fraser's words: that Connor hadn't been carrying a phone at his time of death. That seemed unlikely to Jason. Most people did, especially Millennial journalists like Connor. As Jason left the precinct, he looked through the wallet. Several cards and bills were still inside, including Connor's driver's license.

Whoever had killed him hadn't cared about those things but had taken his phone. Jason was sure of it.

His feet took him in the direction of the nearest subway station, but his mind was far away, recreating the moment of Connor's death. The details were hazy, smearing together like the world did on a rainy day, but his brother stood as the vivid centerpiece in white and blue. Jason played the confrontation over and over, replacing the assailant with a different person each time, with a different angle of approach. Imaginary gunshots echoed in his head again and again. The more he envisioned the encounter, the less it mattered that he didn't know the killer's face. He saw a wicked grin, or perhaps a sneer. Greedy eyes. A mocking laugh.

The charade of sadness fell away. Cold fury swept through Jason in its wake, no longer stifled by skepticism or performance. He descended into the underground, his hands clenched into white-knuckled fists.

Chapter Seven

The hours following Connor's autopsy were a blur. Detectives from the Lerwick Square Police Station arrived to receive the initial findings; when they learned Ayana was the deceased's sister-in-law, they interviewed her in the sitting room. She called Jason after they left to relay what happened, but not long after, the details of their questions and her answers spiraled out of her head like blood down a drain. Shock, perhaps. Though Connor's organs had been normal, she read his report several times, memorizing the details, gripped with a sudden fear that the computer would delete the file overnight.

Work proved a necessary balm. She hyperfocused on the next autopsies, retreating into the comfort of their mechanical rote: external examination, chest incision, organ removal, dissection, weighing. By the time Rahul wheeled in the last decedent of the day, Ayana had compartmentalized the morning's revelation for later perusal.

"Who do we have here?" She removed the cloth covering the corpse. The gaunt, pallid face of a middle-aged woman emerged from beneath the white fabric. Strands of silver threaded through her hair.

"Lisa Templeton, fifty years old. Her niece found her dead in her apartment yesterday."

Ayana's eyes flickered over scabs and sores from multiple injection sites, as well as scratches on the dead woman's skin, likely caused by irritation. "So she died alone?"

"Yeah. Rough way to go."

The autopsy began without cause for alarm, but when Ayana peeled back the flesh of the chest and abdomen to reveal the body cavity, the sight that greeted her shattered the illusion of normalcy she'd built up over the past few hours. Rahul saw it, too, and gasped.

Countless small holes, as black as the void, trembled along organs and bone. The John Doe's cadaver from the previous week had possessed only a patchwork arrangement of the nightmarish condition, leaving parts of him unblemished. Not so with Lisa. Every inch of her innards shivered with an affliction that pulsed and twitched like something alive.

"Harvey," Ayana said, remembering her promise. "Wait here. I'm getting him to look at this while we have her open."

After removing her protective equipment and washing her hands, she marched up to his office and knocked on the door. His voice ushered her inside. He sat at his desk, typing at his computer, but paused and looked up as she entered. Sympathy settled into his face—an expected reaction, but one she didn't want from *him*.

"Hudson, my condolences for your loss. If you need to take bereavement, I completely understand."

"I'm fine. Thank you." The shock of Connor's death was already fading, replaced with a more urgent matter. "Can you please come into the autopsy suite? We have another instance of the abnormality. I need you to look at it, Harvey, and tell me why you got rid of the first one."

All the compassion bled from his face, leaving only a tension she could not name. Still, he followed her down the hall. An autopsy technician helped him into a set of protective equipment while Ayana managed her own in a quarter of the time. She waited for him at the entrance to the suite, then led him to the station where Rahul stood sentinel. Harvey's face paled beneath his mask and face shield when he laid eyes on the corpse, yet he maintained a stoic, professional demeanor while surveying the body.

Ayana frowned. Had she and Rahul been so calm upon seeing the holes for the first time?

"The first decedent with this phenomenon didn't have nearly these many holes," she said. "We can't know if this woman's condition is a more advanced stage of the disease, or if it afflicts people in different ways, or *anything*. We need more data and our first sample is gone." She leveled a pointed look at Harvey.

He clasped his gloved hands behind his back. "You're right, Hudson. We *do* need to do something about this."

She stood straighter and lifted her chin in triumph. Finally, she had gotten through to him. Finally, he understood the gravity of the situation.

"Sew her back up," he said, dashing her victory on jagged rocks. "I'll call the crematorium to pick her up this evening."

Ayana staggered back as if he'd punched her in the gut. "What?"

"You're an intelligent woman, Hudson. I don't think I should have to repeat myself."

Her hands shook so violently that balling them into fists did nothing to quell the tremor. "With all due respect, Harvey," she said, hearing the quiver in her voice as well and hating how it made her sound, "this is a situation that we, as doctors, have never seen before. It is our *scientific imperative* to study it in the lab, to understand what's causing it and how it's affecting patients. We don't even know if it's what caused their deaths."

He scanned the cadaver a second time with the same stoicism from earlier, his gaze lingering on the pockmarked arms. "This woman was a drug addict. Cause of death: heroin overdose." He met Ayana's gaze with the authority of a man who expected to be obeyed. "You can put that in the report, Hudson. Now sew her back up. I won't say it again."

"How can you be so dismissive?" she exploded. "What kind of conspiracy are you part of? How many of these bodies have you seen? And how many have you covered up?"

He flushed a bright scarlet. "How dare you!"

"How dare *me*? How dare *you* insult my profession like this! I have half a mind to report you to the Board unless you tell us exactly what you're up to."

"No, I don't think you will." His tone took on a dangerous edge, the kind mothers warned their daughters about. "I think the Board of Physicians would have some serious concerns if one of their licensed doctors started raving about strange holes in cadavers without any evidence. It would be a shame to lose a license that way, wouldn't it?"

The raging fire in Ayana extinguished all at once, as if she'd plunged into a vat of ice water. Every part of her went numb. She did not trust herself to speak, not while Harvey remained in the room with her.

Sweat glistened on his wide forehead. His eyes above his face mask wrinkled in smug satisfaction; he must have taken her silence as a sign of complacency. "Why don't you take bereavement for the rest of the week? Clearly the stress from losing a beloved family member is affecting your judgment. Take the rest of the day off after this last task. Just remember to fill out your timesheet before you go."

With a farewell nod to Rahul, Harvey ambled out of the autopsy suite, leaving the pair alone with the corpse. Ayana remained frozen where she stood, her gaze fixed upon a groove in one of the machines on the other side of the chamber.

"Dr. Hudson? What should we do?" her assistant asked in his meek voice.

Scream, she wanted to say. Break something. Rage at the injustice against women of her caliber while weak men threw their weight around like unworthy gods. But she forced herself to recover her composure. She did not know how serious Harvey was about reporting her to the Board, but she couldn't take the chance. Not after how long she'd worked, nor how hard.

She looked first at the cadaver, then at Rahul. "We do our jobs."

As they sewed up Lisa Templeton in silence, Ayana wished she'd had the foresight to sneak her personal phone into the autopsy suite for pictures. With her forced bereavement, she didn't know when she'd get another opportunity. In the break room afterward, she poured herself another cup of coffee, not caring that it was already late afternoon. Rahul joined her after returning the decedent to the cold lockers.

"I'm sorry about what happened back there," he said.

She arched a quizzical eyebrow. "Why?"

"I know you want to get to the bottom of whatever *that* is, but we won't get another chance. I agree with you, though. We should be studying it. What Mr. Blumenthal is doing is wrong."

Ayana pursed her lips. An idea had formed in her head while she waited for the coffee to finish brewing. She chose her next words carefully. "You have friends among the nurses at Upper Kemsing Hospital, don't you?" she asked, lowering her voice.

"Yeah."

"Can you ask them if they've seen any signs of the affliction among living patients? And if so, we need to understand if there's some kind of trend among them. We need their medical history, their family's medical history, their socioeconomic status—anything. Everything."

He stared at her in disbelief. "You're asking me to breach patient confidentiality."

"I can pay you. You need money for your husband's medication, right? Name your price."

The incredulity on his face transformed into quiet outrage. "Dr. Hudson, you've just crossed a line. I will *not* be bribed to do something illegal. Out of the respect I once had for you, I won't tell Harvey you just said this to me, but you can cease considering us friends."

Before she could respond, he turned and stomped out of the break room. She watched his retreating back until he turned a corner and disappeared from view, then sighed. To the empty air, she said, "I don't have any friends, Rahul."

· · · · **·** · **·** · · ·

The mouthwatering aroma of sesame oil, ginger, garlic, and chili invaded Ayana's nose the moment she entered her townhouse. In the kitchen on the second floor, she found her husband's familiar figure by the stove, a ladle in one hand, a fistful of basil leaves in the other. After dropping her tote bag onto an armchair in the living room, she sidled up to him and wrapped her arms around his midsection.

"What's for dinner?" She rested her chin on his shoulder.

"Three cup chicken." He tossed the basil into the wok and stirred the food with vigor, forcing her to step back and give him room. "There's fresh rice in the rice cooker."

Hot steam bloomed in her face when she opened the appliance. "I took bereavement leave for the rest of the week, so I can help you with the funeral and anything else you might need to do for Connor. We work with a few different funeral homes at the office, so I'll give you their numbers tomorrow."

"Sure. Thanks."

"How'd the police interview go?"

Jason scooped the chicken onto a serving dish and set it down on the table next to the bowl of rice. Plates and chopsticks were already arranged at their respective seats. "Fine."

Sitting near him, she noticed the tension in his jaw and furrow of his brow. "Do they suspect you?"

He scoffed. "Of course not. I have an alibi."

Silence stretched between them as they began to eat. The hot rice and tender, savory meat were grounding, rooting her in a version of the world where corpses didn't carry impossible secrets.

Halfway through the meal, Jason spoke. "What did you learn from the autopsy?"

Ayana drank some water and cleared her throat before rattling off the details from memory: "Cause of death was multiple gunshot wounds, three total to the torso. Two caused injury to the left lung, one to his left lung and heart. The direction of each injury was front to back, with minor lateral and vertical movement. They were clustered approximately ten to thirteen inches from the top of the head and two to four inches from the left of the midline. No exit wounds. We extracted all three bullets from the chest cavity for analysis with the firearms team. There were also minor abrasions from when the body hit the ground."

He absorbed her report in stony silence. "So the killer stood directly in front of Connor and caught him off guard."

Though reconstructing the crime scene was the responsibility of the police, her imagination had reached the same conclusion. "That's the most likely scenario, yes."

More silence. She could almost see the gears turning in her husband's head. Eventually, he asked, "Do you remember what I taught you about shooting a gun?"

Frowning, she shifted in her chair, recalling the

memory of her first lesson. He'd taken her to a local gun range soon after their courthouse wedding. The gunshots around her had been deafening, and the heavy steel of the pistol unwieldy in her hands. "Not really."

Jason put down his chopsticks and walked over to a wooden decoration mounted on the nearby wall, little more than a foot-long box with a stylized tree burned onto its front face. He gave the right side a sharp tug and it swung open, revealing a handgun nestled within black foam.

Ayana tensed when he returned with the gun in hand. Moving with practiced ease, he pulled back the slide, removed its magazine of bullets, and placed both pieces on the table between them.

"This is a Walther PDP." He tapped its dark gray frame with a finger. "A magazine shoots ten rounds, and I've loaded it with the kind of ammo that should stop someone coming at you at a close distance."

He reassembled the gun and presented it to her with his hand around the grip, his index finger lying flat along its side, and the muzzle pointed away from them both.

"Hold it like this. Don't put your finger on the trigger until you're ready to shoot, and don't aim the gun at someone unless you're going to shoot them."

"I remember," she said, averting her gaze from the weapon.

He lowered the gun. "Ayana, this is serious. Connor didn't die because he was mugged or as some kind of collateral damage in a nearby shootout. Three bullets in a tight cluster, point-blank in the chest? This was a hit, and he was the target. We need to be more vigilant. The murderer might come after me next."

"Because you kill people for a living?" She didn't mean to sound accusatory, but the thought of having to defend herself from an attacker was too much to bear. Between the unexplainable condition of two cadavers and her boss' suspicious behavior, she had enough to worry about. Jason was a killer, too; let him deal with any threats to their safety.

"I know a lot of criminals," he conceded. "They'll use whatever convenient excuse to kill someone. Trust me—I've heard them all."

She forced herself to look at him. "When we got married, you said you can handle anyone who tries to hurt us."

"I can, but in case I'm not around, I need you to know what you're doing."

"I can't carry a gun around the city, Jason. I'm not like you."

"No, but you should at least know how to shoot one. You remember where I put all the guns around the house, right?"

"There." She tilted her chin at the small cabinet, its door still hanging open. "In the console by the front door. The desk in your office. Your bedside table. And the basement room."

"Good." Leaving the loaded gun on the table, he resumed his meal. "The police told me where they found Connor, so I'm going there tomorrow. His apartment, too. Maybe they missed some clue or evidence pointing to the killer."

Ayana had lost her appetite. She stared at the gun, wishing Jason would put it away. "Why? Just leave the investigation to them. They're professionals."

"I'm a professional, too."

Anxiety clawed at her stomach, sudden and acute. "Do you know who could've done it?"

When he met her gaze, his eyes were as hard and unforgiving as steel. "Not yet, but I'll find out, one way or another. And when I do, I'm going to kill them."

Chapter Eight

The basement level of Centerpoint Parking Garage was spotless. The crime scene cleaners had pressure-washed away the bloodstain where Connor had fallen, cradled between two parking spaces, leaving a patch of concrete brighter than its surroundings. Jason stood at the edge of it, tracing the outline of the area with his eyes. When he lifted his gaze, he spied a security camera affixed to the ceiling a few yards away. Though its lens pointed outward to capture as much of the basement as possible, a strategic placement of parked cars would block its line of sight.

Turning away from the site of Connor's death, Jason walked a slow circuit around the garage floor, sweeping the ground for anything unusual: a forgotten bullet casing, a discarded candy wrapper—anything at all. But the police had picked the place clean; not even a glint of an abandoned penny caught his attention. He left empty-handed.

Twenty minutes later, he disembarked the subway in Oldtown to walk the familiar streets to Connor's apartment. At night, its neighborhoods were full of lights and life, with laughter spilling from the various bars, beer gardens, and restaurants of the district. In the clear light of mid-morning, however, the streets were tranquil. The few residents Jason passed were out walking their dogs, jogging, or procuring coffee from the hipster cafés that flourished there. Outside Connor's residence, Jason didn't notice any strange vehicles parked along the curb or suspicious individuals loitering on the sidewalk. A good sign, he thought.

In the lobby of the apartment building, he retrieved Connor's mail from the double row of thin, metal rectangles that served as mailboxes. Thumbing through the white envelopes revealed them as either spam or overdue bills.

"Sorry, but I really don't know anything about Connor Ridley."

Jason's head jerked up at the voice. An older woman stood within an open door marked EMPLOYEES ONLY. She was speaking with a lanky, dark-skinned man in a button-up shirt and jeans, who was holding up his phone between them. From where Jason stood, he saw an app open on the screen, scrolling to the left at a steady pace—the kind used for recording voice memos.

"That's okay," the man said. "Can I give you my phone number, at least? That way, if you learn anything new, you can give me a call."

She looked uncertain. "Sure... What's your name again, kid?"

"Trey Simmons."

Jason stepped up to the pair and addressed the woman. "Excuse me. Are you the owner of this apartment complex?"

Both of them looked over at him. "I am," she said. "Who're you?"

"Jason Ridley. My brother Connor—"

"Died. Yeah, I know. Police came by. Sorry to hear."

"Thank you. I need to get everything from his unit, but I won't be able to do it in the next few days, with the funeral and all. How much time are you willing to give me?"

She sighed. "Well, he never paid rent for this month. It's due tomorrow, and I have a feeling he was gonna be late on it. If you can pay it on time, I'll give you the whole month to move his things out. How's that sound?"

Jason flashed her his most charming smile. "You're amazing. How much is rent?"

"Eighteen hundred."

Trey winced, but Jason was nonplussed. He plucked a blank check from his wallet, filled it out in neat, legible handwriting, and handed it to the landlady. She beamed at him, revealing a gap between her front teeth.

"You let me know if you need anything else, all right, dear?" she said.

"Of course. Thanks again."

Trey, who'd been peering at Jason with keen interest ever since his interruption, jumped in—as Jason expected he would. "You're Connor's brother? Do you mind if I interview you? I'm Trey Simmons, with the *Lancing Daily*."

That information gave Jason pause. "You worked with Connor?"

"Sort of? He was my senior. I talked with him a few times, but we weren't really friends. I'm writing an article about his—you know, the incident."

"The murder."

Trey's mouth widened in an awkward smile. "Well, technically, it's a homicide until a suspect is charged with murder, but yeah, the murder."

Jason considered the request. The only factor preventing the police from interrogating him more thoroughly was his alibi with Ayana. If Trey published an article describing what a good relationship the Ridley brothers had and highlighting Jason's sorrow over Connor's death, it could lessen whatever suspicions the police still harbored.

"Sure, I don't mind answering some questions. I'm going to check on Connor's apartment right now, actually. You're welcome to come along."

Trey hurried into the elevator after Jason, almost with a skip in his step. He kept glancing over as he started a new recording and began his line of questioning. "Okay, so... Can you please state your name for the record and your relationship with Connor Ridley?"

"Jason Ridley, Connor's older brother."

"And what was your relationship like? What was your childhood like?"

"It was good," he lied. "Connor was the kind of little brother who followed me around everywhere. We were close enough in age that he tried to get into everything I was into. He'd play the same sports, read the same books... But, at the same time, we had enough of a gap in our ages that he eventually became his own person after I left home."

"Yeah? You left?"

"After I graduated high school."

"Right, right. Did Connor follow you to the same college?"

"No, I enlisted in the Army. By the time I ended my service, Connor had moved here to attend Lancing University."

The elevator arrived at the fifth floor. Jason exited, Trey at his heels.

"So you're not originally from Lancing?"

"No, we grew up in the Virginia suburbs, just outside Washington DC." Fishing Connor's key ring from his pocket, Jason unlocked the door of his brother's apartment and stepped inside. Nothing had changed since his last visit. He dropped the mail onto the kitchen table and peered into the refrigerator. Its inventory consisted almost entirely of condiment bottles, except for an open packet of bacon, a half-empty carton of eggs, and leftovers from Friday's dinner. He popped the cover off the food container of dumplings and walked over to the trash can.

Trey appeared at Jason's side in a flash. "Wait, don't throw those out! I'll eat them. I only had coffee for breakfast today."

After a moment's hesitation, Jason handed over the container. "Suit yourself."

While Trey waited for the food to heat up in the microwave, he examined a collection of framed photographs on a nearby bookshelf. He picked one up and showed it to Jason. "Is this your family?"

Jason recognized it from when he was a teenager. His grandmother had endured a long flight from Taiwan to visit them, so his family took her into the nation's capital for a day of tourism. Fourteen-year-old Jason slouched at the old woman's side, glowering at the camera, while ten-year-old Connor hugged her with a beaming grin. His white father and half-Taiwanese mother stood on either side of the boys, each with a hand on a son's shoulder. In the background behind them, the Washington Monument reached for the sky.

"Yeah."

"Huh, cool." Trey put the photo back with the others. "Hey, you think I could interview your parents for my article? Would they be up for it?"

"Not possible." Jason paused, knowing people hesitated before speaking about bad memories. "They're dead. Car crash."

"Shit, man. I'm sorry."

"It's fine. It happened a long time ago."

After emptying the refrigerator and freezer, Jason explored the rest of the apartment, searching for clues. Nothing seemed amiss, however. In fact, each room existed in a state of limbo, frozen in time until a return that would never come. A load of laundry sat in the dryer, waiting for someone to put it away. Plants thirsted in their pots. A pile of crumpled receipts and spare change occupied the center of the coffee table.

"How's the article coming, by the way?" Jason asked as he walked into Connor's bedroom. An unmade bed took up most of the space inside; a dresser and small desk squeezed into what remained. The closet door was open, revealing a colorful row of shirts on hangers. Jason made his way to the desk, drawn by the laptop resting on its surface.

Trey lingered in the doorway with his reheated dumplings. "Not well." The color on his cheeks deepened as he blushed. "The cops are being super secretive. They told me they're interviewing family members and friends right now to narrow down possible suspects. Somehow, I can't help feeling like I'm trying to catch up to them with my own investigation."

"So you don't have anything at all."

"That's not true! I'm just—I'm working on it."

The laptop prompted Jason for a password, offering "summer 2006" as its hint. He drummed his fingers against the top of the desk, stumped.

"What happened in 2006?" Trey asked, leaning over

Jason's shoulder.

"We went on our last trip to Taipei to visit our grandmother. We were there for six weeks." Jason reached back through the decades of memories. Piercing the haze of time, he recalled the sweltering humidity, late afternoon rains, and the sting of sunburn on his too-white shoulders. Shaved ice had been the brothers' favorite snack during those torturous days, especially when served with fresh fruit and condensed milk.

How dull and pointless those days had been.

Jason typed a few different word combinations into the laptop. It accepted his fourth guess.

"Nice!" Trey said. "So what are you hoping to find in Connor's files?"

"Anything that explains what he was doing in Lerwick Square on Saturday."

The triumphant grin faded from Trey's face. "Right."

However, a quick look through the folders revealed they were empty, even the recycling bin. It was as if Connor hadn't used his laptop at all.

"This ain't right," said Trey, shaking his head. "Your brother brought his laptop into the office every day to write articles. Someone must've tampered with it. Not the cops, but someone else."

All at once, Jason knew. He looked around the bedroom, seeing it with new eyes. "The killer. They got here before we did."

Trey rubbed the back of his neck. "Shit. You really think so?"

"There's no other explanation."

"What can we do?"

Jason considered the other man. "You said Connor brought his laptop to work. Do you have some kind of cloud service where he might've uploaded notes or documents? Maybe even photos?"

"Uh, yeah. I can check."

"Thanks. Let me know if you find anything. Here—my number."

"Cool. I'll let you know if I learn more from the police, too."

A grateful smile spread across Jason's face. "I owe you one."

Trey mirrored his smile. "No, man, you helped a lot by talking about your childhood with Connor. It's the least I could do."

They left the apartment building with the laptop and its charger in a backpack Jason took from Connor's closet. On the sidewalk, Jason paused, a potential solution to a particular problem forming in his mind. He turned to Trey. "Hey, are you looking for other people to interview for your article?"

"Yeah, why? Got someone in mind?"

"I do. Someone who's been around Connor a lot recently and probably knows more about what he was doing in the days leading up to his murder."

"Who?"

"His girlfriend, Sabrina Kopanski."

Chapter Nine

Ayana flashed Sabrina a friendly smile as soon as she caught the other woman's gaze from across the bistro. Sabrina hurried over and wrapped her arms around Ayana in a fierce hug. Caught off guard, Ayana stiffened, but the other woman didn't seem to notice.

"I'm so glad to see you," she said, pulling away and holding Ayana at arm's length. Her reddened eyes and fragile smile suggested recent tears.

Of course. She was grieving.

Ayana wondered if she'd ever looked so miserable over a man she'd only known for four months. "I'm glad to see you, too. Are you okay?"

Sabrina barked out a strained, sad laugh. "No."

"Let's get some food. That'll make you feel better."

They sat down with their meals not long after ordering: chicken Caesar salad for Ayana and a shrimp alfredo bowl for Sabrina. Ayana debated the best way to approach conversation when her companion opened with the most obvious topic: "Have you heard the news about Connor?"

"Yes. I actually performed his autopsy myself."

Sabrina paused and looked up, the surprise on her face quickly morphing into recognition. "Oh, right. Makes sense." She resumed eating. "The police told me it's a homicide. Someone gunned him down."

"It couldn't have been an accident," Ayana said, uninterested in entertaining other possibilities. Facts were facts. "Connor was my brother-in-law, but you probably knew him better than I did. Do you know of anyone who might've had a grudge against him?"

"No. I have no idea. The police asked me that, too."

So Sabrina had agreed to an interview as well. Ayana pursed her lips. "What else did they ask? Wait, let me guess—when you last saw Connor and what you were doing Saturday afternoon?"

"Yeah. You too, huh?"

"Me too."

"I wish I knew more." Sabrina heaved a deep sigh. "Connor told me he was going to do some research for this new article he's writing, but he didn't say what kind. I don't know how it could've gotten him shot."

That was new information. "Did he at least share what he was writing about?"

"No. I think he was still in the early stages of researching it."

Ayana sank into her musings while she ate. Sabrina's

interview with the police was a potential risk for Jason. He was so confident she'd never reveal how she'd stumbled upon him in the middle of a murder, but Ayana wasn't so sure. Though religious belief was no guarantee of virtuous morals, Sabrina worked for a nonprofit that provided charitable relief to unfortunate groups. If anyone were to tattle on Jason at risk of their own life, Sabrina was a prime candidate.

"Did you have a good weekend? Do anything exciting?" Sabrina asked, the whiplash of her sudden questions momentarily knocking Ayana off-balance.

She recalled the importance of her husband's alibi. "Oh, yes. Jason and I stayed at home, made egg tarts together, and watched a movie. The one where two astronauts try to get back to Earth after their space shuttle is destroyed."

"So you were home all weekend? Jason too? He didn't go out at all?"

There it was. "Why does it matter?"

"I just—" Sabrina looked away. "I guess it doesn't."

"If you're trying to insinuate something, I'd like to hear it."

"No, I'm not. It's just..." A long, tense pause. "Connor looked bad Friday after you left. He said he was fine, that he'd just tripped in the dark and hit his head on the wall. I asked him about the yelling and he said he and Jason got into an argument, but it wasn't a big deal. But it *was*, Ayana." Fury and hurt flashed in her eyes. "They were arguing about *me*."

Ayana's mind raced for an appropriate response, but Sabrina barreled forward with her rant.

"Jason apparently doesn't think I was good enough for Connor, but when I got mad about how much of a judgmental asshole your husband is, guess what? Connor *defended him*, saying that Jason's always had his best interests at heart. Can you believe that? In a single breath, Connor said how he was arguing with his brother about me, then defended his brother *to* me!" She leaned in and grasped Ayana's wrist. "Are *you* okay, Ayana? He doesn't hurt you, does he?"

Ayana yanked her wrist from the other woman's grip. "I would never have married Jason if I thought he was going to hurt me. I have too much self-respect for that," she said, enunciating each word with deliberate slowness. She took a deep, steadying breath through her nose. "I agreed to meet you because I wanted to get to know you, as a friend, but if you're just going to sit there and disparage my husband, I'd prefer to leave."

At least Sabrina had the grace to look chastised. "I'm sorry. I—I don't know what came over me. My emotions have been all over the place since Connor died. It hurts a lot more than I expected."

Ayana did not respond for a long moment while she struggled to rein in her own emotions. "Did you love him?" she finally asked.

"I don't think so, but I was starting to see the potential in him as someone I could spend the rest of my life with. We liked a lot of the same things, had a lot of the same preferences. I'd started spending the night at his place, too. Not every weekend, but I had a toothbrush and hairbrush there, just in case. He even gave me his spare key."

"Liking the same things doesn't necessarily mean you're compatible."

"Of course not, but I also got the sense he was... This is going to sound silly, but it felt like he completed me."

Ayana bit back a derisive laugh. "The other night, you said you wanted advice. If you're going to heed anything I say, heed this: do not seek a future partner who will complete you. You're a complete person, all by yourself. Instead, seek one who enhances the life you already have. You're young, Sabrina. This isn't the end, even if it feels like it. No matter what pain you're feeling, it will pass, and you'll move on."

Sabrina fell into a contemplative silence and picked at her food. Ayana forced herself to resume eating, too. Though her salad no longer appealed to her, the ritual of eating brought with it a sense of calm.

Eventually, Sabrina spoke again in a more subdued voice. "If you don't mind me asking, how does your marriage enhance your life?"

Ayana had pondered the same question before—two years ago, in fact, when she watched over Jason while he slept, recovering from the ordeal that ended up binding them together. She was ready with the answer. "It brings me a sense of security. Jason is dependable and predictable. I never have to wonder about him. I find that comforting."

Perhaps others in her situation would struggle with his temperament and personality, but once she knew how to classify her husband, managing him became easy. He was a person like anyone else, with his own triggers, desires, expectations, and interests. What set him apart, in her mind, was how much simpler his were. He demanded her loyalty, her competence, some privacy, and little else. Even her affection was optional; she could give it, or not, however she wished. That alone had been enough to encourage fondness of him during the first year of their relationship.

Sabrina's surprise was plain on her face. "Really? Did something happen to you before?"

It was a logical conclusion. Ayana hesitated, a deflection perched on her tongue, ready to spare her from baring an old wound to a stranger. But she'd promised Jason she'd keep an eye on Sabrina, and the best way to do that was to secure her friendship. People didn't share their inner thoughts and plots with acquaintances, after all. Swallowing the deflection, Ayana said, "I dated someone while I was in medical school and doing my residency. We were together for four years. Unfortunately, it ended when I found out she was cheating on me."

"Oh, God, that's horrible."

"When I asked her why, she said she'd grown frustrated with our relationship. I was too busy with school and work to pay her the attention she wanted. I reminded her that when she first asked me out, I told her I was going to prioritize my career; it was important to me, after all. She was fine with it, until she wasn't."

Sabrina sat back in her chair. "Four years. Were you thinking of marrying her?"

"At the time, no. It wasn't something I wanted to think about until after I finished everything and secured a job. But maybe I would've, if things had turned out differently." Ayana sighed. "I'll be honest: I was devastated. Breaking up with me would've still hurt, but the fact that she didn't have the courage to end our relationship before starting another one... It made me feel expendable."

"I'm sorry."

"Don't be. It was a long time ago. I'm happily married now, to a husband I know would never hurt me." She leveled a pointed look at Sabrina. "In that way, or in any other."

Sabrina fiddled with her fork. "I see." Another long pause. "Listen, I'm sorry. It was wrong of me to insult Jason like that, let alone to your face. I guess I just jumped to conclusions because of behavior I've seen in other people. I didn't mean to insult you."

Ayana forced a reassuring smile. "I forgive you. Now, why don't we talk about something a bit more lighthearted?"

The two women chatted for another half-hour before Ayana reached her limit for social interaction and excused herself. She learned nothing of note in the interim; Sabrina seemed like an average young woman, fresh out of graduate school and eager for real world experience. Unfortunately, she also had a sharp mind. She'd pierced the veil of Jason's deception and seen his true face. Though she hadn't mentioned their encounter and had even apologized for mischaracterizing him, no person lived under a death threat with eyes wide shut. Sabrina was smarter than she was letting on; Ayana was sure of it. And sooner or later, one of their lies would unravel first. She had to ensure it wasn't hers.

With no other plans after lunch, she went straight home. The familiar, dark red brick of her townhouse's façade greeted her like an old friend. At the front door, she slid her key into the lock, as she'd done hundreds of times before, and turned it.

It did not budge.

Ayana froze. Was the lock broken? There was no way she'd used the wrong key. Grasping the doorknob with her other hand, she made to remove the key and try something else, but the knob turned as she twisted it and the door swung open, unlocked.

She peeked into the darkness of the entryway. Had she forgotten to lock the door when she'd left the house that morning? No, she'd tested the knob to be sure, and it hadn't budged then. Was Jason home from visiting Connor's apartment, then, and he'd simply forgotten to lock it? Another no. His profession made him careful with everything. His shoes, coat, and keys were missing from the entrance, anyway. He was still out.

Her shoulders tight with tension, she stepped inside, careful not to make a noise. She slipped off her heels and slowly placed her bag and keys on the floor. After wiping her sweaty palms on her coat, she glanced at the wooden console next to the door. Jason's instructions unfurled in her mind, revealing the hidden compartment where he'd stashed one of his handguns. She removed the slim weapon with shaking hands and crept toward the stairs.

Above her, the floorboards creaked as someone walked through her house.

Chapter Ten

Jason pounded on Izzy Espino's front door with a heavy fist. He stood in the hallway outside her studio apartment, ignoring the sharp scent of piss emanating from the nearby stairwell. Down the hall, a couple screamed at each other in a language he hadn't learned yet. A huge rat scurried across the filthy floor, saw him, and fled in the opposite direction.

The pumping bass of heavy metal music thudded through Izzy's door, muffled by the thick metal. Sighing, Jason knocked again, with greater force. After waiting another minute, he raised his fist a third time, but the door opened before he could strike it. The guttural screaming of a song poured out, blasting his eardrums. A woman who was *not* Izzy stared at him with wide eyes before squeezing past and hurrying down the hall. Izzy herself appeared a half-second later, her shoulder-length black hair askew, her dark eyes sparkling with mirth. An oversize black T-shirt sporting Japanese kanji covered her thin frame. Burgundy sweatpants and mismatched socks completed her appearance.

She slung Jason a crooked grin and opened the door wider so he could enter. "Sorry to keep you waiting. Cass had to get dressed first."

He said nothing as he surveyed the inside of her cramped studio. It barely had space for the enormous, L-shaped desk that housed her prized possession, a custom computer rig glowing with rainbow-colored lights. The headache-inducing music poured from its speakers, causing her army of intricate plastic models to shake on their stands. Lunch in the form of takeout lumpia spread out on the narrow kitchen counter, while a stack of empty Monster Energy cans formed a delicate pyramid at its far end.

"Turn off this noise," he said. "I can't hear myself think."

With an exaggerated sigh, she paused her music. The sudden silence was jarring and made all other sounds louder in comparison: the whir of computer fans, the muffled yelling from another apartment unit, the traffic from the street.

Izzy collapsed into her computer chair. "Okay, boss. What brings you to my humble abode?"

He unshouldered the backpack he'd brought with him and took out Connor's laptop. "File recovery."

She shot him a bewildered look. "I'm not standard IT service, Jason. You can go to any old computer repair shop for that."

"This is my brother's computer."

"Oh, did you steal it?"

"No. He's dead."

Her eyes bugged out. "Holy shit! How'd he go?"

"Gunshots to the chest."

"No way. Was it a hit?"

"Likely. The laptop, Izzy."

Shoving aside a pile of comic books, she cleared space on her desk and set the laptop down on it. When the password prompt appeared on its screen, she looked up at Jason expectantly.

"Fulian zero six, all lowercase," he said, then spelled it out for her.

She wrote it down on a piece of paper decorated with cute cartoon animals. "Does that mean anything?"

Fulian Park was the playground in Taipei where he and Connor spent their days whenever they visited their grandmother. Jason sat on the benches with her, his nose stuck in books about world wars and human anatomy, while Connor shouted in broken Mandarin and ran around with other kids.

"No."

Accepting his answer with an indifferent shrug, she clicked around the folders he'd already checked. "Damn, this thing's empty. You sure it's been used?"

"Yeah. Connor's coworker said he brought it to work every day."

"So you want everything restored?"

"As much as you can grab."

Izzy cracked her knuckles, another crooked grin splitting her face. "You got it. It'll be two hundred upfront, non-refundable."

"That's not all. I need security footage from the basement level security camera at Centerpoint Parking Garage in Lerwick Square."

She whistled. "Date and time?"

"Saturday, February first at four twenty p.m."

"I can get you the full twenty-four hours. Anything else?"

"Any and all personal information you can get on Detectives Fraser and Silva of the Lerwick Square Police Station, a *Lancing Daily* reporter named Trey Simmons, and a woman named Sabrina Kopanski who works for a nonprofit called St. Julian's Foundation."

Izzy shifted in her chair, frowning. "What's going on, Jason? Who are these people?"

He stared her down. "I don't pay you to ask unnecessary questions, Izzy."

She cleared her throat. "You're right. Sorry. Uh, yes, I can get all that for you. It'll be six hundred instead. I'll take half now, half later."

The cash exchanged hands. He left the laptop, charger, and backpack with her and departed with the promise she'd have everything for him in a few days' time. From her apartment, he trekked through dilapidated streets and caught the subway to the docks.

Grosmont Fish Market sat in the epicenter of the

city's harbor district. In the massive, warehouse-like building along its west end, fishermen sold their daily catches to vendors, who sold them to customers in turn. The rest of the market was outdoors, taking the form of small, family-owned restaurants and shops. There, visitors dined on the freshest catches, indulged in local snacks, and purchased souvenirs. Bypassing these tourist traps, Jason made his way into the building. Rows upon rows of vendor stalls greeted him upon entry. Bins and baskets overflowing with ice displayed fresh shellfish, while live specimens—from fish to lobsters to octopi—awaited their deaths in saltwater tanks. Because they were still alive, the cavernous building lacked the pungent, briny smell of most fish markets, making his visit all the more bearable.

Instead of entering the gridwork of stalls, Jason hugged the wall and ducked into a wide corridor. Market staff hustled to and fro, paying him no heed. He navigated the labyrinth of back rooms with ease, following familiar landmarks until he reached a closed, unmarked door. He announced himself with a predetermined pattern: two knocks, a pause for two heartbeats, another three knocks. Without waiting for a response, he shoved the door open and strode into a small, narrow office. Metal filing cabinets lined the opposite wall beneath a window shaded by white blinds. A shelf crammed with binders and hardcover books stood to Jason's immediate right, while a wooden desk occupied the far end of the room to his left. Vince sat in an office chair behind the desk. Another chair closer to Jason was empty.

"Have a seat, Jason." Vince pecked away at his keyboard with only his pointer fingers. "I'll be with you in a moment. Just finishing this email."

Jason lowered himself onto the empty chair. The old wood creaked under his weight. While he waited, he regarded the poster on the wall behind Vince's desk for the dozenth time. *Local Saltwater Fish of the Northeast*, it said at the top. Beneath the title were rows and columns of different species: albacore, bluefish, black sea bass, cod, all the way down the alphabet until tuna, wahoo, and weakfish. He read the whole list five times before Vince finished his email.

Directing his full attention to his guest, the older man laced his fingers together in front of him. "I don't have any new info on Kopanski, if that's what you're here for. Or any new contracts, either—for you, anyway. The Panzieri boy wants to avenge his father, but I'm giving that to someone else."

Vince meant Tyler Panzieri, Robert's son, the heir to both his shipping and criminal empires.

"Who does he think ordered the hit?" Jason asked. It didn't occur to him to ask if Tyler knew who'd pulled the trigger.

"The Monahans, of course. Whether that's true or not, Tyler has plenty of reason to think so. They murdered a Panzieri lieutenant and three of his soldiers a few years back."

That had been Jason's work. The Panzieri lieutenant had killed the Monahan heir, Desmond, in an ugly bout of gang violence. Desmond's father demanded vengeance and hired Jason through Vince. In their line of business, though, the weapon never took the blame, only the one who aimed it.

"Interesting, but not why I'm here. There's something else."

A bushy eyebrow rose into Vince's forehead. "Do tell."

"Someone murdered my brother in Lerwick Square on Saturday." Vince opened his mouth to speak, but Jason held up his hand. "Save it. I'm done hearing condolences."

"Lerwick Square is Monahan territory. Have the cops arrested anyone yet?"

"No. They're digging around, though."

A pregnant pause filled the space between them before Vince asked, "Did *you* kill him?"

Heat flared through Jason. He glared at the older man. "He was my *brother*," he said through clenched teeth. "He was too emotional and made stupid choices and liked to talk too much, but he still had his uses. I had no reason to kill him."

Vince raised his hands in surrender. "Men have killed their brothers for less. So, what do you want from me?"

"If you hear anything in your circles about a man or woman or group of people who killed a man in a white shirt and blue jacket at Centerpoint Parking Garage on Saturday afternoon, let me know. I want to find out who killed Connor before the police do."

"Why? Let them handle it."

Jason's lip curled into a snarl. "Because the motherfucker stole my property, Vince. He trespassed against *me*. And I'm going to make him pay."

Vince pinned Jason with a stern look. "Don't be stupid, son. You've been in this business long enough; you know what happens when things get personal. Tyler Panzieri is going to find himself under the guillotine sooner or later if he continues down this path of vengeance. His family will recover, but it's different for you. Your wife is your only family now, and she's a civilian. You need to consider her safety in all this."

Jason stood with such abruptness that his chair scraped the floor. "I'm not your son, Vince, and you know nothing about my marriage. Don't speak about it as if you do."

Vince did not flinch. "Maybe not, but over the past forty years, I've seen others fall into the same trap and their loved ones suffer for it. Remember, the entire reason we can operate at all in this political hellscape is because we keep things professional. People hire you to be their weapon. No one blames the weapon for the crime, but if the weapon were to start committing crimes all on his own—"

"Spare me the lecture." Jason stomped toward the door.

"Damn it, Jason, I'm trying to help you!" Vince slammed his hands on his desk and shot to his feet. "You have everything going for you right now! Don't throw it away!"

His warning fell on deaf ears. Jason wrenched the door open and banged it shut on his way out. Darkness eclipsed the edge of his vision as he stormed out of the fish market, narrowing the world to a single, violent focus. His blood pounded in his ears, so loudly that he failed to hear the discordant droning trailing him down the street.

Chapter Eleven

Ayana crept up the stairs, her racing heart fit to burst from her chest, her stomach twisted into knots. Swallowing hard, she poked her head over the edge of the second floor and scanned the open area that combined the living room, dining room, and kitchen. Upon first glance, nothing was amiss. The footsteps had stopped, too. The silence permeating the townhouse carried a palpable tension, raising the small hairs on her arms and neck.

The gun was heavy in her hands. Jason had picked a small one—easier to conceal and more ergonomic for her grip, he'd said—but to her, it was little more than an unwieldy block of metal. Wracking her brain to remember his lessons, she flipped the safety off and tugged the slide to chamber the first round. It barely budged. Her heart rate rocketed and fresh sweat soaked her blouse. Pointing the pistol at the floor, she pulled harder. Finally, the slide gave and snapped back into place with a loud clack.

She froze and strained her ears. Whoever else was in the townhouse must've heard the sound, but there was only silence.

In that moment, it occurred to her that she had no idea what she was doing. Even if she found the intruder, was she really going to shoot him? And then what?

She couldn't think about that. She had no time to plan, only act.

Grasping the gun in both hands, Ayana sneaked through the empty kitchen and past the dining table. A door at the far end led to the small office Jason used for his day job. It stood open ajar. She couldn't remember if it had been like that when she'd left the house. Reaching out a trembling hand, she pushed it aside, revealing its simple furnishings, his closed laptop resting atop the wooden desk.

No one was inside. The invader was on the third floor.

A creak from behind turned her blood to ice. "Don't move," said a man's deep voice. Though she didn't recognize it, the accent was one she'd heard before. Bostonian? "I don't want to shoot you, but I will if I have to."

"Okay." Her own voice was barely louder than a whisper. "Not moving."

"Put the gun down—*slowly*. No sudden movements."

The vivid mental image of a pistol pointed at her head compelled her to obey. Bending at the knee, she set her useless weapon down at her feet.

"Now stand up again, slowly, with your hands in the air." When she was upright once more, the man said, "Come away from the door and stand in the center of the room."

She turned and regarded him at last. Though he was only a few inches taller than her, he cut a dreadful figure in his dark, loose clothing and black balaclava. All she could see of his face underneath were a pair of dispassionate eyes that tracked her every move. He kept his gun trained on her while she walked into the kitchen. In the periphery of her vision, she spotted the block of cooking knives Jason kept in razor-sharp condition—too far away.

"We don't keep cash in the house," she blurted out, assuming the man's intention, hoping he hadn't seen the fireproof safe in the master closet where she and Jason kept their emergency fund. "I can give you jewelry, though—gold and gemstones. My husband has a luxury watch, too, a Rolex. It's real, not fake. Just leave the tech, please."

The man stepped between her and the gun he'd forced her to discard—not that she was quick enough to lunge for it before he shot her. "I don't care about that."

Her gaze snapped to meet his.

"Your husband. When will he come home?"

What had Jason done? "I don't know. He didn't tell

me. Why does it matter?"

"Never mind that. I know what he's done—what he's capable of doing. A man like him doesn't deserve to roam the streets freely. So, you're going to cooperate with me, all right? Tell me where he keeps his guns and gear."

Ayana swallowed hard, shoving down the taste of bile alongside her rising dread. Was this man a rival in Jason's main line of work? Or perhaps this was his punishment for letting a civilian witness a murder. Did that mean Sabrina had leaked what she'd seen? The police wouldn't send someone to sneak into a suspect's house, though; they'd barge through the front door with an arrest warrant. And even then, they had no proof of his crimes. If the man wanted Jason's equipment, was he trying to collect evidence to prove her husband's guilt?

"Th-that one's the only gun," Ayana stammered, fear and instinct loosing the lie from her lips before she could stop herself. "We don't own any others. We're normal—"

"Don't bullshit me. I know they're here somewhere."

She glanced past him at the stairwell leading down to the first floor. If she ducked his weapon and ran—

"Down there, huh? In the basement?" The man half-turned toward the stairs but kept his gaze fixed on her. "Show me, and I'll leave you unharmed."

She weighed her options, forcing herself not to think about the kind of harm he could inflict on her if she refused. Simply owning firearms was not illegal, but she had no idea whether Jason's were legal purchases. And while one or two were normal for the average city-dwelling gun owner, the dozens racked on the basement wall were another matter. It could be enough to arrest him. Still, leading the man into the basement and barricading him inside might buy her time to call Jason for help.

Hyperaware of the pistol aimed at her back, she took the stairs at a slow, careful pace. The front door hung open by a sliver, letting in a thin beam of bright light from outside. Her shoes and bag sat nearby. How far could she run if she bolted right now? No, she couldn't; running wouldn't stop the man from ransacking their house for the evidence he sought.

Before she knew it, they reached the bottom of the stairs.

He nudged her with his gun. "Keep going. Where's the basement?"

She spoke without thinking. "This way."

Around the corner, a short hallway led to a small utility room, its concrete floor unfinished. A hot water heater, HVAC unit, and exposed pipes occupied much of the space. Against the far wall, two large, plastic storage containers sat stacked atop each other next to a metal shelving unit. As she crossed the room, Ayana recalled the boxes' combined weight and calculated how quickly she could move them.

"There's nothing here," the man said. The click of his gun sent a fresh spike of adrenaline through her veins.

"You better not be messing with me, woman, or I'll—"

"They're right here," she said, her voice quaking, her fingers clumsy around the replacement air filters she'd grabbed from the shelf. One clattered on the floor at her feet. She snatched it up and set the small pile on top of the plastic bins. Then she grasped the nearer side of the shelf and yanked hard. The entire unit and part of the wall attached to it swung into the room.

Beyond the rough, rectangular hole was total blackness.

Her hands still gripping the shelf, she looked over her shoulder at the man, who stood in the center of the utility room. His eyes narrowed, but they no longer focused on her. They stared into the dark emptiness past the yawning mouth she'd unveiled.

"Careful, there's a step," she said, hoping he'd go first. "The light switch is on the right."

He gestured for her with his gun. "After you."

Panic surged through her. "I—I don't think I should—"

"I said *after you*." His free hand whipped out toward her. Releasing the shelf, she jerked back and stumbled against the wall. Her eyes darted for the door to the hallway, but he closed in, moving fast, blocking her escape. He reached for her again—

A hand dragged him back by the collar. Metal flashed in the dim light. A knife pressed against his neck, right above his carotid artery.

Ayana's breath caught in her throat. Jason stood behind the man, his imposing frame tense as he held the blade to the other's flesh. Wrath darkened his face and turned his eyes into chips of ice. A vein stood out on his temple.

"Listen closely," Jason snarled in the man's ear, his voice low and rough in a way that made her stomach flutter and her skin flush with heat. "I'm going to give you very specific instructions. If you so much as *breathe* wrong, I'm going to kill you."

His wide-eyed captive swallowed hard.

"My wife is going to take your gun from you. Give it to her willingly. Afterward, you're going to put your hands up where I can see them."

Meeting Ayana's gaze, the man turned his gun around so its handle pointed at her. She dashed forward and tore it from his grasp. Wrapping her slim fingers around its bulky grip, she pointed it at him uncertainly. His hands rose into the air.

With startling speed, Jason smashed the handle of his knife against the side of the man's skull. He fell to the floor like a stone.

Ayana stared at the unconscious man, still holding the pistol in both hands. Then her knees buckled and her arms trembled anew. Tears pricked her eyes as she exhaled a sob of relief. Jason took the gun from her and set it aside before folding his arms around her. Burying her face in his shoulder, she curled her fingers in the thick fabric of his coat and cried.

"I'm here," he murmured into her hair. The knife

he'd wielded had disappeared into a pocket; both of his hands cradled her, one at her back and the other at the base of her neck. "You're safe now."

"He knows about you, Jason," she sobbed. "He was asking about your guns, your gear. I think he was trying to collect proof—evidence of crime. Who is he? How does he know all this?"

The edge returned to his voice. "I intend to find out."

She lifted her tearstained face and met his unforgiving gaze. His thumbs rubbed her cheeks, wiping the wetness away. "We can't call the cops, can we?"

"No." He extricated himself from her embrace, prompting a voice inside her to wail with selfish want. "We have only a limited time before—*if*—he wakes up again. Help me with him."

Fighting every urge to draw him back to her and curl up against his chest, she asked, "What do you need me to do?"

"Come with me."

Jason led Ayana into the darkness behind the wall. Flipping the light switch near the entrance brought to life the single lightbulb in the ceiling. Firearms of all shapes and sizes lined one wall, grouped together by similar design. A long folding table, the kind used for buffets, stood against the opposite wall, while at the far end, several metal shelves held an organized assortment of objects. She recognized a few of them, such as a pair of binoculars and several pocket-sized flashlights; others, however, escaped her recognition.

He unrolled a large spool of clear, plastic tarp across the center of the room, spreading it out to cover as much of the concrete floor as possible. Afterward, he gestured to a metal chair, folded up and leaning against the table. "Bring that over here."

She unfolded it while he selected a bundle of thick, synthetic rope from a shelf. He repositioned the chair to his liking, dropped the rope onto the tarp next to it, and ushered her out of the room.

"Quickly. Grab his ankles."

While Ayana lifted the man's legs, Jason hauled him up by the armpits. The dead weight strained her arms and shoulders, but she gritted her teeth and managed not to drop him as they carried him into the chair. While she held him upright, Jason bound the man to the seat with the rope. She watched, enraptured, as his expert hands tied complicated knots she didn't know how to begin unraveling.

"Anything else?" she asked, stepping back.

He shook his head and handed her his coat. "I don't think you should stay down here. Why don't you lie down upstairs? I won't take long."

Her gaze dropped to his free hand hanging at his side. Held in his fingers was his knife, its blade folded into its handle.

Looking him in the eye again, she leaned up and kissed him, pouring every ounce of her gratitude into the gesture. He gripped her waist with a possessive hand. It took all of her willpower not to tug him closer.

"Try not to kill him," she murmured, pulling away despite the sudden flare of desire within her.

A terrible, handsome smile split her husband's face. "No promises."

Chapter Twelve

While the man was still unconscious, Jason closed the door to his hidden room, rolled up his sleeves, and put on a pair of black latex gloves. He checked the man's pockets, finding a lockpicking tool and nothing else, and removed the balaclava covering his head. Only then did the man awaken, blinking away his disorientation. His eyes met Jason's and grew wide with understanding—but, curiously, not fear.

Closing his fist around the handle of his sheathed knife, Jason strode over. The man lifted his chin and set his jaw, his eyes flashing with defiance. Jason punched him across the face. The force of the blow snapped the man's head to the side, but his bindings kept him upright. Grunting, he raised his head again. Blood began trickling from his nose.

"That's for frightening my wife," Jason said, holding back the enormous urge to beat the man into a bloody pulp. Judging by his mild reaction to a fist to the face, he was used to pain. A run-of-the-mill beating would not be enough to extract information from him. Seizing tufts of the man's short, auburn hair, Jason wrenched his head back. "Who do you work for?"

The man grinned. "I'm an agent of God."

Jason punched him again. Scarlet smeared across his knuckles. "Try again."

"You think I'm lying, but I'm not. You're a sinner, Jason Ridley. Killing people for material gain? How arrogant. Who are you to decide who lives or dies?" The man scoffed. Despite his fanatical words, his tone was calm, his gaze bright and clear. "You bear the black mark of the Abyssal King. When the end times come, he will feed upon your corpse along with all the other sinners on this forsaken world. Only those blessed by God's grace will be saved."

Jason flicked open his knife and buried it in the man's shoulder, ripping a scream from his throat. The corner of Jason's mouth twitched in satisfaction. He yanked his blade free from flesh and stood back as the man squirmed in his bonds, breathing hard through his smashed nose.

"I'm going to give you the same terms you gave my wife: cooperate or die," Jason said. Blood dripped from the knife onto the plastic tarp underfoot. "And if I were you, I'd cooperate. God isn't here to save you from me."

A slow, gasping chuckle fell from the man's lips. "What makes you think I'm going to tell you anything?

You think I care if you kill me? I'm not afraid of you. You're only one man, but I'm not alone in my mission. Divine retribution will come for you if I fail. You'll be banished to Hell where you belong."

Jason drove his blade deep into the meat of the man's thigh, above the kneecap. His quiet laugh twisted into a howl of pain.

"How do you know about me?" Jason's last conversation with Vince flashed through his mind. Sabrina. The Panzieris. "Why were you looking for my things? To frame me?"

The man panted harder, sweat beading on his forehead. His smile was tight with agony. "They were right. You're a fucking sociopath." The grin transformed into a crimson-flecked sneer. "The world's better off without your evil. Your *wife's* better off without you. Poor woman."

There was no getting through to him, not with standard techniques. Jason stepped back, prying his knife from the man's wound. He uttered a strangled cry, shoulders shaking. His breath came in ragged gasps. A person with such mental fortitude had to be insane or highly trained. Perhaps both.

"You don't deserve her," the man said, interrupting Jason's thoughts. "She ought to be saved from sinners like you. God will save her. All she'd have to do is forsake you and your sinful ways."

Jason's grip tightened around the handle of his knife. His eyes narrowed.

The man smirked, a haughty gleam in his eye. "She's your weakness, isn't she? It's so obvious. Makes me wonder what you'd have done if I *had* killed her. I wasn't going to, but now I'm thinking I should've. That would've done the trick. Forcing you to find her on the floor, covered in blood, while I'm standing over her—"

Jason's vision went red, his mind blank. He shoved his blade into the man's neck with medical precision, severing an artery. Blood spewed from the wound. The man spasmed in his bindings, a wet gurgle rising in his throat. Jason stood over him, panting, nostrils flaring, eyes blazing fury.

· · · • • • • • · · ·

Later that night, the doorbell rang, announcing Vince's arrival. Jason heard Ayana welcome their guest while he waited in his secret room. As they exchanged pleasantries, it occurred to him they had never met before. Not once had he thought to introduce them to each other—and for good reason. Ignorance of the world that created men like Vince and Jason kept Ayana safe.

Stepping up beside Jason, Vince took one look at the bloody scene and sighed. "I see why you asked for the body van. Who was he?"

"He never said his name. My guess is ex-military, based on the way he smiled through the torture." Jason tossed a white hazmat coverall to Vince, identical to the one he himself was wearing. After killing the home invader, he'd changed into a new set of clothes and washed his stained ones with cold water, hydrogen peroxide, bar soap, and bleach. Cleaning up a body, however, was messier business, and hazmat suits protected them from infections as well as stains.

Vince raised an eyebrow. "Smiled?"

"He was some religious fanatic. I couldn't get any straight answers out of him."

"I see." He shook out the hazmat suit. "Before we begin, do you have any nosy neighbors we should worry about?"

Jason shook his head. It was late enough that the other people living on his street were likely winding down for the night, if not already asleep. "Did you park in the back?"

"Of course. This isn't my first rodeo, Jason."

"Then we'll be fine."

"Good. Let's get started. I'm getting too old for all-nighters."

The men finished gearing up in personal protective equipment and freed the corpse from the chair. They cut the clothes away, stuffed them and the rope into a trash bag, and zipped the victim into a black body bag. His spilled blood had congealed, making it easy for Jason and Vince to roll up the plastic tarp without liquid leaking onto the concrete. They packed it away into a second trash bag and shed their PPE into a third. Within fifteen minutes, they loaded everything into the black, unmarked van parked behind the row of townhouses.

Vince climbed into the driver's seat to call their disposal contact and arrange the drop-off.

Before joining him, Jason approached Ayana. She'd reappeared from upstairs and lingered in the hall with an unreadable expression. Ever since the incident in the utility room, she'd been quieter than usual, her body tense even under his touch, her gaze unable to settle anywhere for long. When he told her he'd killed the intruder, she accepted his decision with a silent nod before drawing him into a tight embrace. He stayed in her arms for as long as she needed, comforting her with his body until she finally, reluctantly released him. Only afterward did he make his preparations and call Vince.

The light citrus scent of her bath soap filled Jason's nose when he kissed her forehead. "I'll be gone for a few hours, so go to bed without me," he murmured, stroking her cheek with a thumb.

"Be safe," she whispered. "Don't get caught."

"I won't."

While the men drove to their destination, Jason caught Vince up on what had transpired, including what he'd learned of the break-in from Ayana. "You saw the body. He had no identifying marks except for a few minor scars and birthmarks," he said. "No tattoos, no jewelry, and his clothes were all plain."

"He was a professional like us, then," Vince said. "Or... at least, that's what I'd assume, if he hadn't specifically been looking for *items*, not *people*."

"Right. Between Sabrina showing up at the penthouse and Connor's death, someone is trying to get me in trouble."

"Seems like it, but I'm struggling to think of who."

"What about the Sons of Saints? Aren't they religious?"

Vince snorted. "Not any more than me. Sure, they're mostly Catholic Latinos, but they named themselves after Saintfield, their territory, not actual saints. No, our mysterious interloper must be part of a new group. I'll do some digging."

Jason rubbed his face with a hand. Finding and killing the person responsible for murdering Connor was already a substantial enough effort on its own; he was used to hunting people whose names and faces he already knew—or, at least, could easily look up. Now he had another mystery on his plate, with a dead man as his only clue.

"Is your wife okay?" Vince asked, cutting through Jason's thoughts. The city around them darkened as they left the busier, livelier neighborhoods and entered the industrial district. "The whole ordeal must've been a fright for her."

Jason considered lying, but Vince had seen Ayana for himself when she'd greeted him at the door. "She's shaken, but she'll recover soon."

"Maybe, but civilians aren't like you and me. It may take her much longer than you think to feel safe again in her own home. This is why you need to let go of revenge, Jason. You'll only put her in *more* danger."

Jason scowled into his side view mirror. The light from outside the van cast angular shadows across his face.

After five minutes of silence, they drew up to the closed gate of a massive, fenced parking lot. Vince lowered his window. The gray-bearded security guard looked up from his crossword puzzle and smiled in recognition. He exchanged a knowing nod with Vince and waved them through the gate. In the gloom, Jason made out the hulking shapes of city buses, garbage trucks, and other municipal vehicles. Beyond them, a squat warehouse with large bay doors stood dark and empty.

"Vince, have you heard of something called the Abyssal King?" he asked as they parked behind a row of garbage trucks.

The older man paused with his hand on the door handle and stared at Jason with an admonishing frown. "Where'd you hear that name?"

"The guy mentioned it a couple of times but never said what it is. Sounded like Satan or something."

"Not quite. Worse."

Jason arched an eyebrow. "You know about it?"

Vince's eyes were as dark and hard as flint. "I've *seen* it."

Before Jason could respond, Vince shoved the door open and exited the car. Jason caught up with him as a man-shaped silhouette peeled from the shadow of a truck. The figure stepped into the beam of the van's headlights, revealing himself as a short man around Jason's age.

"Good evening, Simon," said Vince in a gruff voice. He handed over a wad of cash, which Simon counted on the spot.

"Five hundred. Perfect." He slid the money into his back pocket. "Let's move quickly. My wife thinks I'm still downstairs watching TV."

Working together, the men lifted the body bag out of the van and carried it to one of the garbage trucks. They were top-loading vehicles with metal ladders built into their sides. Simon climbed up first, tossing down one end of a thick cable once he was in position. Working by the headlights of Vince's van, Jason and Vince secured the cable around the corpse.

"Do you hear that?" Simon called down to them.

Jason's head jerked up, expecting approaching sirens but hearing nothing amiss. Police usually didn't come sniffing around that parking lot, anyway, not with the gate guard in Vince's pocket.

"What is it?" Jason asked.

"Not sure. Sounds like... white noise? Radio static?"

He strained his ears. At first, there was only silence. Then he caught it—a faint humming or droning.

Vince cast a nervous glance at the deepening darkness. "Quickly. We don't have time to waste."

Still atop the garbage truck, Simon grabbed his end of the cable, preparing to haul the body up alongside him. Jason started climbing the ladder to lend him a hand, but a sudden, insatiable hunger clawed at his stomach, freezing him in place. The droning grew louder with the steady approach of something unearthly. He sensed it deep in the marrow of his bones. Sweat drenched his skin. Every animal instinct screamed for him to run.

"Get back!" Vince shouted, abandoning the corpse and bolting for the van.

Jason flung himself off the ladder and raced after Vince. Simon was not as quick. The other two glanced over their shoulders to see him halfway to the ground, caught in an unnatural blackness. His mouth hung open in a soundless scream, and his round, terrified eyes locked with Jason's for a split-second before they froze over with ice. Steam rose into the air from Simon's pores. Flesh bruised purple-red beneath spreading frost, pale and cancerous. All the while, his body twisted into thin, elongated shapes, spiraling into the center of the all-consuming void. In a matter of seconds, he was gone, vanished into the ether as if he'd never existed at all.

Jason stood transfixed. How fascinating. How *incredible*.

A shove from Vince jolted him back to the present danger. "Hurry! Before we're next!" the older man shouted.

Jason jumped into the van while Vince scrambled into the driver's seat. The engine roared and they hurtled backward from the darkness. The car's headlights did nothing to pierce the blackness; in fact, what light struck it warped around it before siphoning into its formless shape, devoured. Jason watched as it next fell upon the corpse in the body bag, removing all trace of his deed.

"What the fuck was that?" he asked as they peeled out of the parking lot.

The blood had drained from Vince's face. He clutched the steering wheel with both hands, his knuckles bone-white. "The Abyssal King."

Chapter Thirteen

The front door of the townhouse slammed shut, jolting Ayana from her fitful sleep. She lay frozen in bed, the covers pulled up to her chin. Straining her ears, she listened for the creeping footsteps of another intruder, her imagination spiraling into dreadful nightmares of what might come. But soon she recognized the familiar sounds of Jason putting away his shoes, hanging his coat and keys, and making his way up the stairs. The bedroom door stood open ajar; through the gap, she watched the hallway lights come on, banishing the blackness. A moment later, his silhouette darkened the doorway.

Ayana sat up. The digital clock on her bedside table read one thirty in the morning. "Hey."

The mattress creaked as he sat down next to her. "You're still awake."

"I couldn't sleep." She took his hand. "Is the body...?"

"I've taken care of it."

Anxiety loosened its grip on her nerves. Fighting back a fresh wave of tears, she pressed his palm against her cheek. "Thank you."

He wrapped his arms around her and held her tightly. She melted against him, savoring the warmth and strength of his body against hers.

"I should've been braver," she whispered.

"Don't worry about it." Jason stroked her back with a gentle hand, soothing her. "No one will touch you as long as I'm around."

Closing her eyes, Ayana allowed herself to believe him. He had survived military service and was a veteran in his chosen career. Time and time again, after carrying out deeds that would have doomed lesser men, he returned home to her. Though she'd accepted that he lied as easily as he breathed, no other man was more capable of keeping his word to her, especially since the law did not restrict him. Most importantly, he seemed to *want* to keep the promises he made to her, when he never showed interest in doing the same for others. From what she'd observed, Connor had never enjoyed the privilege while he'd lived.

Thoughts of her dead brother-in-law jogged her recent memory. Her eyes flew open. Lifting her head, she looked into her husband's shadowed face. "Sabrina spoke with the police." In the wake of her heart-hammering encounter with the strange man, she'd forgotten all about her lunch date with the younger woman.

"She's furious and out to ruin you, Jason. She called you an abuser to my face."

His grip on Ayana tightened. "And what did you say?"

"I told her I wasn't going to listen to such slander. She seemed genuinely apologetic, but I don't trust her. Also, I said you were with me all Saturday, so you couldn't have killed Connor."

"She must've told the cops that Connor and I fought at his place after dinner." Jason heaved a weary sigh. "Learn anything else?"

"Nothing substantial. I told her that you and I are making arrangements for the funeral tomorrow. I plan to text her the details so she can attend, if she wants."

"Make sure she does. I'll give a eulogy for Connor that changes her mind."

· · · · ● · ● · · · ·

Nightmares plagued Ayana while she slept, filling her mind with dark shapes that looked like men one moment, only to twist into unspeakable horrors the next. They chased her through the familiar rooms of her townhouse, until suddenly she was no longer home but caught in a labyrinth of white walls, sterile as a hospital and just as sickly. Barefoot, she sprinted from one dead end to another. Her monstrous pursuers closed in, their hideous droning growing louder and louder. She pressed herself against a wall, a scream ripping from her throat as her body unraveled at their touch.

"Those dreams again?" Jason asked, rubbing her arm. She lay beside him, panting, her heart racing in her chest. Dawn had come, sending pale fingers of sunlight through the gap between their curtains. The sight did not fill her with any comfort, however, for in the deepest shadows of the room, she caught glimpses of quivering holes.

She forced herself to focus on the day's errands—namely, accompanying her husband to the funeral home they'd chosen. The staff had already picked up Connor's corpse from the forensic center and were storing him in their cooler. After reviewing the myriad package options and shaking their heads at the exorbitant costs, Jason and Ayana chose a traditional funeral service and visitation. He grumbled later about how pricy taking care of Connor had always been; even in death, his brother made demands of his bank accounts. She made noises of agreement, though she knew from her meticulous records of their finances that they could shoulder the expense without worry.

The couple went their separate ways after eating lunch together: he returned home to handle the legal matters of Connor's death, while she took the subway to Lancing University's library. Harvey had blocked her chances to research the strange, new affliction at work, but his reach did not extend beyond the forensic center's walls.

She disembarked the subway at Upper Kemsing and

walked the rest of the way along a bustling street lined with restaurants. Ahead of her on the opposite sidewalk was the bistro where she'd met Sabrina the previous day. Her pace slowed as she passed it, her gaze drawn not to its familiar façade but to the window of the Italian restaurant next door. She stopped in her tracks, her brain scrambling to make sense of the scene before her eyes.

Harvey sat at a table in plain view, looking chastised, arms crossed and shoulders hunched. Across from him, Sabrina was speaking vehemently and gesticulating with both hands, her face twisted in frustration.

Questions about their relationship swirled in Ayana's head. Though she couldn't make out their words, their interaction ruled out a romantic rendezvous; they kept their distance from each other, leaning away from an invisible line drawn between them. A business meeting, then. But what business did a marketing agent for a religious nonprofit have with the city's coroner? And why did Sabrina, who was young enough to be his daughter, look like she was *berating* him?

Suspicion took root within Ayana. Sabrina's pretense as a frightened girl, upset by the death of her boyfriend, fell away. She was orchestrating something—she had to be. But as much as Ayana wanted to confront the pair in the restaurant, she couldn't act on a mere hunch. She needed more information first. More knowledge.

She continued down the street toward Lancing University.

· · · · • · • · • · ·

The sight of the library's main entrance transported Ayana back to her undergraduate years. Little had changed. Flyers still covered the bulletin board in the lobby, advertising school clubs and campus events. A new generation of students huddled at desks, listening to music through headphones while they typed at laptops, read books, and scribbled notes. Stairs she had traversed dozens of times led to upper floors and maze-like stacks.

At the Service Desk, she obtained a guest ID, password, and directions to the computer room. A dozen PCs in tidy rows greeted her upon arrival, each one with an identical setup. They were all newer models than the ones in her memories, and faster, too. Within a few minutes, she was logged in and searching the Internet. A few clicks of her mouse brought up several medical journals. She took her time browsing their databases, seeking articles about recent discoveries that matched what she knew about the strange, black holes.

Half an hour passed without success.

Hoping to cast a wider net, Ayana took her search to an enormous database containing every major scholarly journal and several smaller ones in every subject known to academia. She pored over each one she thought relevant but came away empty-handed, still at square one.

Blowing the air from her cheeks, she stood and paced to the nearest window, stretching her legs as she went. She paused in the rectangle of daylight and checked her phone for new messages. Nothing of note caught her eye, though, not even word from Rahul about new cases. Not that she'd expected him to write after their last conversation.

Forcing away the memory, she returned to her borrowed computer. She drummed her fingertips against the desk as she considered her next angle of approach. Medical school had trained her to go straight to academic sources, to trust little else beyond the thorough and scientific research of her peers. But if academia was a bountiful river teeming with verifiable data, there also existed another body of information as broad and deep as the ocean. In its metaphorical waters lurked innumerable uneducated discussions and questionable conclusions in the form of online forums.

Ayana hesitated, her hands hovering over the keyboard. Then she committed, posing her queries to the entirety of the Internet. Only a few clicks later, she found speculation about a Russian astronaut who had worked on the International Space Station in 2002. Forum posters claimed he returned earlier than planned, suffering from an illness the doctors had not seen before in other astronauts. While official documents claimed the usual space sickness, conspiracy theorists believed another truth entirely: that his organs had turned into Swiss cheese, their gaps filled with pockets of void.

Links took her from one forum to the next. She read through threads claiming to have bona fide English translations of the astronaut's fever-induced ramblings. They spoke of enigmatic beings living on faraway planets or in the dark spaces between the stars, as old and vast as the universe itself. That they were powerful deities too incomprehensible for the human mind. Forum users debated the validity of these ravings, some believing them to be true, others demanding proof. The former group suggested readings from the book *Liber Devorationis*, a title foreign to Ayana in both subject and language. One account described it as the foremost primer on the Abyssal King, known also as the Lord of Hungering Skies and the Void Between the Stars.

She paused at those words. Why were they so familiar?

After jotting down the phrases in her phone's Notes app, she clicked a link on a post claiming to have photographic evidence. Several large photos loaded on the computer screen, forcing her to zoom out to see them properly. The first few depicted the same six people gathered in a room with sofas and chairs, their heads turned toward the camera. They wore the same hairstyles and clothes in each photo, but instead of faces, black holes filled the empty spaces between hairline and chin. Ayana shuddered, gooseflesh rising on her arms. Her animal instinct reared its head, screaming for her to flee. Fighting the urge to avert her gaze or close the tab, she scrolled down to the remaining photographs. She found more faceless people, their edges warping in inverted curves. Bodies contorted in grotesque, painful, impossible ways. The final images depicted hazy, dark silhouettes, their shapes both human and monstrous, their eyes aglow with preternatural light.

The same horrors from her nightmare.

Ayana's stomach churned. Sweat broke out all over her skin. Her head throbbed with a sudden, acute ache. Her hands moved of their own accord, logging her out of the computer and gathering her possessions. She stood on shaky legs and stumbled from the room, squinting through a veil of scintillating light at the signs on the walls. Their letters melted together like dripping wax, and the accompanying symbols bloomed with trembling, pulsing holes.

"Shit," she whispered. She had to rely on her own memory to find the exit. Bracing herself with a hand on the wall, she started down the corridor. Footsteps echoed off the walls as a drumbeat in her ears. She rushed ahead, turning a corner and slamming into another woman coming from the opposite direction.

Except the woman stared at her with a dozen eyes glowing orange-gold like dying stars. Black tendrils extended from the dark cavity of her chest.

Ayana screamed, heedless of her surroundings. She bolted down another hall, throwing open doors at random until she found the women's restroom. Hurrying into the nearest empty stall, she locked its door and stepped up onto the toilet seat—a precarious perch, but necessary. She didn't want her feet visible in the bottom gap in case the monster tracked her there. She fought each heaving breath, desperate to silence herself.

The bathroom door opened with a sigh. Biting her bottom lip, she strained to hear the creature's movement across the tiles, but nothing of the sort reached her ears. Instead, a human woman's voice called out, carrying a note of concern:

"Miss? Are you all right?"

A ludicrous thought crossed Ayana's mind, likening the woman to a siren that used her hypnotic voice to lure her prey into tentacled clutches. No writhing mass slithered along the floor, however, only the soft steps of a two-legged animal with shoes on her feet.

"Miss? Are you in here?"

Saying nothing, Ayana focused on suppressing the rumble of her guts, hoping they wouldn't reveal her position with an explosive burst of her half-digested lunch.

Eventually, the woman left. Alone again, Ayana climbed off the toilet and bent over it, expecting to vomit. Nothing came up. Though her headache remained, her nausea was subsiding. She chanced a peek at her phone; the words on its screen were normal and unchanging. Releasing a heavy sigh, she exited the stall and walked over to the row of sinks. Her reflection in the mirror looked haunted. She yearned to splash her face with cool water, but a face full of makeup meant that was out of the question. Instead, she settled on dabbing at her slick forehead with a damp paper towel until she was no longer feverish.

She did not move from the sink for a long time afterward. The last ten minutes replayed on repeat in her head, looping through the strange online discoveries and her abrupt physical symptoms. Perhaps she was getting sick. That explained the nausea, the flashing lights in her vision, and the horrific migraine causing her to hallucinate. Her panic attack from looking at the photographs made sense, too. Anyone would have an extreme reaction to their disturbing content. They *had* to be doctored. She could think of no other explanation for their fantastical imagery.

She exhaled, comforted by her logical conclusions. The quivering holes in her cadavers had to be grounded in science, too, not in occult theories espoused by the chronically online.

Still, doubt scratched at the back of her mind. She'd never recovered the tools she lost in the autopsy suite.

She left the bathroom and followed the signs back to the circulation desk at the front of the library. A young woman sat behind its computer. Her long brown hair and sideswept bangs framed her bespectacled countenance, while a purple cardigan sweater and long skirt completed her look.

Ayana strode up and cleared her throat. "Excuse me.

Do you know anything about a book called *Liber Devorationis*?"

A bright smile spread across the librarian's face. "Yes! I'm familiar with it."

Ayana hesitated. That voice.

The woman who'd followed her into the bathroom had the same voice. Right? Or had she imagined it?

A glint of gold against the librarian's white blouse caught Ayana's eye—a pendant of the capital letter N, flanked by a bundle of grain on its left and a rolled scroll on its right.

If the librarian noticed Ayana's alarm, she did not show it. "It's a very rare occult text dating from the 1500s and published by the Nisaba Society. There are only six copies in existence."

Ayana recovered her composure at last. "Wait, so it's real?"

"Of course! Why wouldn't it be?"

She had no answer to that—at least, none she thought wise to give. "How can I read it? Do you have a copy here?"

The librarian's smile faded. "No, I'm sorry. There was only one copy in the US until very recently. Now we're not sure if it's even in the country anymore."

"Why? What happened?"

Her face darkened. Behind her glasses, her eyes flashed with unmistakable contempt. "It was stolen."

Chapter Fourteen

Jason sat back in his office chair and rubbed his face with both hands. His laptop was open on the desk in front of him, displaying his calendar for the upcoming month. Several new appointments graced the next few weeks, each one colored bright red: Connor's funeral, a meeting with an estates lawyer, another meeting with an accountant. A paper checklist bore additional tasks, several of them crossed off. Those that weren't outnumbered those that were. In the paper's margin, he'd recorded different phone numbers to the *Lancing Daily*, Connor's landlady, a moving service, and a cleaning service.

"What a pain in the ass," he muttered before getting up and padding into the kitchen. At the same moment, the front door opened, announcing Ayana's return. While he waited for her to join him in the kitchen, he prepared another double-shot of espresso.

His wife greeted him with a kiss on the cheek. "You look exhausted."

She did too, he thought. Her eyes and mouth were tight with tension, and the artful bun of braids atop her head was askew, though it had been perfectly upright earlier that day.

"Connor never bothered writing a will, so there's extra hassle getting his shit together. I've made all the immediately important phone calls, but there's still a lot to do," Jason said.

"Anything I can help with?"

"No. The courts, the banks, and the lawyer will only talk to me since I'm next-of-kin."

"I see. Makes sense." Ayana set her purse down on a chair and opened the refrigerator. She withdrew a tub of Greek yogurt and a small container of fresh blueberries. "What are we having for dinner later?"

He glanced at the clock on the wall. "Let's order pizza. I'm going out tonight and won't have time to cook and clean up."

The espresso machine finished brewing, filling the kitchen with the decadent, rich aroma of coffee—and reinforcing his intention of a late night. He removed his cup and took a tentative sip of the scalding drink.

"Oh?" She paused in the middle of reaching for a bowl. "Where are you going?"

"To meet some associates of mine."

She continued to stare at him with uncharacteristic intensity. "For?"

He frowned. If she was nervous about him leaving her alone at home for a few hours, their future together did not look as perfect and bright as it once had. His lifestyle—especially his career—demanded her self-sufficiency. "I'll only be out for a few hours."

"That's not what I asked, Jason."

"Ayana, I need you to trust me—"

"It's not about trust." She lowered her arm and turned toward him. "Of course I trust you. I let you kill a man in our basement, then bury the body in the middle of the night. What part of all that gives you the impression I don't trust you?"

A tense silence settled into the space between them, prompted in part by her word choice. *Let*. No one *let* him do anything. He neither sought nor needed permission to act as he wished, least of all from the woman who'd decided to turn a blind eye to his unlawful deeds.

"You told me you don't care about where I go or what I do," he reminded her. "This was part of our agreement."

"I know." Though she held his gaze, her tone softened. "But lately, it feels like events are conspiring against us. Not just you, not just me—*us*. And the more I think about it, the more I realize I don't want to be left in the dark."

Sighing, he set down his coffee on the kitchen counter. He wanted to argue that expanding her knowledge of his activities put her in a precarious position, as people could use her to get information about him.

But that had already happened. A stranger had broken into their home and threatened her with death if she didn't comply. In a court of law, denying awareness of Jason's criminal acts kept Ayana safe; in the real world, however, no such guarantee existed.

"There's a poker den in Lerwick Square owned by the Monahans," he said at last. To her credit, she didn't ask who they were. Instead, she resumed making her yogurt bowl. "I've worked for them before. They may know more information about the man I killed or something he called the Abyssal King."

Her head snapped in his direction and her hands froze in place. "The Abyssal King?"

"You know about it?"

Abandoning her snack, she dashed to her purse and pulled out her phone. "I just learned about it at the library." She showed him a bulleted list of random words and phrases saved in her Notes app. "The Abyssal King is some kind of... I don't know how to describe it. A myth, I guess. People believe it lives in space and infects humans with these... deformities."

The vivid memory of Simon's contorted body flashed in his mind's eye. "What kind of deformities?"

She shook her head. "I wish I knew the right words. I thought it was a new disease when I first saw it —"

Jason seized her arm. "You *saw* it? When?"

Ayana blinked at him. "At work, in a couple of our decedents. The organs were perforated in a strange way. I couldn't see into the holes because they were so unnaturally black, and when I tried touching them with a scalpel, the metal twisted all on its own until it became unusable. It sounds crazy, but I know what I saw."

So she *hadn't* encountered the same amorphous darkness, only its effects in other humans. He forced himself to relax, though tension lingered in his posture and the clenching of his jaw. "I believe you. I've seen it, too." There was no point in keeping the information from her. "Twice. Once after my last job, and again last night."

He described both encounters, from the sensation of ravenous hunger to the glimpses of something alien in the farthest reaches of its darkness. In turn, she explained the recent events at her workplace in greater detail, including her boss' dismissive attitude and suspicious behavior.

"That's not all," she said. "I saw Harvey with Sabrina on my way to Lancing U. He regularly has lunch with business contacts, like people from the Health Department, but I don't think this was that kind of meeting. She was scolding him for something. I'm sure of it."

Jason crossed his arms over his chest and drummed his fingers against his bicep. "If he's covering up the bodies, then he's connected to the Abyssal King somehow, just like the man from yesterday. Your boss might be part of this religious cult, then. Sabrina, too. Her family's nonprofit is Catholic, and her actions these past couple of weeks aren't adding up."

"You mean with your last assignment?"

"Yeah."

Ayana chewed on her lower lip, deep in thought. "She wants to be my friend, and I can take advantage of that. I'll arrange to meet up with her tomorrow and try to get her to open up." She began typing on her phone, then paused and looked at him. "Do you think Connor's death is wrapped up in this, too?"

"It wouldn't surprise me at this point. I'll find out more in the next few days, and then we'll know."

"If this is all part of some larger conspiracy, then we need to work together. We had our comfortable arrangement, but we're not going to figure anything out if we're doing things separately, on our own. So, no more secrets."

The instinct to lie reared its head. Agree and mollify her, it told Jason, but keep your secrets anyway. Except his wife was right: there were more elements at play than he'd anticipated, and the best, most practical way to address them was with a multi-pronged approach. Continuing to lie to her lowered their chance of a swift success.

"No more secrets," he agreed.

She smiled with relief. "Thank you." Another pause. Her smile faltered as she dropped her gaze, an unexpected blush coloring her cheeks. "Also... I want to resume shooting lessons."

He raised an eyebrow.

"I can't expect you to be completely honest with me when I refused to accept what marrying you really meant, back then. I thought it would be easy to keep our lives separate—you with your business, and me with my work. You were just being pragmatic, caring for my safety, but I didn't want to imagine ever needing to protect myself like that. It was too frightening to think about. I was naïve." When she looked at him again, her eyes were steely with determination. "If I want us to work together, I have to acknowledge my place in your world, too."

There was the woman he'd chosen.

It was Jason's turn to smile. He took Ayana's hand and rubbed his thumb across her knuckles. "If you're sure."

She grasped his hand, lacing their fingers together. "I'm sure."

· · · · ● · ● · · ·

The pungent odor of cigarette smoke greeted Jason when he strode into the secret basement beneath Pete's Bar and Grill in Lerwick Square. A gray haze swaddled the ceiling lamps hanging over each square table, a dozen in total. The majority were already occupied with chain-smoking regulars—mostly men, a few women. Hands held cards and glasses of liquor with comfortable ease. Cash crossed each table at regular intervals, each exchange accompanied by jubilant shouts, snappy remarks, or dark rumbles. Explosive laughter peppered the constant buzz of conversation. Two additional doors led to other parts of the gambling den: a storeroom Pete kept well-stocked, and a cramped bathroom the Monahans sometimes used for punishing troublemakers.

"Jason! Hey!" a familiar voice shouted over the din. Nick Monahan split off from the crowd at the bar, dressed in a baby blue suit and matching trousers. His dirty blonde hair fell to his shoulders, and at least five rings decorated the fingers of both hands. "What brings you here, man? Been a long time since you came around."

Jason didn't bother answering Nick. Instead, he simply stared at the other man and waited.

"You know what," Nick said after a beat, "you're right. I don't need to know. But listen, let me buy you a drink, huh? It's the least I can do for all the good help you've given my family over the years."

He gave Jason a cheeky wink before hailing the bartender on duty for two glasses of Midleton Irish whiskey, served neat. A moment later, he pressed one of them into Jason's hand.

"You hear the news, by the way?" Nick asked, grinning, as he escorted Jason to an empty table. "Old Bobby P. got killed the other week."

"I did." Jason sipped his drink. "I also heard his son Tyler took over and is looking for revenge."

Both of Nick's eyebrows shot up into his forehead. He sat in the chair to Jason's left. "That right? Huh. Guess I don't blame the guy. He's hot-blooded, like me. But does he actually know who did it?"

"Of course not."

"Yeah, of course not. Still, it's good to be cautious." Turning, he gestured for someone in the crowd. An older man stepped up and bent his ear toward Nick. Though Jason couldn't hear the Monahan heir's instructions over the surrounding murmur of conversation, he read lips well enough to get the gist.

Increase patrols. Don't let the Panzieris target us.

The older man disappeared again. Nick turned a pleased, open smile toward Jason. "For that, my friend, the second drink's on me, too. But first, how about a game?"

"Sure." Jason reached into his wallet and pulled out several twenty-dollar bills.

Nick waved a hand and hollered, "Helen! Eddie! Get your asses over here. We're playing with *Jason fuckin' Ridley* tonight!"

A muscular woman with colorful tattoos on her arms and a lean, freckle-faced man took the remaining seats. Nick shuffled and cut a deck of cards, then dealt two facedown to each player, including himself. Jason peeked at his hand. Ten of clubs, king of diamonds. Not great odds, but he could still bluff his way into winning. He tossed forty dollars into the pot. The others did the same.

"Hey Jason, you up for a contract?" Nick flipped three cards off the top of the deck. Ace of diamonds, four of diamonds, queen of spades. "The guys and gals here have been itching to join the fun after we all heard about Robert's death. We wanna take down another of the Big Three."

Jason watched the subtle shifts in his opponent's faces. When he added another forty dollars to the pot, Helen's jaw clenched, while Eddie's eyes darted between his cards and Jason's concealed hand. Only Nick remained unfazed by the dealer's draw.

"Which one, the Sons of Saints or the Novikovs?" Jason asked, keeping his expression and tone neutral.

"The Sons. Everyone knows they have some serious drug operations going down in Saintfield. I want to run them out of their own territory and seize control of what's there. If we fail, at least we can do a little arson and theft to give 'em trouble. But I figure if we have you on our side, we can even take down Rodrigo the Red himself."

"The Sons outnumber you."

"In associates, yeah, but not in made men. And women," Nick added quickly, throwing an apologetic look at Helen. "We've been growing our numbers steadily, and we've got a big shipment of guns coming in this week, too. With that extra oomph in firepower, we can take 'em, easy."

Jason shook his head. "I'm not taking any contracts right now."

"Yeah? Too bad."

The three gangsters met Jason's bet. Nick flipped a fourth card off the top of the deck, a jack of hearts. Just like that, Jason had a winning hand, even if the combination itself was middling. He doubted Eddie or Helen had anything better, but Nick hadn't given any tells.

"Speaking of which, have you heard of any new groups forming? Especially any that are religious fanatics?" Jason tossed another forty into the pile in the center of the table. Nick, Eddie, and Helen exchanged blank looks and shook their heads. "Then what about something called the Abyssal King?"

"What is that, some kind of cryptid?" Nick snorted, matching Jason's bet.

"No, wait, I've heard of it," said Eddie. "There was a story a while back about a guy who was super obsessed with this chick, right? He'd visit her at work all the time, invite her out on dates, ask for her number—you know, the whole works."

Helen rolled her eyes. "Yeah, creep shit."

"Well, he gets so mad that she keeps rejecting him that he kidnaps her one day, after she gets off work. It's all subtle, like, he asks her for help with something in his house, then spikes her drink so she passes out."

"Does this story have a happy ending?" Nick asked, raising an eyebrow.

"No, no, listen—it's like one of them old wives' tales. There's a *moral*. Anyway, a couple of days into the torture, something finds the guy's hiding place. But it's not an animal, right, and not human, neither. It fucks the guy up."

"Wait, I've heard this story, too, but it's a little different," Helen said. "I heard some dickhead locked a woman up in his basement and raped her repeatedly, but got torn to pieces by somethin'. The cops only found some parts of him, not everything."

Eddie pointed at her. "Same thing! Like he'd been eaten!"

Nick cut in with a sharp gesture of his hand. "Wait a minute—*eaten*? But you said it wasn't some kind of animal?"

"Yeah, boss. Exactly," Helen said. "He got what he deserved, as far as I'm concerned."

She peeked at her cards again and threw more bills into the pot. Eddie considered his own hand and folded, prompting Nick to reveal the final card: three of spades. Jason raised his bet again, bringing the total pot to four hundred eighty dollars. Nick uttered a low whistle and folded. Helen took one final look at her hands and folded, too. They all flipped over their cards. She had no hand to speak of, but Nick's was one point stronger than Jason's. While Jason collected the pot, Nick shook his head, chuckling.

"Damn, I should've kept going. Another round?"

Jason nodded and gathered the deck into his hands. "So what happened to the girl?" he asked Eddie and Helen. "The cops rescued her?"

"Nah, that's the thing," said Eddie. "There wasn't any girl when the cops showed up, just evidence that something nasty had happened in the basement. But they did find something *else*, something not quite human."

Nick shoved Eddie's shoulder playfully. "Stop with this spooky shit, man. What do you mean, 'something else'?"

But Eddie wasn't laughing. "Something the Abyssal King made in his own image. It was drawn to the girl's pain and suffering, see? It took her and it... *changed* her."

"Into what, some kind of mutant?"

"No. A monster."

Chapter Fifteen

Ayana went with Jason to the shooting range the next morning. In a claustrophobic lane, bombarded on all sides by deafening gunshots, she paid close attention to his instructions. How to stand, how to hold the gun, how to aim and shoot—echoes of her first lesson with him two years ago. Back then, the deluge of new information and the sensory overload had frayed her nerves, making her irritable and resistant to learning. With the fresh fear of finding herself at the wrong end of a gun, however, she rallied herself and remained attentive throughout his brief lecture. When it was time to put theory to practice, she squeezed the trigger of the Walther PDP. The boom and the recoil nearly had her jumping out of her skin, and the shot went wide, but she'd fired the gun. It wasn't so frightening after that.

A few hours later, after changing her clothes and ridding herself of the acrid gunpowder smell, she took the subway to Oldtown. The winter sun had already set, but plenty of shops were still open, crowds of customers bustling through their doors. One cheese shop in particular held wine tastings in the evenings, pairing different vintages with their specialty products. She'd chosen the location for her meeting with Sabrina, counting on the alcohol to help her socialize outside her comfort zone. When Ayana arrived, Sabrina was already there, browsing the blocks of cheese on display.

"Thanks for coming on such short notice," Ayana said, suppressing the urge to flinch away when Sabrina hugged her. She returned the embrace with as much warmth and as little awkwardness as she could muster.

"Thanks for inviting me!" Sabrina said, beaming. Her eyes weren't as red as they were two days ago, and she'd done her makeup and curled her hair. "I wasn't about to say 'no' to a wine tasting. I've always wanted to try something like this."

"It's your first time?"

She nodded. "Never had the time or opportunity before. All the drinking I did in undergrad was with my sorority, and I was too busy in grad school to think about going anywhere but local bars."

"What about in Lancing?"

"My coworkers go out to happy hour sometimes, but never to wine tastings."

How curious that Sabrina didn't mention having any friends.

A store employee ushered the women into a side

room, where colorful wine bottles and a variety of cheeses decorated all four walls. Other guests sat grouped at square tables, engaged in hushed conversations while they sampled the shop's offerings. After Ayana and Sabrina chose a table near a corner of the room, another employee brought out a large wooden platter with crackers, grapes, and eight different cheeses, pre-sliced for their enjoyment. Accompanying the artful arrangement were eight wines divided across two flights.

Ayana speared a slice of Manchego with a tiny fork and raised it in toast. "Cheers."

Sabrina laughed and did the same. "Cheers!"

Both food and drinks were excellent, much to Ayana's delight. Conversation started light, with comments on the depth of flavors in the wines and how well they paired with the cheeses. The shallow waters of small talk were where she excelled and found herself most comfortable, but it wouldn't last. While she drank, she kept tabs on her own sobriety, waiting for the moment when the wine loosened her tongue enough to invite more personal topics. Striking a careful balance was key. Too sober and her aversion to conversation would hinder her, but too drunk and she risked stumbling on her own lies.

"You've been in Lancing for a little while already, haven't you?" she asked. "How are you liking it?"

Sabrina paused her nibbling on a piece of Gruyère. "Oh, it's a beautiful city, but also kind of mind-blowing with how big it is. I didn't realize until coming here that you can pretty much live your entire life in your district and never need to leave it. Connor even said he only visited some districts once or twice a year."

"It's true."

"I've never seen anything like it. But I haven't traveled much, either, so I guess that's not surprising." Sighing, she swirled the wine in her glass. "I want to, though. When you talked about your honeymoon in France, it made me really want to go, but I feel like I can't take a break from work right now."

Sipping her own wine, Ayana maintained a cool, casual demeanor. "Why not?"

"My parents want to see me do well and succeed. To prove I have what it takes to take over the nonprofit one day."

"Is that what you want?"

Sabrina rested her elbow on the table and her chin in her palm. "Sometimes I think about doing other work, but I really do believe in our mission at St. Julian's. It feels like we're saving the world. That's why I don't resent my parents too much for dictating my life for me. Attending private Catholic school, joining the National Honor Society, studying business at Boston College—these were all the things they chose for me, but I can't say I hated any of it."

The first inkling of a pleasant buzz pricked at Ayana's brain. "My parents don't understand why I chose my specific career, but they're happy enough I can take care of myself financially. I racked up quite a lot of student loans over the years."

"Did they want you to be something else?"

She chuckled. "No, they were very happy I wanted to be a doctor. Anything that made a lot of money, really. We weren't exactly poor, but we lived in a poor area, and my parents took on side jobs occasionally so we could have some extra spending money. Fortunately, we had a very close-knit community. Our neighbors and other families from our church were always helping each other out."

Her inclusion of that last statement produced the desired effect. Sabrina leaned in, her eyes bright, her expression eager. "Are you religious?"

"No."

"But you just said you used to go to church?"

"My parents were Methodist. They took me to church every Sunday and enrolled me in class meetings. They were good friends with a lot of other church members, so that was our main community growing up."

Her friends' shrieking laughter mixed with the quieter rumble of adult conversation in her memories. Lazy summer cookouts, school trips, and late-night card games had peppered her childhood, ensuring she was never alone and never lonely, even as an only child. Those early years of innocence had been idyllic, not yet tainted by prejudice and interpersonal strife.

"What changed?" Sabrina asked.

A wide hand striking Ayana's youthful cheek. Scripture brandished at her like a weapon. The sting of rejection and otherness.

"I figured out I'm bi and brought a girlfriend home. Let's say my dad wasn't happy about that."

Glancing away, Sabrina cleared her throat. "Oh. I'm sorry."

Ayana tossed back the rest of her wine. "It was a long time ago. We're on speaking terms again, especially now that he's mellowed out with age."

But also because she'd married a man, in the end. She still hadn't forgiven her father for almost kicking her out of the house as a teen, nor did she think marrying Jason erased her identity as a queer woman—a concept her parents still struggled to acknowledge as real. It was easier to keep her father at arm's length and treat him as an acquaintance than open herself up to that betrayal again.

Not just her father, but everyone.

Everyone except Jason.

"If anything," Ayana said, "my mom's angrier about the fact I never had a proper wedding. She says a courthouse wedding doesn't count, especially because I never invited her."

Sabrina's eyes bugged out. "You didn't?"

"It was just the clerk, Jason, Connor, and me. Connor was our witness."

A veil of somberness fell over her face. Picking at the selection of cheeses, she said, "My mom would kill me if I didn't have a proper wedding one day, with a full

Catholic Mass and everything. Fortunately, she and my dad want me to focus on my career for now. Even if Connor hadn't died and our relationship became serious, I think they'd want me to put off marriage until I felt more confident about running St. Julian's."

Ayana found herself nodding in agreement. A lull in the conversation followed while she groped for the next thing to say, eventually settling on: "Who's this saint it's named after, anyway?"

"St. Julian the Hospitaller. Do you know his story?"

"No, not at all. Enlighten me?"

Sabrina popped a cube of cheese into her mouth and chewed before launching into the tale. "When he was born, witches cursed him with the fate that he'd kill his parents one day. Julian's father wanted to send him away, but his mother refused to allow it. When Julian was old enough to learn about the curse, he willingly left his home to get as far away from his parents as possible. He traveled to a new country and got married. Many years passed, and Julian's parents decided to look for him. During their travels, they asked a woman sitting outside a church if she could shelter them for the night, as they were tired. She agreed and gave them her and her husband's bed to sleep in while he was out hunting."

"Let me guess," Ayana said. "The woman outside the church was Julian's wife, and when he got home later, he thought she was sleeping with another man. In a fit of rage, he killed them—his parents—and only found out afterward."

"You got it."

"How's he a saint, then?"

"He devoted the rest of his life to charity after that night, and even built a hospice where he and his wife took care of sick and weary travelers."

Ayana raised an eyebrow. "That doesn't seem like enough to make up for killing his parents."

"No? That was one instance of sin, but he made up for it many times over with a lifetime of goodness." Sabrina contemplated her half-empty wine glass. "We all make mistakes, after all. As long as we strive to do good every day, we have a chance at grace."

Ayana had nothing to say to that. Doing good had never been one of her concerns, only doing *well*, even as a child. People assumed she'd studied medicine out of a desire to help others, but in truth, illness fascinated her. She'd turned the study of trauma on the physical body into her specialty, and cadavers neither complained nor sought reassurance before she cut into them to learn more.

Still, saving lives was part of her profession, whether she cared for it or not. "Doing well" as a doctor meant ensuring humankind wasn't devastated by a new disease with catastrophic effects to vital organs. She and her colleagues needed to research, analyze, and catalog it. To do otherwise was gross neglect, a crime against humanity.

The memory of Sabrina and Harvey sitting together in that restaurant resurfaced in Ayana's mind. How many crimes had they committed already? Did Sabrina really think she could atone for them with all her good deeds?

Ayana selected another glass from the flight and drank deeply. "I'm guessing your grandfather named his nonprofit after St. Julian because of that later charity work."

"Exactly."

"Besides fundraisers, what else do you do?"

"Food drives, building houses with Habitat for Humanity, volunteering at homeless shelters, soup kitchens." Sabrina counted them on her fingers. "Connor actually started going with me to the soup kitchen we host on Sundays. We went a few times before he died."

"You must be busy all the time, handling the marketing for all those events."

"It's a team effort, so it's not too bad. Once you establish a schedule, it's easy enough to keep the cadence going. It's trickier when there's a one-off event, or when we're considering taking on something new."

"Still, it's admirable." Ayana held Sabrina's gaze and smiled. "Truly."

The other woman smiled back. "Thanks. I try. It's a dangerous, scary world out there, you know? I'm not perfect, but if I can do anything to make it safer for us all, I will." Her eyes unfocused. Ayana had the distinct impression Sabrina was no longer seeing her surroundings but looking at something inside herself. Determination set into the lines of her face, and her voice dropped to a low murmur. "I'm not afraid to do what's right—or necessary."

Chapter Sixteen

After chatting with Sabrina for another hour at the cheese shop, Ayana returned home by taxi, preferring solitude and silence to the jostle of the subway in her tipsy state. Upon arrival, she went looking for her husband and found him in his office, hunched in front of his laptop, the screen's blue glow soft upon his angular features. Her quiet knock on his open door drew his attention from the computer to her face.

The corners of his mouth curled up in an amused smile. "You look like you had a good time."

Chuckling, she pushed off the doorframe and strolled over to his desk. The warm flush of alcohol suffused her, loosening her body, prying away the claws of worry and decorum from her mind. "The wine and cheese were surprisingly good. The company... It wasn't as bad as I thought it'd be. Sabrina had a *lot* to say about herself—her childhood in Boston, her strict parents, blah blah blah."

He swiveled his chair around to face Ayana, his smirk fading into his usual stoic neutrality. "Anything related to your boss?"

She took his hand in both of hers and caressed his palm with her fingertips. "No, nothing. Nothing about Connor or the Abyssal King, either. I was mostly trying to make friends, remember? She'll open up more if she thinks I care about her." Pouting as she recalled the argument with Harvey, she added, "Unlike you, I can't brute force information out of people."

"You have time. There's still the funeral."

Ayana nodded, her eyes sliding to Jason's laptop and the text document open on its screen. After skimming the words, she realized what it was. "Connor's eulogy? You finished it?"

"Almost. I'm still fine-tuning."

"Show me?"

Much to her dismay, her husband withdrew his hand from hers and walked to the other side of his office with his phone, his thumb swiping across its screen. At the far wall, he paused with his back to her, then turned around, transformed. Sadness lined his face, softening his eyes and mouth, furrowing his brow. He glanced down at his phone and began.

"When Connor and I were kids, our grandma didn't like that we didn't know Mandarin, so she made a point to teach us whenever we visited Taiwan. Part of our lessons meant listening to her read famous Chinese poems. I thought they were boring, but Connor loved them. He found everything interesting. But it wasn't enough for him to just *know* things, either; he had to dig down until he got to the truth of things. And people were no exception."

Ayana watched, fascinated, as Jason mimicked grief. His soulful gaze locked with hers, summoning a faint ache into her own heart. A rueful smile ghosted across his lips.

"Everyone who's had the pleasure of speaking with Connor knows he always gave you his full attention. He was curious, insightful, and patient. He never brushed you off or made you feel unwanted. These qualities led him to excel in journalism, which he used to uncover the beauty—or the tragedy—of ordinary people's lives and share their stories with the world."

Jason swallowed hard and cleared his throat, a subtle movement with tremendous effect.

"When Connor was eight, he found a young cat wandering the neighborhood in the middle of winter. She was hungry, shivering—a scrawny thing, probably the runt of the litter. He begged our parents to let him keep her. They eventually relented, and he took such great care of her for the next two weeks, feeding her and going with our mom to the vet for all her checkups. He named her Penny. You knew they were going to be best friends just by looking at them. I've never seen a kid so happy—or so devastated when she escaped the house. He cried for days. That's how much Connor cared, not just for people and their stories, but for all living beings. His well of compassion ran deep, and the world is that much colder with his loss.

"Over the past few days, I've wrestled with putting the depth of my feelings into words, but English keeps failing me. So I thought I'd consult the poet Li Bai, who lived in China in the eighth century. He once wrote—"

Without looking at his phone, Jason recited some words in Mandarin. Though Ayana didn't know their meaning, his thoughtful cadence and sorrowful intonation made the ache in her chest all the more acute.

"—which means, 'Beside my bed a pool of light—is it hoarfrost on the ground? I lift my eyes and see the moon; I bend my head and think of home.' In the days following Connor's death, I found myself thinking about this poem again and again. 'Home' can mean a lot of things: the physical space where we live, of course, or where we grew up, but also people. The way they made us feel, and the nostalgia of fond memories with them. When I think of Connor, I can't help but think of our childhood home in Virginia, with our parents, and the hot summer days in Taipei, and all the birthdays and Christmases and family vacations. And even when we grew up and started living our own, separate lives, we could look up at the same moon and feel that connection to something only we shared, as brothers. Now when I look at it, I see everything that Connor was: his joys, hopes, passions, and dreams. And despite how much my heart aches at his passing, as long as we have these memories of him, he's not truly gone. Not while we remember." Jason paused for two heartbeats, his eyes downcast. Then he offered Ayana a small, sad smile and murmured a soft, "Thank you for coming."

Before her eyes, his persona vanished, evaporating from his body like mist. His expression reverted to its unsmiling intensity, and the slouch rolled out of his shoulders.

She took a deep breath, breaking his spell over her. "It's really good, but it'd be more convincing if you can look teary-eyed, especially at the end."

He rubbed his chin. "I've only had tears from pain."

"Maybe eyedrops? You could go to the bathroom before we leave for the cemetery."

"Not a bad idea." He sat at his desk again. "I want to practice a few more times before Saturday."

"I'll be around." She had nowhere else to be. "How much of that cat story was true, by the way? I've never heard it before." She didn't need to ask about his true feelings regarding his brother. He'd made *those* perfectly clear over the past two years.

"Most of it." Jason tapped at his keyboard, making edits to the eulogy. "I left out the details no one needs to know."

Previously, Ayana would've left his answer at that. He rarely spoke of his past, especially his childhood, and she never mustered enough interest to ask. But circumstances had changed. They'd agreed to tear down the boundary separating their lives and work together. To live together.

No more secrets.

"What really happened?" she asked before she could change her mind.

He glanced at her. "I killed the cat."

Somehow, that was the least surprising thing he could've said. "Tell me the true story?"

He only stared at her at first, his blue eyes scrutinizing her. She waited for him to finish his silent assessment, her expression open, her mouth turned up in a small, encouraging smile.

"I was in middle school and Connor was still in third grade at the time," Jason said at last. "His bus dropped him off at home sooner than mine did, which wasn't ever a problem. Usually, I stayed in my room while he watched TV until our parents got home from work. One day, though, I got home to find out Connor had invited a friend over, and they were both in my room."

Ayana curled her fingers around her husband's hand again. He turned his wrist so she could massage his palm, another sign of his acceptance. "I'm guessing your room was strictly off-limits."

"Of course. I made sure Connor knew it, too, so he shouldn't have been in there, let alone with a friend."

She could only imagine young Jason's ire, though the man before her remained relaxed in his chair. "What were they doing?"

He rolled his eyes. "Playing with my airsoft stuff, pretending to shoot at each other. I kept my gun in a box under my bed, but my helmet and gloves were on my dresser. I beat the shit out of Connor and his friend when I found them. Connor's friend ran away crying."

Brawls between brothers were common enough that she didn't bat an eye. She had a feeling, though, that the injuries Jason had inflicted weren't the worst of what happened. "How does the cat factor in?"

In a calm, almost dismissive tone, he said, "I wanted to make sure Connor learned his lesson. I made him bring the cat into the backyard. Since I didn't have knives of my own at that age, I grabbed one from the kitchen. A chef's knife. I forced him to sit and watch as I gutted his animal."

"Alive?"

Jason pushed back his left sleeve, revealing a familiar series of long, thin scars on his forearm. She'd always wondered how he'd gotten them. "Alive."

Ayana absorbed the new knowledge in silence. Again, none of it surprised her. Before proposing to him, she'd read every article and anecdote she could get her hands on about his condition—or what she thought was his condition, at least. Not once had he mentioned it during their year of dating, so she had to go off intuition and educated guesses. He finally admitted to it when she confronted him with the question, armed with her research and greater understanding. His cold, dreadful smile when he answered told her he was impressed, and his honesty was her reward.

She also knew symptoms manifested early in children as violence, compulsive lying, theft, and isolation. As an adult, he was an expert at controlling his urges, but an impulsive, emotional child had no such self-discipline.

"What happened after?" she asked, wondering if he'd turned the knife on his brother, steeling herself for the worst answer.

"Connor was a mess, but he eventually promised not to do it again," Jason said. "I left the corpse in the yard as a reminder he could see whenever he looked out the window, but our parents found it a few days later. They thought a dog must've killed it."

"And Connor never did anything like that again?"

"Never again."

A mild ending, all things considered. Satisfied, Ayana squeezed Jason's hand. "Thanks for sharing the story with me."

A smile tugged at the corner of his mouth as he laced their fingers together. "Why'd you want to know?"

She hesitated, a dismissive excuse on the tip of her tongue. "I don't want us to be strangers to each other," she said instead, meaning it. "I know it's not your nature to care about people, but if you ever want to know something about me, or about my past, just ask."

His smile took on an edge of amusement. "I'll keep that in mind."

She noticed he didn't make the same offer to her, but he'd humored her with the cat story when she'd asked, and that was enough. "Aren't some of your relatives coming to the funeral? Won't they notice discrepancies in your speech?"

He shook his head. "We didn't spend much time with them growing up, and I stayed quiet whenever we did get together. My parents were too embarrassed after my doctor's visit to talk about it with anyone, too."

The infamous doctor's visit. Despite her expressed desire, Ayana knew enough not to ask about *that*. A few weeks after meeting Connor on her wedding day, he told her in private that Jason wasn't the same after his formal diagnosis with a psychiatrist. In fact, he only worsened. Connor thought Jason was in denial, unwilling to accept his condition as his reality, and hoped therapy would help him cope with the truth. But Ayana had observed enough of her new husband by then to reach a different conclusion:

Jason wasn't in denial. He knew exactly who he was, who he wanted to be. Not a single person could change him—not a therapist, not his brother, not even his wife.

And she liked him that way.

Chapter Seventeen

The next day, Izzy stopped by the Ridley-Hudson household. She stood on their doorstep in a puffy green coat, a laptop bag slung around her body and Connor's backpack hoisted on one shoulder. "Hey boss!" she said when Jason opened the front door. Grinning, she patted the laptop bag. "I have the stuff you asked for."

Without a word, he stepped aside so she could enter.

She gazed curiously around the entryway. "Damn, this is your house? It's nothing like your old apartment. It has *character*, like someone actually lives here. When'd you move in, again?"

"Two years ago." He and Ayana had purchased the house soon after they married, once they realized paying for two homes was absurd.

"And this is my first time visiting? The fuck, Jason."

Unfortunately, moving in together meant rearranging his habits so they could keep their lives separate. He stopped bringing work home with him, which had the added benefit of keeping his wife safe from harm. The past few days had changed everything, however, even their arrangement.

He locked the door and gestured at his guest's feet with his chin. "Shoes, Izzy."

She kicked off her sneakers. "Dude, I know. I'm more Asian than you, remember?"

Grinning again, she bounded up the stairs. He followed at a walk, arriving at the second floor in time to see Ayana stiffen when Izzy greeted her. As with Vince, Jason had never bothered introducing the two women; the former only knew the latter as his associate, someone he paid to steal other people's data. In fact, he was certain they'd met just once before, when Izzy "ran into" Jason and Ayana on the street and handed off an unlabeled envelope. Inside it had been detailed information on his next target.

Ayana smiled in the guarded way he recognized as a sign of her social discomfort. "Izzy, right? Do you want something to drink?"

Izzy unloaded her bags at the dining table and shrugged out of her coat. "Sure! What've you got?"

"Water, sweet tea, coffee—"

"Coffee's great, thanks!"

While his wife rummaged around in the kitchen, Jason joined Izzy at the table. "Well? What'd you find?"

She withdrew a stack of papers, divided into four stapled packets, from her laptop bag. "It took some elbow grease, but I got everything you wanted. First, here's all the info I could get on those people. Fraser, Silva, Simmons, and Kopanski."

Jason flipped through the first packet, an intrusive look at Fraser's Internet and call histories from his personal devices, bank statements from the past three months, and a comprehensive background check.

"Second, I dug through your brother's accounts using the password you gave me and managed to get some photos. It's not a complete recovery, but maybe you can make sense of them." Izzy removed Connor's laptop from his backpack and booted it up. "I did notice something really spooky, though."

Jason glanced sidelong at her. "Spooky?"

"Yeah. Look, I'll show you."

Putting the papers aside, he sat in the nearest chair and waited while she logged into the computer. Ayana came over and hovered at his shoulder.

"These are all empty, like we saw before." Izzy pointed to the list of folders on the screen. "But look at what happens when I enable the 'date modified' column when we're viewing them like this. Look at the date."

"February second," Jason read aloud. His head snapped up. "That's the day after Connor died."

"Yep. Exactly. Someone was tampering with his shit *after he died*. Where'd you find his laptop, again? At his work?"

"No, his apartment." Jason leaned back in his chair,

arms crossed over his chest, his mind racing to make sense of the mystery. "The only people who likely entered his apartment beside me were the police when they swept it for evidence, and it couldn't have been them. They would've just confiscated the computer and brought it back to the precinct."

Ayana seized his shoulder. When she spoke, her voice was tight with revelation. "Sabrina has a spare key."

He and Izzy turned in their chairs and stared at her. Of course. The apartment's front door had no signs of forced entry. A spare key made perfect sense.

"The Kopanski chick? The one you asked me to look up?" Izzy asked him, her brow furrowed in confusion.

"Yeah," he said, his voice terse. Addressing Ayana, he asked, "How do you know this?"

"She told me at lunch the other day. I forgot to bring it up because of the break-in."

"Wait, who's Sabrina, exactly?" Izzy asked. "What break-in?"

Ignoring her, Jason squeezed Ayana's hand. "It's all right. At least we know who tampered with Connor's computer."

A slight crease formed between her eyebrows, and she opened her mouth only to shut it again. He waited to see if she had some argument to make, but instead, the discontent cleared from her face.

Good. He'd reward her for that decision later.

She looked at Izzy and said, "Sabrina Kopanski was

the woman dating Connor when he died."

"And the break-in?" the younger woman asked.

Ayana's eyes narrowed. "Why?"

"I have what's called a natural curiosity."

"Let it go, Izzy," Jason said, reinforcing his wife's show of support with his own. "Where are the photos you restored?"

While Izzy took control of the computer again, Ayana gave his shoulder a gentler squeeze, communicating her gratitude to him. Without taking his eyes off the screen, he reached up and patted her hand.

"I put all the photos in this folder so you can easily find them all again," Izzy said. "Most of them are of random crap like sunsets and food, but look through it yourself. See if anything stands out to you."

Ayana leaned over his shoulder as he scrolled through the gallery. Most of the pictures were as Izzy described: sunsets, food, the rooms of his apartment. They possessed the moody, artistic quality of something he might find in a magazine, but in the end, they were still random crap.

After twenty or so similar images, the nature of the photos changed. A smiling Sabrina posed in front of different buildings and landmarks around Lancing, sometimes by herself, sometimes with Connor. Jason recognized the zoo, a famous restaurant in Upper Kemsing, and the movie theater in Oldtown. More random crap. Frustrated, he opened his mouth, another disparaging comment about his brother on the tip of his tongue.

Then he scrolled to the last image and froze.

Connor and Sabrina stood before a brick building, their arms around each other's waists. The building's façade had no obvious signage, except for the large wall decoration affixed above their heads. Flat and brass-colored, it was cut from several thick, metal sheets and had been bolted together into a shape Jason had seen before: a European-style, double-edged sword with its blade pointed downward, a stylistic sunburst behind its hilt and cross guard.

The same symbol on Vince's ring.

"Where is that?" Ayana asked.

"Not sure," said Izzy, shrugging. "I checked the image data, but it doesn't include the location."

Removing his hands from the keyboard, Jason turned to Izzy. He could ponder the symbol's meaning—and Vince's connection to it—later. There were more pressing matters. "What about the camera footage?"

"That's the third thing." She closed Connor's laptop and set it aside, only to replace it with her own. Compared to the first one's standard, brushed steel appearance, hers sported a black case and stickers of cartoon characters. Opening it, she brought up a video file but did not press the play button. "Here you go. Twenty-four hours of CCTV camera footage from Centerpoint Parking Garage's basement level, for your viewing pleasure."

She clicked the progress bar at approximately three-quarters of the way through it. The image jumped, showing four ten p.m. Connor's recognizable figure stood in plain view, facing the left side of the video, peering into the space between two cars. When she pressed the play button at last, the scene lurched into motion. There was no sound, but Connor's gestures suggested he was talking to someone outside the camera's line of sight. He withdrew his phone from his pocket and swiped through it, then showed its screen to the other party—and to the watching camera.

Jason squinted and pointed at it. "Some kind of voice memo app. He's recording their conversation."

Standard practice for a journalist. Had Connor been meeting with a contact for a new article? Someone he wanted to interview?

In the video, he stepped closer to his conversation partner, almost disappearing from sight behind the bed of a large pickup truck. Only his head remained visible above it. Jason, Ayana, and Izzy watched in tense silence as Connor's expression transformed from amicable eagerness to outright terror, though the reason remained unseen. He raised his hands in the universal gesture of surrender, his phone clutched in his right hand, the device still recording.

Then he dropped dead and fell out of sight. His phone skittered across the concrete to the middle of the parking aisle.

Jason pointed again. "No muzzle flash, but you can see the smoke. The gun had a suppressor."

A second figure emerged from behind the cabin of the pickup truck, appearing like a shadow in a black coat and newsboy cap. An upturned collar and surgical mask obscured the profile view of their face. The rest of them remained hidden behind the truck's bed as they moved from the left side of the video to the right side, stopping when they reached Connor's phone. They removed the glove from their right hand, crouched, and picked up the device. A moment passed while they thumbed through it. Then they pocketed it and walked away with their back to the camera.

Jason frowned. Not only did he recognize the killer's clothing, but also their posture and gait. But that was impossible.

Izzy paused the video. Ayana exhaled slowly. He could almost hear the tension easing out of her body.

"I had a hunch that's where Connor's phone went," he said. Rewinding the video, he paused it at the moment where his brother raised his hands into the air. "Connor is six-one, so the killer must be five-nine or five-ten based on how much of their head we can see here, compared to how much we can see of Connor's." He resumed the video to illustrate his point.

Vince was five-ten.

"That's a well-tailored coat," Ayana said when the killer was in full view again. "It has a lot of shape and suits their body well. Whoever they are, they must pay close attention to detail and be particular about their preferences. It's possible they're wealthy."

Vince was wealthy. He went to a tailor for all his clothing.

"Interesting," Jason said. "Good eye."

When the killer removed his glove to use Connor's phone, Ayana shouted, "Wait! What's that?"

"On his hand?"

"Yes. Can you zoom in? Enhance the image?"

Jason looked at Izzy, who nodded. "Yeah, but it won't be quick," she said. "Converting even these few seconds to 4K will take around thirty minutes."

"That's fine. Do it," he said.

While Izzy worked, Ayana returned to the kitchen, leaving him alone with his swirling thoughts. Did Vince know someone was impersonating him, mimicking him down to the way he walked and carried himself, to frame him for Connor's murder? Jason could think of no other explanation for the uncanny resemblance. But who, exactly, was trying to pin the blame on Vince? Men like him and Jason were considered neutral parties, existing outside the political machinations of Lancing's crime families and street gangs. Untouchable.

Ayana returned with three steaming mugs of coffee, interrupting his musings. Taking one for himself, he turned his attention to the packets and sifted through them until he found Sabrina's. He usually needed at least a few hours of combing through it with a scrutinizing eye to find anything unusual or damning, but perhaps he could glean something useful in the next half-hour. Ayana disappeared into the kitchen again to start preparing dinner, while Izzy lounged on the couch with her mug and a portable gaming console.

When the upscaling process finished, the trio gathered back at the dining table. The isolated video clip played in remarkable, high-definition detail. Izzy zoomed in on the killer's bare hand, where a ring stood out on their pinkie finger. She enlarged the image a few more times until the ring took up the entirety of the laptop's screen.

It was the same ring Vince owned, except around the sword-and-sunburst symbol was an arc of tiny, capitalized words:

St. Julian's Foundation.

Chapter Eighteen

Ayana's gaze snapped to meet Jason's. The shock on his face mirrored hers. Opening the first laptop again, he pulled up the photo of Connor and Sabrina standing beneath the same symbol cast in metal. "They're in Bracknell," he said. "Vince's people were keeping tabs on Sabrina for me and found out that's where she lives. The office building for St. Julian's is there, too."

"Want me to get the lay of the land for you, boss?" Izzy asked.

"Do it. I'll stop by Vince's place this weekend to get updates about Sabrina, too."

"She'll be at the funeral tomorrow," said Ayana. "I'll tell her I want to visit St. Julian's. Maybe I can learn something."

Jason looked at her for a brief, tense moment. Then, without breaking eye contact with her, he nodded and said, "Izzy, get me a map of the neighborhood and blueprints for the building by tomorrow."

"You got it. Oh, here, let me give you the video files."

After finishing her coffee, Izzy packed up her belongings and pocketed a wad of cash Jason handed her. Ayana escorted her down to the entryway and hovered nearby while she tied on her sneakers.

"Thanks for the coffee, by the way," Izzy said. "It was really good."

Ayana forced another polite smile. "I'm glad."

"How're you holding up, by the way?"

"What do you mean?"

"Your brother-in-law just got iced a few days ago. I know Jason doesn't give a shit about other people, but... I don't know, I thought maybe you'd be upset."

"I'm fine. Connor and I weren't close."

"Oh, well... If you ever want to vent and need someone to listen, just let me know. My girlfriend says I'm a good listener."

Frowning, Ayana narrowed her eyes at the other woman. "Izzy, you and I barely know each other. This is only our second time meeting. I don't appreciate you making assumptions about me *or* my husband, or trying to insert yourself into my private life."

Izzy blinked, clearly taken aback. "Whoa, I was just trying to be nice. You don't have to be an asshole about it." Shaking her head, she opened the front door and stood on the threshold. "Man, when Jason got married, I kinda worried about the woman he'd picked as his wife. He can be a cruel motherfucker, but I thought maybe you were different. Guess I was wrong. You were meant for each other."

She stepped the rest of the way out the door and slammed it shut behind her.

Ayana exhaled slowly. Finally, that business was finished. Jason had informed her of Izzy's visit beforehand, but she hadn't anticipated how uncomfortable it was to feel like an outsider in her own home. Watching the pair interact made her wonder about the specifics of their working relationship: how long they'd been associates, what jobs Izzy had helped him with, and if she'd been a frequent visitor of Jason's home in the past. The first inkling of discontent wormed its way through Ayana, though she couldn't place why.

Shrugging away the nagging emotion, she rejoined Jason at the dining table. Her eyes fell upon the open file with Sabrina's information. "This is bigger than we thought."

"Yeah." Sighing, Jason flipped the packet to the first page and tossed it onto the pile with the others. "The ring—I've seen it before."

Ayana's brow creased in another frown. "Why didn't you say something about the building in the photo, then?"

"I wanted to confirm my suspicions first." A beat. "Vince has a similar ring, just without the words."

"The man who helped you with the body? He's a member of St. Julian's?" Dread rose like bile in her throat.

"No. He didn't know anything about Sabrina when I told him about her. Anyway, he's had that ring for a couple of years now. It's possible that sword symbol is used by other religious groups, not just St. Julian's. I'll ask him about it when I see him again."

She wasn't convinced, but very little changed Jason's mind when he thought he knew the right answer to a question. Earlier, she'd wanted to argue that Sabrina possessing Connor's spare key only made her a likely candidate of the sabotage, not the confirmed culprit, but she knew better than to press the issue. And in Vince's case, Ayana didn't know enough to suggest an alternative. Again, a trickle of dissatisfaction wound through her chest. "What does he do, exactly?"

"He's a broker of sorts, and before that, he worked in my profession. I've known him for a long time." Jason replayed the unenhanced camera footage. His eyes never left the screen. "The Army taught me how to kill people, but he taught me how to hunt them down."

· · · · ● · ● ● ● · ·

On the morning of Connor's funeral, Ayana dressed in her most conservative black outfit, a knee-length dress with long sleeves and a neckline that covered her collarbone. Opaque tights and plain heels completed the look, while simple pearl jewelry adorned her ears and throat. She chose a small clutch purse for the occasion, expecting to return straight home with her husband after the ceremony.

As she passed the open door to the master bathroom, she spied Jason's reflection in the large mirror above the double sink. He gazed at himself, his expression full of subtle sorrow: soft eyes, a downturned mouth, slight tension in his eyebrows. Then he dropped the look, resuming blank neutrality for a second before putting it back on with the most minute variations.

After a few repetitions, he caught her staring. She nodded in approval.

At the funeral home, Connor's grieving friends and family members gathered for the viewing. To them, Jason was the perfect picture of an older brother in mourning. He introduced Ayana to the aunts, uncles, and cousins who had traveled from out of state to attend. She remembered their names only for that afternoon, knowing that outside the once-in-a-lifetime circumstance of Connor's death, she'd never see them again. His friends and colleagues were a different matter altogether, for they knew neither Jason nor Ayana well. She found herself forced to entertain them, mixing sympathetic small talk with her deeper ponderings on human mortality. When Jason asked her to join him in saying their final goodbyes to his brother, she was never more grateful for a reprieve.

The funeral home set up the casket at the head of the room, inviting guests to gaze upon the features of the late Connor Ridley, fixed in quiet repose. A classic black suit hid the bullet wounds and autopsy incisions from mourners' sight. Ayana had already observed her brother-in-law's body days before, but Jason hadn't laid eyes on Connor since their last dinner together. She noted the twitch in her husband's jaw and the way his clenched fist shook at his side. Stepping closer to him, she held his hand in both of hers and gave it a gentle squeeze, an unspoken reminder to maintain his façade. After a few seconds, the strain eased from his body. He laced their fingers together.

"I'm fine," he murmured without taking his eyes off Connor.

"I know," she whispered back. She stroked his wrist anyway and glanced over their shoulders at Sabrina, who was chatting at the other end of the room with a young, dark-skinned man. Ayana had met him just minutes earlier. His name was Trey, she recalled. "They'll pay for this, one way or another."

Jason made a soft, pleased noise in the back of his throat—though she couldn't tell if it was because of her vocal support or the thought of revenge. Perhaps both.

Extricating herself from him, she wove her way through the crowd to reach Sabrina's side. "Allow me to steal you from Mr. Simmons for a moment," Ayana said to the other woman, flashing Trey a small grin at the same time.

He obliged with an embarrassed smile of his own and excused himself to catch up with a colleague.

Ayana fixed Sabrina with a concerned look. Though the younger woman's hair, makeup, and clothing showed special care for her appearance, they did nothing to hide the slump of her body and the redness of her eyes from recent tears. Reaching out, Ayana patted Sabrina's arm. "How're you holding up?"

"I'm... all right." She sounded exhausted.

"Have you had a chance to be alone with Connor?"

She peeked sidelong at the casket but quickly looked away. "Yeah. It was hard, standing up there with him. Just a week ago, he was full of life. Now he doesn't even look real. Like someone dressed a doll to look like him."

"I'm sorry. I hope you can focus on the good memories you had with him instead of... *that*."

She nodded, her eyes unfocused.

"I've been thinking about our conversation the other day," Ayana continued. "About St. Julian the Hospitaller."

That comment shook Sabrina out of her thoughts. "What about him?"

"You said he made up for a single act of sin with a lifetime of good deeds. If Connor's murderer confessed, showed guilt, and wanted to repent, would you forgive him?"

She stared at Ayana in stunned silence for a long moment, clearly taken aback by the question. Finally, she said, "I don't know. I asked myself the same thing, but I'm torn. I should forgive them, though, I think. It's what God would want. It's what He'd do."

Ayana wasn't convinced, but she nodded anyway. "You have a bigger heart than I do. I don't know if I could forgive anyone who hurt the people I love." She glanced at Jason from across the room. "I'd want to make them pay."

Sabrina's expression was unreadable.

"Speaking of St. Julian's, though, I'd like to visit. Can I? The charity work you've described is really compelling."

"You think so?"

"I do. I'm a health professional; helping people and improving their lives is part of my field, even if my current job is examining the deceased. It's clear St. Julian's is interested in doing the same. If there's any way I can contribute or participate, I'd like to know."

For a moment, Sabrina said nothing. Then she gave a single nod of her head, her eyes flashing with determination, her entire demeanor shifting as if rejuvenated with purpose. "In that case, how about you meet me at our office tomorrow at six p.m.? I can give you directions from Bracknell Station."

Ayana smiled. "I'd love that."

The funeral, a graveside service, directly followed the viewing. Jason had chosen a small plot in a shaded, well-maintained cemetery near their neighborhood. He wanted to give the impression to other mourners that the Ridleys in Lancing would be buried together. The ceremony itself was simple, without fanfare. One of the funeral directors led the service and read a poignant poem about death. Then Jason gave his eulogy, the same one he'd recited to Ayana, with some minor changes. She observed how the mask of grief he displayed to the assembled crowd did little to detract from his charisma. In fact, it had the opposite effect, offering false connection to those gathered to honor his brother, inviting false vulnerability. More than once during the speech, she heard faint sniffles. Even Sabrina dabbed her eyes with a tissue.

Though Ayana kept her expression somber and eyes downcast, inwardly, she flushed with pride. No other man could con an entire crowd quite like Jason.

After the ceremony, Jason and Ayana lingered at the grave to receive the last condolences and parting words from guests. The crowd trickled out, some in small groups, others in pairs or individually. Last to remain was Trey, whose gaze lingered on the other mourners' retreating backs before he approached the couple. He acknowledged Ayana with a brief flicker of his eyes before addressing Jason.

"Before you two leave, could I have a word?"

His façade remained fixed to his face. "Sure, Trey. What is it?"

"First, that ceremony was beautiful. Your eulogy really hit me right here." Trey tapped his chest above his heart. "It motivated me to keep working hard on the coverage for Connor's case."

"Thank you."

"The second thing's related to that." Trey's serious expression darkened, and he lowered his voice. "I found out what Connor was researching for work when he died."

Ayana raised an eyebrow. Next to her, Jason tensed. "The last article he told me about was the one on refugees entering the country," her husband said. "I thought that one had already been published."

"It was. I'm talking about a different article, a new one. One of our senior writers mentioned it to me yesterday when I told her I was coming to the funeral. She said Connor wanted to dig into a new topic and shared his preliminary notes. She knew about my coverage of the homicide investigation, too, so she forwarded them to me in case they'd help." Trey paused, licking his lips. Despite the chilly February air, sweat beaded on his forehead. "Connor was looking into some crazy shit, man."

"Crazy how?"

"Like conspiracy levels of shit. He thought the city's police department has been corrupted all the way up to the chief's office, if not the commissioner's office. Connor's theory was they're all in collusion with several crime groups—big ones, too."

Ayana's eyes widened, but Jason's narrowed. "Which ones?" he asked.

"His notes didn't say, but if I had to guess, he was looking at the Big Three: the Novikovs, the Sons of Saints, and the Panzieris."

A muscle in Jason's jaw twitched, though his mask of confusion and concern did not slip. "Did your coworker say if anyone else knows about this?"

Trey hesitated. "I don't think anyone does. It sounded like Connor was still in the very early stages of his research and didn't have anything substantial, only theories. His notes mention how strange it is that recent public records show an increase in poverty, arrests, and other crime-related activities in certain districts and not others. Makes you wonder, though, right? Connor's death was a homicide. The police haven't arrested anyone yet, but if Connor got in trouble with one of the gangs because he was snooping around, it's possible the killer was one of them."

"Or the police themselves," Ayana said.

Trey glanced at her, nodding. "They'll want to make someone a scapegoat."

Every imagined scenario of Jason handcuffed and behind bars raced through her head at lightning speed. Schooling her expression to the best of her ability, she resisted the urge to look at her husband. The last thing she wanted was to give Trey any reason to suspect Jason like Sabrina did. Earlier that week, she'd read Trey's first article in the paper. It had painted an appropriate picture of Jason in grief, the last of his immediate family left alive. Manipulating Trey to continue writing along those lines was crucial.

"And that's not all," he was saying. "I looked into Connor's girlfriend like you suggested. Her family runs a nonprofit organization—"

"St. Julian's Foundation," Jason said. "We know."

"Okay, but did you know that ever since they set up

here in Lancing three years ago, they've made enormous annual donations to various organizations in the city? I'm talking in the range of three to five *hundred thousand* dollars. Can you guess which ones?"

Jason and Ayana exchanged the same grim looks. "The police," he said.

"And the mayor's office," said Trey. He looked right at Ayana. "And the Lancing Board of Physicians."

Chapter Nineteen

Jason turned Trey's revelation over in his head. At his side, Ayana stared at the reporter in mute, wide-eyed shock. "If St. Julian's is manipulating multiple influential groups in the city, then their agenda goes beyond helping the poor and homeless," Jason said.

"It has to," Trey agreed. "But it also makes you wonder where the hell they're getting all that money from. It can't be from all their fundraising, can it? Because otherwise, how do they succeed with actually helping people if that's their front, right?"

"They must get donations from private supporters."

"The Roman Catholic Church," Ayana said, though the furrow of her brow suggested she wasn't certain. "Sabrina told me her family's close with Church officials."

"That's possible," Trey said. "But why? What's the point? Makes no damn sense." He sighed. "I tried talking to her during the viewing, but it didn't feel right, pestering her about her family while she's upset about Connor."

"I can ask her about it. She invited me to meet her tomorrow at St. Julian's office in Bracknell."

He looked at her in surprise, but Jason only nodded. "For what?" Trey asked.

"I told her I want to help."

He took a step forward. "I'll go with you."

She gave him a single, sharp shake of her head. "No. Sabrina will be more likely to open up with one person, not two, and especially if they're another woman. But keep in mind she's unlikely to know anything about the donations since she's in marketing, not finance."

Ayana's reasoning made sense to Jason. "Be safe when you go."

She smiled at him. "I will."

Trey bid them goodbye at last. When he was out of sight, Jason released a slow exhale. Though he was practiced at maintaining a persona for several hours, he'd only had to feign grief once before when his parents died. Back then, he'd used Connor's genuine sorrow as a shield, putting his brother between the other mourners and himself. They directed their sympathy toward Connor's outward distress, leaving Jason alone to plot the lawsuit against the drunk driver responsible for the car accident. At Connor's own funeral, however, Jason had no shield. Ayana was occupied by her own task, and Sabrina hadn't been dating Connor for long enough to qualify as a serious partner. As a result, Jason was the center of his guests' attention and the primary target of their pointless sympathies. He weathered the inanity with spectacular deception, but after three hours of nonstop acting, he wanted nothing more than to return to the privacy of his house and take a nap.

"Let's go home," he said to Ayana, turning away from his brother's grave.

She slipped her hand into the crook of his elbow and drew up against him. "That boy was awfully generous with his information."

"He's an eager kid looking to impress his bosses."

"He told you that?"

"No, but you can tell just by how he talks."

She chuckled. "You're right." They fell into a comfortable silence as they walked past rows of gray tombstones toward their car, parked around the corner and at the bottom of a gentle slope. Before long, she spoke up again. "What if his bosses are part of this weird conspiracy? What if St. Julian's is giving them money, too?"

"It wouldn't surprise me. Media's always being bribed by one party or another. Trey said he doesn't think his coworker said anything to anyone, but I doubt it. People talk. Connor could've mentioned doing the same research to an editor or someone higher up the chain. That could be how they knew to silence him."

"How can we trust Trey, then?"

"We can't." Jason looked her in the eye and held her gaze. "Only each other."

Ayana nodded, though the slight crease between her eyebrows remained. After another moment of silence, she said, "You know, it's possible Sabrina's the reason behind everything. She told me Connor had started joining her at the soup kitchen hosted by St. Julian's. She wasn't coy about sharing her workplace with us, so I wonder if he was trying to learn more information from her. But if that's what happened, he must've raised her suspicions somehow."

"That's why you have to be careful when you go tomorrow. Don't give her any reason to suspect you."

"I'll bring my self-defense key ring and pepper spray."

Jason wanted her to bring a gun instead, but she still wasn't skilled at handling one, and its presence would only cause alarm. As they rounded the bend and their parked car came into view, he opened his mouth to suggest another visit to the shooting range. Two figures standing alongside their vehicle, however, gave him pause. Even from a distance, he recognized the man with his sandy blonde hair. The other person was a black-haired woman Jason had never met, but her presence as the man's companion confirmed her identity.

Detectives Fraser and Silva.

Ayana noticed them right away, too. "What do they want?" she whispered, her grip tightening around Jason's arm. The news about Connor's investigation must have planted new anxieties in her mind, still fearful from the break-in on Tuesday.

Jason patted her gloved fingers with his other hand to reassure her. He slowed their pace by a fraction, if only to muster the last of his social battery. "To offer us condolences, probably." As they neared, he raised his voice to normal speaking levels. "We didn't expect to see you today, Detectives."

He unlinked his arm from Ayana's to shake their hands.

"I tried calling, but since you didn't answer your phones, I assumed you were still at the funeral, and we didn't want to disturb the ceremony," Fraser said.

"I know we've already said it, but we're so sorry for your loss, Mr. Ridley, Dr. Hudson," said Silva, shooting Ayana a sympathetic look.

More empty, meaningless words. "Thank you," Jason said. He took a step toward the passenger's side door of his car. "Now, if you'll excuse me, my wife and I have had a long day, and we'd like to go home."

"Of course," Fraser said. "I thought we'd just update you on the latest news from the investigation."

As Jason expected. He gave the other man his full attention. "Go on."

"Forensics determined the make and model of the gun used to kill your brother. We'll be able to use that information to identify the original seller and learn if there've been other crimes associated with the weapon. The more we know, the higher the chance we'll be able to locate and capture the perpetrator."

Ayana smiled. "That sounds promising."

"What kind of gun was it?" Jason asked. The footage from the parking garage's security camera hadn't shown the firearm.

Fraser shook his head, hands on his hips. "I'm sorry, Mr. Ridley, but that's not information we can share at this moment."

Suppressing a sigh, Jason flashed an apologetic smile. "Of course not. Thanks for the update. If there's nothing else..." He waited, expecting the two detectives to step away from his car.

"Actually, we also have some additional questions for you," Silva said, glancing at Fraser before assuming a careful mask of professionalism. "We understand you served in the Army after graduating high school. Is that correct?"

Jason cocked his head at her. "What does that have to do with my brother's murder?"

"If you'd rather not answer the question, we understand, but we'd appreciate your cooperation, Mr. Ridley."

He sighed that time. "That's correct."

"Which years? How long did you serve?"

"Between June 2007 and April 2013, so almost six years." He had no reason to lie; his military service was a matter of public record, available for the police to confirm for themselves. The impromptu interview was a test of his willingness to help, not a way for them to obtain knowledge. "I was eighteen when I enlisted," he added as an afterthought. Normal people tended to answer with more information than the question required.

"And what was your rank when you left?"

"Eighteen-B. Special Forces Weapons Sergeant."

"In other words, a Green Beret," Fraser said, rubbing his chin. "What was your overall experience in the Army?"

In his mind, Jason reached back through the years, rewinding time to the first days of Basic Combat Training. His memories played out in rapid-fire, the details hazy but the broad strokes still vivid. The Drill Sergeants had targeted him early, able to sniff out his teenage ego and antisocial behavior. Their cruel punishments taught him how to lay low and keep his head down. A chaplain who took pity on him advised him to make friends. Anyone not engaging in camaraderie stood out too much and appeared suspicious. He learned to smile and laugh like the others, blending in until he was invisible. The Drill Sergeants redirected their attention after that.

After Basic Combat Training, Infantry School was more of the same tiring bullshit. At least graduating meant leaving the hot, humid training grounds of Fort Moore, Georgia for the hot, arid warzone of Iraq, where all the bullshit became worth it. The memories that followed were more colorful: weekly mortar attacks, endless weapons cleaning, capturing and dismembering desert lizards when bored, the exhilarating twilight of a dust storm, the first time he killed a man. A tour in

Afghanistan came later, followed by his acquisition of the coveted green hat that made him elite.

"It was the most difficult, challenging thing I'd ever done in my life," Jason said, "but if I had to go back and do it all again, I would. I got to see parts of the world I never thought I'd visit and met many people who shaped the course of my life, for better or worse."

Silva spoke up again. "Were there any specific experiences or moments during your time in the Army that you regret?"

His smile did not reach his eyes. "I'd rather not share stories from my service. In fact..." Looking at Ayana, he read the silent plea in the subtle lines of her face. She must have sensed his intent, for she took his arm again. "I think it's about time we left."

Fraser held up his hand. "Hold on, Mr. Ridley. We appreciate your patience, really. We just have a couple more questions we want to ask."

Jason allowed some of his exasperation to show in the glare he gave the other man. "I don't see how any of this is relevant to Connor or the man who killed him."

"It could be very relevant." A beat. "Detective Silva and I had the chance to speak with one of your former comrades in Special Forces, a gentleman who had to take extended medical leave for a broken wrist at the same time you left the Army. His injury healed, and he returned to work after a few months, but he's never forgotten what happened."

Jason's fight or flight alarms rang in his head. The

details of his discharge from the military were private, but that didn't stop lowlifes from blabbing their mouths, especially ones with grudges. He imagined a broken shell of a man suffering from PTSD and depression, speaking on the phone with the two detectives, unraveling over a decade of pent-up resentment.

"His name was Duane Bower. Do you remember him, Mr. Ridley? He was an Engineer Sergeant at the time of the assault."

Though the bruises had long faded from his knuckles, Jason still recalled the satisfying crunch of bone breaking beneath his hands. Bower had been bigger, but by the time the rest of their team pulled them apart, Jason wasn't the one with a battered and bloody face. Nor had he been the one wailing in agony, cradling his wrist to his chest.

Back then, he thought his commanding officers would overlook a single incident. After it happened, though, someone leaked a rumor that it wasn't the first time he'd broken the bones of another soldier in a fit of violence. Someone else mentioned the lizards. Before he could plan his retaliation, he was in his captain's office, staring down two options: transfer out of Special Forces and take a demotion, or leave.

"Bower sounds familiar, but I don't know what you mean about an assault." Jason met Fraser's steady gaze with a bemused expression. "A lot happens in the line of duty, Detective. The things we witness and live through change us permanently. Bower sounds haunted by the ghosts of war."

"I don't think so." Fraser took a step toward Jason. "I think something happened to make you snap, and Bower was your unfortunate victim."

Every muscle in Jason's body tensed, ready to spring into action. The only weapon he'd brought to the funeral was a small knife hidden inside the waistband of his pants. If he moved quickly enough, he could kill both cops with it before they fired their guns, but Ayana, still clinging to his arm, was likely to slow him down.

He had to resort to intimidation and lies.

"All you have is his word against mine," he said, forcing himself to remain cool in the face of Fraser's accusation. "So frankly, this is all a waste of time. I'm going to go home now, Detective. And if you don't step aside so I can leave, you can bet I'm going to pay a visit to your captain. It's your call."

Chapter Twenty

Ayana's eyes flickered between Fraser and Silva, watching their reactions with bated breath. All thoughts of Trey's earlier news, especially of St. Julian's sway over the Board of Physicians, had fled her mind. In that moment, she could only focus on the sudden and real threat embodied by the police. If an altercation broke out, the life she'd crafted with Jason was doomed to end. Either they put him in handcuffs for attacking a cop, or they shot him dead before her eyes. One wrong move and they would gun her down, too. His ability to pass as white would not save them. She gripped his arm harder, hoping he'd understand her desperate warning.

He didn't look at her. His unflinching gaze remained fixed on the two cops. A muscle in his jaw tensed. She wanted to admonish him for his idiocy, but the words caught in her throat. She didn't trust herself to speak.

Silva's mouth twisted into a frown. She looked ready

to argue, but her partner spoke first, offering Jason a strained smile. "There's no need for that, Mr. Ridley." Fraser removed his hands from the waistband of his pants. Ayana's gaze lowered to the holstered gun hanging at his right hip. "Perhaps you're right and Bower simply misremembered. It's been ten years, after all."

Jason said nothing. He glared at the detectives, waiting.

Fraser stepped away at last. Silva followed a half-beat after him, though she did nothing to hide her frustration. "Thank you for your service," Fraser said, his eyes never leaving Jason's face.

Jason opened the passenger's side door for Ayana. She ducked into the car with a final, tight-lipped smile at the cops and pretended to check her emails on her phone while her husband climbed into the driver's seat. Only when they were leaving the cemetery by its single, narrow road did she peer into her side-view mirror. Fraser and Silva lingered on the grassy curb, watching them depart. As soon as they were out of sight, Ayana relaxed into her seat. She glanced at Jason, whose knuckles were white as he gripped the steering wheel.

They sat in silence for several minutes while she waited for his anger to ebb away and her own panic to die down. Eventually, she regained a sense of calm, her heart rate returning to normal. Next to her, he released a heavy exhale through his mouth and leaned back into his seat. She reached across the space between them and stroked his thigh. He responded in kind, squeezing her hand in his and rubbing her knuckles with his thumb. A fleeting smile touched her lips, tempered by the seriousness of the moment.

"That Bower man remembers correctly, doesn't he?" She looked into her husband's face. Her tone lacked accusation. "You broke his wrist. Your punishment was leaving."

Annoyance flashed in his eyes, but he did not direct it at her. "Yeah. Either that, or be kicked out of Special Forces and demoted back down to Private."

"Can the police do anything with that knowledge, if they decide to believe Bower?"

"No. They don't have proof without my discharge information, which is private and won't become public for another fifty years. If they want to see it, they'd have to ask me for signed permission or get an arrest warrant."

She relaxed into her seat. "And they can't get one without proper cause, because you have an alibi. Thank God."

Humming an affirmative note, he lifted his hand to the steering wheel again. Her own hand remained on his leg as she gazed out the front windshield, mulling over the recent conversations—first with Trey, then with the detectives. Even if the Lancing Police Department received bribes from St. Julian's Foundation in the form of donations, she didn't know if the U.S. Army was so easily swayed. The convoluted politics of the American military complex prevented the influence of a private corporation from taking root—or so she hoped. Individuals, though, were far more susceptible to manipulation.

"Is there any chance someone with access to those discharge records—an archivist or something else administrative—might be persuaded to leak your information to the police?" she asked.

"Of course. But they wouldn't dare. If they're stupid enough to use it as evidence against me, we can sue for invasion of privacy."

She nodded, accepting the answer and the comfort it brought. Caressing his thigh again, she murmured, "I, for one, am glad you left when you did. We wouldn't have met otherwise."

For the first time since his brother's viewing, Jason graced her with a genuine smile. Though it was nothing more than the tired curl of the corner of his mouth, it warmed her all the same. "No, we wouldn't have."

The car turned into the familiar street of their neighborhood. Dark, rough trees lined the boulevard, forming an interlocking archway of skeletal branches overhead. Ayana peered up through the gaps between them at the pale sky beyond. "What about the 'Big Three' Trey mentioned? Do we have to worry about them? Could they have anything to do with the man who broke into our house?"

"No. They have no reason to come after me." When she shot him a quizzical look, he continued, "I've spent a lot of time and effort building up my reputation over the past ten years. I'm in good standing with every major criminal group, not just in Lancing but outside of it. The ones who don't know me personally know what I'm capable of. It's why I get paid so well."

"How well? Out of curiosity."

"People in my profession don't have official rankings, but we all know of each other—if not by name, then by price. I'm in the top five."

She regarded her husband with a new appreciation. Despite his tendency to lie and embellish, he took enough pride in his work that she didn't think he was exaggerating. The incredible paychecks that passed through his money laundering contacts only reinforced his claim.

"So the Novikovs, the Panzieris, and Sons of Saints won't fuck with me. Not if they know what's good for them," he said.

"Those names sound familiar. At least, the Novikovs and Panzieris do. The Novikov Group is that luxury real estate agency, isn't it? And aren't the Panzieris a big name in international shipping?"

"That's right. Milena Novikova and Robert Panzieri are—well, *were*—the heads of two very old, very influential crime families in Lancing."

"'Were'?"

"Robert's dead. His son's taken over."

"And the Sons of Saints? What about them?"

"They're a major player in the city's drug trade right now. Cocaine, heroin, prescription drugs like oxycodone and morphine—you name it."

Jason parked the car in front of their townhouse, and the couple retreated at last into the sanctuary of their home. He lingered in the entrance for a moment, looking both ways down the sidewalk before ducking into the entryway and locking the door. Ayana proceeded up the stairs ahead of him, heading straight for their bedroom to change out of her formal mourning clothes. He followed close behind, already removing his knife from its hiding place. Sitting at her vanity, she watched as he placed the sheathed blade on his bedside table.

"So what do we do?" she asked, removing her jewelry and stowing them away. "What *can* we do?"

"*You* will continue to get whatever information you can from Sabrina, about both her family's nonprofit and the Abyssal King." He shrugged out of his suit jacket. "It's obvious the man who broke into our house is connected to them in some way. Meanwhile, I'll visit Vince tomorrow. I want to ask him about that ring, and he might know something about the partnership between the Big Three and the police. I don't think he knows that they're connected to St. Julian's, though."

"I'm guessing he's well connected to all those criminal groups."

"Very."

Ayana closed her jewelry box, pausing with her hand on the lid. She twisted in her chair to look at her husband, who was hanging his suit jacket in their walk-in closet. "Can we really trust him like this? Earlier, you said we can only trust each other."

Jason glanced at her. "I *don't* trust him. I know how to use him to my advantage."

Of course. She should've expected that. "What if he's part of the conspiracy?"

"He's not. He has no reason to accept bribes—not for any financial or political reasons. Considering the nature of our work, we exist outside any alliances between crime groups. Siding with one or another hurts us more than it helps us."

She exhaled, nodding. "Okay. That makes sense."

Leaving her vanity, she reached behind her neck, seeking the zipper pull at its base. Before she could grasp it, though, large hands swatted hers away. She lowered her arms and examined her reflection in the full-length mirror as Jason unzipped her dress. He lingered at her back while she peeled the heavy, black fabric off her body, his fingers grazing the curve of her spine. Once she'd stripped down to her underwear and tights, he pulled her backwards by the hips against his chest—bare, she noted, thrilled by the feel of hard muscle and warm skin.

"Thank you for today," he murmured into her ear. His mouth fell upon the sensitive flesh of her neck, and his hands roamed her stomach and chest.

Despite the worries still running through her mind, she smiled. "Which part?"

"All of it."

Ayana turned to face him. His mask had fallen away,

revealing both exhaustion from the day's events and annoyance at whatever thoughts still preoccupied him. The intimacy and trust behind his display of vulnerability melted her heart. Her smile widened, softened. Reaching up, she stroked his rough, stubbled cheek. "Of course, Jason." Standing on her toes, she planted a sweet kiss on his lips. "We're a team, and I love you."

He answered with another kiss, fervent and needy. Closing her eyes, she willed herself to let go of her anxieties, to give in to his soothing touch and allow herself to relax. But though their kisses grew in passion and urgency, a nagging question remained rooted in her mind.

Jason must have sensed her distractedness. He stopped and looked her in the eye. "What?"

She resisted the urge to shake her head and bit down on the word "nothing" before it escaped her lips. Her cheeks and ears burning, she lowered her gaze and began in a low, halting voice, "Lately... well, I've been wondering what you'd do if something were to happen to *me*."

His fingertips dug into her flesh, prompting her to look back up at him. On his face was a fierce protectiveness—no, possessiveness—she'd never seen before. Her heart leaped in her throat at the sight, and her skin prickled from the heat surging through her.

"That will *never* happen. I won't allow it," he said. "No one is going to take you from me. Not the cops, not that unhinged religious cult, and certainly not any crime lord who thinks they're untouchable. I would kill every man, woman, and child in this city—on this whole fucking *planet*—before I let any harm come to you."

Knees weak, she clung to him, basking in his unusual yet unmistakable declaration of affection. "Even the children?" She chuckled from the absurdity. Before he could reply, she said, "And here I thought you didn't know how to love people."

Jason neither smiled nor laughed, which only made him more endearing. Instead, he pulled her closer until their foreheads touched. "You're my wife, Ayana. You *chose* to belong to me, and I protect what's mine."

Belonging. Yes. That was why she'd decided to marry him. Staring at him from across her old apartment's kitchen table, she'd borne witness to his darkest truth. With her own two hands, she'd lifted the mask off his face and saw the man beneath it. A man with whom she was able to envision a secure, happy future.

A future where she *belonged*.

Wrapping her arms around his neck, she pressed herself flush against his chest. The growl that sprang from his throat was everything she wanted. "You're mine, too," she whispered before capturing his lips in a searing kiss.

To her utter delight, he maneuvered them to the bed, his hands undoing the clasp of her bra. Discarding the rest of their clothes, they tumbled onto the mattress in a mess of tangled limbs. He trailed kisses down her neck, her chest, her stomach—all the way to the intimate place between her thighs. Pleasure became her whole world. She arched into it, threading her fingers through his hair.

All thoughts of her brother-in-law's murder, dangerous conspiracies, and the nightmares that haunted her vanished from her mind. Instead, wondrous bliss dominated each of her senses. When she welcomed her husband inside her, an undeniable, unending love surged through her entire being. And later, while cuddling together in the aftermath of their coupling, she mused how fortunate she was to find someone who finally made her feel safe, wanted, and—most importantly—understood.

Chapter Twenty-One

The following day, Jason walked the familiar Grosmont streets leading to Vince's fish market. As the sun dipped toward the horizon, its final rays set the sky ablaze with orange hues and cast the skyscrapers in a ruddy glow, their windows flashing with momentary brilliance. Shadows lengthened along the street. Other pedestrians streamed past him—tourists, mostly, seeking dinner at one of the many seafood restaurants that made the district famous. Dressed in a black wool coat and dark jeans, he blended in with them, slipping through the thinning crowds without drawing their attention. No one had reason to suspect the Glock 19 holstered inside his waistband, nor the extra magazine of ammunition and silencer in his pocket.

Not that he expected to use them that evening, but he was a creature of habit, and his habits kept him alive.

Unlike its neighbors, with their colorful neon signs

and storefront lights coming to life as the sun set, Grosmont Fish Market sat alone in darkness. Its main building loomed above a grid of closed and empty shops. Though he couldn't see them well from the street, he knew a few lights were still on inside the former. Vince tended to work late into the night, long after the last vendor stall took down its tables and most of his staff went home. At that hour, he kept only a skeleton crew onsite, men and women he'd recruited into his *other* business.

Ignoring the fish market's main entrance, Jason skirted its perimeter until he reached the first narrow alleyway leading inside. He walked a zigzagging route to the main building, avoiding the single road cutting through the market's center, the only one wide enough to accommodate cars. Though it led straight to his destination, walking it left him wide open. The sharp corners, angled awnings, and assorted clutter of the surrounding side streets, on the other hand, provided plenty of cover. He stuck to their shadows as he surveyed the building ahead, catching glimpses of the front of it in the gaps between stalls.

When the last row of shops stood between him and the building, he slowed his pace. Three unfamiliar cars—two black, one red—sat parked in the open space before the main entrance. Five dark-clothed figures loitered nearby, standing apart from each other in ones and twos. Not Vince's people, Jason knew at once; *they* guarded the entrance from inside, not outside on the curb. Street lamps cast a yellow glow upon the scene, but he was too far away to distinguish the strangers' individual features. A quick examination of the vehicles, however, revealed the license plate of the sleek, crimson-colored one nearest him.

THE RED, it said in bold, black letters.

His lips pressed together in a grim line. Rodrigo the Red, leader of the Sons of Saints, was there to see Vince.

Jason had a hunch he knew who owned the other cars.

Turning away, he took a detour to the side of the building, remaining within the shadows of the surrounding stalls until he spotted a familiar, unmarked door. The staff entrance. A single man stood outside, arms crossed over a pair of stained, gray coveralls, smoking a cigarette. Jason stepped out of the gloom and strode toward him. He looked up as Jason neared.

"Mr. Ridley, it's you." He removed his cigarette from his mouth. "Sorry to tell you, but Mr. Moynier is busy tonight, so it's better if you come back tomorrow."

Jason pulled out his Glock. Holding it close to his body, he aimed it at the man's stomach. "My business with Vince can't wait."

The man hesitated, eyes trained on the weapon.

"You should take the night off," Jason continued in a calm, even tone. "Your wife and kids will be happy to spend the time with you."

He counted to ten in his head while waiting to see what Vince's henchman would do, but did not even reach six before the man folded. "S-sure. That's a great idea. The door's unlocked."

"Thank you."

Jason watched the man's retreating figure until it disappeared into the shadows between two stalls. Then, screwing the silencer onto his gun, he slipped into the building. As expected, a few hallways and rooms—the ones Vince and his staff used throughout the night—remained lit. Darkness shrouded the rest, including the open space where vendors sold their living wares. Jason followed his usual route to Vince's office, sneaking past open doors and well-lit rooms where workers carried out their tasks. In no time at all, he reached his destination.

A sliver of light shone between the closed door and the floor. Moving with silent steps, he sidled up to the door and leaned his ear against it.

"We need to do *something*, fellas," came a loud, rough voice he recognized as Rodrigo's. "I don't care if we have to take it into our own hands and come up with our own plans. Shit's getting way more dangerous in Saintfield by the day. I can't afford to wait much longer."

"Why do we have to adhere to plans laid by an uptight religious cult, anyway?" another man asked—not Vince. The arrogant voice belonged to someone much younger.

Jason cocked his head. "Uptight religious cult" could only mean—

"St. Julian's has been fighting monsters like the

Abyssal King for the past seventy years," Vince said. Jason imagined him seated behind his desk, hands folded in front of him, a stern look on his face. "And their tactics have worked so far. Compared to their knowledge, we are fighting blind against an impossible foe."

"You've really eaten up all this supernatural bullshit, haven't you, Moynier?"

"You wouldn't call it bullshit if you'd witnessed what we have, Mr. Panzieri," said an older woman in a smooth, cultured voice. The faint notes of a Russian accent revealed her identity right away: Milena Novikova. Which meant the unknown man was Tyler.

Trey, and therefore Connor, had been right.

"Your father was wise enough to see that working together was the only way we'd stand a chance against that *thing*," Milena continued. The creak of old wood implied she sat in the visitor's chair. "It's not something you can face alone, with your own soldiers. The whole city is at stake—all our livelihoods, and Lancing is too big for one man to protect on his own."

"But that makes us dependent on a group of outsiders!"

"It's an *arrangement*," Vince said. "Your father and Milena and Rod have all benefited as much as St. Julian's these past three years. You've been involved in your family's smuggling operations for a while now, so you know how much easier it is when the cops look the other way. St. Julian's has made that even easier with the police in their pocket."

"Yeah, but for how long? How do we know they're not going to turn around and stab us in the back?"

"Look, kid," Rodrigo said, sounding heated, "maybe it's because you ain't seen it yet yourself, but this Abyssal King ain't the kind of thing you stab yourself in the back over. The way it kills people is somethin' you ain't ever seen in your life, I guarantee. And bullets, fire—nothing hurts it."

"So how exactly does St. Julian's intend to get rid of it?" A tense silence followed Tyler's question until he barked out a derisive laugh. "You don't know? Great. Just fucking great."

"Not like you've got anythin' better."

"Enough," Vince said. "We'll continue to trust St. Julian's. Their methods have worked so far. Once they've formed a solution to the Abyssal King's increased activity outside its usual territory, we'll be ready to help them implement it. We *must*, or we will lose everything our families have worked so hard to achieve."

"Where outside the usual districts have you seen it?" Milena asked.

"I heard the Hellhounds MC have been losing members to somethin' eating them alive out by Keady Woods," said Rodrigo.

"Bracknell, too," said Vince. "I was out at the county lot with Jason Ridley early last week, and the Abyssal King attacked us."

Jason's breath caught in his throat at the mention of his name. Every muscle in his body tensed with anticipation. He shot a quick glance down the hall for escape routes. To his left were two other doors, their signs indicating a supply closet and an all-gender bathroom.

"What? Why?" Tyler was asking.

"Why does it do anything? It's attracted to cruelty."

"No, I mean about Ridley. What was he doing out there with you?"

"He killed the man St. Julian's sent to his house—the one who was supposed to look for evidence to arrest him." Vince's tone grew frustrated. Jason forced himself to resume breathing at a steady, normal rate. "It was a stupid idea. I said as much, but..."

"They seem determined to put Mr. Ridley behind bars," Milena said. "If they have the police in their pocket, why don't the cops make up an excuse like they usually do?"

"He has a solid alibi for Connor's death and a clean record besides that. I should know; I helped him maintain it these past ten years. The only thing they *might* be able to use is the hint I gave them about his sudden discharge from the Army, but that's no guarantee, either."

Jason's eyes narrowed. What?

"Do you suspect or anticipate any retaliation from him?"

A pause, followed by an uneasy reply: "I'm not sure. At the very least, I don't think he suspects me, and I'm certain he knows nothing about *us*."

Tyler spoke up again. "Why don't you just kill him like you killed his brother? You know, the journalist."

Jason reeled from the door as if pummeled by a sledgehammer. He barely heard Rodrigo's exclamation of disbelief, Milena's sharp admonishment, and Vince's low warning. Swaying on his feet, Jason fought to maintain deep, even, silent breaths despite the anger surging through his chest. He weighed his options, imagining a half-dozen scenarios where he burst through the door and gunned down the collaborators before they could react. First, the man opposite the door, then the one closest to it. Then Milena in the chair. Then Vince.

Footsteps from down the corridor, growing louder by the second, snapped Jason out of his mental calculations. He darted into the bathroom and slapped the switch by the door, turning off the motion-sensing light. Easing the door shut, he pressed his ear against it and strained to listen over the rapid beating of his own heart. The footsteps passed his hiding place and stopped where he'd been standing moments ago, outside Vince's office. A soft knock followed. Though Jason no longer heard the conversation in the room, he caught the muffled sound of the newcomer's voice.

"Mr. Moynier, our guests waiting outside caught someone snooping around the fish market. They have him out front."

Vince answered, but his exact words were indecipherable.

"Not sure, sir. A young guy. Claims to be some kind of reporter."

Conversation from inside the office followed the announcement, too indistinct to Jason's ears. Only when several pairs of footsteps exited into the hall did he hear Vince speak. "I'll handle whatever this is. You three go home. I'll contact you all when I hear back from our friends."

A door clicked shut as the group walked together down the passageway, five different voices speaking in low tones among themselves. Jason waited until the sounds faded into silence before he opened the bathroom door. The corridor was dark and empty. Adjusting his grip on his gun, he stalked after the group. Fewer lights were on in the main building compared to when he'd entered, but he knew the way back to the side entrance by heart. He slipped outside with ease, then, hugging the wall like a shadow, snuck around to the front.

The sight that greeted him when he peered around the corner was what he'd expected: Vince with his hands in his coat pockets, speaking with a man held at gunpoint by two different henchmen. The intruder held his hands in the air by his head, palms out. Wide eyes fixed Vince with a pleading stare.

"I—I promise I'm not here to cause trouble. I'll leave right now, I swear," Trey said, his voice overly loud in the tense quiet of the fish market at night. "God, please don't kill me."

Chapter Twenty-Two

Ayana's gaze fell upon the two-foot-tall replica of the sword and sunburst she last saw on the ring of the man who'd killed Connor. Wrought in stainless steel, the decoration hung upon the façade of the multistoried building before her, its metal surface alight with a fiery glow from the setting sun. Intricate stonework around the building's windows and along its edges lent it a noble air that contrasted with the more rundown, modest apartment buildings and row houses of the district. Glancing to her left and right, she searched for a sign with the words "St. Julian's Foundation" on it but found none; only the symbol confirmed she'd reached her destination.

How odd.

After shooting a quick text to Sabrina announcing her arrival, Ayana walked through the glass door of the main entrance. A spacious lobby greeted her, as joyless and sterile as most corporate foyers. To her left was the front desk, manned by a gray-haired woman in a pink cardigan sweater. She peered at Ayana over the rim of her glasses but said nothing. Ayana offered the receptionist the faintest of smiles, but the woman only lowered her eyes to the book in her hands.

That was fine. Ayana was not there to make small talk with strangers. Ignoring the receptionist, she peered at the tri-fold brochures arranged in neat stacks along the front edge of the desk. Each one was a different color, depicting smiling adults and children beneath bold words that said, "Through Service, to God," "Healing the World," and "Our Future in God's Hands." A frown began pulling at the corners of her mouth. She turned away before the receptionist noticed.

Crossing the room, Ayana made her way toward a cluster of sofas and armchairs situated around a low coffee table. Above them on the wall hung a massive portrait of a suited gentleman, his mild smile carrying a patronizing note as he gazed outward. His full head of blonde hair, youthful appearance, and vintage clothing meant the painting had to be several decades old. She assumed the man was none other than Sabrina's grandfather, founder of the organization.

The elevator at the far end of the lobby pinged. Ayana glanced from the portrait in time to see Sabrina emerge from the carriage, beaming. She strode over with all the confidence of a marketing agent, showing a side of herself Ayana had not seen before. "Hey! So glad you could make it!"

The women shared a warm embrace that Ayana was getting better at faking. "It wasn't too difficult. Thank you for the directions, though, because I didn't see a sign on the building."

Izzy's aerial maps had helped, too.

"Of course!" Sabrina said. "Since this is your first time here, I thought we could start with a tour of the ground floor—our public area. Then there are some people I'd like you to meet. How's that sound?"

"Perfect." What was the harm, after all?

The women started down the hall to the left of the elevator, past two bulletin boards covered in colorful flyers and notices. Sabrina explained that members often posted requests, from dog walking jobs to sales of secondhand items. The community-centric impression continued as she took Ayana around to various rooms: a large library divided into adults', teens', and children's books; a play area; classrooms equipped with desks, chairs, and whiteboards; conference rooms; and the large dining hall where St. Julian's hosted their soup kitchens. Throughout the tour, Sabrina explained the services the nonprofit provided its members, but she was tight-lipped about anything financial, only sharing information about flexible membership payment plans to accommodate lower-income families.

"So, what did you think?" she asked when the tour ended. The pair were making their way back through a corridor lined with conference rooms and classrooms.

"It's all very impressive. There's something for everyone here."

"We try to do our best for the community here in Bracknell. It's not enough for the whole city, but maybe one day, we can expand to other districts. Anyway, ready to meet some cool people?"

"Sure, but who, exactly?"

"You'll see." Sabrina flashed her an enigmatic smile before stopping in front of a door labeled Conference Room C and poking her head into the room. "Hey, hey! Are you ready?" she asked its occupants.

"Hey Sabrina! Whenever you are," came a man's voice.

She ushered Ayana inside. Two men and one woman stood from their seats around a long, rectangular table with rounded corners. One-by-one, they shook Ayana's hand. Sabrina introduced them as Derek Imai, Tim Guberman, and Phoebe Jansen—former professors from Harvard, Brown, and Cornell, respectively. From their khaki slacks to their cozy-looking sweaters, they certainly looked the part.

"A pleasure to make your acquaintance," Ayana told them as they all took their seats around the table once more, "but I don't understand why we're meeting."

"We're St. Julian's research team," said Phoebe, as if that explained everything. In front of her was a large tablet in a slim, leather case.

"I didn't realize the marketing team needed Ivy League professors."

The trio exchanged a look. "We're not part of marketing," Tim said with a laugh. "We have a more important mission, and based on what Sabrina's shared with us about you, we believe your contributions would be invaluable—if you choose to join us, of course."

Ayana glanced at Sabrina, who sat at the head of the table. "And what has she shared?"

Derek spoke up. "That you're a doctor of medicine and specialize in body trauma. Phoebe, Tim, and I all have PhDs—mine in classical archaeology, Phoebe's in medieval literature, and Tim's in theoretical astrophysics—but unlike us, *you* have hands-on experience with patients. We hope you can provide new, expert insight into what we've been studying from a purely academic standpoint thus far."

In her mind's eye, empty pockets of deepest black writhed and pulsated across dead organs, hypnotic and terrifying all at once. She recalled her visit to Lancing University's library—the melting signs, the tendrils of the many-eyed woman—and the ghastly shadow-figures that haunted her dreams. Her breath quickened into shallow gasps, and her heart thudded in her stomach, sending tremors through her whole body.

Sabrina cocked her head. "Are you okay, Ayana?"

"I'm fine." Swallowing hard, Ayana removed her water bottle from her purse and took a sip. "Go on, please."

Phoebe turned on her tablet and swiped her finger across the screen. "We'd like you to look at some pictures, Ayana. Can we call you Ayana? They're disturbing in nature, so if you start feeling queasy or lightheaded, please tell us right away."

"As you said, I'm a doctor. I can handle the sight of most things."

Phoebe's smile was a thin, grim line. "This isn't like most things."

Ayana took the tablet and examined the first photograph. It depicted a standard hospital room, complete with bed, CPAP machine, IV stand, and various monitors. On the bed lay a malnourished, middle-aged woman—pale skin, head shaved bald, eyes closed. A blanket covered her up to the waist, but her chest was bare. Small holes riddled her torso from collarbone to sternum, and the surrounding skin gleamed with an unnatural, metallic sheen.

"We've looked at many subjects like her," Phoebe said in a detached tone. "Each one is afflicted with a curse. Some of the symptoms are the same, but there are variations. That one, for example—what flesh of her chest remains has turned into solid silver."

Fresh sweat broke out over Ayana's skin. The photograph was impossible. Doctored, she thought, like the ones she found on the conspiracy forum. Why would Ivy League professors hand her a manipulated photo? She looked up at Phoebe. "Don't tell me this is real. It's a joke, right?"

But the expression on Phoebe's face was far too serious for a joke. "It's very real, I'm afraid."

While part of Ayana searched for a rational explanation, another part of her swelled with triumph, vindicated. She and Rahul weren't alone in their findings after all. Other persons of great intelligence and learning had discovered the anomaly, too. "Where'd you take this photo?"

Sabrina answered instead. "In our patient suite on the fourth floor."

"Here? You have a medical team?"

"Just nurses, to keep them alive. They don't know the details about our mission, and we haven't found a surgeon we trust yet."

"You've seen this phenomenon before, haven't you?" Derek interrupted, gesturing to the tablet. "If you swipe, you'll see more photos of other subjects."

Sure enough, a series of men and women in hospital beds followed the first one. Most looked between fifty and seventy, though a few were older and others were quite young. One was still a child.

With shaking hands, Ayana returned the tablet to Phoebe, who put it back to sleep and flipped the case's cover over the dark screen. "This is what you're researching?" Ayana asked, looking each professor in the eye.

"Part of it," said Tim. "Our research topic is actually much broader in scope. Cosmic, really."

"I don't understand."

He took a deep breath. "I suppose I should explain, since it's my field of expertise. How much do you know about our universe, Ayana?"

"Just what's taught through high school. I never took astronomy in undergrad."

"Please correct me if my presumptions are wrong, but as scientists, you and I have been taught to look at the world through a lens of logic and reason. Facts, the scientific theory, our research—all are fundamental to understanding our world and what lies beyond. Do you agree?"

"I do."

He adjusted his glasses and cleared his throat. "For most people, that's enough. They don't desire to know more. But theoretical astrophysics explores possibilities and hypotheticals, and thanks to the generous resources of St. Julian's Foundation," he acknowledged Sabrina with a nod, "we've made a startling discovery about the nature of the universe."

Dread unfurled in Ayana's gut. "Startling in what way?"

"It's inherently illogical. Physics, calculus, chemistry—everything we use to explain natural phenomena is merely a veneer. The truth is much deeper and much more unknowable."

He was avoiding saying it outright. "What are you talking about?" she pressed. "And what does that have to do with the disease afflicting all these people?"

Tim hesitated and glanced at Sabrina, as if seeking her permission. She nodded. When he addressed Ayana again, his eyebrows scrunched together. "The universe as we know it operates on the whims of ancient, cosmic beings we call Elder Gods."

Ayana stared at him. "Excuse me?"

"Unfortunately, they defy classification, at least according to the research my colleagues here have compiled. What we do know is that Elder Gods are older than time itself and can travel across many planes of existence, including our own. Generally, we don't perceive them, and *they* don't perceive *us*. Our Earth is one tiny planet in the vast expanse of the universe, so most of the time, we're too small and irrelevant to register on their scale. But on occasion, an Elder God will cause a disturbance across time and space that threatens to destroy Earth."

Ayana heard his words, but, strung together, they were ridiculous. A low chuckle escaped her lips before she could stop it. She looked at Sabrina. "So... what, are you telling me St. Julian's is some kind of cult that worships ancient aliens?"

Anger flashed in Sabrina's eyes, catching Ayana off guard. "Absolutely not. St. Julian's is committed to *stopping* them."

That answer did not lend much more credibility to the explanation. "I'm sorry, but wouldn't we all know when the world is under the threat of destruction by some extraterrestrial force? It would be all over the news."

"It's not as simple as that. UFO sightings and fleets of spaceships are the stuff of science fiction. The signs of oncoming doom are much more insidious and confounding, showing up first as eccentricities, then developing into what has traditionally been called madness."

Again, the terrible images from her nightmares flashed through Ayana's mind. Her gaze fell upon Phoebe's tablet.

"You said you wanted to help people, Ayana. To improve their lives," Sabrina continued. "We need a medical professional of your caliber, someone willing to look beyond the ordinary. We have a few doctors contracted to us in Boston, but they're busy with their own projects and can't afford to split their focus to help us. Please consider joining our cause. You'll be working with the best—experts in their fields—and have St. Julian's backing to conduct research on all the subjects affected by the curse."

"We believe their bodies hold answers we haven't been able to piece together yet," said Derek. "Tim, Phoebe, and I—our knowledge is critical for the mission in other ways, but human biology could hold the key to understanding and stopping our enemy."

"That's what the scholarship has led us to believe, anyway," Phoebe added.

Ayana took a moment to process their words. "Who is the enemy, exactly? What cursed these people?"

Sabrina grimaced. "It goes by many names, but a few crop up again and again in the literature. Lord of the Hungering Skies, He Who Arrived Before Time, and the Void Between the Stars... but here at St. Julian's, we call it by its oldest name: the Abyssal King."

Chapter Twenty-Three

The way behind Jason was clear. No one guarded his side of Grosmont Fish Market's main building, not with their attention on the intruder out front. No one had spotted him yet, either—not the men holding Trey at gunpoint nor the crime family leaders who had exited with Vince. Leaving unnoticed was the easiest choice Jason could make, yet he could not abandon Trey to his doom. The journalist had already seen too much in the faces of Milena, Tyler, and Rodrigo. Trey would not leave the fish market alive. But first, Vince would subject Trey to brutal interrogations until he revealed everything he knew: Connor's investigations, his own findings, and his collaboration with Jason.

And Jason could not let that happen.

He stepped out from behind the corner and raised his Glock at the same time. Aimed. Fired. The nearest gunman jerked from the two bullets hitting his torso.

Two more followed. He dropped to the ground, spasming.

Everyone scattered, seeking cover. Jason ducked behind the nearest car—the red one—as bullets from the other henchmen flew at him. They punched through steel and shattered glass. Amid the gunfire, Rodrigo bellowed in outraged Spanish, berating his men for damaging his vehicle.

Jason yelled, too. "Simmons! Get over here!"

Trey scampered into view, skidded to a stop next to him, and gaped at him with eyes as wide as saucers. "Jason?"

"Shut up and keep your head down!"

The car at their backs rocked with every gunshot. Jason listened for the pause as his assailants either reloaded or waited for him to move. As soon as it happened, he popped up over the hood. Sighted his next target. Squeezed the trigger twice. Another henchman tumbled to the ground, blood oozing from his chest. Jason crouched again as a new hail of bullets whizzed toward him.

"What do we do?" Trey asked, panic written all over his face.

Jason ran the options through his head. Picking off the other gunmen would take too much time; they'd surround him and Trey long beforehand. Stealing Rodrigo's car was too risky with the damage it had already sustained, and the Sons of Saints leader likely had the keys in his pocket, anyway. "We have to keep moving.

See that alley over there? Run for it, and keep running until you reach the main street. Don't slow down or stop. I'll provide cover fire."

Before Trey could protest, Jason grabbed the collar of his coat and shoved him toward the narrow opening. In the same motion, Jason stood again and fired at a big, brutish man he recognized as Milena's bodyguard. The bullets slammed into the wooden wall by his head, forcing him behind cover. Running backward after Trey, Jason gunned down another assailant and took a mental tally of his remaining bullets. Three left. Reaching the mouth of the alley, he pivoted for another shot.

Searing pain seized his right arm as a bullet tore through his triceps. He stumbled backward into the darkness, dropping his gun into his left hand. Wet, warm liquid trickled along his skin beneath his clothing, spreading outward quickly.

Blood.

Jason emptied the rest of his Glock's magazine into the tires of Rodrigo's car, deflating them. Then he raced after Trey, catching up to the other man with ease, reloading as he ran. A bullet ricocheted off a nearby wall. They both flinched.

"Left!" Jason shouted, shooting back at their pursuers. Trey dodged into the next left turn. Jason followed a half-second behind him, barking out a zigzagging route to the main street. They burst out of the alley onto a wide sidewalk, Trey gasping for breath, Jason pressing his good hand against the gushing wound in his injured arm. He turned to the younger man. "Keep moving. Hail us a cab."

Trey took one look at Jason's arm and jumped to obey. They jogged down the street, Trey with his hand out as he surveyed traffic. Meanwhile, Jason flipped on his gun's safety, unscrewed the silencer, and slipped both pieces into their hiding places on his body. By the time the familiar yellow vehicle pulled up alongside them, he'd shrugged out of his coat. Bunching it up between his hands, he jumped after Trey into the back seat.

Before Trey could speak, Jason gave his home address to the driver. "We'll pay double if you don't ask questions and don't tell anyone about giving us a ride."

Their eyes met in the rearview mirror. The driver gave a silent nod. The taxi peeled from the curb and merged with the rest of the nighttime rush at the same moment a black-clothed figure emerged from one of the fish market's alleys.

Not bothering to buckle his seatbelt, Jason sat at an angle and cradled his injured arm in his lap, using his coat to soak up the blood. Getting it anywhere on the car's interior was a bad idea. "Take off your scarf," he said to Trey.

"Dude, we should be taking you to the hospital." Still, Trey unwrapped the fabric from his neck.

"Put it around my arm here, above the wound. Good. Tie a knot as tightly as you can."

Though Trey's hands were shaking, he did as instructed.

"Do you have a pen?" Jason asked.

"Yeah, always do."

"Put it on the knot, then tie another knot around it." He waited until the other man finished. "Now turn the pen until the bleeding stops."

Trey applied the tourniquet. Jason screamed through gritted teeth against the life-saving pressure. He panted for a few seconds, head bowed, then checked and double-checked the wound. Afterward, he taught Trey how to complete the wrapping so the pen stayed in place.

"Okay, now call my wife. Tell her to meet us at home right now."

"Why—"

"Don't argue." Jason glowered at Trey. "This is more important than your fucking questions."

"Okay, okay, geez. What's her number?"

Jason recited it from memory. He focused on steadying his breathing while Trey placed the call.

"Ayana, hey! It's Trey. From the funeral, yeah. Listen, uh, I don't mean to alarm you, but Jason's hurt. He's—uh, his arm. Oh, okay. Yeah, we're on our way. Cool. See you there." He hung up and turned to Jason. "She said she's leaving now and should be home in thirty minutes."

Grosmont was closer to their destination than Bracknell, so they would arrive before Ayana. Jason would have to rely on Trey's assistance until she got home. "Do you have any first aid or medical training?"

"No, none."

"Then you need to do everything exactly as I tell you until Ayana can take over, just like with the tourniquet. Understood?"

Trey's face blanched. "I... Yeah, man. Whatever you need."

Twenty minutes later, the taxi pulled up in front of Jason's townhouse. He eyed the price on the dashboard. "Pay the man in cash," he said to Trey.

"Uh, I don't carry cash."

Jason rolled his eyes. "My wallet is in my back left pocket. Take out sixty bucks in twenties and hand it to him."

While the money exchanged hands, Jason pinned the driver with an unforgiving stare. "Remember, you saw nothing. You've never been to this address before."

"Yes, sir."

"Good. Trey, the door. Keys are in my right coat pocket."

They stumbled into the house as the taxi drove away. Jason kicked off his shoes and stomped up the stairs with Trey at his heels. As they navigated the dark second floor, he barked out orders:

"Lights are over on that wall. Trash bags are under the sink. Grab one and bring it here." When Trey returned, Jason stuffed his soiled coat into it. "Tie that up and leave it on the kitchen floor." After washing his hands, he spread out a kitchen towel on the granite island, where he dumped his gun, silencer, and other everyday carry items. "Now come with me upstairs."

In the bathroom on the third floor, he removed the handheld shower head and passed it to Trey. "The bullet hit the back of my arm, so I can't see the wound. You need to clean it out for me, and you need to be really fucking thorough. Dislodge any clothing scraps that are in there."

Trey swallowed hard. "Sure."

Jason steeled himself for the sting of water on raw, ruined flesh. He watched as his blood swirled down the drain.

"Jesus, this is nasty," Trey muttered from behind. In a louder voice, he asked, "What the *fuck* happened back there, anyway?"

"I could ask you the same thing. What did you think you were doing?"

"I was checking out some rumors that the fish market's a front for money laundering. I thought maybe I could check the place out while it's closed for... you know, clues."

Jason laughed, a rough, harsh sound that punctured the nervous tension in the room.

Trey lifted Jason's arm for a better angle at the wound. "What about you? What were *you* doing back there? And why did you have a gun on you?"

"It's better if you don't ask questions."

"I'm a reporter, man. It's my job to ask questions."

"Then I'll pay you to shut the fuck up, too."

"Too late for that. I've already looked into you, actually. I was digging around for info about Connor and called up your old high school. I talked to your old teachers. They remember you, you know."

Finally, the water ran clear. Lowering his arm, Jason turned and met Trey's gaze. Whatever he was about to say didn't matter. Jason had saved his life, and if he didn't think that was enough reason to keep his newfound knowledge to himself, Jason knew a few ways to convince him.

Trey looked away and turned the water off. "They said you were a loner and didn't have any friends. That you ate lunch by yourself for four straight years. That you got into fights a lot with other kids."

Jason exited the bathroom without a word. Drying his hands and arms with a clean towel from the closet, he waited for Trey to finish his unnecessary, theatrical buildup. The adrenaline had left Jason's system, making the pain of his injury all the more acute.

Trey followed him out into the hallway. "And apparently, one of your teachers found a bunch of crazy shit in your locker once. Photos of dead and butchered animals, a dozen knives, clippings of newspaper articles on local murders. That kind of shit doesn't stop after childhood, you know. I watched a documentary about a psychopath once, and he was just like that."

More silence, long enough that Trey began to fidget with his wristwatch.

"Who fucking *are* you?" he asked after a beat, his

voice pitched with terror. "You live in a rich part of the city. You have a happy marriage to a nice, beautiful lady. Your speech at the funeral was really moving—it felt so sincere. Nothing about you screams, 'I kill people.' And then you just..." He gestured at Jason's arm. "Fuck, man. Are you with the Monahans or something?"

"No," Jason said at last. "And the less you know about me, the better. I helped you tonight, but nothing's stopping me from killing you, too, if you keep sticking your nose where it doesn't belong."

Trey fell silent.

Chapter Twenty-Four

Ayana burst through the front door of her house and kicked off her heels. Without bothering to shed her coat or hang her keys, she surged up the stairs to the well-lit second floor. Jason sat at the kitchen island, a roll of paper towels and their plastic bin of first aid supplies already on the countertop in front of him. Trey paced nearby, hands on his hips, stopping only when she appeared.

"Thank God!" he exclaimed. Her husband, on the other hand, simply looked at her with a note of relief.

She dropped her belongings onto an armchair as she passed through the living room and drew up to Jason's side. A makeshift tourniquet, held fast with a ballpoint pen, wrapped around his upper arm. The cleanliness of his skin and the site meant they'd already washed it at least once.

She removed two latex gloves from the bin. "Show

me."

Jason angled the back of his injured arm toward her. Gently, she gripped it with one hand and examined the wound with a small flashlight from the box. Its bright beam revealed a few tiny scraps of fabric still clinging to his torn muscle.

"Trey, there's a small, white case in the bin. I need the tweezers inside it, please," she said, her tone clipped and professional. He rummaged around for it. A few seconds later, they swapped tools. "Hold the light for me so I can see clearly."

With great care, Ayana removed the fabric from Jason's wound and dropped them onto a paper towel. Once she was sure she'd found everything, she put down the tweezers. "One more quick rinse, then I'll stitch you up," she said to him.

Huddled together over the sink in the nearby powder room, she splashed warm, soapy water onto the gash. "You're lucky the bullet didn't hit any bones or arteries. What's your pain level right now?" she asked him, keeping her voice low.

He grimaced. "Five or six."

She patted his arm dry with a paper towel, careful to avoid the jagged edges of his ripped flesh. "How did this happen, Jason?"

"I went to see Vince at Grosmont Fish Market and found him holding Trey at gunpoint. I intervened, but there were more hostiles than expected."

She suspected there was more to the story he didn't

want to share with their guest still present. When they exited the bathroom, Trey was sitting on their sofa, looking around as if unsure what to do with himself. "You can go home now, Trey," she said. "Thank you for helping Jason until I got here."

"Oh, sure," he said, though he didn't get up from his seat. "But I don't mind staying a bit longer and offering a hand until he's all set."

She arched her eyebrow at him. Was it a sense of debt that compelled him to linger, or some other reason? "In that case, come help me sew him up."

Fifteen minutes later, Ayana closed Jason's wound with dissolvable stitches and wrapped them in bandages. She bid him sit on the couch with his arm propped up by pillows while she removed the tourniquet. Afterward, she lingered at his side, her hand on his wrist. Looking into his eyes, she murmured, "I'm glad you're safe."

He leaned in and kissed her. All the tension she'd been holding eased out of her at his touch. She cupped his face with her other hand, her fingers caressing his cheek.

"Thank you," he said.

She smiled at the sudden déjà vu. Two years had passed since he'd shown up on a warm summer night at her old apartment, bleeding from a long but shallow gash across his back. She'd ushered him into her kitchen to tend to the wound. It paled in comparison to this new injury, just as her fear back then had not nearly been so acute. At the time, she hadn't known his whole truth, but it fed the suspicion she'd been harboring: that her charming, easygoing boyfriend was not as he appeared.

Since that night, she'd revisited that memory many times, wondering what would've happened if Jason had gone elsewhere for help. Perhaps she would've still learned about him eventually. She didn't put much stock in fate, but she couldn't imagine their lives playing out any differently. She didn't *want* to.

"How many more times will I have to patch you up in my house like this?" Ayana asked, half-joking. "First the knife attack, and now you've been shot."

His lip curled at their shared memory. "I go to you because I trust you."

Cheeks flushing with warmth, she rose from the couch. As much as she yearned for intimacy with her husband, Trey hovered like an awkward third wheel in the kitchen. "Stay put and keep your arm elevated," she told Jason. "I'll be back in a minute."

The other man must have sensed the mood, for he'd put his coat back on. "I don't need the scarf back," he said, eyeing the bloodstains on the pale blue fabric. He did take his pen, though, and allowed her to escort him to the front door. "Are you two, uh, going to be okay?"

"Of course. You take care, too, Trey."

But he did not hurry to leave after putting on his sneakers. Instead, he paused, glancing up at the stairwell before asking in a hushed voice, "Are *you* okay, Ayana?"

Another wave of déjà vu hit her, that time carrying a note of sourness. She stared at him, reading his meaning in the inflection of his tone. Answering his unspoken assumption, however, would only confirm his suspicions as correct when they were not. "What do you mean?"

"Jason was *shot*. No one gets shot just because they were minding their own business. And judging by your reaction, you know, don't you? About *him*?"

"What *about* him, Trey?"

"He killed those guys at the fish market without a second thought! I knew he was Army, but..." Trey shook his head as his words trailed off. "He didn't want to go to the hospital, either. I get doing whatever it takes to avoid the cops, but there's something else going on, isn't there? There's something fucked up about him."

She shot him a look of warning. "Jason saved your life."

To Trey's credit, he hesitated. "I know. Fuck, I *know*." Looking torn, he reached for the doorknob. "I just... If you need anything, let me know, okay? You or him."

"You already paid him back by bringing him here. You don't owe him anymore."

Annoyance flashed across Trey's face, catching her off guard. "It's not about that. Whatever's going on with Connor's murder is bigger than the two of you. It'd be wrong to abandon you both just because things have gotten scary. Anyway, you have my number now. I'll be in touch."

He bid her goodnight and slipped out the door. She watched his receding figure from the threshold before retreating back inside.

When she returned to the living room, Jason was no longer on the sofa. Footsteps from the floor above meant he was in their bedroom, but for the briefest moment, Ayana was back on the first floor, her stomach twisting into knots as a stranger walked through their home. Squeezing her eyes shut, she breathed through the memory until the spike of anxiety faded.

She jogged up the steps. The bedroom door was wide open. "I thought I told you to stay put," she said before pausing in the doorway. Her silver-and-white suitcase lay on the bed. Her husband dropped a second suitcase, his black one, next to it with his good arm. Her eyes snapped to meet his. "Jason?"

"We can't stay here." He grabbed some shirts out of their shared dresser. "Pack a few days' worth of clothing and whatever essentials you need."

Ayana's thoughts flew to her job at the forensic center. Her bereavement leave was over; her boss and coworkers were expecting her to show up for work the following day. And then there was the matter of St. Julian's Foundation. "We can't just leave," she said, trying and failing to reconcile two truths in her head: that Jason was not a man who feared anything, yet he was acting like he was trying to flee.

He must have read her thoughts, for he stopped what he was doing and came to her side. Cradling her face in both of his hands, he said, "We're staying in Lancing. We just need to live in hotels until I'm done killing them all."

Relief washed over here. *There* was the man she knew. She grabbed at his wrists. "What really happened tonight?"

"I found out Vince is in league with the leaders of the Big Three I told you about yesterday. They were all there discussing the Abyssal King."

"What about it?"

Gently extricating himself from her grip, he shared the details of the encounter, from the revelations unveiled by the four collaborators to the confirmation that St. Julian's had sent the home invader. While she listened, Ayana packed her suitcase alongside him, filling it with several days' worth of coordinating outfits. She assembled a travel-sized kit of her toiletries and makeup, then picked out some simple jewelry from her vanity.

"Most importantly, though, I found out Vince killed Connor," Jason said as he zipped up his luggage.

She froze. "What? The man who trained you? Who came to our house and helped you dispose of a corpse?"

"The same one."

Reaching out, she steadied herself on her bedside table. Her ears rang with a high-pitched noise, and her breathing grew shallow. "Jason... He knows where we live."

"I know. That's why we have to leave."

Her knees buckled. She lowered herself onto the mattress. "How long will it take you to kill them?"

He crouched in front of her, took her hands in his, and squeezed her fingers reassuringly. "Not long. But I need you to keep moving, Ayana."

They changed into different outfits and hauled their suitcases to the ground floor. While she fetched her keys and purse, he retreated into his secret chamber behind the shelf in the utility room. When he reemerged, she knew he was armed to the teeth, though she didn't see a single weapon on his body. The knowledge sent a thrill up her spine.

After leaving their house, they rode the subway for an hour, switching stations and lines several times until he was satisfied no one was following them. They ended their journey at a modest hotel in Dunston, checking in for two nights under one of his false identities. Once inside the room, he scoured it for hidden bugs and cameras. Finding none, he finally allowed them both to relax for the night.

"How'd your visit to Bracknell go?" Jason asked as they sat on the couch, eating the Chinese takeout they'd picked up on the way. The television on the opposite wall was tuned to the news, its volume set to a low murmur.

"I don't even know where to begin," Ayana said, shaking her head. Yet she proceeded to recount her evening, starting with the tour of the building and ending with the revelation of the accursed. She even picked up her phone and showed him the profiles of the three professors on their respective universities' websites, proving their identities as well-studied academics.

He listened in stony silence, speaking only after she finished. "Do you believe Sabrina and her research team?"

"Yes. I wish I didn't. It seems insane, but I can't deny what we've seen between my decedents, your encounters, and the photographs of their patients. The symptoms were similar to what I found—worse, even. More advanced." She looked at him. "I have to know more, Jason. Joining St. Julian's mission might be the key to getting the answers we seek, including why Connor had to die."

Jason said nothing at first while he chewed his food. "Vince was the man in the CCTV footage Izzy acquired. He must be a member of St. Julian's, too."

Knowing how much her husband despised others' pity, Ayana considered her next words carefully. "You said you didn't trust him, but he still betrayed you. You've gone to him for help, advice, and work in the past, expecting him to be your ally all this time. But in the end, none of that mattered."

Sabrina was the same. As much as she preached about saving the world, an innocent man was dead because of her family's nonprofit. Moreover, Ayana was certain Sabrina had spoken ill of Jason to the police in an attempt to cast suspicions on him. As far as she was concerned, they were all hypocrites—Sabrina, Vince, and the entire St. Julian's Foundation.

Her husband was right: the only people the two of them could trust were each other. All other monsters be damned.

"No, it didn't," Jason said, bringing her out of her thoughts. He glanced over at her. "I don't like the idea of you walking into any traps, but if Sabrina trusts you..."

"I don't think she does, but she sounded desperate for my expertise. And sometimes that's enough reason to work alongside your enemy."

He nodded. "Then tell them you'll join them."

"I'll text her tomorrow. What about you?"

He raised his gaze to the window and the dazzling skyline of Dunston that lay beyond. "I'm going to pay an old acquaintance a visit."

Chapter Twenty-Five

At first glance, Dunston Auto Body Repair appeared like any ordinary business, with a small waiting room affixed to a larger garage. As Jason stepped through the front door into the former, the bell tied to the handle chimed, announcing his presence. He scanned the cramped space, noting the front desk, the door behind it painted black, and the three empty, plastic chairs to his right. A coffee maker and water cooler stood next to each other in the corner. The back wall had no windows, preventing customers from peering into the garage.

Behind the desk sat a member of the Monahans, a young man dressed in a navy blue coverall with the shop's logo embroidered on the front left breast. He glanced up from his phone at the sound of the bell. "Oh hey, Mr. Ridley. Are you here to see the boss?"

"Yeah. Is he in today?"

He jerked his thumb over his shoulder at the door. "Workin' on his newest set of wheels."

Compared to the reception area, the garage was massive and high-ceilinged, built from a gutted warehouse. Bright ceiling lights illuminated at least a dozen cars on ramps and lifts, stacks of tires and rims, and shelves covered in tools. Mechanics dressed in oil-stained coveralls shouted at each other over the scream of electric drills and the pumping bass of a hip-hop song. They glanced at Jason but otherwise kept working. All the bays were closed to keep out the winter chill, but large fans swept the stinking air out through ducts in the ceiling.

The cars themselves were all civilian vehicles: Hondas, Toyotas, Kias. Half were legitimate work requests, Jason knew, and would return to their owners at the end of the afternoon. The other half, however, were designated spare parts, disassembled and packed away in record time before his eyes.

At the far end of the garage was a bright blue sports car, so shiny it must have just rolled off the lot. Its hood was open, and Nick had both hands in its dark guts. He had traded his suit for a pair of stained blue jeans and a dark gray, long-sleeved shirt, the sleeves rolled up to his elbows. A rag stuck out of his back pocket, and black stained his forearms. He finished fiddling with the car's engine, wiped his hands on the rag, and shut the hood. Only then did he turn and notice Jason standing a few feet away.

A grin split Nick's face. "Look who it is! You didn't drop your car off here, did you?"

"No. I want to talk about work."

The Monahan heir arched an eyebrow but nodded. "Sure. We can talk in the back. But first!" He gestured to his car with both hands. "You like her? Brand new Toyota Supra. Picked her up just the other day. Once I get a few mods in her, I'll be ready for the spring races."

"You're racing again?"

"Yeah, why not? It's not like I'm too old or rusty or anything. Hell, I'm younger than you, I think."

Jason said nothing. Nick took the hint and led the way to another door. Two tall men in dark, unassuming clothing fell into step behind the pair—Nick's bodyguards. They kept their distance as he and Jason walked down a narrow corridor to a small office, the word MANAGEMENT on the nameplate affixed to its door. Sitting behind the desk with a phone to his ear was a rotund man with a bad comb-over. He looked up, startled, when they entered.

"Boss!" He scrambled to mute himself on the call. "Can I help you with something?"

"Out," said Nick with a wave of his hand. He closed the door after his employee scurried away; his bodyguards remained in the hallway. Then he lowered himself into the chair behind the desk. "So, work. I thought you weren't taking contracts right now."

Jason took the less comfortable seat, a metal chair, on the other side of the desk. "I wasn't, but circumstances changed. Are you still planning raids on the Sons of Saints' drug dens?"

Nick grinned and fished a pack of cigarettes from his pocket. He removed one and offered the rest to Jason. "We might be."

Jason accepted a cigarette and lit it with his own lighter. "I want in, but I have two conditions. One, I want Rodrigo captured for questioning first. You can do whatever you want afterward—kill him, imprison him, I don't care."

Nick took a long, contemplative drag and blew out a cloud of smoke. "Why? What does Rodrigo know that you wanna know?"

"It's a personal matter."

"I thought nothin' was ever personal for your type." Assassins, he meant.

"Not this time."

Nick said nothing while he searched Jason's face for the answer, but Jason maintained his mask of neutrality with practiced ease. Smoke curled around his head as he exhaled. After a tense moment, Nick relented. "All right, fine, that's no problem. What's your second condition?"

"It needs to happen tonight."

His eyes widened. "No way. That's too soon. We're not ready."

It was Jason's turn to raise an eyebrow. "You have nothing prepared?"

"I mean, we got the guns, yeah. We have the firepower and the means to get there, but we're still in the middle of scoping out Saintfield to figure out the best place to strike. It ain't easy, you know. *You* can walk around wherever you want and no one will fuck with you, but once the Sons gets a whiff we're sneaking around their territory, they'll do whatever it takes to run us out of it."

"What've you learned so far?"

"We think we've identified the locations of their biggest drug dens, most of which are deeper in the district than others. There are a couple near the edge, which is how they sell to people from neighboring districts. No one outside Saintfield wants to wander too far into Saintfield, you know?" Nick sighed and took another pull from his cigarette. "The problem is, we don't know where Rodrigo's gonna be at any given time. We're still trying to work out his schedule, stuff like that. Which is what I was *hoping* you'd be able to help us out with, since you do all that kinda stuff for your jobs anyway."

"Normally, yes, but that won't be necessary this time. I'll draw Rodrigo out."

"Yeah? And how exactly are you gonna do that?"

The office door slammed open. Jason turned in his chair, his right hand falling to the holster hidden at his waist. A lanky teenager stood in the doorway, wild-eyed and hyperventilating. One of Nick's bodyguards loomed behind the intruder. "Mr. Monahan!" the boy shouted. "It's Eddie and Helen! They're back—and Eddie's been shot!"

Nick surged to his feet, quickly putting out his cigarette in the ashtray on the desk. He raced past the boy through the open door, his bodyguards hurrying after him. Jason followed at a walk, one hand tucked loosely in his pocket, the other cradling his cigarette. The boy darted ahead of him, toward the sound of agonized screaming, curses, and a woman's frenetic yelling. The hallway led Jason to an employee break room. Eddie sprawled on his back on a long table in the center, his entire midsection dark with blood. Helen leaned over him, her arms stained crimson up to the elbow, her hands pressed against his gut. She barked out orders to two garage workers hovering nearby. "I need hot water and clean bandages! You—there's a first aid kit over there!"

Eddie's wordless screams and incoherent sobs grew quieter as the strength seeped out of his wounds. Jason watched as every breath became shallower than the last, as Eddie's eyes unfocused, as his thrashing slowed.

Nick snatched up a handful of clean rags and rushed to Helen's side. He handed a few to her. "Here, use these." She blocked up the wound with them, staining the white with scarlet in a matter of seconds. Meanwhile, Nick wiped up the blood on Eddie's face. "Look at me, man. Hey. Eyes on me."

Eddie's head jerked as he gazed up at his boss, his features contorted in agony.

"You're gonna be all right. You hear me? It'll be all right." Nick's voice cracked with emotion. "We'll patch you up and you'll get a whole fucking month's vacation, then you'll be right as rain again. I'll buy you a drink at Pete's as soon as you're better. Top shelf stuff, I promise. You'd like that, wouldn't you, buddy? Yeah?"

Eddie's eyes unfocused. He uttered a shuddering gasp as blood bubbled between his lips.

Nick's head snapped up. "Where's the fucking first aid kit?" he hollered.

"It won't help him," Jason said, his even voice cutting through the chaos.

Nick whirled upon him. "We can't just let him die!"

Jason met the other man's glower with an unflinching stare. "He's already dead."

The sudden patter of heavy footsteps heralded the arrival of a garage worker, a metal carafe in his hands. He froze mid-stride and stared at the table, mouth agape. Jason and Nick turned to look. Eddie had fallen still, his eyes glazed over, his body limp. Helen stood over him for several shocked seconds before she stepped backward and lowered herself onto a chair, head in her hands. Fury flashed across Nick's face. He cranked his arm back and hurled the bloody rags in his hand to the floor at his feet. They smacked against the linoleum with a thick, wet sound. No one spoke.

Regaining his composure, Nick pointed to the two employees who looked like deer ready to bolt. "You and you. Get some mops and clean the floor." He turned to one of his bodyguards. "Call the cleaners. Tell them we'll pay extra if they get here ASAP."

While his underlings hopped to their tasks, he grabbed another clean rag from a nearby bin and walked over to Helen. He offered it to her without comment. After a moment's hesitation, she took it and started wiping the blood from her hands.

"You gonna tell me what happened?" he asked her, his hands on his hips.

She straightened in her chair and took a deep breath. "Me, Eddie, and Liam were out in Saintfield like you ordered, keeping as low a profile as we could while we were checking out a possible place for a strike. It's either someone's house or a rental of some kind. There were a lot of cars parked in front of it, more than you'd expect. Some of them were pretty nice, too. Liam wanted a closer look, so he and Eddie got out and walked over. I couldn't see them too well from where I'd parked, but I saw the front door open and some Sons come out."

"How many?"

"Three. They confronted Liam and Eddie, there was some conversation, and then I heard gunshots. I pulled the car out into the street as Eddie was running back. They got him here," she pointed to the left side of her abdomen, "just as he was climbing into the car. I don't know how he managed to hang on till we got here."

"And Liam?"

Her face scrunched up and her jaw set. "Eddie said those motherfuckers killed him."

Nick turned away from her and paced the length of the room, pausing astride the ruined table and Eddie's mangled body. Jason watched where he lingered by the door, smoking in silence, waiting.

"We could declare war on the Sons with this," Nick said, his voice raspy and hollow.

"They might try claiming we fired first," Helen said.

"Doesn't matter. There's a dead Monahan in Saintfield."

"You could use the situation to your advantage," Jason said. "Offer Rodrigo an exchange."

The look on Nick's face meant he understood Jason's meaning at once. "We tell them we won't declare war if they give us Liam's body. In fact, I suggest meeting face-to-face as a reassurance. It's what he'll expect, and he won't wanna deal with a Monahan corpse, so it's a win-win for him... except he doesn't know about the guns we got."

"Or about me."

"Yeah, okay. Okay." Nick gestured to the bodyguard who still had his phone out. "Get all our captains to meet at headquarters in an hour. We have a raid to plan. Helen, get yourself cleaned up. Jason, I want a word with you. In private."

The two men returned to the manager's office. Nick leaned backward against the desk and sighed; his gaze lowered to the flecks of blood on his hands.

"You're leading the raids with my captains," he said without looking at Jason. "I want that premium human-exterminating skill of yours put to good use. But," he finally raised his eyes, "I need to know why you're after Rodrigo."

"My reasons are my own."

"I *need* to know, Jason. I can't have you doin' anything that puts Monahan soldiers in any more danger than they'll already be in."

Jason weighed his options. Nick's immediate usefulness made him a tool Jason had neither the time nor luxury to replace. He simply needed to apply the correct emotional nudge. "Remember when the Panzieris killed your brother?"

Nick's expression hardened. "I'll never forget it for as long as I live."

"Then I don't need to explain myself. Besides, I'm not the one you and your soldiers need to worry about."

Nick waved a hand dismissively. He started toward the door again. "Yeah, yeah. The Sons of Saints will be in their home turf, but we have the numbers now—*and* the element of surprise. We just gotta plan it right."

"I don't mean the Sons."

Nick paused in the hallway. He looked over his shoulder at Jason, a crinkle between his eyebrows. "What do you mean?"

Jason stepped into the corridor beside the other man. A plan was taking shape in his mind, one that could turn the tide in his favor—not just against the Sons of Saints, but the Panzieris and Novikovs, too. As numerous and influential as they were, each and every one of them was human, down to the last man.

And there was one thing they collectively feared.

One thing powerful enough to annihilate them all in one fell swoop.

"There's a monster trapped in Saintfield," Jason said, "and we're going to set it free."

Chapter Twenty-Six

Lancing Forensic Medical Center had not changed in the week since Ayana last set foot inside its sterile, beige-colored halls. The security guards at the front desk greeted her with the same semi-bored tone, and the objects on her desk had not moved an inch from their usual places. Sitting at her computer, she needed to pause for only a few seconds before recalling her password. And when Harvey made his morning rounds, he welcomed her back as if their argument hadn't been the catalyst for her bereavement leave. As if they hadn't argued at all.

Rahul, however, had not looked Ayana in the eye since her return. His answers to her questions were brief and civil, his words lacking the amicable warmth of their previous familiarity. During their first autopsy of the day, he embodied professionalism. She wouldn't have minded at all—in fact, she would have preferred the emotional distance—except for how jarring and strange it felt to work alongside him in that manner.

After logging their notes into the decedent's report, she locked her computer and stood. "I think we've earned ourselves a coffee break," she said to him. "Come with me. I want to catch up."

He cast her an uncertain look, but stood and followed her into the break room without a word.

She rummaged through the cabinet for her preferred bag of ground coffee. "How've you been, Rahul? How's Oscar doing?"

Clearing his throat, he put a filter into the coffee pot. "We're getting by."

She chose her next words carefully. "You know, I admire you. Taking care of a spouse full-time mustn't be easy." When he didn't reply, she added, "I had to take Jason to the ER yesterday. It was terrifying." She willed herself to revisit the panic and terror that had suffocated her during Trey's phone call and the dreadful train ride back home.

Rahul paused. When she glanced at his face, concern furrowed his brow and twisted his mouth into a frown. "Is he okay?"

"Yes, thank God. He'd only cut himself, but there was a lot of blood. I can't imagine what I'd do if he was grievously injured or his life was somehow on the line." A shudder—a genuine one—rolled through her at the thought.

Rahul stepped back, giving her space to pour coffee

grounds into the pot. A solemn pensiveness settled in the air between them. "All I can do is support Oscar as best as I can, from moment to moment. Sometimes he has really good days and we can have a lot of fun together. Other times, when he can't even get out of bed, I just have to be there for him. I'll make him comfortable, bring him food and water, do the housework he meant to do but can't. That sort of thing."

"Does it ever become too much?" Ayana asked, the words slipping out before she could stop them.

He shrugged. "I'd be lying if I said it wasn't a challenge, but I knew all about it before we decided to get married. Oscar showed me how he lived his life and what he'd need from a partner, and I gave it serious consideration. Do I have it in me to support him in the way he needs? For the rest of our lives, even? And I found out that answer was, 'Yes.'"

She observed her assistant in silence as he spoke. His words resonated, stirring up memories of that pivotal conversation two years ago, when the course of her life changed forever. The morning after his knife injury, Jason sat opposite her at the kitchen table. When she'd asked him about it the night before, he'd lied. Or so she guessed. It was only a hunch, but by then she knew better than to ignore her instincts. She waited until breakfast the next day to ask him about that, too, armed with her research into his condition. To her surprise, he told her the truth. In the wake of his chilling confession, she found herself contemplating the same question as

Rahul.

And reaching the same conclusion.

"About last week," she said, lowering her voice. He stiffened, his open expression closing up. "I'm sorry. It was wrong of me to offer you money like that. I shouldn't have asked in the first place."

A half-truth. She *shouldn't* have asked, but she wasn't actually sorry.

Unlike Rahul, she would do anything for her husband.

He rubbed the back of his neck. "Apology accepted," he mumbled, his speech halting, his gaze averted. "I know you were only compelled to find out the truth. I don't blame you for that. It was... It took me by surprise, that's all. I know you're not a bad person, Dr. Hudson."

She flashed him a grateful smile before pouring coffee from the pot into a paper cup. Could she have lied so readily, three years ago?

He spoke again. "I admit, I was curious, too. I ended up talking with some nurse friends from Upper Kemsing Hospital after all, about what we saw in the decedents. I didn't ask for the identifying information you wanted, but my friends confirmed they'd seen similar symptoms in living patients. The hospital always transfers them out to a center specializing in new diseases and long-term care. Some place called St. Julian's."

Ayana released the breath she didn't realize she'd been holding. "So that's how they get their test subjects. Trey was right, then."

"Pardon?"

"Rahul, did you find it odd how Harvey was so calm when we showed him the female decedent? The one whose niece found her dead in her home?"

"He *was* acting strange."

"I think he's seen it before. We must not be the first employees here to report the affliction to him."

Rahul fell into a contemplative silence as he poured coffee into his own cup. "It must be a rare occurrence, then," he said at length.

"*Or* whoever's behind it all—the transfers, the orders for disposal—has been able to keep everything contained until recently."

"But who has that kind of power?"

"I don't know, but I intend to find out."

He paused, narrowing his eyes at her. "How?"

She shook her head. It was better that he didn't know. "I'm glad we got the chance to talk, Rahul." She stepped into the hallway outside the break room. "I'll be in the lab for the next couple of hours."

· · · · · · · · · · ·

Ayana looked up from her lunch as Harvey waddled past her desk. In his booming voice, he announced to everyone who hadn't left the building how excited he was to eat at the newest steak restaurant that had opened nearby. She'd read about it online. The chef and owner had already earned one Michelin star at his other restaurant in the city, and this new location offered a three-course lunch experience "for the busy professional." Harvey would be away from the forensic center for at least an hour, if not longer.

How fortuitous.

Keeping him in the periphery of her vision, she swallowed the final mouthful of her chicken sandwich and wiped her hands clean on a paper napkin. He paused to speak with another forensic pathologist, laughed, and started down the hallway again. Balling up the checkered wrapper that remained of her meal, she walked over to the trash can and recycling bins in the hall. The elevator's familiar chime reached her ears. With a slight turn of her head, she watched her boss disappear into the carriage and out of sight. Then she glanced at the desks where her colleagues sat, working. Most were out, too, enjoying a midday respite from the building's stale air and glaring lights. Of the few who remained, only Rahul was looking at her.

She broke eye contact first.

Harvey never locked his office. Ayana slipped inside, careful not to make noise when she closed the door behind her. Approaching the desk, she memorized the items on it, how they were arranged, and the position of the chair. She sat on it and cringed at the unusual warmth of the cushioned seat. Forcing herself to ignore it, she focused on her task at hand. Time was ticking.

With the computer locked, she turned her attention to the desk. Resting on it were a standard-issue keyboard and mouse, a glossy black fountain pen in a brassy pen holder, and a legal pad with a scribbled to-do list. She recognized a few names, but none were Sabrina Kopanski or the leaders of Lancing's major criminal groups. Undeterred, Ayana pulled out the desk's drawers one by one, rummaging through ordinary office paraphernalia, folders containing thick packets of Department of Health policy, and a stack of tax documents. In the bottom left drawer, she found a square, neon yellow Post-it note with a generic password, the one their IT team handed out to every new employee. The paper's many creases and crinkles suggested its age. She tapped the sequence of letters and numbers into the login prompt. Harvey's desktop, including his email, came up right away.

"Really, Harvey?" she whispered in disbelief. "You never reset your password?"

Scrolling through his inbox, she searched for emails from the previous two weeks, and specifically from the days she'd reported the strange anomaly to him. Finding nothing, she next checked a folder labeled Deleted Items, using the same search criteria as before. The email address skopanski@stjulians.org caught her eye. Her heart hammering against her ribs, she clicked on a message dated the Monday after Connor's death.

There's no need to worry about Ayana, the message said. *I've come up with a plan to distract her from the bodies by redirecting her attention to more personal matters. That, on top of whatever needs to happen with Connor, will keep her busy for weeks, if not months. By the time she remembers what she saw in the bodies, we'll have dealt with the monster. Next time, though, don't make such a snap decision like forcing her to take leave. We were counting on her being at work all day tomorrow as part of our plan. Now our team has less time to work, though I have no doubt they'll succeed either way.*

The email was signed, *Sabrina Kopanski, Director of Operations, Lancing, St. Julian's Foundation.*

Ayana sat back in the chair, reeling from the weight of the words on the screen. The phrasing was full of corporate lingo, but she understood the implicit meaning at once: Sabrina, as Head of Operations, had sent the home invader. Her desire to see Jason arrested for his crimes had driven her to commit her own. Lunch was a distraction to get Ayana out of the house. Had they known Jason wouldn't be home, either? Had Vince orchestrated that half of the plan, knowing her husband's habits?

Rahul's muffled voice reached her ears through the closed door. "Wait, Mr. Blumenthal! Sorry, do you have a second?"

"What is it, Goswami?"

Ayana's pulse skyrocketed. Her eyes darted to the door, then around the room, seeking a hiding place. No closets, no large cabinets. The only place was—

She clicked back to Harvey's inbox, locked the computer, and snatched up the Post-it note. Scooting the chair back to its previous position, she crouched under the desk and pressed herself against the wooden panel facing the front of the office. Despite the adrenaline coursing through her veins, she willed herself to take deep, even, silent breaths.

The door swung open. Harvey's irritated reprimand rang out unimpeded. "I can't stand around and chat about this and that right now, or I'll be late for lunch with the director of the Department of Health."

He approached, his footfalls heavy on the carpet. Ayana clamped her free hand over her mouth. He rounded the desk. Moments later, the wide trunks of his legs, clothed in black trousers, and his polished black shoes came into view. If she stretched out her arm, she could touch them.

"Now where'd I put that notebook?" he muttered to himself. "I swear it was right here."

Had there been a notebook on his desk? Ayana thought back to minutes ago when she'd sat in his chair. No, there hadn't... or maybe she misremembered. Maybe it *had* been sitting there, but in her search, she'd stowed it away in a drawer instead. Harvey would notice the change. He may have never reset his password, but he wasn't in charge of the entire forensic center for no reason.

She stared at his legs, waiting with mounting dread for them to shift. For his knees to bend as he knelt in search of his notebook. For him to meet her gaze and his expression to transform, first into shock, then outrage.

Wood scraped as a drawer on the desk's right side

opened. Harvey uttered a noise of triumph. Paper rustled, then he closed the drawer again. His legs retreated from her field of vision and his footsteps receded back toward the other side of the room. "I said *later*, Goswami," he said before the door shut behind him, leaving Ayana alone with the pounding of her heart in her ears.

Chapter Twenty-Seven

Jason's plan to draw the Abyssal King into the open was simple: pure and brutal carnage.

"While Nick meets with Rodrigo to collect Liam's body, three teams will strike known Sons drug dens at the edge of Saintfield," he said. Behind him, Nick's enormous, flatscreen TV displayed a map of the district in question. Gathered on a semicircle of leather sofas and armchairs in front of him were all of Nick's captains, a dozen scrappy-looking men and women. The Monahan heir himself stood at the back, arms crossed over his chest, his face dark with violent intent.

"According to Eddie, the Abyssal King is drawn to cruelty and despair, but it doesn't distinguish between attackers and victims," Jason continued. "It killed the attacker and helped the victim in his story, but when I encountered it, it killed someone uninvolved in the situation while I, the attacker, escaped."

"How do we free it?" Nick asked.

"With a bloodbath. Annihilate the Sons." Jason looked each Monahan captain in the eye before meeting Nick's gaze. "Doesn't matter if they're old or young, armed or unarmed, awake or sleeping. Kill them all."

Some of the captains nodded, accepting their instructions. None seemed interested in objecting.

"Then what?" Nick asked.

"Then I talk to it," Jason said without missing a beat.

Nick did a double take. "What—*talk* to it? That's it? Can it even understand human speech?"

"It's intelligent." Jason didn't have the words to explain it, but when he, Vince, and Simon encountered the Abyssal King in that darkened parking lot, he'd felt a second consciousness fixate upon his own, pinning him like a moth beneath glass. He hadn't felt it since, but he had a hunch it could happen again. "I *can* talk to it."

The Monahans waited until dusk before moving out in a fleet of dark-colored vehicles, inexpensive civilian sedans built for speeding through the twists and turns of city streets. Jason went with them, observing their surroundings as they crossed the invisible boundary into Saintfield. The buildings aged in an instant around him, sporting graffiti-laden façades and dirty, barred windows. In the gloom of twilight, pedestrians hurried down broken sidewalks dotted with litter. He searched for the telltale signs of scouts and runners: keen-eyed individuals looking with more than a passing interest at anything suspicious in their territory. To avoid attracting attention, the Monahans had dispersed themselves through traffic long before their arrival. They wore ordinary and forgettable clothing in black and dark colors, including masks, scarves, and other face coverings to hide their identities.

Most importantly, they kept their firearms out of sight. Jason's dependable Glock 19 sat in its hidden holster at his waist, while his jacket obscured the H&K MP7 submachine gun under his arm from view. A bandolier of ammunition crossed his chest, each of its three magazines preloaded with thirty bullets. Tucked away in his pocket was a folding tactical knife. Beneath his shirt, he wore a Kevlar vest from his own collection.

Beside him in the driver's seat, Helen turned the car onto a quiet, residential street. "We're almost at the house. Just five more minutes."

"Let's go over the plan one more time," he said, turning to address the other two passengers. Sitting in the back were two broad-shouldered men, both seasoned Monahan soldiers with special expertise in firearms. The older one was a fellow veteran. "We take the house by force, first squad through the front door, second squad through the side by the kitchen. Third squad will stay behind to catch anyone escaping and to transport the injured. Move in pairs through the house, watching each other's backs. Kill all hostiles. Round up anyone who surrenders in the living room. Any questions?"

Silence. Jason nodded and faced forward again.

"Helen, park the car two houses down from the target."

She drew the vehicle to a stop in front of a white, two-story house with a chain-link fence and grimy vinyl siding. Glancing in the side view mirror, he watched as two other plain sedans parked along the curb behind theirs. He dialed into an encrypted group call with a burner phone mounted on the dashboard. "Red team in position," he said over speakerphone.

"Blue team's ready," said the commander of three other Monahans squads at a different drug den in Saintfield.

"Yellow is, too," said a second commander, a woman. Both were captains Nick had picked as leaders due to their tenure in the gang, high rank, and experience with violent crime.

"Let's move," Jason said. "Hit them hard and fast. Don't give them time to fight back. Check in by text when you're done. I'll initiate the call."

He hung up and pushed open his door. The other three followed his lead, their heavy boots stomping onto the sidewalk and street. As he unholstered his MP7, the rest of the Monahan captains and soldiers assigned to his team emerged from their cars, too. He screwed a suppressor onto the end of his firearm, checked it was set to semiautomatic, and started toward the brick house Helen had described during their briefing. The grass in the front yard was brown and patchy, and the chain-link fence was red with rust.

The front door opened as Jason approached. A man

appeared on the threshold, one hand behind his back. Jason raised his gun and fired three times. A pistol slipped out of the man's grip and clattered to the ground seconds before his body fell.

Pain throbbed in Jason's injured arm. Ignoring it, he stepped over the corpse and into the house. A living room opened up before him: couch, armchair, coffee table, and two bodies at ten o'clock, raising guns. He pivoted his hips and squeezed the trigger. Blood and brains splattered across yellowed wallpaper. Jason stepped to the side so his team could enter. The two brawny Monahans went upstairs while Helen moved toward the nearest hallway. Jason followed her. The clicks of silenced shots and the thuds of bodies told him the second squad had breached the kitchen.

In the hall, Helen kicked open the first door to the left. Two young men backed up against the far wall, their hands in the air, begging her not to shoot. She yelled back, ordering them to the ground, hands on their heads. They scrambled to their knees in front of her. Jason stalked past to the next door. He slammed it open. The unmistakable stench of feces smacked him in the face. A man flinched where he sat on the toilet, his pants bunched up around his ankles.

Movement in the right corner of Jason's vision: a fourth man, charging with a knife. Jason spun his gun around. The triceps of his right arm spasmed and screamed in pain.

Silenced gunshots clicked by his ear. The man with

the knife jerked backward before hitting the wall at an angle. Blood oozed from the bullet holes in his chest.

Jason looked over his shoulder. Helen lowered her smoking firearm as another Monahan herded their two captives from the other room. "Good job," he told her. He gestured at the bathroom with his own gun. "Handle this one."

Without waiting for her reply, he skirted around the dead knife-wielder and scanned the final room. A bed without sheets or pillows occupied the far corner. A loveseat, small side table, and television were the only other significant pieces of furniture. Handcuffs hung from the bed's metal frame, but both they and the mattress were unoccupied. He opened the room's closet. Empty.

"All clear!" he shouted, making his way back through the hall.

"Upstairs too," said a Monahan soldier.

"Check downstairs."

Jason strode into the living room, where the three Sons who'd surrendered stood in a line against a wall. He eyed each of them in turn, then fixed the first with a glare. A scrawny kid, he looked no older than twenty. He flinched beneath Jason's gaze.

"You," said Jason. "How many people work for Rodrigo the Red?" He knew the rumors, of course, but did his captives know?

The boy only gawked at him with eyes as wide as saucers. Sweat beaded on his forehead.

"How many places do the Sons operate out of? Where are they?"

More terrified silence. Suppressing a sigh, he raised his MP7 and put a bullet through the boy's head.

Jason aimed his firearm at the next captive, who wasn't much older than his dead friend. "Same questions."

The second boy licked his lips nervously. "I don't know! I don't know anything! I-I'm brand new, I just joined—"

Another bullet silenced him forever.

Jason stared down the remaining prisoner. A new stain darkened the front of his trousers, and the smell of fresh piss hit Jason's nose. Wrinkling his face in disgust, he pointed his gun at the wretched man. "Same questions."

The man stammered out some numbers, locations, and addresses. Jason relayed the information over the phone to the other teams, who'd confirmed their own successes. "Send any injured back to base," he added, turning his back on the living room. "Move fast."

He hung up and tossed the phone back to Helen. Pausing in the doorway, he aimed his gun at the last Son of Saints left standing and fired. The corpse slumped to the floor, leaving a wide streak of red on the wallpaper behind it.

"Is this really going to work?" Helen asked Jason as they jogged back to their parked cars.

He climbed into the front passenger's seat. "It will if

you focus on driving instead of asking questions."

They shot down the street toward their next destination. "I don't mean the raids. You said yourself the Abyssal King doesn't distinguish between attackers and victims. What if it comes for us?"

Jason peered out into the growing darkness. He flexed the fingers of his right hand, willing away the pain of his injury. "Let me worry about that."

· · · · ● · ● ● · · ·

The parking lot where Nick had arranged to meet Rodrigo serviced a derelict strip mall. All the businesses had shuttered their windows and flipped their signs to "Closed." No vehicle occupied the space except for those the two men owned. A yellow-white glow from the parking lot's lights suffused the area, though a couple of lamps flickered, daring to darken. Above, the last rays of daylight dwindled in the face of the coming night.

Jason stepped out of the sedan into the frigid air, holding his MP7 in both hands, angled downward. Fresh blood smeared across his face and knuckles. It soaked into his black, long-sleeved shirt.

Not his own blood, of course.

He walked around Nick's parked car and took in the scene. Nick and three of his most loyal captains surrounded two Sons of Saints, holding them at gunpoint. Both knelt with their hands behind their backs; a third lay several feet away in a pool of his own blood. Jason recognized Rodrigo at once, which meant the other two were his top captains—his left and right hands, in essence.

"About time you got here," Nick said to Jason and his team as they approached. "What's the update?"

"We got 'em all, boss," Helen said, though her face was paler than usual in the light. "Eight locations total. It—it was a bloodbath. Everyone's on their way out of Saintfield."

"Losses?"

She hesitated. "Twenty dead or injured."

To Nick's credit, he didn't flinch. "And the Sons?"

She set her jaw and glared at Rodrigo, who stared back at her with his head cocked. The muscles of his body coiled with tension, as if preparing to spring. "At least fifty dead," she said, her chest puffing up in triumph. "The rest scattered."

Rodrigo unleashed a string of curses in Spanish at her. Jason walked over and crouched in front of him, grabbing his attention. "You," he said, his upper lip curling in a nasty sneer. "The motherfucker who shot up my car."

Jason's smile did not reach his eyes. There was no point correcting the other man. "I'll do worse tonight."

"What about the Abyssal King?" Nick asked. "Has it shown up yet?"

"No, but it will once I'm done with *him*."

Rodrigo laughed, filling the air with its harsh sound.

Spit flew from his mouth and spattered against Jason's cheek. "You think you can control that monster? You don't know a goddamn thing, Ridley. It doesn't answer to humans. It does what ever it fucking wants."

"How much do you know?"

"Enough to know it's gonna tear you apart. Let me guess: you killed my men but left me alive because you wanna know the truth. Is that it?"

"Aren't you curious how we know about it in the first place?"

Rodrigo rolled his eyes. "Nah. If it was just the Monahan whelp over there, that'd be different, but you're smart, Ridley. Like scary smart. But not smart enough to stay the fuck away from *it*, are ya?"

Jason said nothing. He simply held Rodrigo's gaze and waited.

"I've seen what it does to people. Even when it ain't around, it makes them sick, like some medieval Black Death kinda shit, but ten times worse. And when it does show its ugly face, it eats people up. Turns them into fucking spaghetti, then you blink and they're gone. You can't control that. Best thing you can do is isolate it. Direct its focus."

"How?"

Rodrigo grinned. "I ain't telling you that."

Jason stood, aimed his silenced MP7 at the kneeling man to Rodrigo's right, and blew off the top half of his head. The body hit the ground with a heavy thud. Rodrigo flinched but did not take his eyes off Jason. The other Monahans stepped back without lowering their weapons.

A distant, quiet droning scratched at the edge of Jason's hearing. He looked at Rodrigo. "Try again."

"Kill me and you get nothing."

"You aren't the only one with information I need. Novikova or Panzieri—"

"They won't talk. That Milena bitch is frozen shut like a fucking tomb, and Robert's boy doesn't believe half the things we say."

The droning grew louder, its low bass fluctuating in an unnatural pattern. A murmur of confusion rippled through the gathered men and women. A few of the Monahans looked around, frowning. Jason kept his own expression neutral, his eyes locked onto his target. He noted the sheen of sweat on Rodrigo's forehead, the tremble in his shoulders, and the panicked roll of his eyes.

Jason turned his back on the kneeling man and started toward the cars. "Move your men out, Nick. We're leaving."

"Wait!" Rodrigo shouted over the incessant, alien sound. "I can help you take 'em down—the Novikovs, the Panzieries, even Vince. Just take me with you! I don't wanna be here when it arrives!"

"What's happening, Jason?" Nick asked, his raised pistol wavering as the droning reached a fever pitch. It thundered through Jason's veins, rattled his bones, and set his teeth on edge.

Rodrigo glanced at Nick's unsteady hand, then turned and dashed for his car.

The bright red machine warped and twisted in a spiraling explosion of steel. The light illuminating it blotted out a heartbeat later as an otherworldly hunger filled Jason's gut. Rodrigo skidded to a halt before the sudden void, screaming. He started running back in the other direction, but his flesh and clothing ribboned outward before Jason's eyes. Blood, muscle, and organs followed. The screaming cut off, though Rodrigo's agonized expression still hung in the air. Abruptly, it vanished, consumed by darkness.

Every small hair on Jason's body stood on end. The Abyssal King pressed its overwhelming, intelligent consciousness against his own, then advanced.

Chapter Twenty-Eight

Ayana's confident steps through the front doors of St. Julian's Foundation slowed when she spotted the man standing beside Sabrina in the lobby. Garbed all in black, he sported a clean-shaven face and a full head of thick, brown hair. A square of white rested against his throat beneath his Adam's apple. Though Ayana hadn't attended a church in many years, she recognized the unique collar. Methodist priests weren't required to wear one, but her childhood pastor often did.

Sabrina's face broke into a beaming smile. "Ayana! So good to see you again, and so soon, too! This is Father Needham. He'll be assisting today with your induction into the organization. Father, this is Dr. Ayana Hudson."

Ayana shook the priest's hand. "Pleased to meet you."

"Likewise, Doctor." He patted her hand with his free one in a paternal gesture, though he couldn't have been much older than her. "I don't believe I've seen you at my church before. How did you hear about St. Julian's?"

She withdrew her hand and forced a polite smile. "Sabrina here was dating my brother-in-law."

"Ah, of course. I heard about Connor. My deepest condolences."

"Thank you."

"Are you Catholic, by chance?"

"No, but I admire St. Julian's mission. I've been looking for a way to contribute back to the community for some time, and this seemed like the perfect opportunity."

Needham's mild expression conveyed nothing of his true thoughts. "Well, if you ever find yourself seeking religious counsel, I would be more than happy to offer my services."

The sooner she left the priest's company, the better, Ayana decided. Her smile remained on her face. "Thank you again, Father."

Sabrina ushered them toward the elevator. "This way, you two. We'll go through the boring paperwork first, then get the formal stuff out of the way."

"What's the formal stuff if not paperwork?"

Her eyes sparkled. "I'll explain more in a minute."

They rode the elevator to the second floor, which boasted rows of high-walled cubicles arranged in a traditional office space. Ringing the bullpen was a perimeter of offices with closed doors. Most were dark and empty, with only a couple of employees still seated at desks in the central area. Sabrina swept past them to one of the surrounding rooms and flicked on the lights. Inside was a plain, L-shaped desk made of white melamine board, the kind assigned to middle management. A photograph of a younger Sabrina, wearing a blue graduation robe and carrying a large bouquet of flowers, decorated the desk. Two older adults—her parents, perhaps—stood to her left and right. Next to the photo were a leatherbound Bible and a small, ceramic figure of a lamb in repose.

Sabrina sat in the gray mesh office chair behind the desk. Ayana and Needham each took one of the two black hairs opposite her.

"Before we begin, I have a confession to make," Sabrina said, flashing the priest a grin as if sharing a joke with him. To Ayana, she offered an apologetic smile. "I've been dishonest about my job role at St. Julian's. I'm not actually in marketing at all. I'm the Director of Operations of our Lancing office."

Ayana raised her eyebrows to affect surprise. "Why lie?"

"Because the nature of our true mission requires a certain level of secrecy. Posing as a smaller role means I can avoid the inevitable questions about what I really do."

A notion not unfamiliar to her. She couldn't blame Sabrina for the deception, even if she didn't like it. "Any other lies I should know about before I sign the membership form?"

Relief entered Sabrina's face. "No, that's all." She removed a thin packet from a desk drawer and slid it toward Ayana. Using a pen, she gestured to various sections of text. "This explains our mission statement, member benefits, and payment options. Fill out your personal information on these pages, then sign your name on the last page here. Before you do that, though, do you have any questions for me? You can speak freely in front of Father Needham. He knows what we do."

Ayana glanced sidelong at the man before meeting Sabrina's gaze. "Yes, actually. Why all the secrecy in the first place? If your mission is so critical, why not go public with it?"

Sabrina's smile was unexpectedly patronizing. "Because most people—that is, the average person—would find it all impossible to believe. They'd denounce it as a conspiracy theory, even if we showed them proof, because they aren't ready to receive the truth. That's how it is with the Word of God, and that's how it is with the reality of our universe."

"*I* believed you."

"Because you're special, Ayana. You don't shy away from the truth. Why do you think it took us so long to find a doctor to join our research team? Not only has your education placed you in this unique position, but so has your past. You don't just accept the truth; you pursue it."

"Then why not speak with the President and other world leaders? Or maybe the Pope?"

Sabrina's smile transformed into a scowl. "Politicians are too greedy and selfish to stop perpetuating wars across the world. Do you really think they'd band together to stop an interdimensional invasion? No, they're more likely to try to exploit the situation to gain an Elder God's power for themselves. The Abyssal King isn't the only one out there, after all, just the most immediate and pressing threat."

Ayana's gaze lowered to the membership form. "You're probably right." She picked up the document and read through it carefully. Nothing stood out as unusual or uncomfortable, not even a requirement to attend religious events. The benefits involved free attendance at monthly meetings, members-only activities with local parishes, and private social media groups. Though the annual fee was pricey, she and Jason could afford it.

She also had no intention of paying it a second time.

On the second page, she filled out her name, home address, and contact information but left her religious affiliation blank. After signing her name, she slid the packet back across the desk.

Sabrina was smiling again. "Thank you very much." She removed the top page, folded it, and handed it back to Ayana. "This is yours to keep. It's all informational. You can go online to pay the annual membership fee."

Then Sabrina passed over a plastic rectangle on a bright purple lanyard. While she typed at her keyboard, Ayana examined the card. One side sported a yellow sword-and-sunburst logo overlaid by black block letters spelling out St. Julian's Foundation. A six-digit sequence of letters and numbers adorned the bottom, while the reverse side was blank except for the magnetic strip along its left edge.

Sabrina clicked her mouse with a decisive flourish. "There, done! Your ID card's been activated. You now have elevator access to all the upper floors, including this one."

Ayana tucked the precious object into her purse.

"Now for the formality. Father, if you could, please?"

Needham shifted in his chair, resting one ankle on the opposite knee. He laced his hands in his lap. "Exposure to the Abyssal King and its influence, such as the phenomena you've witnessed in its victims, can cause some unfortunate side effects. Anxieties, hallucinations, nightmares—that sort of thing. Have you experienced any of that yourself?"

Ayana hesitated. Nodded.

"Pursuing the truth will put a great deal of pressure on your psyche, which we can't allow to fracture any more than it already has. Over the years, St. Julian's has devised a method to ward against the effects. If you're going to be on the research team, we strongly recommend going through with it yourself."

"And if I don't?"

The corners of his mouth tightened. "Then your mind will shatter. You'll lose your intellect and reason, and succumb to madness."

She bit back the instinctive urge to call him a liar, to demand proof. She had already signed the paperwork to join their initiative; she could no longer lean on disbelief. "All right. I'll do it."

The three of them left Sabrina's office, crossed the full length of the cubicle area, and proceeded through a glass door into a long hallway. They passed a break room, bathrooms, and a couple of small conference rooms before reaching their destination: a wooden door labeled LIBRARY. Affixed to the wall beside it was a black card reader with a small red light. When Sabrina held her ID card to it, the light turned green and the door unlocked with a loud click.

Beyond it was a large, spacious room lined with wooden bookshelves and vintage cabinets. Rectangular, minimalist pedestals and tables occupied the center of the chamber, their surfaces laden with an assortment of esoteric objects. The arrangement reminded Ayana of a museum exhibit. She peered at a set of four statuettes carved from ancient-looking stone as she followed Sabrina through the space, unable to discern their origin or significance.

At the other end of the library was another door. Holding it open, Sabrina gestured for Ayana and Needham to enter first. He obliged without hesitation, but she paused in the doorway. A ring of high-backed, throne-like chairs faced the center of the new, smaller room. Looking down, she noticed a symbol inlaid in the marble floor, a circle with many overlapping lines and unfamiliar letters inside it. At the very heart of the image was a burning star.

"Where are we?" Ayana asked.

"A place of movement and transition." Sabrina closed the door behind her. "We conduct all our rituals here, away from prying eyes and the influence of the eldritch."

"Don't you have a prayer room downstairs for that kind of thing?"

"That room is for the public. *This* one is for *us*."

Needham reappeared from the shadows with a swinging brass censer in hand. Plumes of cloying frankincense wafted toward Ayana from the spherical container. He gestured with his other hand. "If you could please join me in the center of the sigil, Dr. Hudson."

The softness of his disarming smile warred with the way her stomach lurched and twisted. Still, she did as he asked, standing opposite him at the star. Sabrina lingered between two chairs, watching with her hands folded in front of her. Ayana stared at the tile mosaic at her feet, admiring the glimmering sheen of blues and greens that converged within the star.

Before her eyes, a hairline crack formed in the marble.

The priest did not seem to notice. Swinging the burning censer in a gentle arc in front of him, he launched into a Latin chant. She knew just enough to pick out the words for God, Jesus, and the Holy Spirit, but the rest was gibberish.

The crack spiderwebbed out, slow like frost across glass.

Needham began walking in a slow circle around her, his voice taking on the monotonous cadence of a deep trance. Fragrant smoke trailed after him, forming a soft, gray haze in the air between them.

About two-thirds of the way around, he choked on his words. His feet tripped on nothing she could see. She reached out reflexively to steady him, but stopped when he held up his hand. His face contorted in pain, his eyes squeezing shut.

"Father?" she asked.

In the corner of her eye, Sabrina stiffened.

Beneath Ayana's feet, the tiles rattled.

Needham's eyes flew open. Blood streamed from his tear ducts as an unholy scream ripped from his throat. The censer slipped from his hand and broke open as it hit the floor, scattering burning incense. She scrambled backward into a chair, every instinct urging her to flee, her growing curiosity rooting her to the spot. What was she witnessing?

"Stay with him! I'll be right back!" Sabrina shouted as she rushed out the door.

Still screaming, the man fell to his knees. He tore at his clothes with such frenzy that the buttons of his clerical shirt popped off. Black holes bloomed across the pale flesh of his abdomen and chest. The skin around them began sloughing off, then evaporated into the air, exposing the muscle underneath. Ayana leaned forward, drawn by the horrific sight.

He turned his desperate gaze upon her and reached out a hand, his fingers gnarled like claws. "Help me! Please!"

Shrinking back from him, she shook her head, at a loss for words.

"Please!" His shouts turned to sobs. He began crawling toward her chair with slow, jerky movements, as if every motion of his body tortured him.

Ayana found her voice. "Stay back! Don't touch me!"

"Mercy! Please!"

His face split down the middle and she screamed.

The door burst open again. Sabrina rushed inside with two security guards and a male nurse. Shouting among themselves, the three men grabbed Needham and hauled him out of the room. He thrashed all his limbs, but their grip was secure. His chilling, wordless cries faded into silence as they took him away, leaving only a trail of blood on the floor.

"Are you all right?" Sabrina asked Ayana, though her own hands shook violently, her face had lost all color, and her eyes were round with panic.

Ayana checked herself and found she was unharmed. She tugged at her sweat-drenched blouse and tucked away a loose braid. "I'm fine. It didn't get me. But the men who helped him—are they going to be all right? They touched him." Her scalpel, made of stainless steel, had not survived contact with afflicted organs.

Sabrina shot a nervous glance at the open door leading to the library. "They should be. They're trained to touch only the body parts that haven't been affected yet."

The women left the ritual room, careful to step around the blood and the ashen remnants of the incense. The bright lights of the library banished all lingering sense of danger. Sabrina paced across the floor, wringing her hands.

"What happened back there?" Ayana asked, her natural inquisitiveness resurfacing now that the nightmare had passed.

"I don't know. I've never seen—It's never happened before. Not like this."

"What's that supposed to mean?"

Sabrina threw her an exasperated look. "The room is warded, Ayana. The sigil on the floor is supposed to protect it and anyone inside it from the influence of the Elder Gods. Something went wrong."

Ayana spoke the first words that came to mind. "Maybe the protections aren't strong enough anymore."

Genuine terror crept into Sabrina's face. She made the sign of the cross with her right hand, then followed it with another gesture, one Ayana didn't recognize. "I hate to believe you, but I think you're right. The Abyssal King has become too powerful, and more quickly than we could have ever anticipated. I'm sorry. I wanted to spend more time with you this evening to get you up to speed on our research, but I need to speak with the city's leaders and formulate a new plan now that we're on an accelerated timeline."

"The city's leaders? You said you couldn't trust politicians with your mission."

Sabrina hesitated. "I did. Some collaboration is necessary, unfortunately. I've been working with the mayor and the chief of police to protect the city from the eldritch threat. They've been sworn to secrecy, too." She hurried over and took Ayana by the elbow. "I know you probably have a lot of questions, but I don't have the time to talk right now. I have a lot of work to do."

"I understand. I'll head home."

"Thank you."

As the pair passed the last of the display tables on their way to the exit, Ayana glanced at the book resting on it, a thick tome cradled by a wooden stand. She had only a few seconds to read the title on the front cover before Sabrina ushered her out into the hallway. The words burned in Ayana's mind, dredging up memories from a different library, a different nightmare.

Liber Devorationis.

Chapter Twenty-Nine

Jason clenched his fists, willing his body to stop shaking from the sheer exhilaration of his brush with the impossible. Nearby, Nick had fallen flat on his backside. Sweat streamed down his face, plastering his hair to his forehead; a massive stain had formed on the front of his shirt. Around them, the Monahan soldiers stood in stunned silence.

Nick rose on shaky legs. He shoved his pistol into its holster and wiped his palms on his jeans. "Jason," he said, his voice wavering and cracking, "what the *fucking hell* was that?"

In contrast, Jason's voice was steady. "What I came here to free."

"*That* thing? Are you fucking crazy?" Nick grabbed Jason's collar. "It almost fucking killed us! Look at what it did to Rodrigo! To his car!"

The ruined vehicle still stood several yards away,

transformed into an art installation of shredded steel, leather, rubber, and electrical wiring. That it hadn't combusted intrigued Jason, but probing the remnants of the Abyssal King's passing was not on the agenda for the night. He moved to leave. "We can talk about it on the ride back to Lerwick Square. Right now, we have to get out of here before the cops start mobilizing."

A muscle in Nick's jaw clenched, but he gave a curt nod. "Everyone, move out!"

His soldiers snapped back to reality. They piled into their cars, drove out of the parking lot, and dispersed into the night. Jason rode with Nick in the back of the latter's gray sedan, his bodyguards occupying the front seats.

"I thought we were goners for sure," the Monahan heir said. "When that thing came for us, and you said bullets don't work on it... Shit, man. I wanted to strangle you for leading us to our deaths. Still do."

"Well, we're alive, and the Sons of Saints have been decimated. If you're quick, they'll never recover."

"How'd you get that thing to stop before it killed us the way it did Rodrigo? Didn't he say it doesn't answer to humans or something?"

Jason hadn't done anything. When the alien consciousness brushed against his own, overwhelming incomprehension froze him where he stood, made his tongue heavy, and filled him with feverish levels of adrenaline. Its impenetrable presence probed his mind, sizing him up as one predator would another. Any lingering doubt of its keen discernment or the depth of its understanding vanished. Finally, something existed that matched his own supremacy.

And then it left. Before the cloud of nothingness reached Jason and the Monahans, it vanished into thin air, the wound in reality reknitting as if it had never been there. As far as he could tell, nothing had triggered its departure, nor had it left any sign or reason behind.

"Like Rodrigo said, it's smart," Jason said at length. He removed his phone from a zippered pocket of his jacket and turned it on. No new messages. "It knew we weren't there to fight it."

"Neither was Rodrigo, though."

"Not tonight, but they've clashed before. And the Sons of Saints aren't the only ones, either. If the Abyssal King is as intelligent as I think it is, I can use it against the others who've been trying to contain it."

"Rodrigo said something about that before he died. 'Isolate it.' What exactly is going on?"

Jason looked Nick in the eye. "Conspiracy." As the car made its way through the city, he caught the other man up on everything he'd learned. "Three years ago, the Sons of Saints encountered the Abyssal King in Saintfield. At the same time, an organization named St. Julian's Foundation set up an office over in Bracknell. Somehow, they got the Sons, the Novikovs, and the Panzieris working together to keep the Abyssal King from spreading outside specific districts in the city and killing people. The police are involved, too. There must be some kind of business deal between the Big Three and the cops so they don't mess with each other; otherwise, I can't see why they'd agree to anything."

Nick shook his head. "Damn. I'm as Catholic as they come, and I've never heard any of that occult movie shit in my life."

"Your father's been looking for opportunities to tear down the Big Three and take over their operations and territory."

"Yeah, he has. *We* have."

"Well, here's your chance."

Nick blew the air from his cheeks and tapped his knee with a finger. "So the Novikovs are your next target?"

"That's right. Milena will be harder to hit, though."

"She basically has celebrity status, hanging out with all those millionaires who can afford her fancy houses. Rodrigo might've made a fuckton of money off all those drugs, but she's got her claws in a different kinda crowd."

"And it's not like she runs brothels and strip clubs we can raid. Her girls go straight to their clients, not the other way around."

"Yeah. Tell you what—I'll talk to my old man, see if he has any ideas."

The familiar sights of Lerwick Square surrounded them as they passed into the district. Jason spied an entrance to the subway up ahead, a block away. He removed the magazine from his MP7, pulled the bolt to eject the remaining round, and handed the weapon to Nick. Then he unbuckled the bandolier from his body and left it on the middle seat. "The sooner we come up with a plan, the better. Word travels fast. Now that we've destroyed the Sons, we'll have a harder time catching the others by surprise. Especially Vince."

The car pulled to a stop beside the subway entrance. "I'll call you," Nick said. "Don't let the cops get you before then."

Jason nodded, his only gesture of farewell. He stepped out of the car and shut the door. It zoomed off into the night.

His phone buzzed. Ayana was calling. He answered while descending the steps into the station. "What is it?"

"Hey. Finished with your errand for the night?" Her voice sounded strained.

"Yeah, why?"

"I am, too. I'm heading home now."

Never in the three years of their relationship had she called him for something so mundane. He paused in front of a large map on the wall showing every subway line and their stops. "What's going on?"

"Oh, I don't know. Thirty minutes, maybe?" The non sequitur set off the alarms in his head. "I'm coming from Bracknell, after all."

He traced the route from Lerwick Square to Bracknell with his eyes. It was too far. "Are you in danger, Ayana?"

"Yeah, that's a good idea." A note of relief. He'd

cracked her code. "What did you have in mind?"

His eyes darted across the map, searching for the station equidistant from their two locations. As soon as he identified it, he rushed for the correct platform. "Can you take the orange line to Gullane?"

"Yeah."

"Okay. Do that. Once there, head for the opera house exit."

"Love it."

At that hour, Lerwick Square's subway station thronged with citizens on their way home from work and after-school clubs, or seeking dinner at one of the district's many restaurants. Jason wove between them, one hand holding his phone to his ear, the other extended in front of him as he maneuvered through the crowd. More than once, he shouldered aside a stranger. Their yelps and curse-laden shouts did nothing to deter him.

"Is someone following you, Ayana?"

"Oh, yeah, that works."

He reached the right platform and got into line behind a middle-aged man in an ill-fitting suit. Above their heads, the electronic display showed one minute until the next train's arrival. "Describe him for me."

Ayana didn't respond. Jason waited ten seconds before checking his phone.

He'd lost the call.

"Fuck," he muttered, prompting the man beside him to raise a judgmental eyebrow. Fighting the urge to pace, he peered down the dark tunnel. Distant light heralded the train's arrival. Moments later, it slowed to a stop alongside the platform. He rushed aboard and counted the stops until Gullane—five, a nine-minute trip. While other passengers took up seats or squeezed into the space around him, he remained rooted by the door, one hand on the nearest metal grab rail.

Two stops later, his phone buzzed with a text. *White male, reddish-brown hair, beard. Tall, maybe your height. Dark brown jacket, jeans, white shirt, a black-and-orange baseball cap.*

He typed back, *Is he on the train with you?*
Yes. He's at the other end of the car.

The train sped out of the station and Jason lost signal. He put away his phone again, repeating the description of his wife's stalker over and over in his head. If he intercepted the threat in the station, the pedestrians around them would make pulling a gun on the other man a challenge. Moreover, a well-meaning but idiotic stranger might call for security. That meant he had two options: rely on intimidation or confront the threat on the street. Either way, he had to reach Ayana first.

At Gullane Station, he burst out of the doors first. He hurried toward the exits, running up the escalator two steps at a time, his heart hammering in his chest. Congestion at the turnstiles brought him to an abrupt stop. While he waited his turn, he scanned the throng for his wife or the man she'd described but spotted neither of them.

A minute later, he passed through the turnstiles. Signs on the wall pointed him in the direction of the opera house. He raced past couples and families strolling toward the same exit, his head swiveling to and fro. At the bottom of the stairs leading up to the street, he paused and looked around.

No Ayana. No threat.

Jason dashed up the stairs and emerged into the brisk February night. All around him, the dazzling lights of Lancing's glitzy, glamorous entertainment district sparkled against darkness. He took in deep lungfuls of cold air, wrestling his heart rate back to its normal pace. Panic helped no one, his wife least of all.

While he focused on his breathing, he retreated to the side of the entrance, out of sight of anyone ascending the steps. From there, he could peer down the well-lit stairwell. Though he didn't know what Ayana had worn for her visit to St. Julian's Foundation, he was familiar with all the clothing she'd packed in her suitcase. A black-and-orange cap was easy to spot from his vantage point, too.

Not once did it occur to him that he might have arrived too late, that she was already in Gullane, running from a predator and praying for someone to intervene. Nor did it occur to him that the threat might have already overtaken her, killed her, and pushed her body into the tracks. No other possibility existed in his mind, except that he had arrived first to save his wife from imminent danger.

A familiar gait drew his attention to a black-haired woman clad in white clothing. She carried a brown purse he'd seen hundreds of times. And sure enough, several yards behind her stalked a man in a cap with the right colors. When she reached the top of the stairs, Jason stepped from the shadows into the light. "Ayana!" he called out.

She whirled around, eyes wide. The panic in her face transformed into immediate relief. "There you are!"

She hurried to him. He folded his arms around her as she pressed herself against his chest, her nose buried into his jacket. Moments later, the man with the baseball cap stepped into view. He hesitated, looking first to his left, then his right. When he glanced over his shoulder in their direction, he locked eyes with Jason. Instinctively, Jason's hand fell from Ayana's shoulder to his hidden Glock. He imagined the necessary movement: a half-turn, pivoting with Ayana, shielding her with his body while he raised his pistol at the would-be assailant. Two or three shots to the chest were all he needed to take the man down.

But the stranger looked away and continued across the intersection.

Jason slid his half-drawn gun back into its holster. "Come on," he said to his wife in a low voice. "Let's get back to the hotel."

Chapter Thirty

Ayana lay in bed in their hotel room, garbed in a comfortable cotton robe and staring into space. The sound of running shower water filled the silence through the open bathroom door. A house renovation show played on the muted television, the smiling hosts walking their audience through the latest additions to a beautiful, Victorian-style residence located upstate. But instead of enjoying the mindless program, she relived the events of the evening. The bizarre Catholic ritual and Needham's affliction. The discovery of *Liber Devorationis* in St. Julian's library. The terrifying possibility of someone following her from the building.

Did Sabrina suspect Ayana of duplicity? Had she ordered one of her employees to follow their newest member? Whatever the case, Ayana planned to exercise more discretion when—not if—she returned. She needed the knowledge in that book. Avoiding St. Julian's Foundation was not an option.

The shower noise stopped, plunging the room into silence and drawing her from her thoughts. She set aside her half-eaten chocolate bar and picked up the first aid kit. A few minutes later, Jason stepped out of the bathroom, a white towel hugging his waist, his hair still damp. Sitting up on the edge of the bed, she snuck an admiring glance over the planes of hard muscle on his arms and torso. When he sat down next to her, she kissed his shoulder.

"Thank you again," she murmured before examining his gunshot wound. Though he'd put stress on it during his visit to Saintfield, the stitches hadn't come undone. It was healing nicely.

Jason held his arm still while she applied a new bandage. "Are you sure he was someone from St. Julian's?"

"I'm not certain. He could've just been a random man who saw me as I was leaving, but I don't think so. Either way, I thought I could dissuade him if I talked on the phone, but..."

Her husband's mouth pressed into a thin line. "Not all men are so easily discouraged."

A shudder ran through her at the comment. She closed the lid on the first aid kit. "I hate that."

He wrapped his arm around her and pulled her against his side. She turned toward him, comforted by the kisses he pressed to her forehead. "I don't want you going to work tomorrow," he said. "We need to check out in the morning and move to a different hotel. If they're trying to track your movements, they'll expect to see you at the forensic center."

She'd anticipated this and already made peace with it. Nodding, she withdrew just enough to look him in the eyes. "Okay, but I don't want to hide away uselessly, either. I have to go back to St. Julian's. Something happened tonight that scared Sabrina, and now she's trying to figure out how to seal away the Abyssal King as soon as possible."

He frowned. "We can't let that happen. I want to use it to exact our revenge."

Ayana gaped at him. A terrible chill seized her for the third time that evening. "You know what it can do, Jason."

"Exactly."

She knew that tone of voice, that hard gleam in his eye. Nothing could dissuade him from his path, and she needed to keep pace. "Then we need to stop her. If I can learn what her plan is, I can relay the information to you."

When he didn't respond right away, she knew he was weighing their options. Finally, he asked, "What happened tonight?"

She recounted the ritual, the fracturing marble floor, and the priest's transformation. Afterward, he agreed with her assessment: the Abyssal King must've accumulated enough strength to break through whatever supernatural barriers St. Julian's had erected.

"Then tonight's raid succeeded in two ways," he

said. "We eliminated one gang and freed the Abyssal King."

"You saw it, then?"

"Yeah. And it knows my intention."

Ayana sighed, bone-weary, and rested her head on Jason's shoulder. "I'm glad you came back," she said softly, her fingers running down his chest, tracing faded scars half-hidden by hair. He'd survived knife attacks and gunshots, but the wounds inflicted by the Elder God were a different matter entirely. Could *anyone* recover from them?

As if sensing her worry, he lifted her chin with a hand and covered her mouth with his. Closing her eyes, she leaned into the kiss, allowing the taste of him on her tongue and the heat radiating from his naked body to wipe away her anxieties for the night. When he lowered her onto her back, she reached between them and tugged the towel free.

· · · · · • · • • · · ·

The next morning, Ayana finished her skincare routine and stepped out of the bathroom to find her husband standing by the bed, the TV remote in hand. He frowned at the screen, the lines of his face sharp with focus. She drew closer, curious. On the TV, a female reporter stood in an unfamiliar neighborhood, the houses rundown and the road broken with potholes. Yellow police tape stretched out behind her, while cops and crime scene investigators worked quietly in the background.

"Saintfield residents reported hearing gunshots throughout the district last night. The officers who responded to the calls have described the crime scenes as 'massacres,' tallying up a total of fifty-seven victims across eight locations, most of them men between the ages of eighteen and sixty," the woman said, her brow furrowed in picture-perfect concern.

Ayana sat on the edge of the mattress, trying to frame such immense violence in terms she understood. Fifty-seven cadavers were nineteen days' worth of autopsies for a single forensic pathologist—almost a month of work, if she took off weekends.

"Police are calling this mass shooting, the largest in Lancing's history, a terrorist attack against its citizens," the reporter continued. "Officers across the city are mobilizing to bring the perpetrators to justice and are requesting the cooperation of all civilians who may have information about last night's attack."

Ayana looked at Jason. "What does this mean for us?"

"It means we need to move." He tossed the remote onto the bed and reached for his phone. "Finish packing. I need to make some calls, then we're out of here."

An hour later, they checked out of their hotel room. He'd slicked his hair into a style he didn't usually wear, and both of them donned sunglasses to obscure their faces. They spent another hour on the subway, switching lines every ten minutes, until they disembarked at

Keady Woods. He led the way to a personal storage facility, where, for the first time, she saw some of the equipment he kept outside their house. They swapped their suitcases for ones he'd prepared years ago, then changed out of their coats to a different pair. Afterward, they dropped their luggage off at a hotel ten minutes away, once again using one of his false identities and the bank account tied to it.

By noon, the couple were back in Dunston, walking toward a car repair shop she had never visited before. He led her around the side of the building and knocked on a normal-sized service door beside a row of much larger bay doors, all of them closed. Only a few seconds passed before the service door opened, revealing a tall, hulking man. Recognition entered his face when his eyes fell upon Jason. He gave Ayana a quick once-over, then waved them inside.

Despite the time of day, the spacious garage was dead silent. Cars lined up in the center of the space, one in front of each bay door, but no hardworking mechanics bustled around them. Instead, only one other man stood inside next to a bright blue sports car. His dirty blonde hair was tied up in a small bun, and he wore a plain black T-shirt, black leather jacket, and ripped blue jeans.

He grinned as the couple approached. "Glad I heard from you earlier, man," he said to Jason, shaking his hand. "The news ain't good."

"No," Jason agreed. "Nick, this is my wife, Ayana.

Ayana, Nick Monahan. He and his soldiers helped carry out the plan last night."

"Soldiers?" she asked.

Nick smiled. "Slang for our full-time employees. All good, loyal people."

"I see." She reached out to shake his hand. "A pleasure to meet you."

To her surprise, he brought her hand to his lips and graced the back of it with the barest kiss, then released her with a wink. "All mine, trust me."

If her husband thought anything of the gesture, it did not show on his face. Not that she expected him to care. He had a possessive streak, but she'd never known him to be jealous.

"How do you and Jason know each other?" she asked Nick.

"My dad hired him a while back after the Panzieris murdered my brother Desmond. Jason killed all four of them. We've been on good terms ever since." He slapped Jason on the shoulder. Jason did not smile, but neither did he scowl. "Knowing a man like him is always good for business, anyway."

"And what sort of business does your family do?"

Nick's disarming smile told Ayana she would never know the whole truth. "Cars, of course."

The service door opened again, heralding another arrival. Izzy strode inside as if she belonged there, dressed in her signature puffy coat and a pair of black combat boots. A laptop bag hung from her shoulder, and she carried a plastic cup of bubble tea in one hand. The drink's tapioca pearls sent an involuntary shiver up Ayana's spine. She turned away as Izzy joined them and Jason introduced her to Nick.

"I've always wanted to meet the baby-faced Monahan heir!" she said.

He laughed. "I know you, too. Heard your name in my network a few times."

"Yeah? Then when are you hiring me, huh?"

Their banter continued as she set up her laptop at a tall toolbox on wheels. Ayana stood to the side, listening. The gnawing discomfort from before had returned. Knowing Jason's profession and supporting the lengths he took to evade detection afforded only shallow, infrequent glimpses of the life he'd lived for years before meeting her. Until Connor's death, she hadn't wanted to know any details; that had been their agreement. But there, in the company of three bona fide criminals, she realized for the first time how different Jason's world was from hers.

And how much she hated not knowing.

She walked over to Izzy during a lull in the chatter. The younger woman was clicking around her computer but looked up when she noticed Ayana beside her. Her expression became guarded, and she stood a little straighter.

"Hey," she said.

"Hey." A pause. "I'm sorry for my rude behavior last week. I had no reason to treat you like that when all you were doing was trying to be a good friend."

Izzy stared at Ayana. Blinked. "What brought this on?"

"A lot's happened these past few days. I've learned that nothing is what it seems, and people will lie through their teeth to get what they want. I know that shouldn't surprise me, considering..." Ayana glanced at Jason, who was conversing with Nick.

"No shit, Sherlock."

"I know, I know. But I mean it. I'm sorry. I..." She froze, her words perched on the tip of her tongue. Instinct made her want to swallow them, but this was Izzy, Jason's trusted accomplice—not an innocent civilian unaware of the dangers of associating with Ayana, nor a cultist with a secret agenda. "It's hard for me to be vulnerable with others. My parents betrayed me deeply when I was a kid, so I thought, why should I share anything about myself with anyone when they will only hurt me? It's better if I go through life without opening up emotionally."

Even her relationship with Jason had started that way: passionate nights in his bed or hers, without commitment or attachment. The last thing she'd wanted was yet another person breaking her heart. But even in those early days, they had an uncanny compatibility that went beyond surface similarities. Unspoken tension drew them together again and again, until fondness bloomed into genuine affection and love. And when she finally proposed over breakfast, her eyes wide open to the depth of his deceptions, she'd wanted nothing more than to keep him in her life. For her own safety, she was prepared to stop seeing him if he rejected her offer. But when he accepted, she couldn't recall a more profound happiness—or a greater relief.

Izzy's expression softened. "I'm sorry. I can relate. My parents kicked me out of the house when they found out I'm gay. It's why I do this kind of job now." She gestured to her computer. "I just kind of fell into it when I first left home and haven't found my way back out. But it pays the bills better than anything else I *could* do."

Ayana exhaled, feeling like she'd shed ten pounds of bricks that had been weighing her down for years. "We have to stick together, don't we?"

"Yeah, I'd say so. But at least you have Jason, right? I mean, I figured that's why you married him, despite all his obvious red flags. He doesn't want to get to know anyone."

A low chuckle fell from her lips. "You're right. He's never demanded emotional vulnerability from me, which is ironic, because he's the only person I feel like I can be vulnerable around."

Izzy smirked. "I bet you're the only person he tolerates it from, too. I was so right. You two *are* perfect for each other." Turning, she placed her hand on Ayana's shoulder. "Apology accepted. And my offer still stands: if you ever want to vent or talk about anything, I'm happy to listen. So, friends?"

The word filled Ayana with an uncommon, warm

fuzziness. She smiled. "Friends."

The service door opened once more. Curious to see who else Jason had invited to their meeting, she looked over at the newest arrival, then did a double take.

Trey stood in the doorway, wearing a nervous expression as he glanced around the garage.

Chapter Thirty-One

Though Jason approached Trey with calm, measured steps, the nervous tension emanating from the younger man was so palpable, they could slice through it with a knife. To Trey's credit, he stood his ground, though he watched Jason like a spooked prey animal watching a predator. Behind him, Nick's bodyguard closed the service door, cutting off all avenues of escape. Trey flinched at the sound and quickly glanced past Jason's shoulder at the others gathered in the garage.

"Hey, Jason. I guess I'm in the right place?"

Looming over Trey, Jason pinned him with a stern look that brooked no argument. "You are, and since I'm in charge here, you will listen to me."

Trey swallowed. "Sure, man."

"I invited you here because you've been helpful to Ayana and me thus far, but if you so much as breathe in the wrong direction—such as toward law enforcement—I will make you regret it. Understood?"

"Yeah. Totally."

If Trey was smart, he would've reported Jason to the police and stayed far away from the garage. Instead, he'd appeared like a summoned hound, anxious but agreeable, despite Jason's threats two nights ago. Whatever misplaced loyalty Trey felt might get him killed, but until then, Jason was going to use it to his advantage.

"Good."

He made another round of introductions, referring to Trey as a journalist for the *Lancing Daily*, Nick as the garage's owner, and Izzy as a genius with technology. They all shook hands before gathering around the rolling toolbox. Ayana returned to where she belonged at Jason's side.

"Did you bring what I asked for?" he asked Nick.

"Sure did." Nick beckoned for his bodyguard. The large man set down a police scanner next to Izzy's laptop. When Nick turned it on, its dull, inert screen brightened with an orange glow and displayed LANCING PD DISPATCH, CH 003 in black block letters. He turned the scanner's dial until he found the right channel, catching the last words of a woman's crackling command:

"—set up a checkpoint on the highway southbound out of the city."

"Here's the situation," Jason said. "I need to eliminate Milena Novikova and Tyler Panzieri. Police involvement after the Sons of Saints massacre is only going to complicate matters further."

Trey's eyes widened. He looked like he wanted to say something but wisely kept his mouth shut.

"Unfortunately, even with the Monahans' help, the Novikovs and Panzieris have greater numbers, and we no longer have the element of surprise. They're going to expect an attack now, so we have to switch up tactics."

"My dad's in talks with some of the other groups in the city," Nick said. "The Hellhounds Motorcycle Club is on board, at least, since they have beef with the Novikovs, but there's no guarantee any of the others will agree to help."

Izzy piped up. "You know what's a strategy that doesn't depend on sheer numbers?" She mimed squinting down the scope of a rifle and pulling the trigger. "Boom, headshot."

Jason nodded at her. "It should work for Milena. Drawing her out into the open would be a poor move, since she's known for holing up in her penthouse to avoid danger."

"Besides, her security is unmatched," Nick said. "She's an old lady, so she doesn't have the arrogance of a young prick like Tyler thinkin' he's immortal. Trying to break into her place like you did with old Bobby is next to suicide, even for a crazy motherfucker like you."

Trey stared at Jason, mouth agape.

Jason ignored him. "Which of Milena's penthouses is she most likely to retreat to?"

Izzy's hands flew over her laptop's keyboard. "Probably the one with a good back door, just in case things go belly-up. She's got a place in Lower Kemsing and another in Gullane."

Nick threw a finger gun at the hacker. "Lower Kemsing. Centralized, with access to all major highways leading into and out of the city. It's Novikov headquarters. That's gotta be it."

"I'm pulling up the floor plan for her penthouse apartment, and also blueprints for each of the buildings immediately next to it," Izzy said to Jason.

"Good. Send those to me encrypted."

"You got it, boss."

Nick drummed his fingers on the top of the toolbox. "In that case, my people will keep an eye on Tyler's movements. Maybe he'll fuck up somewhere down the line. We'll find an ideal time for the hit. Once you're done with Milena, let me know and I'll give you what updates we have."

"That works." Jason crossed his arms over his chest. "That just leaves Vince, then."

Trey perked up at the name. "Vince? Like Moynier?"

"The same."

"What's his connection to all this?"

"Yeah, actually. I'm wondering that, too," Nick said, frowning. "I know what you said about the whole conspiracy thing, but what's Vince getting out of the whole arrangement?"

"Conspiracy? Wait, you mean with St. Julian's Foundation?" Trey's visible confusion morphed into horrified realization. "Connor had been right all along? The Big Three are all involved, plus the money launderer, Vince Moynier?"

Nick and Izzy exchanged an amused look.

"You think Vince is a money launderer?" she asked Trey, laughter on her tongue.

"Is... isn't he?"

"It doesn't matter what Vince is or isn't, or what he's getting out of the arrangement," Jason said. "All that matters is he's involved, which means he has to die, too."

The good humor vanished from Nick's face. "Vince is a decent guy, though. I don't know what beef you have with him, but he's never been in our way. In fact, he's an asset to all of us. We Monahans have no reason to target him."

Jason considered the best tactic to bend Nick to his will. With the bodyguard watching them, physical coercion was out of the question; he would jump to protect Nick at the first hint of an altercation. Jason had no leverage against the Monahans, either. Their relationship up to that point was based on mutual benefit and the acknowledgement of his unmatched reputation. Or so he'd assumed.

Ayana touched his arm, drawing his attention. "Tell them," she said in a soft, encouraging tone. "They're our allies, aren't they? They can't help us if they don't know the whole story."

She was right, of course. Sometimes, unlocking a tool's maximum potential required disclosing private information. Such was the case when he'd revealed his identity to her two years ago. She'd deduced the truth for herself and didn't flinch away from it, proving her loyalty to him instead. Intrigued by her choice and no longer seeing a reason to deceive her, he decided to reward her by involving her in his deception instead. Now she was invaluable as his partner and confidante.

He met her gaze and nodded, accepting her suggestion, then turned to the other three. They stared at him with expressions of open curiosity and anticipation. "Vince murdered my brother," he said.

Trey's face paled, and Izzy's jaw dropped.

"No way!" she said. "He was the guy in the security footage?"

"Yes. He's my real target. Everyone else is his partner in the conspiracy. Killing them off will force him into a corner, without allies."

Uttering a low whistle, Nick scratched the back of his neck. "Well, shit. When you mentioned Desmond, I didn't realize…" His face darkened with grim understanding. He looked Jason in the eye and nodded. "Guess you gotta kill Vince, then. He must still be in the city. I doubt word got to him before the police started locking down the highways."

"The police are working with them, though," Ayana said, her hand still resting on Jason's arm. "Sabrina confirmed as much with me last night. She's not just part of St. Julian's marketing team; she's in charge of their entire operation in Lancing."

"For what purpose? Why?" Trey asked, pulling a notebook and pen from his coat pockets. When Jason glowered at him, he put them back, chastised.

"Religious fanaticism," Ayana said. "They believe the world is doomed and it's their mission to save it."

"The Abyssal King, right?" Nick asked. She nodded. Shaking his head, he uttered a strained laugh. "I'd call it crazy, but after last night, I don't know what to believe anymore."

"Even if the police are working with St. Julian's, only the highest ranks will know what's going on," Jason said. "We can sow confusion among the lower ranks and make them think Vince participated in the slaughter in Saintfield. This is where you come in, Trey."

The reporter looked up, startled. "Me?"

"Nick's right—there's no chance Vince has left the city, not if he's as loyal to St. Julian's as he seems to be. In fact, he's probably helping them carry out their retaliation to last night's incident right now. I need you to leak Vince's physical description to the police and the press as if you were a witness to the attack. That *should* send them on the hunt for Vince for several hours, if not the whole day, until word to stand down works its way through the chain of command."

"Okay, but how do I do that? It's not like I can use my cell phone. They'll trace and ID me."

"I can help with that," Izzy said. "You can borrow one

of my burners, and I can hook you up with a really good voice changer app. We should go somewhere else in the city, too, so when the burner broadcasts its location, it's nowhere near Monahan territory."

He stared at her for a beat, then bobbed his head in a hesitant nod. "Sure, okay. Cool."

Jason regarded each of his allies in turn. "I'll keep in touch with each of you over the next few days. If we can take down Milena and Tyler in one fell swoop and flush Vince out of hiding, all of this should be over by the end of the week." He picked up the police scanner. "I'll need this. Any other questions?"

Nick shook his head again, and Izzy shut her laptop with a grin.

"I'm good! I sent the files over to you, Jason," she said as she put away her belongings. "Trey, how about we get some lunch on the way? I know a really awesome taco place by the station here. Authentic birria and everything."

Jason and Ayana left the garage and took the subway back to Keady Woods. At their hotel, they collected their luggage and checked into their room. While she unpacked her toiletries, he changed clothes for the second time that day into an all-black ensemble. Alongside his usual suitcase, he'd retrieved a black backpack from his storage unit. Unzipping it revealed all the disassembled components of his Remington Modular Sniper Rifle: barrel, suppressor, buttstock, bolt. He searched a smaller pocket containing boxes of ammunition until he found the long-range .338 Lapua bullets. He loaded five of these into the gun's magazine.

After he packed everything back up, he put on a thick jacket and a warm beanie. Shouldering his bag, he turned to find his wife sitting on the edge of the hotel bed, watching him. She stood when he walked over.

"I won't be back until after I've dealt with Milena," he said in a low voice, "and probably not until after the business with Tyler is over, too."

"I know."

Wrapping her arms around his neck, she leaned up to kiss him. The faint citrus scent of her perfume filled his nose. His hands encircled her waist, pulling her flush against the front of his body. Desire flared inside him; their kisses deepened and grew more urgent.

Abruptly, Ayana drew back, her eyes bright with hunger but her brow furrowed with worry. "Please be careful," she whispered.

"I'm always careful." Jason dipped his head and kissed her again. Her grip on him tightened, and she arched her back to press herself against him. With great reluctance, he clamped down on his own cravings. Wrenching himself away, he stepped past her, toward the door. "Remember to check out after two nights and move to the next hotel if I haven't returned by then."

She grasped his hand. "But you will."

He squeezed her fingers. "I will."

Chapter Thirty-Two

After Jason left the hotel, Ayana waited thirty minutes, then departed for her own errand. She took a taxi to Bracknell, paid the driver in cash, and walked the remaining two blocks to St. Julian's Foundation. A security guard in a black uniform stood in the lobby, but otherwise, nothing had changed since the previous evening. The old woman behind the front desk was even wearing the same pink sweater from Ayana's first visit.

"Excuse me," Ayana said to the receptionist. "Is Miss Kopanski still in the building?"

"No, she left an hour ago."

"Did she say when she'd be back?"

"She didn't tell me anything. Want me to call her office and leave a message, Miss...?"

Ayana flashed her most pleasant smile. "Oh, no need. Thank you."

She strode toward the elevator, making a show of

removing her new ID card from her purse in case the receptionist was watching. In the carriage, she waved her card in front of the security panel and pressed the button for the second floor. Upon reaching her destination, she saw the offices were busier: employees, young and old alike, typed at their computers and talked in quiet tones. She walked past them with her shoulders back and chin raised, embodying the confidence of someone who belonged among them. No one stopped her.

Retracing her steps, she reached the library without incident. The security panel on the wall accepted her ID and unlocked the door for her. She slipped inside without a backward glance.

The room was as quiet and empty as a tomb. Relieved to be alone, she navigated the tables and pedestals until she stood in front of the book that had caught her eye. *Liber Devorationis.* Beneath the gleaming, golden title was a circle stamped into the dark leather of the front cover; several smaller circles divided it, reminding her of bubbles or compound eyes.

Or the holes in her cadavers.

The sight sent a shiver up her spine. Taking a deep, steadying breath, she opened the book to the inside title page. A familiar symbol in black caught her eye: a capital letter N, flanked by a bundle of grain to its left and a rolled scroll to its right. Underneath it, typed in small, black letters, were the words: PROPERTY OF THE NISABA SOCIETY.

Where had she heard that name before?

Shaking her head, Ayana turned several pages. Black-and-white illustrations flickered in and out of sight, teasing her with strange geometry and impossible biology. She forced herself to focus on the table of contents. Unfortunately, its information was scant, with sections titled, "On rituals," "On the physical," and "On the subliminal." She hesitated, her fingertip sliding across the delicate, off-white paper. Physical matters were familiar; she already knew how human bodies transformed under the Abyssal King's influence. Though learning more about it was alluring, her eyes kept drifting back to the words "On rituals."

She was there to stop Sabrina, after all.

Steeling herself for the absurd, Ayana flipped to the start of the chapter.

Thirteen years of higher education had trained her to read dense texts full of jargon, but her schoolwork paled in comparison to the paragraphs in that ancient tome. When she thought she grasped the meaning behind a handful of sentences, the next one confounded her. Words in languages not spoken by any human tongue peppered the text, but no footnotes nor glossary provided their definitions.

The drawings and diagrams were no better. Some resembled pictographs she'd seen online, and one symbol in particular reminded her of the burning star that had cracked during Needham's ritual. But when she thought she understood an image, a second glance at it revealed something new that hadn't been on the page before. More than once, she wondered if she was hallucinating again, but no black holes opened up in her vision. The words bled together only in the usual manner of obtuse text. She forged on, turning the pages, searching for any hint of Sabrina's machinations.

Eventually, something shifted—perhaps in the book, or perhaps within Ayana herself. While puzzling over yet another foreign word that defied human language, trying and failing to sound it out under her breath, it changed before her eyes. She could read it. When she read it aloud again, syllables she'd never uttered before rolled off her tongue.

"What the fuck?" she blurted out.

Seized by the implication of her abrupt understanding, she flipped back to the first page of the chapter. All the alien words were different—*legible*.

She threw herself into a second pass at the text, her eyes darting across the paragraphs with renewed fervor. Sweat beaded on her forehead. Her fingers trembled across the paper. So engrossed was she in her reading that she didn't notice the intruder until too late. It brushed against her consciousness, sending her hurtling through space with a sharp lurch of vertigo. She scrambled for the edges of the pedestal, grasping the sharp corners as the world tilted.

Colors burst in her vision, a spectrum of otherworldly hues. Entire landscapes stretched around her for miles, incomprehensible structures reaching for a sinuous sky. They flickered and vanished, replaced in an instant by entirely new geography. An ocean of vapor caressed her skin, every molecule visible to the naked eye.

She blinked, and the world shifted again. She recognized oak trees and conifers, reservoirs of water and vast deserts. They cycled through the seasons and ages in a millennia-long timelapse. Animals arose from their ancient ancestors, propagated, and died. Primates stood upright and never walked on four limbs again. In a fertile valley, humans gathered with bundles of grain and danced around a stone statue shimmering with preternatural light.

Centuries passed in a flash. Civilization advanced, yet the people in that same valley shook carved talismans at the same statuette and poured libations over a sheep's decapitated head. A few of the ritual's attendees made the same gesture Sabrina had drawn into the air—not the Christian sign of the cross, but the other one. A wizened priestess raised a knife into the air. Its black iron flashed like an omen in the flickering torchlight.

Ayana blinked again and found herself on the bank of a fjord, a range of gray mountains rising at her back like jagged teeth. Pale-faced men in bright, colorful clothing gutted a lamb with a knife identical to what the old priestess had held. The meaning of the slaughter reverberated in Ayana's bones; it was no mundane task but a ritual of warding. A heartbeat later, she stood within a limestone hallway adorned with countless hieroglyphs. The same black blade glittered in a priest's hand as he padded down the corridor toward a stone door. Above the entrance, a sprawling mural depicted a row of small people bowing down before an enormous, black-headed figure seated upon a throne.

After that, the visions picked up speed until they were a blur before her eyes. Yet she observed each one with crystal clarity, the repeating images, gestures, and symbols etching themselves into her memory. Interspersed among them were glimpses of human flesh running red with blood, limbs stretched out toward the stars, and bodies unraveling. A yearning filled her, a glowing warmth that swelled inside her chest. The birth of a child, the love of a spouse, the bond of friendship—none of these compared to the sudden injection of transcendent awe that shook her soul.

And then she was back in the library.

Her knees buckled as if another's hand had been holding her aloft and suddenly disappeared. Her body shook with the beating of her heart, so hard and fast she thought it would burst. As she gulped lungfuls of stale air, the bewildering ecstasy faded, leaving her bereft. The acute loss was a yawning void inside her.

Sabrina was right. The universe contained far greater depths than humanity dared to dream. Ayana had borne witness to it, smelled it in the air, felt the vibrations upon her skin.

And it was out of their grasp.

Biting back a sob at that revelation, she closed *Liber*

Devorationis with reverent hands and stepped away to compose herself. Her wandering gaze fell upon the other objects in the room. The stone statuettes she'd seen before were different from the ones in her vision; their luster was gone, and their details had eroded with time. She passed over them, her eyes drawn to another item on display. The black knife formed a gentle crescent shape, its handle adorned with gold, its blade shining with unnatural sharpness. As she drew nearer, an urge to pick it up pressed against her mind.

She raised a hand toward it. Its slim handle looked like it belonged in her palm.

The door clicked as it unlocked. She snatched her hand away and whirled around. A second later, Sabrina appeared in the doorway and froze.

"Ayana? I didn't know you were coming today. What are you doing here?"

"I couldn't stop thinking about what happened to Father Needham last night," Ayana said, recovering enough to deliver the answer she'd prepared. "It was the scariest thing I'd ever seen, and I've seen some horrific things at work."

Sabrina's expression softened. "I know. It was terrible, especially because he was such a devoted man of God."

"It made me realize how serious this all is." Ayana waved her arm in a vague gesture. "You could say it reaffirmed my commitment to the cause. I thought I could start by getting a full picture of what exactly we're dealing with."

The other woman said nothing at first. She closed the door and crossed the room until she stood in front of *Liber Devorationis*. Ayana's chest tightened with a brief possessiveness. How dare St. Julian's Foundation acquire that book, she thought. It didn't belong to them.

"It's difficult to get a full picture, unfortunately," Sabrina was saying. "All our knowledge about the Abyssal King is contained in this book, but unless you're properly warded against its influence, reading it is impossible. In the early days after we'd first procured it, two members of our research team lost their minds. We couldn't continue until we made the proper revisions to our protection ritual."

Except Father Needham hadn't been able to complete the ritual for Ayana. Her own mind should've fractured with how much she'd read, but as soon as the thought occurred to her, another took its place:

The Key must know the wisdom and the will.

"Does the book say anything about how to seal away the Abyssal King?" Ayana asked, careful to maintain an air of ignorance.

"It's… not simple to explain."

"Try me. The worst that can happen is I'll be confused."

A dry chuckle escaped Sabrina's lips. "Well, based on the team's reading and interpretations, they believe a precise ritual formula is required for a proper sealing. They're confident they know the right sigil to use, the right combination of Greek, Latin, and Etruscan letters—things like that. But one component keeps coming up again and again that we haven't deciphered yet."

"What?"

"The blood of the heretic."

Bodies spread out on stone altars. Glassy eyes and open mouths crawling with flies. Sheep's heads soaked in crimson. "What's that supposed to mean?"

"We still don't know. We've performed a battery of tests to figure it out, but none have worked."

The scientist in Ayana, the person she'd been for the majority of her life, reared her head at that statement. "How do you test that kind of thing?"

Clearing her throat, Sabrina shifted from one foot to the other. Her fingers plucked at the hem of her blazer. "We, ah, have attempted the ritual with different prisoners to determine who is 'heretical enough.' Unfortunately, murderers, rapists, and pedophiles haven't made the cut, so we're considering more extreme options."

Ayana stared at the other woman for a long moment, at a loss for words. She considered asking what those options were, but instinct told her not to press the topic. Instead, she asked, "What happened to the prisoners when your tests failed?"

Sabrina's shoulders dropped as she relaxed; a flicker of relief passed across her face. "They were transformed, much like Father Needham was last night, some to the point of death."

"Does that mean some of them are alive?"

"Yes, actually. The most recent one's upstairs in the patient suite."

Ayana hurried for the door. "Their symptoms might hold answers." She paused, seeing Sabrina's startled expression. "This is why you invited me to join, isn't it? To help you seal away an Elder God?"

Sabrina exhaled. "That's right."

"Then show me."

Chapter Thirty-Three

Of the options Izzy provided him, Jason picked the roof of an adjacent apartment building for his sniper's nest. Though the parapet running along its edge provided some cover, it lacked materials to make his wait more comfortable, making it less than ideal. However, the other locations had poor sightlines into Milena's spacious balcony and the floor-to-ceiling windows that afforded him a view into her penthouse. He also had to consider wind direction, the setting sun, and the glare from its final rays on the glass. Taking everything into account, the apartment roof was the best choice despite its suboptimal conditions.

Fortunately, he came prepared. He withdrew a collapsible plastic stool from the hidden pocket of his backpack and set it up beside the parapet. Crouching, he pulled on a pair of black gloves, removed all the pieces of the Remington MSR from his bag, and slotted them together. Next, he took out the police scanner, turned it on, and tuned it to the right channel. The air crackled with radio conversation at a low volume.

"...white man in his fifties, about five-foot-ten, full head of gray hair," said dispatch, sharing Vince's physical description.

"Copy," said a chorus of police officers scattered throughout the city.

Taking a seat on the stool, Jason adjusted the butt of his rifle until it was comfortable against his shoulder. He lowered the bipod and rested it on the top of the parapet. Hunched over to reduce his silhouette as much as possible, he peered through the scope and honed in on Milena's living room.

And then he waited.

The sun set to his left with a swiftness common for that time of year. As the city plunged into darkness, lights came to life within countless windows, mirroring the stars that twinkled in the sky. The penthouse remained unlit, however. He kept still, practicing his breathing, allowing his eyes to adjust to the growing gloom as visibility into Milena's home decreased. His injured arm throbbed. He released his grip on the rifle to shake it out, but only for a moment.

The penthouse's living room lit up. His heart jumped in his chest, but he maintained his slow, deep breathing to counter the sudden spike in his heart rate. Sniping required steadiness in the entire body. Hands too jittery from nerves or excitement missed every shot. When

Milena appeared in his scope, he tracked her movement across the floor, giving himself time to regain total calm. Plants and decorations obscured her on occasion, but he wasn't concerned. The opportunity for a clear and unobstructed headshot would come; he was certain of that.

The woman spoke as she paced, though she held no phone to her ear, nor was she wearing a wireless headset. Another person was in the room with her, he realized—someone he couldn't see. That was fine. Expected, even. She kept her bodyguards close, though based on how engrossed she was in the conversation, he doubted that was their identity.

While he waited and watched, he reviewed his escape plan in his head. The mental exercise ceased as soon as the second person in Milena's living room appeared in his scope.

It was Vince.

Jason tensed, his heart rate picking back up. His rifle's magazine held five bullets, but as soon as either Vince or Milena died, the other would flee; neither was stupid enough to stay behind and risk joining the other as a corpse. A person didn't reach old age in their field of work without a heightened sense of survival. That meant Jason had to use a single bullet on both of them. But Vince stood with his profile half-hidden by the marble bust of a youthful man, while Milena continued to pace at the other side of the room, her gestures agitated. If they didn't move to stand next to each other in Jason's window of opportunity, he wouldn't be able to hit them both. He had to choose one.

Vince was Jason's primary target. Killing him that evening meant finally getting revenge on the person who'd stolen Connor. The moment of retribution had arrived. Vince stepped out from behind the marble bust and turned his full body toward Jason's hiding place. He would not have a better shot. Taking distance, trajectory, and the wind into account, he centered his sights on the old man's head. He inhaled. Exhaled. With a twitch of his trigger finger, he'd end it all. Vince would never know what hit him.

Jason froze at the thought.

No. Vince had to know. He had to die knowing Jason had hunted him down.

That *no one* outsmarted, outran, or outgunned Jason Ridley.

He readjusted, searching for Milena through his scope. She was stalking toward Vince, her arms crossed. She stopped in front of him, the back of her head in Jason's sights. The alignment wasn't perfect, but if the bullet grazed Vince's body after passing through her skull, it could still kill him.

And if it didn't? Let him run. Let him hide. Jason was coming either way.

Once more, he centered his rifle. Inhaled. Exhaled. Squeezed the trigger.

Milena's head exploded in a pink mist. As Jason recovered from the recoil, Vince darted out of sight through an open door. Jason disassembled the MSR in a matter of seconds. He packed each piece of the rifle into his backpack, along with the police scanner and collapsible stool. He picked up the empty brass casing on the roof by his feet, stuffed it into his jacket's pocket, and raced for the stairs.

A few minutes later, he stepped out of the apartment building's back door into a shadowed alley. Turning away from the bustling main street, he started toward Lower Kemsing's subway terminal at a brisk walk. On the way, he tossed his gloves and the empty bullet casing into one trash can, his beanie into another. Half a block from the station, he removed his jacket and dropped it onto the lap of a homeless woman. He kept his backpack, though, its incriminating cargo still inside.

At the underground subway platform, he reached a row of lockers and punched a code into one of them. Its door swung open, revealing his brown bomber jacket. Putting it on, he checked its pockets for his keys, wallet, and cell phone. The last of these showed no new messages or missed calls.

In line behind other pedestrians waiting for the train, Jason sent a quick text to Nick: *Done with M.*

Seconds later, the phone buzzed with a call from Nick. "Jason! The package is on the move, heading northeast from Upper Kemsing! We're tracking it now. Black BMW, probably armored."

In other words, Tyler was traveling through the city.

Was he trying to leave?

Jason left the queue to look at a map of the subway lines. "Reroute through Stagsden Commons and have your friends there slow it down. Pick me up from the station in seven minutes."

"You got it, man."

They hung up as the train arrived at the platform. He squeezed onto the nearest car. Seven minutes later, he jogged through the subway station at Stagsden Commons and burst out aboveground. The distant roars of speeding cars filled the air, an uncommon noise in that district, with its abundance of green space and distinct lack of skyscrapers. A thunderous rumble announced the arrival of Nick's blue Supra as it barreled down the street to stop in front of him.

Jason hopped into the passenger's seat. Nick floored the gas, and they sped off into the night. The phone mounted on the dashboard connected to a group call with Monahans barking updates on Tyler's location. Nick adjusted his route based on their information, weaving through traffic with unparalleled agility and speed.

"How'd it go?" he asked Jason.

"Fine. Vince was there."

"*What?*" Nick risked a sideways glance. "Did you get him?"

"No. I only had time for one shot." After easing his bag onto the back seat, Jason removed a Sig Sauer P365 and suppressor from the glove compartment. He fitted them together, checked that the pistol was loaded, and flicked off the safety.

"Shit, I bet this is why Tyler suddenly ran like that. Vince tipped him off."

"Where was Tyler?"

"At his company's headquarters, probably in some kind of board meeting or whatever. My boys followed him there from the restaurant where he had lunch, and he didn't leave until just a minute before I called you. He was rushing out and had a bunch of security with him."

A voice on the group call announced that Tyler's car had broken free from traffic congestion and was heading for the ramp out of the city. Nick turned a hard right, peeling away from the main boulevard in hot pursuit. Jason peered out the tinted window at unfamiliar streets. Scenery zoomed past in a dark blur. Ahead, signs pointed them toward the highway.

"I'll shoot out the tires," he said. "Expect them to return fire, so get ready to dodge."

"Easier said than done, but sure," Nick said, shifting into fifth gear as they hit the freeway. The digital speedometer ticked up into the seventies.

"Just saw you pass, boss," said a Monahan soldier over the phone. "Panzy Junior is ahead of you, three cars up. Second lane from the left. Can't miss it."

"Thanks, Duffy."

The engine revved as their car picked up speed. They passed a minivan, a pickup truck, and a four-door sedan. Finally, Tyler's car was just ahead. Jason rolled down his window, aimed his gun at the back left tire, and fired. The rubber blew. The rear of the BMW swerved to the left, but its driver straightened it out and switched to the other lane. Nick drew up his Supra alongside it. The back window facing them rolled down to reveal the muzzle of an automatic rifle.

"Get behind!" Jason shouted. He yanked the lever to lower the back of his seat and fell with it, ducking out of sight.

Nick hit the brakes as a volley of bullets sprayed across the front of his vehicle. He shifted gears and slipped behind the other car. "Shit!"

Jason sat back up as they chased the BMW to the far side of the road. He fired several shots at the open window, but the angle was poor and his right arm screamed with a persistent ache. His bullets embedded into the armored door instead. "Ram into them!"

"Are you fucking crazy? This is a Toyota!"

"Just do it!"

Nick hesitated a half-second, then whipped the wheel around and hit the gas. The gap between the cars shrank with dangerous speed. Jason spied the glint of the rifle's muzzle, then the grizzled face of the bodyguard holding it. He raised his pistol and fired. The bodyguard collapsed back against his seat, blood streaming down his face between his eyes.

Nick's Supra slammed into the BMW. The two vehicles skidded across the highway until they struck the guardrail. Metal screeched as it shredded. The cars spun apart and stopped perpendicular to each other. Nick killed the engine and shoved his door open, grabbing another Sig from the center console as he went. Jason followed him out the driver's side door, crouching behind it as another volley of bullets from the BMW tore through the Supra. Glass from the window shattered and fell over Jason's head and shoulders. Shaking off the shards, he popped up as Nick gunned down the other driver, who dropped another automatic rifle to the ground.

The front passenger's side door of the BMW opened. A lean figure in a navy suit rushed out and bolted down the street.

Tyler.

Jason tossed his pistol back into the Supra and dashed to the BMW. He scooped up the rifle, aimed at the retreating silhouette, and waited for Tyler to pass beneath the nearest streetlight.

Its orange-yellow glow illuminated him for a brief moment.

Jason pulled the trigger. Twelve bullets tore through Tyler's body in the span of a second. He crumpled to the ground and did not move.

Only then did Jason notice the wail of police sirens, louder and closer than they should have been. Nick was yelling, but a blast of wind and the unmistakable whir of helicopter blades drowned him out. Jason spun around as a blinding searchlight bore down upon the wreckage.

"This is the police," said a woman's voice over a loudspeaker. "Drop your weapons. Do not attempt to flee."

At least eight interceptors, their light bars blazing red and blue, sped toward them. Jason's gaze snapped to Nick to see he'd already surrendered his Sig Sauer and raised his hands, palms out. Jason, however, still held onto the automatic rifle.

"I repeat: drop your weapons," said the cop.

He considered the police cruisers as they surrounded him and Nick. Armed officers poured out of the vehicles, two per car.

The gun in his hands could fire seven hundred rounds per minute.

"Don't fucking do it!" Nick yelled at Jason, barely audible over the helicopter's roar.

A dozen firearms leveled at them. One cop kept screaming at Jason to relinquish his gun. Jaw clenched, eyes radiating malice, he slowly lowered the rifle to the ground. Then he stood, hands in the air by his head.

The police descended upon him.

Chapter Thirty-Four

The fourth floor of St. Julian's Foundation resembled a long-term care unit for patients at a hospital, complete with a small team of nurses in dark scrubs. One of them led Ayana to the room assigned to Matthew Whitcomb, the latest victim of Sabrina's questionable experiment. Inside, Ayana found a similar setup to what she'd seen in the research group's photographs: hospital bed, monitoring machines, a computer in the corner. Whitcomb lay in the bed and appeared to sleep. Settling in the chair by the curtain-covered window, she began to read his report.

A forty-seven-year-old man, he'd been incarcerated for double homicide when he was twenty-one. Prison had not aged him well. His hair was gray with only a few streaks of its original black, and his hairline had crept so far back across his skull that he resembled a tonsured monk. Deep lines from stress and isolation gouged his face. Angry red burns covered the rest of his skin, as if he'd thrown himself into boiling water. His exposed chest did not bear the pulsating black holes that had become so familiar to her, though. Instead, a single gaping wound split his flesh, exposing organs and veins that didn't usually see the light of day. Two rows of human teeth rimmed the opening. Saliva dribbled between them onto the blanket drawn up to his waist. Dozens of human eyes blinked open along his collarbone and arms, staring at her. Their irises were green, matching his original eye color, according to the report. She stared back with a clinical detachment.

The door opened and a young nurse entered. She smiled at Ayana. "You're the new doctor, aren't you?"

"Yes, with the research team."

The nurse's eyes widened. She swiped into the computer in the corner and started clicking around. "I'll get out of your way in a sec. I just need to record his vitals."

"Take your time."

Silence reigned for only a moment before she spoke again. "Absolutely wild stuff, isn't it? I never thought I'd see anything this extreme when I was in nursing school."

"Have you been working for St. Julian's for a while?"

"About six months."

"And have you seen a lot of different afflictions in that time?"

The nurse's hands stilled over the keyboard. "A few, but nothing quite like this. Most of the time, there are the holes in the body cavity, but there's never anything *in* them. Have you seen those yet?"

"Yes, I'm familiar with them."

"There was another subject in here a few months back whose soft tissue had hardened. On the surface, it looked like a severe case of fibrodysplasia ossificans progressiva, but once we got a look inside him, we discovered that the tissue wasn't turning into bone but metal."

"You performed surgery without a surgeon?"

"Oh, no, nothing like that. His body split open by itself."

Like what happened with Needham. "Is he still here?"

"No, he didn't live for more than a couple of weeks. Organ failure."

"And Whitcomb?" Ayana glanced at the man on the bed between them. "How long has he been here?"

"A month. His vitals are surprisingly stable, though his heart rate refuses to go below one-twenty, and his burns aren't healing. It's like his body is stuck in limbo, unable to make a full recovery."

The nurse wasn't wrong. The thought occurred to Ayana as if she'd always known it. "What happens to the patients... sorry, the subjects in the long-term?"

"We keep them alive here until they expire, or until the research team decides they've obtained all the information they can. When that happens, we administer a precise formula and dosage of medication to help them pass on."

"So, forced euthanasia."

The nurse flinched. "Their quality of life is already so poor. We're doing them a mercy."

Ayana said nothing. The question of human ethics had never interested her, but having read *Liber Devorationis*, they were less relevant than ever.

Whitcomb's body eyes watched the nurse as she updated his record with readings from the machines. After she left the room, the eyes shifted back to Ayana. A wheezing sound rushed from the opening in the man's chest, but he spoke through his regular mouth.

"Do you pity me?" His voice was frail and quiet, as if he hadn't used it in a long time.

"No," she said. "You weren't worthy."

He stirred in the bed. When he opened his regular eyes, they were milky white. They stared at a fixed point on the ceiling. "I know. My flesh—I was not willing. It came for me and I... I was afraid."

"Only willing flesh can act as the Key for its Becoming." The words tumbled from her lips as if someone else had placed them on her tongue. "And its Vessel on this plane cannot know fear."

"How will we know we've found the Vessel?"

"By the cataclysm of their existence." Ayana let the weight of her words settle on the air between them for a moment, then asked, "When it came for you, did you see it?"

"A glimpse, yeah, just before..." Whitcomb hesitated,

closing his eyes again.

"What did you see?"

Silence stretched between them for several seconds before he answered. "It was immense. Terrible. The hunger..." He shuddered. "It was crushing me. I couldn't move, couldn't scream. My body turned inside-out. Everything burned, and the light..." He choked out a sob. "The unholy light!"

Her gaze flickered to his burns. "And then what happened?"

"Rejection," he whispered. "Pain."

Sighing, she placed his report on a nearby table. "You're suffering because you were weak. Now you must wait until your flesh succumbs, or until it returns for what it gave you."

He burst into tears. "I know."

She'd seen everything she needed to see, heard what she needed to hear. Leaving the doomed man to his quiet weeping, she stepped into the hall and retrieved her phone from her purse. Though she didn't expect to hear from Jason for a while, she reasoned that live, local reports were the quickest way to learn if something had happened yet to Milena Novikova or Tyler Panzieri. A video popped up as soon as Ayana opened the news app on her phone. Aerial footage of the highway filled her screen. Brilliant light from a police helicopter bathed a two-car crash along the right shoulder, as well as two figures standing amid the wreckage. One of the vehicles was a black sedan, while the other was a bright blue sports car.

She stopped dead in her tracks. She'd seen the second car before. Earlier that day, in fact.

"We're back with the latest updates on the high-speed car chase on I-95," said a male broadcaster, his voice superimposed over the video. "Police have apprehended two suspects, both of whom were seen emerging from the blue Toyota that crashed into a black BMW. Both cars were sighted exceeding the speed limit by twenty miles an hour before their fatal collision. Three unidentified individuals were confirmed dead upon arrival, but not because of the crash."

The video switched to a cop's bodycam. Red and blue lights flashed back and forth against the darkness. Holding his pistol with both hands, the officer pointed it at a man standing several yards in front of him.

Ayana's heart dropped into the cold pit of her stomach. Though the footage was grainy at that distance, she recognized the suspect at once. She knew that aggressive stance, that haircut, that brown jacket he'd been wearing the night he brought home a bottle of French wine. She knew those hands raised in surrender—hands that had touched her intimately, held her face while he kissed her, and caressed her to sleep when nightmares plagued her.

As she looked on, three officers wrestled Jason to his knees and forced him into handcuffs.

The news broadcaster resumed speaking, but a high-pitched ringing noise in her ears drowned out his words. The world around her spun; she reached out a shaky hand and leaned it against a wall. With every blink of her eyes, she saw the police subduing her husband. Each time, her thoughts ground to a halt.

Jason said they'd never catch him. He'd *promised*.

"Ma'am? Are you okay?"

Ayana's head snapped up. The nurse from earlier stared at her, brows furrowed in concern.

Straightening, she closed the news app and held her phone with both hands to keep them from trembling. "I'm just tired. I'll head home now. Have a good night."

She continued to the elevator without a backward glance, forcing herself to walk with calm, measured steps. Once the doors closed, she dialed Izzy's number.

Izzy picked up after one ring. "Ayana! Are you okay? Where are you right now? I saw the news!"

Ayana's sigh of relief came out as a sob. "I need your help," she whispered urgently. "I'm at St. Julian's in Bracknell and I'm trying to leave. If they have Jason, they'll try to get me next."

"What can I do?"

"I—I don't know. I have to get back to our hotel, get rid of anything—"

"Where's the hotel?"

"Keady Woods. It's the Luna Bright Hotel on Palmer Street."

"Got it. I'll call you when I get there. And Ayana? Try to breathe. It'll be okay. We've got this."

"Thank you, Izzy. I'll see you soon."

The elevator arrived at the ground floor with a soft chime. Ayana stepped out, withdrawing the phone from her ear to hang up. Before her thumb tapped the red button, however, a different woman's voice froze her in place:

"Where are you going, Ayana?"

Sabrina blocked the path to the building's front entrance. Flanking her were four security personnel. Clad in black uniforms and brandishing rifles, they formed an imposing, impenetrable wall. Three other guards approached from either side of Ayana and also behind her, cutting off all escape routes.

In the corner of her eye, she noticed that the phone call with Izzy had not ended yet. Was the hacker listening?

"I have to go home," Ayana said. "There's been an emergency."

Sabrina had the audacity to look apologetic. "I'm afraid that won't be possible. We've just completed preparations for another trial of the sealing ritual, and the rest of the research team could really use your help with it."

"I haven't familiarized myself with all the material yet. I'm not sure how much help I can be."

"Nonsense." Sabrina's smile cut across her face. "Your mind is razor sharp, so you're already an asset. I'm sure you'll be able to catch on quick once we get started. Also, we've finally figured out the right formula."

"The blood of the heretic, you mean?"

"Exactly. You don't want to miss such a momentous occasion, do you? We can celebrate together, as colleagues."

A chill ran down Ayana's spine. Every instinct screamed at her to flee, but how? And where? After taking a deep breath, she returned the other woman's smile. "When you put it that way, how can I refuse?"

"I knew you'd be agreeable. Before we leave, though, please hand over your belongings. We'll make sure you get them back by the end of the night."

One of the security guards slung his rifle over his shoulder and stepped toward Ayana with a hand outstretched. She considered refusing, but six other armed guards were watching her. After a moment's pause, she relinquished her purse. Up close, she saw clearly the distinct sword-and-sunburst badge pinned to the front of his uniform.

He took her phone from her and ended the call. Her heartbeat quickened, pounding against her abdomen like a jackhammer. She didn't know what Izzy could do with the conversation she'd overheard, but any advantage was better than none.

In silence, Sabrina and her security detail escorted Ayana out of the building and into one of two black SUVs parked on the street. Inside, the seats were transverse, with the middle row facing the back. Sabrina and Ayana sat diagonally across from each other. Two security guards joined them while two others climbed into the front seats. The guard with Ayana's purse boarded the other car.

"Where's the ritual taking place?" she asked as they drove down the main road through Bracknell.

Shadows fell across the upper half of Sabrina's face so that only her teeth were visible when she grinned. "Somewhere we won't be interrupted."

Chapter Thirty-Five

Jason sat alone in the back of the police interceptor, hands cuffed behind his back; a partition of steel mesh separated him from the officers up front. Nick had disappeared into a second car. That was the last time Jason saw him before both vehicles started back toward the city. For some time, one car followed the other, but they eventually went different directions at an intersection. Jason watched the changing landscape of buildings, taking note of street signs to orient himself and anticipate his destination. Upper Kemsing, where the car chase began, was the most likely possibility, but he had to be ready for anything.

He reviewed the usual arrest procedure in his head. After arrival at the police station, the cops recorded a suspect's name, birth date, and address; filed his fingerprints; took samples of his handwriting, saliva, and hair; and photographed his mug shot. An interrogation followed. Suspects stayed in holding cells—or even prison—until their hearings before a judge. Jason doubted a judge would set him bail, considering the severity of the charges against him. Murder. Illegal possession of a firearm. He knew to plead "not guilty," but without bail, the court would send him to prison. The possibility of escape was already low; it would lower further at the police station. At jail, it was next to zero.

Which meant he had to run as soon as they opened the door to let him out.

The familiar silhouette of Grosmont's subway terminal jolted him out of his mental preparations. Based on other landmarks and street names, the car was heading deeper into the district, in the opposite direction of its police station. Within a few minutes, Grosmont Fish Market came into view, the bottom half of its main building illuminated by the soft glow of the surrounding street lamps. Its windows, on the other hand, were dark.

As the interceptor neared the fish market, he discarded his original escape plan. The police were taking him to Vince. Jason was sure of it, even when they continued past the market's front gate. The noise of Grosmont at night receded into the background as they proceeded down the narrow, winding streets toward the harbor. He knew the neighborhoods well, having walked the same routes countless times in the past. Ahead of them, invisible in the gloom, was the warehouse district.

"This place at night always gives me the creeps," said the cop in the front passenger's seat. "I don't like driving through here."

"We'll be in and out in no time," said his partner. "After we drop off Rambo back there, we can stop by the Neptune and get a bite to eat."

"Only if you're paying."

"Yeah, yeah."

The first cop, a white man, turned in his seat to look at Jason. "I don't envy you, man. You're gonna wish you were back at the station with us."

Jason stared back in silence, waiting to see what else the officer might reveal. However, his partner, an older Black man, intervened with a sharp scolding. "Shut up, will you?"

"Eh, he's already dead."

"Yeah, so don't talk to him. No use talking to a corpse."

A few minutes later, the car drew up to the gate of a large, fenced-in area Jason recognized as Vince's property. Though he couldn't see them in the darkness, he envisioned the three brick warehouses in his mind's eye. He'd first visited them six months into his new career, approximately a year after his discharge from the Army. Vince had scouted Jason out via word of mouth, impressed with his work during his first few contracts, and invited to train him as a professional in their career.

After a brief exchange with the Black cop, the gate guard waved them inside. Jason shifted in his seat for a better look through the front windshield. He spotted two small lights affixed to the front of the farthest warehouse, glowing like twin beacons in otherwise impenetrable blackness. As they approached, the interceptor's headlights revealed two sedans parked in front of the building. He recognized the navy one as Vince's.

The cops parked a short distance away, positioning their car so its headlights shone upon the front of the warehouse. The white cop hopped out with a shotgun in hand and pointed it at Jason through the window. His partner came around the back of the car and opened Jason's door.

"Out," said the Black cop.

With a shotgun in Jason's face, running was out of the question. He stepped out of the car and let the police herd him toward the building. Its front door opened and Vince emerged, surrounded by four of his employees, a mix of men and women. Among them, they carried another shotgun, a submachine gun, and two pistols. Vince himself appeared empty-handed, but Jason knew better.

"Good evening, gentlemen," Vince said when both groups stood in front of each other. "Thank you for your cooperation. My people will take over from here."

"You know," said the Black cop, "we arrested two men on the freeway today. The media and public will expect to see this guy alongside his friend in future news reports."

"I appreciate your concern, Officer Newkirk, but

I encourage you to trust your commanding officers. They'll know how best to spin this story."

"Sure. I supposed it's above my paygrade."

"That's right."

"We need the handcuffs back," said the white cop. "We can't just let you have them."

Vince's smile did not falter. "Not a problem. We have zip ties."

On cue, one of his employees stepped forward with a strip of thin, black plastic. Jason waited to see if they were stupid enough to remove the handcuffs first before putting the zip tie around his wrists, but such was not the case. The material was heavy-duty, military-grade plastic, difficult to snap with strength alone. He'd have to wiggle out of his binds one finger at a time. As the zip tie encircled his wrists, he twisted them to create slack. His shoulders ached from having his hands behind his back for the entire trip to the harbor, and the wound in his arm throbbed with pain.

The police took back their handcuffs and drove off. Visibility fell as the headlights turned away. Vince and his henchmen became a wall of five black silhouettes haloed by cold, white lights. But the darkness benefited Jason, too. Keeping his arms as still as possible, he started easing his hands out of the zip tie.

Vince sighed. "I truly regret that it came to this, Jason. I'd hoped to keep you uninvolved and out of the picture, but you just had to take your brother's death personally."

"Why'd you kill Connor?" Jason demanded to buy himself time. "What had he done?"

"Nothing—*yet*. But he was sticking his nose into places where it didn't belong. Investigative journalists are the worst, you know. They're persistent little rats that'll do anything, even illegal things, to get their story."

"He got close to the truth of your alliance." It wasn't a question, but a litmus test to see how much Vince was willing to divulge.

Vince spun the ring on the pinkie of his right hand. Though Jason couldn't see its details in the gloom, he imagined its sword and sunburst in his mind's eye. "He was discouraged many times. He had chances to back out, but he never took a single one."

Jason tilted his head. "Discouraged? You mean by Sabrina."

"That's one thing you brothers had in common: your stubbornness. Your persistence."

Avoiding the question meant Jason was right. "So Connor's own girlfriend gave the order to kill him."

Vince scoffed. "Her? No. She's nothing more than a frightened little girl. She came running to me for advice when your brother wouldn't give up. She wanted to scare him off, but all her tactics had already failed. It was *my* decision to kill him. It was the best way to ensure he never unearthed anything." A pause. "I didn't think you'd care. In fact, I thought I'd done you a favor, getting rid of that nuisance for you."

It was Jason's turn to scoff. "You don't know a fucking thing about me."

His eyesight had adjusted to the darkness enough to catch the twitch of annoyance in Vince's cheek.

Jason's right thumb was halfway free. "So what's in it for you, then? You were never religious, so why side with St. Julian's? Is the Kopanski girl keeping your dick warm for you?"

He expected Vince to recoil or, if not, to defend himself. Instead, his voice grew somber. "You saw it, Jason. You've seen what it's capable of. I was with Rod when it first manifested in Saintfield three years ago. It attacked his men and nearly brought ruin to the Sons of Saints. The little tantrum you threw last night was *nothing* compared to the way it brutalized the district."

"How come no one heard about it, if it was so bad?"

"Because of St. Julian's. They stopped the Abyssal King from breaking through before it could annihilate Saintfield. Don't ask me to explain it—I don't understand it myself. Something about magical wards between dimensions. What matters is they bought us time, Jason, and came up with a plan to isolate the monster to certain districts in the city, until they can banish it away forever."

"And how exactly do you isolate a thing like that?"

"By giving it what it wants, in small doses and only in certain areas. It feeds off cruelty. At first, the mayor and chief of police wouldn't agree to ignore certain criminal activities in those areas, but St. Julian's convinced them.

It was the only way. That's why no one could know—not the public, not your brother, not you."

"But you're telling me now."

A hard edge entered Vince's tone. "Yes. I suppose you deserve to know, considering what they'll do to you."

Jason's head snapped up.

Vince wasn't going to kill him. The weapons were for show.

With a single, hard twist of his wrists, Jason slipped his thumb from the zip tie, then his right hand. Stepping up to Vince, Jason swung a fist at the older man's solar plexus. Vince jerked away. Too slow. Jason's fist connected. Vince stumbled backward, wheezing.

His henchmen rushed at Jason. He pivoted, grabbing one of them by the wrist and upper arm. A sharp twist of his hands snapped her elbow. Her high-pitched shriek cut through the night's stillness. Agony shot through his injured arm as his muscles seized up from the force of the maneuver. Releasing the woman, he tucked his arm close to his body, gritting his teeth against the searing pain.

Those few, precious seconds cost him. A blow to the back of the head knocked him to his knees. His vision swam and blurred. Clinging to consciousness, he tried to stand, but a heavy boot slammed into his ribs, sending him sprawling. Before he could recover, Vince's thugs swarmed, raining kicks onto Jason's prone form. He lashed out, but the butt of the shotgun smacked him in the temple and everything went black.

Chapter Thirty-Six

As the SUVs made their way through Lancing, Ayana peered out the tinted window, looking for familiar landmarks and buildings to orient herself to their location in the city. Neither Sabrina nor her security personnel had bothered to blindfold Ayana, which meant one of two things: either the research team really did need her assistance with the ritual, or St. Julian's Foundation did not intend to let her survive the night. Considering the armed escort, she doubted the former.

The car radio played at a low volume during the drive, tuned to the news. "Police have arrested several members of the Monahan crime family and the Hellhounds Motorcycle Club this evening, linking them to earlier reckless driving through Upper Kemsing and Stagsden Commons, as well as the high-speed car chase on I-95," a female radio host reported, her tone warm and full-bodied, perfect for her profession. "Officers at

Stagsden Commons have identified the man at the subsequent car crash as thirty-three-year-old Nick Monahan. Monahan was apprehended after his blue Toyota crashed into the black BMW belonging to one of the victims, Tyler Panzieri. Panzieri, whose father passed away only three weeks ago, was shot dead alongside two other male individuals. Monahan has been taken into custody at the Stagsden Commons police station for processing."

Another radio host spoke up, a man with a smooth, deep baritone. "What's interesting, Nicole, is that the live helicopter and bodycam footage showed a second man with Monahan at the crash. Have the police released anything about him yet?"

Ayana leaned forward in anticipation.

"Not yet, Arthur, though I'm sure he's being processed alongside Monahan at Stagsden Commons and his identity just hasn't been revealed yet."

"Could there be another reason the police haven't released his information?"

"Maybe. Either way, our listeners will be the first to hear updates about tonight's breaking news as it unfolds."

Ayana sat back, trying to school the worry from her face. Sabrina must have glimpsed it, though, for she pinned Ayana with an icy glare. "It's what Jason deserves, you know," she said, her tone abrasive and hateful. "The police should've arrested him days ago at the funeral, but their bureaucracy is idiotic."

Ayana stared at her for a long moment. "You sent the detectives to Connor's funeral?"

"Not directly, but I was putting pressure on their captain as the bereaved ex-girlfriend. He interviewed me after Connor's murder and told me to call the station if anything else came up. I blew up their number demanding updates and action so they'd put your husband in the fucking hole already."

Heat flushed Ayana's face. She returned Sabrina's look with a sharp one of her own. "Jason didn't kill Connor."

Sabrina's eyes flashed in the darkness. "He might as well have! He abused Connor! Whenever Connor brought up Jason, he got all nervous and tense, even when he was saying what a great brother Jason was. It was all bullshit, Ayana. A relationship built on fear."

Ayana said nothing. Connor should've known better than to talk about his brother with anyone.

"Did you really think I believed you when you said how great your marriage is?" Sabrina laughed contemptuously. "A monster like Jason doesn't care about people. He doesn't know how to love. He just takes and takes, and when he doesn't get what he wants, he hurts people until he does."

"Don't you dare talk about my husband as if you know anything about him."

"I know *enough*. I met him before dinner at Connor's." She paused, watching Ayana's face. Ayana continued to scowl, anticipating Sabrina's next words as the memory of Jason's confession flashed through her mind. "The man in the news report—Tyler Panzieri? His father Robert was one of our allies. He knew about the Abyssal King. He'd donated hundreds of thousands of dollars to St. Julian's over the last three years so we could conduct our research. He died three weeks ago, and guess who killed him. That's right, your husband."

"Do you have proof?"

"Proof?" Sabrina's laugh was more unhinged that time. "I *am* the proof! I was there! I showed up to Robert's apartment to talk about the impending doom of the world and how to stop it, but Jason had just killed him! And you know what else, Ayana? He pointed his gun at *me*. He threatened to *kill* me if I breathed a word about it to anyone else!"

She paused again, waiting for a reaction. Ayana refused to give her the satisfaction of one.

Several seconds of expectant silence passed before Sabrina's eyes widened with revelation. "You knew all along."

It wasn't a question, so Ayana did not deign to answer. "If St. Julian's was so influential, why didn't you tell the police?"

The reversal of roles snapped Sabrina out of her shock. "I did, but I was outvoted. No one wanted to go after Jason." She sneered. "They're all fucking cowards, but they somehow convinced me to leave him alone. That we could adjust and Tyler would step up as an ally. I didn't realize how much of a terror Jason would be until we met again at Connor's. That's when I knew he'd be a thorn in my side unless I got rid of him."

"Is that why you ordered Connor's murder?"

To Ayana's surprise, Sabrina flinched. "Why the fuck would you ask that? You think I'm capable of *that*?"

"The man who shot and killed Connor, a man named Vince Moynier, was wearing a ring with St. Julian's symbol on it." Ayana gestured to the badge affixed to the nearest guard's uniform. "If you're in charge of all operations in Lancing, that means you gave Moynier the order to kill Connor."

"No!"

Ayana blinked, taken aback. Sabrina's hands were white-clenched fists on her knees. Light from a passing street lamp gave Ayana a glimpse of her face, contorted in anguish.

"I'd never do that! I never wanted Connor to die, just to stop his investigation!"

Nothing Ayana had to say could match the knife of guilt she imagined twisting through Sabrina's heart every day since Connor's death. Instead, she let the weight of her admonishing stare convey her thoughts. Sabrina had failed her relationship in every way Ayana's own had succeeded, and she had to live with the consequences.

"Is that why you started dating Connor? To stop him?" Ayana asked at last.

Squeezing her eyes shut, Sabrina turned her face away. It was all the answer Ayana needed. She leaned back in her seat and looked out the opposite window.

"I really liked him, you know," Sabrina said unprompted, her words choked with emotion. "I didn't expect to, but he was really funny. Kind. And there was a sadness in him I wanted to heal. I thought if I could get him to stop snooping around, we could have a proper relationship."

Ayana didn't bother looking at her. "You can't lie to each other and call it a relationship."

"Ma'am, we're here," said the driver. His announcement cut through the emotional strain inside the vehicle, but Ayana remained tense. The SUV passed through a gated fence and parked alongside two sedans in front of a large, brick warehouse. Two lights on either side of the building's doors provided some illumination, but not enough to get a good sense of their surroundings. The lights of the city did not reach that secluded area, though she caught a whiff of saltwater when she stepped out. They were in Grosmont by the harbor.

Four security guards surrounded Ayana and pointed their rifles at her. She glanced at the weapons before turning to Sabrina. "What exactly should I expect to happen during this sealing ritual?"

Sabrina had composed herself in the few minutes it took to park. She smiled at Ayana. "Patience. You'll find out in just a few minutes."

She led the way into the warehouse. They passed a dark stain on the asphalt that reminded Ayana of blood splatters in crime scene photos. The mental image of

Jason, bleeding all over the ground, sprang unbidden in her mind's eye, but she banished it at once and took a shaky breath.

Her husband was alive. He had to be.

The inside of the warehouse was a sharp contrast to the dark, empty world outside. Ceiling lights blazed above an expansive space full of unrelated clutter. In one corner hung three heavy-looking punching bags, while standing near them were two wooden poles. Short, blunt spokes protruded from them at different angles. Multiple racks of clothing took up another corner, a single full-length mirror set up next to them. Workbenches, toolboxes, computers, and other electronic contraptions she couldn't name occupied a third corner. Strangest of all was the massive, elaborate sigil drawn on the floor in the center of the warehouse. It was similar to the one in St. Julian's Foundation from the night of Needham's transformation.

Standing by the sigil's outer edge were Tim, Derek, and Phoebe. They talked in low voices and glanced toward Ayana, then quickly looked away. A different group—men she didn't recognize—loitered on the other side of the central space, dressed in ordinary clothing and carrying guns. One of them pointed his firearm at a solitary man kneeling within the sigil itself, just off-center, hunched and unmoving. His hands were drawn behind his back. As her own group neared, Ayana recognized his brown jacket and his swollen, bloody face. Her heart plunged into her stomach when his eyes locked with hers.

"Jason!" she screamed.

Her body moved toward him of its own accord. One of her guards shoved the muzzle of his rifle against her chest, but she'd seen the truth of the universe; bullets meant nothing to her. Shoving aside the gun, she took three steps before two more guards grabbed her arms and held her back.

She squirmed in their unrelenting grip. "Let me go! I want to see my husband!"

Jason's snarl echoed in the building. "Let her go or I'll tear your fucking throats out."

"You're in no condition to make threats," said one of the men watching over Jason. Only then did she recognize him as Vince. He walked over to Sabrina, who'd been watching the exchange with a cool expression. "You need to subdue her," he said, gesturing with his chin at Ayana.

Sabrina pursed her lips, then addressed Ayana. "You have two options: either you cooperate and we won't have to tie you up, or you can suffer the same fate as your husband."

Vince frowned. "Why are you giving her a choice?"

"Because I'm not a monster."

A mocking laugh burst from Ayana. "Of course you aren't. You just lock up people in your 'hospital,' perform experiments on them until they die, and execute prisoners in search of a solution to your cosmic problem."

Sabrina whirled upon her, arm snapping out. Pain bloomed in Ayana's cheek from the flat of Sabrina's palm, bringing tears to her eyes. Sabrina's chest heaved, her pale face burning bright red, her fists trembling at her sides.

She turned to the nearest security guard. "Bind her wrists and put her in position," she said before turning on her heel and stalking away.

Chapter Thirty-Seven

A heavy, gloved fist slammed into Ayana's stomach. She folded over, gasping from the agony, coughing up spit and bile. Two guards dragged her to the center of the sigil and threw her onto the floor next to Jason. He tried to lunge at them, but one kicked him back down while the second shackled Ayana's wrists in front of her with a zip tie. She winced as the plastic bit into her skin.

Vince directed his people outside to keep watch, leaving the guards from St. Julian's to level their rifles at Ayana and Jason. Meanwhile, Phoebe and Derek walked up to Sabrina, carrying a familiar leatherbound book and a roll of thick cloth. From where she lay, Ayana couldn't hear their conversation, but when Sabrina nodded, she knew the ritual was about to start. She tried sitting up, but her abdomen throbbed with pain, forcing her to remain curled on the floor next to her husband.

"Jason," she whispered, "we have to do something."

Next to her, he pulled himself back upright on his knees. Together, they watched Phoebe open the book in her hands. She began chanting in Latin, her sonorous voice filling the air. At her side, Derek unrolled the cloth and unveiled a crescent-shaped knife. When he held it aloft, its black blade appeared to absorb all light. He sliced his other palm with it and dripped blood onto the sigil in front of him.

Neither of them looked at Ayana.

"Ayana, I need you to trust me," Jason said, his gaze fixed upon the two professors.

She closed her eyes, took a deep breath, and opened them again. "I trust you."

He surged to his feet and took two wobbly steps forward. An icy hand gripped her heart at his heavy, pained breathing, but she'd already granted him permission. All she could do was watch.

With a burst of strength, he charged at Phoebe and Derek.

Two guards swiveled, their rifles tracking Jason across the open space, but Sabrina's shrill cry cut through the air: "Don't shoot! You might hit them!"

Phoebe screamed. Jason slammed into her, knocking her over. Then he spun and smashed his forehead into Derek's nose. The knife clattered to the floor and skidded a few feet away.

Three deafening gunshots filled the warehouse. Jason swayed on his feet as blood darkened the back of his jacket, spreading from three separate bullet holes.

He crumpled to the ground.

Next to Sabrina, Vince lowered his smoking pistol.

It took Ayana several seconds to notice she was screaming. Tears streamed down her face. Distantly, she registered Sabrina and Vince arguing, then Sabrina calling for her team to resume the ritual. It didn't matter that Jason was dead; they only needed his blood.

The entire building shuddered, and the air filled with a tremendous droning.

Shouts rose up around Ayana. Heavy boots pounded across the floor. She pushed herself up into a sitting position—and froze.

Another consciousness slithered against her own and coiled its tendrils around her soul. Her mind burst open. Visions flashed before her eyes: her blood flowing out of her veins like great rivers into the vast universe. Her essence twined together with its cosmic threads and sank into the fabric of reality itself. Comets peppered her body like the soft drizzle of rain. Ahead, Jason burned, brighter than anything else in the sky. The very substance of him exploded with supernovas, and light poured from his eyes. Power emanated from every pore.

He turned his gaze upon their world.

Vesuvius erupted. Ash and fire swallowed a city whole.

Drought choked the land, bringing famine. Skeletal livestock keeled over while crops withered and died.

Plague. Rats swarmed filthy streets. Boils burst open

fragile skin and wept sickening pus.

Wars ravaged populations. Civilizations fell. Stone wore away beneath the winds of time. Artifacts gleaming with unnatural light disappeared into darkness, removed from collective human memory for thousands of years. A crescent-shaped dagger turned up one day in the Museum of London. A young monk saw God in his dreams and wrote down his revelations, until his brothers found him devouring live worms in the dead of night. All exorcisms on him failed.

All exorcisms on him failed.

All exorcisms—

Ayana snapped back to reality. Phoebe had resumed the ritual, her chanting punctuated by gunshots and the occasional, bloodcurdling scream from outside. Next to her, Sabrina fidgeted, casting frequent glances at the front door. The droning continued, unabated.

A ravenous hunger clawed at Ayana's stomach, demanding sacrifice. She rose to her feet. The black knife gleamed a few feet away, abandoned and forgotten. Walking over, she picked it up with her bound hands. The handle fit in her palm like it belonged there. Her blood surged through her veins, seeking release. In her mind's eye, a youthful man pointed the same knife at his exposed chest, his face lifted to the sky in sublime ecstasy.

"Willing flesh," she murmured. Her heart sang between her ribs. "The Key." She looked at her husband, who groaned and shifted where he lay face-down on the floor. Once more, she saw the world burning beneath his gaze. "The Vessel."

Turning, she spotted Derek and Tim nearby. The former sat on a folding chair, looking dazed as the latter fussed over him. A moment later, Tim walked away with a handful of bloody tissues, leaving Derek alone.

Ayana saw her chance.

Derek noticed her at the last moment of her approach. He raised his head. Countless hours of studying medicine helped her pinpoint the carotid artery in his throat right away. It pulsed, beckoning.

"Wait, you can't—" he said.

"Ayana, stop! What are you doing?" Sabrina shouted, her voice a weak hum against the roar of the Abyssal King.

The ebony blade slid into Derek's neck, severing the artery. When Ayana yanked it back out, blood spewed forth in steady bursts. He clutched at the wound, but it didn't matter.

Sabrina rushed over, snatching at Ayana's wrist. Ayana lashed out with the dagger, slicing the other woman's hand and drawing blood. A cry of pain ripped from Sabrina's lips. She clutched the wrist of her injured hand and backed away, her eyes trained on the blade coated in crimson.

"You think this will stop the ritual?" she demanded, though her eyes were wide and her voice shook. "We have everything we need! We *will* stop the Abyssal King, no matter what you do!"

Ayana said nothing as she stepped sideways around Jason's body, the knife extended to keep Sabrina at bay. He was still alive, but not for long. Ayana had only a few minutes.

"You're just one woman!" Sabrina shouted. She matched Ayana's steps as they circled each other. Phoebe was just outside arm's reach, still reading from the book and chanting. "What can you do against us? Against years of scholarship and research? Against our funding and firepower? Nothing! You don't even have your precious husband anymore!"

As if in defiance, Jason tried pushing himself up with his good arm but collapsed again, screaming in agony. Though Ayana's chest tightened at the sound, she made no move to help him. She had a mission to accomplish; she couldn't afford distractions. Whipping around, she plunged the dagger into Phoebe's neck. Both Phoebe and Sabrina shrieked; the book tumbled from the former's hands. Ayana pulled out the blade and shoved Phoebe away. Sabrina scrambled for the professor while Ayana dove for the tome.

Sabrina pressed her palm against Phoebe's throat in a desperate attempt to staunch the bleeding. Wild-eyed, she shot Ayana an incredulous, terrified look. "You've lost your fucking mind!"

Ayana mirrored the cool expression Sabrina had worn earlier. "It doesn't matter what I tell you. For all your talk about the true nature of the universe, you'll never understand something you fear."

The warehouse shuddered again. Dust and small debris from the ceiling rained down upon the women.

"Just... just hand over the book, Ayana! Please! We can still save the world!"

"That comment just proves my point." Ayana moved to stand over Jason. "Goodbye, Sabrina."

Kneeling beside her husband, she put *Liber Devorationis* and the black knife on the floor and helped him roll onto his back. No exit wounds. The bullets were still inside him. Hurrying, she placed the book on his chest and pressed his hand against the cover. His arm was so heavy, like dead weight. She leaned in close and held his gaze.

"Jason, listen to me," she said over the beautiful droning, the gunfire, and the shouts from outside. Everything was louder; someone had opened the warehouse doors. "Whatever happens next, you have to say yes. If you want us to win, you have to say yes. Do you understand?"

He stared at her for several long seconds, his shallow breaths filling the space between them, then gave the slightest nod of his head.

Ayana let out the breath she was holding and sat up. Wrapping both hands around the handle of the knife, she pointed its blade at her own chest.

The boom of a single gunshot rocked the air like thunder. She lurched forward, her midsection burning with the most agonizing pain she'd ever felt. Tears pricked her eyes again. Warm blood seeped out of the bullet hole in her abdomen, soaking her blouse.

"Vince!" Sabrina's voice. So far away, a lifetime away. "Vince, stop shooting people for a goddamn minute and help me with Phoebe!"

"You can't save her, you fool!" he shouted back. "We need to get out of here before we all die!"

Ayana swayed as the strength drained from her body, but she refused to release the knife she still held aloft. If she dropped it, everything was lost. Gritting her teeth, she rammed the blade into her heart.

The warehouse's roof exploded, shredding into a million ribbons. Darkness descended, consuming brick and glass and iron alike. Malevolence radiated off its formlessness, sending the research team's sole survivor running for the door. Shoving his handgun under his coat, Vince rushed to Sabrina's side and grabbed her arm to haul her out. Ayana watched from high above as her own body collapsed onto Jason's, her blood spilling onto *Liber Devorationis* and siphoning into its hungry pages.

In a blink, she was no longer in Grosmont. Lancing was far away, a microscopic speck on the grain of dust called Earth. Stardust swirled all around her, while in the distance, clouds of gas shone with all the colors of the spectrum. She stared for several seconds before realizing she was seeing ultraviolet and infrared, as well as colors without names.

The universe shifted. Her consciousness hurtled through time and space. An explosion of light and matter sent galaxies blasting past her. Nearby, a planet formed, its surface erupting with tremendous violence until the land settled. Water gathered. Life emerged. Stars died before her eyes. They collapsed into inescapable, hungering voids, consuming everything in their paths. The sudden urge to look into their depths seized her. Reaching out, she wrapped her hands around the rim of the nearest one. Her fingers, blazing with light, warped and twisted, but she felt no pain, no fear.

Smiling, she plunged into the yawning expanse. Both the blackness and the ring of light around it contorted, transforming from a perfect circle into an oval. The light split away and soared above her, revealing bands of stars within its composition. In the distance, the chain of galaxies making up the universe bent into an arc. The deeper she dove, the more the fiery halo spun around her, deforming and bending and separating and encircling and merging together again. Meanwhile, the void rose up on all sides, elongating. Ahead of her, the universe dwindled into a thin strip of stars at the farthest edge of her vision. It dispersed as the bands of light vanished, leaving her in total darkness.

Chapter Thirty-Eight

Jason floated in nothing for an eternity. In and out of his consciousness slipped hazy images, faint recollections of a life lived a millennia ago.

A childhood of isolation and otherness. The steaming, stinking innards of the rats he'd captured and dissected with a stolen knife. His mother's screams when she found the mutilated corpse of Connor's dead cat.

A schoolyard fight. The ache of broken ribs and a black eye paled in comparison to the humiliation of defeat. The first taste of murderous intent.

A doctor in a white coat. The diagnosis, antisocial personality disorder. His parents, fighting over the cost of treatments—and whether he was even human. His mother, crying. His father, drowning in drink. His brother, begging the other kids to believe Jason was normal.

Their looks of shame, guilt, and revulsion.

Ayana's gentle smile bloomed in the darkness, her eyes alight with quiet joy. He stirred at the memory of her laughter and wit, of the velvet softness of her skin and the warmth of her body. She was his drug, drawing him to her again and again like the gravity of a star.

He had to return to her.

Coming back into his awareness, Jason struggled for control over the vast and oppressive blackness. At first, nothing happened. Then the center of the universe materialized before him. Brilliant white light wreathed a colossal form crafted from its absence. Debris swirled around it and disintegrated into its body. From the figure emanated a plethora of new scents, yet he knew them all by name. Hydrogen. Helium. Silicone. When the entity moved, every atom shifted to realign itself with its creator.

The figure reached for him. In the face of its approach, his soul vibrated.

A question hung in the air, asked without words. His mind raced to interpret the sensation. Complex concepts pulsed along an invisible thread connecting him to the figure. Some were recognizable, like hate, anger, and lust. Others were foreign, though he knew their names: fear, anxiety, loneliness. Others still were too complicated, encompassing ideas beyond the bounds of his human existence. All these he cast aside until one remained, its essence distilled into words he could comprehend.

Kinship. Symbiosis. Power.

Jason thought of Ayana.

He raised his head and looked straight into the waiting void. Though he did not open his mouth, his answer flowed out from him, fierce with conviction:

"I accept."

Tendrils of darkness snaked out from the center of the universe and pierced his body. Every nerve burned with the fire of a thousand suns, ripping a tortured scream from his throat.

His eyes snapped open.

The sky above him blazed—not with skyglow from light pollution, but with the full intensity of a billion stars circling each other in the farthest reaches of space. They bathed the world with their illumination. Every small detail stood out to him with crystal clarity, from the grain pattern of the wooden strike dummies in the corner to the scales on the wings of moths fluttering around the lights outside the warehouse.

He took a deep breath and tasted dozens of potent smells, both familiar and strange. Rich iron from the pool of blood at his feet. Rot from the dumpster behind the fish market's main building. The salty brine of seawater and the acidity of sulfur dioxide in the air. And humans. So many humans, with their sweat and perfumes and recent meals amalgamating into distinct combinations. Cars roared in his hearing as they zoomed along the distant streets of Grosmont. He picked up the chatter of low, private conversation along the main boulevard, each word clear as if spoken directly into his ears. A cat leaped from one rooftop to the next; he heard the whisper of its landing. His brain filtered through all these sensations, noting them, then regulating them to the background of his awareness.

And beneath it all lurked a second consciousness, vaster than him by every measure and entwined with his.

Jason reeled in his perception to his immediate surroundings. The doors of the warehouse stood wide open, Vince and Sabrina upon its threshold. They stared at him with slack jaws and wide eyes. Fear rolled off them in waves. Three security guards wearing the logo of St. Julian's Foundation rushed in around them, guns clutched in white-knuckled hands, their pale faces blood-splattered and sweat-drenched. Jason contemplated them, then looked down. Ayana's lifeless body lay on its side at his feet, the dagger still protruding from her chest.

"What the fuck is that thing?" a security guard demanded. "Where'd the Abyssal King go?"

"Doesn't matter!" said another. "Kill it!"

Bullets flew through the air at Jason. Before they reached him, the halo of light around him brightened, incinerating them. They dropped to the floor as molten balls of lead, still glowing bright red with residual heat.

"You *dared* put your hands on *my wife*," he said, his voice echoing with an alien reverberation.

The confusion on the guards' faces lasted for only a heartbeat. The miasma of darkness surrounding Jason flared and raced toward them. A blade of pure void sliced through them, removing the tops of their heads. Their corpses fell forward, pink brain matter oozing from the open cavities of their skulls.

Vince and Sabrina had already fled. Jason strolled to the front of the warehouse. As he neared, the doors warped and crumpled on their hinges before disintegrating into their base atoms. The same happened to the bricks surrounding them until a jagged hole formed in the wall. Emerging from the building, he picked out a pair of tail lights and the rumble of an engine as Vince's car sped through the gate. Sabrina's distinct fear-perfume wafted from the passenger's seat.

With a mere thought, Jason tore a hole between the threads of reality and stepped through. His perception shifted to permeate the entire city. He was every street and building, every service tunnel and security camera. He rode the current of every power line and Internet cable. From his vantage point, he watched Vince's car travel north from Grosmont.

The pair were heading toward Bracknell. To St. Julian's Foundation.

As Jason swept his consciousness through the city, following the vehicle, he paused in Stagsden Commons. The bright lights in the police station illuminated cops as they bustled to and fro, processing all the criminals they'd arrested that day. Nonstop conversation, the bitter taste of black coffee, and the oily smell of takeout assaulted his senses. He unfolded the building's secrets and saw the layout was identical to the one in Lerwick Square. The front lobby. The interrogation rooms. The holding cell with Nick Monahan sitting inside, surrounded by his loyal soldiers.

Jason reformed himself before the main entrance of the police station and peeled away the doors without lifting a finger. A young officer behind the bulletproof glass of the front desk shouted and scrambled for the alarm. Shrill noise blared all around Jason, but his mind reduced it to a murmur. The cop rushed out from behind the barrier with his gun drawn. He fired. The bullets disintegrated in midair, mere seconds before his skin boiled and sloughed off. Spots of void bloomed across his face and neck, silencing him before he could scream again. He was dead before he hit the floor.

The walk through the rest of the police station was more of the same. Cops rushed at Jason, then fell, reduced to corpses. Eventually, he reached the holding cell. The Monahans had heard the commotion; he registered their terror long before they came into view, their bodies pressed flat against the far walls of their cage to escape his reach. Nick stood between them and danger, his shirt soaked with fresh sweat. Jason regarded the group for a moment, then turned his attention to the locked door. The steel shattered, siphoning into him and leaving a man-sized hole in the bars.

He fixed his gaze upon Nick, who cringed but stood his ground in front of his men. "You should not encounter any resistance on the way out," Jason said.

"Take their weapons if you need, and their cars."

The confusion cleared from Nick's face. "Jason? Is that you?"

"The man you knew is no more."

He took a step forward. "It *is* you! What... what the fuck happened?"

"What matters is what *will* happen. You and your family should leave Lancing."

"Wait, what? Why? What's going to happen?"

Jason searched for the words Nick would understand. "The end has come. The city will not survive it," he said at length. "Consider this warning the payment for all your help these past few days."

As he turned to go, Nick rushed through the hole in the cell. "Wait! What about your wife? Don't you care about her? Won't she die, too, if Lancing is destroyed?"

Jason did not need to look back to see the other man's bewildered expression. "Worry about yourself. This is our final goodbye, Nick. If we meet again, it will not be as allies."

• • • • • • • • • • •

Gasoline gushed out of Vince's empty, parked car as Jason crushed it with his mind. Looking up from the ruin, he searched the building in front of him, observing every floor, every room, and every crack in its walls. He found Vince and Sabrina on the second floor, rushing around a private library, throwing books and other small items into a suitcase. The fourth floor, however, contained something even more curious.

He warped there, materializing in front of a long desk and the nurse sitting behind it. She shrieked and tumbled backward off her chair. Ignoring her, he stepped into the nearest room and drew up alongside the bed. A man in his forties lay beneath thin, white blankets. Dozens of green eyes peered at Jason before widening in recognition. A gush of air escaped the mouth-wound in the man's chest.

"The Vessel," he sobbed, his expression a mix of terror and ecstasy. "Please, mercy. I wasn't worthy."

Jason held his hand over the man's body. His soft weeping pitched into a tortured wail, only to cut off when he burst into stardust. The cloud of shimmering colors spiraled into Jason as he inhaled, warming him with the heat of the universe. It spread from his chest to every part of his body, while the light encircling him shone with even greater brilliance.

He left the room and proceeded through the floor, reabsorbing every soul that belonged to him, realigning their cosmic signatures to his own.

When he finished, he turned his attention back to Vince and Sabrina. They stood outside the main entrance of St. Julian's Foundation, staring at the remnants of the former's car. The woman gripped the long handle of the suitcase in one hand.

"Any other brilliant ideas?" Vince asked, his words echoing through space to reach Jason.

"There's a garage at the corner where we keep the company cars," Sabrina said. "The keys are in the security office. I have badge access, and we can leave through a side exit that's closer to the garage, too."

They hurried back inside and down a corridor. Jason observed them as they swiped into a room with a computer against one wall and a row of lockers against another. Sabrina opened a box mounted on the first wall and grabbed a key from inside it. She handed it to Vince as they left the room.

Jason stepped out of a tear in reality, barring their way.

"Monster!" Sabrina cried. She withdrew an agate talisman from her coat and brandished it at him. "Vessel of the Hungering One, begone!"

A tendril of darkness snaked across the floor toward her and sliced off her hand at the wrist. Screaming, her face contorting with horror, she staggered against the wall and clutched at the stump of her arm as it spewed blood. Vince swore, turned, and fled, leaving the woman and the suitcase behind.

Her howls of agony filled the hall. As darkness encircled her, her thrashing grew more frantic. Angry, red blotches bloomed across her face and neck, swelling and blistering as they spread. She clawed at her clothes, ripping the fabric until her fingernails tore through her skin. Yellowish pus oozed from the open wounds. Her flesh blackened, then peeled away in curling chunks, and still she shredded herself bloody. Finally, her body burst at the seams, muscle and sinew and bone ribboning out in all directions, into the maw of the waiting void.

The darkness retreated. Nothing of Sabrina Kopanski remained.

Jason left for the garage. He materialized next to a row of company cars as Vince rushed for them, forcing the older man to skid to a stop. Vince's eyes darted around the area. He spotted a green sedan at the far corner of the floor and ran for it. Without warning, blades of darkness erupted from the asphalt beneath him. One slashed the outside of his thigh as he danced aside. The tendrils shot toward the car, skewering its tires before he could reach it.

Panting, he spun around, wobbled, and fell hard on his knees. Blood darkened the leg of his trousers around the wound. Jason walked over, taking his time. As he neared, Vince flinched away, teeth bared, wild-eyed. He struggled to his feet and limped toward the low outer wall of the garage. Grasping the stone, he peered over the edge of it. The sidewalk lay far below, five floors of open air between them.

He turned around as Jason's hand shot out. He grabbed Vince's collar with human fingers, bare of light or transformation. The aurora around him lifted away to reveal his human face. Vince stared, his mouth opening and closing several times before words finally tumbled out.

"But I shot you! You should be dead!"

Jason said nothing. He shoved Vince against the wall, wrapping both hands around the other man's neck, and squeezed.

Vince's eyes went as wide as they could go, almost popping from their sockets. Frantic fists pummeled Jason's arms, shoulders, and face, while Vince's good leg kicked Jason's lower half. Gritting his teeth against the assault, Jason bore down harder. Minutes passed. Vince's efforts weakened and faltered. He resorted to clawing at Jason's wrists and jerking his head from side to side—both fruitless endeavors. Blood vessels burst in his left eye while dark liquid trickled from his nose.

At last, Jason felt bone crack between his hands. Vince gurgled and gasped. His eyes rolled back into his skull and his body went limp.

Jason tossed the broken carcass of his prey aside. As cold starlight rippled around him, he cast a final glance at Vince's terror-stricken face and smiled.

Chapter Thirty-Nine

The gentle sensation of the breeze against her bare skin stirred Ayana from her slumber. She opened her eyes to the night sky above her and the cold, hard floor of the warehouse at her back. Looking down, she discovered all her clothing and the zip tie around her wrists were gone. Instead, her arms lay relaxed at her sides. The dagger no longer protruded from her chest, either, but rested in the palm of her right hand. She tried to sit up, but all she managed was the twitch of a finger.

"I wouldn't do that yet if I were you," said another woman's voice, a familiar one. "Your body's still in the process of reforming itself. You should lay still until it's finished."

Ayana turned her head to the left. A young woman with long brown hair and glasses crouched a couple of feet away. She wore a purple cardigan sweater and a floor-length skirt, while a gold pendant hung around her neck.

"I know you," said Ayana, recalling dark tendrils and glowing eyes. "You're the Librarian."

"That's right."

"My body is reforming?"

The Librarian pointed to a distant spot to Ayana's right. "See for yourself."

She looked. Five mutilated corpses lay several yards away, their blood and viscera unraveling in long streams and wriggling toward her like enormous, gruesome earthworms. When the first one reached her, it crawled up her side and slid into the jagged exit wound in her abdomen. Another one inched across her chest to the stab wound through her heart. Her organs itched as they accepted the gift of replacement tissue.

"Fascinating," Ayana murmured. "How am I alive?"

"Our King wills it." The Librarian strolled over to the open space in the middle of the warehouse. She examined the sigil on the floor with pursed lips, her hands clasped behind her back. "This ritual circle never would've worked."

"Would *anything* have worked?"

"Yes, but only to delay the inevitable. There are secret formulas and signs that can seal up the rifts between planes, but that knowledge comes at great cost. Fortunately, the meddlesome ants in St. Julian's only know some minor wards—strong enough to stop servants like me, but nowhere near enough to contain our King. And anyway, new rifts open up all the time."

"So then the circle, the artifacts, the chanting...?"

"A truly awful misinterpretation of the text." The Librarian walked back, stepping around the trails of gore feeding into Ayana's body, and picked up *Liber Devorationis*. "We scholars of the Nisaba Society maintain strict standards of accuracy in our publications. It's not our fault—nor the faults of those who first penned the writings—if someone can't manage to open themselves up to the universe. You understand, don't you, sister?" She smiled as if divulging a secret.

"Sister?"

"Oh yes. You've been chosen to join the ranks of those who serve the Lord of Hungering Skies. Your role among us is quite unique, too: Bride of the Cosmos, the most powerful and esteemed of us all, meant to usher in the new age of this world by molding it according to His will. If I were still human, I'd be envious."

Ayana closed her eyes. Chosen. Yes. She belonged at the side of her King. A delightful warmth spread through her chest at the thought.

"You know," the Librarian said, "the Nisaba Society would benefit a great deal from your assistance. Once you've gotten accustomed to your new form and all your powers, of course. Humans have received so many revelations of the universe's truth, but much of it is still uncatalogued. The Society's job is to collect and safeguard it all, but there are so few of us."

"Of course. I'll reach out to you as soon as I can," Ayana said, opening her eyes.

"There's no rush. Lancing's a large city, and its transformation into His seat of power will take some time. I'll be at the Library when you're ready to meet. Oh, and I'll take this, too."

She plucked the knife from Ayana's fingers. Cradling both blade and book against her chest, she disappeared in a flash of coruscating light, leaving Ayana alone in the warehouse. The last of the blood and entrails disappeared into her body, which promptly stitched itself together with nary a scar. Sitting up, she noticed a flash of black as countless small, pulsating holes opened across her abdomen. In the blink of an eye, they closed again, leaving no sign of their passing.

In the distance, voices called her name.

Two sets of frantic footsteps drew her attention to the gaping hole in the front wall of the building. Izzy and Trey paused within it, both of them panting hard and holding powerful LED flashlights. They took in the grisly scene, from the eviscerated bodies to the occult ritual circle on the floor.

"Holy fucking shit," Izzy breathed, her face taking on a greenish tinge. "I'm gonna be sick."

The beam of Trey's flashlight fell upon Ayana. "Oh my God," he said, shoving the device into Izzy's hands and tearing off his red parka. "Ayana, are you okay?"

The pair picked their way across the filthy floor to reach Ayana's side. Without looking at her, he wrapped his coat around her shoulders to cover her nakedness, then helped her to her feet.

"Thank you. I'm okay," she said. Though the parka was unnecessary—the February chill was pleasant on her skin—she clutched it closed around her in case more black holes manifested on her body. "What're you two doing here?"

"I heard something going on with you before our call ended earlier. It sounded pretty suspicious, so when you finally hung up, I called Trey for help," Izzy said. "Thankfully your phone was still on so I could trace it, but it took us a while to get here."

"There are a ton of cops out on the streets tonight," Trey said. "When Izzy saw where you'd stopped, we thought it'd be easier to walk part of the way than hire a taxi."

"We, uh, we had to climb the fence to avoid the gate. Surprisingly not as easy as it looks in movies."

Ayana's first instinct was to scold them, but she suppressed the urge and smiled.

Izzy handed back Trey's flashlight and pointed hers around the warehouse, sweeping the beam across the surrounding destruction. "What happened here?"

"It's a long story," Ayana said with a laugh. "I'm not sure you'd believe me. But we don't have to worry about St. Julian's anymore."

Both of Trey's eyebrows shot up into his forehead. "What's that supposed to mean?"

"Sabrina's dead." The truth echoed back to Ayana across the threads of blood and essence connecting her to the universe. "All the people on Jason's kill list are dead."

"What? How?"

"Never mind how. Where's Jason now?" Izzy cut in. "Last I saw on the news, the police arrested him and Nick at the car crash. That's why the cops are swarming the streets."

Tilting her head back, Ayana unfocused her gaze to search for her husband's unmistakable signature. Beyond their immediate area, the city of Lancing loomed within a dark, obscuring fog. But within that haze burned a brilliant light, an aurora of splendor and triumph. It hurtled toward her like a thunderbolt, growing bigger and brighter within her consciousness.

Returning to her physical body, she smiled at her companions. "He's on his way."

A beautiful melody filled the air—the song of the universe. Though Trey and Izzy winced and clamped their hands over their ears, a broad smile spread across Ayana's face. Glorious hunger filled her. Along one wall of the warehouse, reality split open, peeling back to reveal the nothingness of the void. Jason emerged from it in all his monstrous perfection. A dozen eyes of blazing starlight pierced her soul.

Izzy and Trey screamed. The latter reached out long arms to herd the women behind him, though he himself started hyperventilating, and sweat beaded on his brow.

Ayana placed a hand on his shoulder. "It's all right."

Though he frowned at her, he lowered his arms.

Withdrawing her hand, she stepped out from behind him and faced her husband. Jason stood several feet away, far enough that his mere presence would not harm them.

"They were worried about me," she said to him, more for their benefit than his. He already knew.

He fixed the two humans with his unreadable gaze. "You two have done well," he said. His thundering voice surrounded them, coming from everywhere at once.

Izzy blinked as recognition dawned on her face. Trey caught on a split-second afterward. "Jason?" they asked in unison.

"Leave the city," he said. "Take your loved ones and go. You have until dawn."

"What are you talking about?" Izzy asked. "Ayana, what does he mean?"

"Exactly what he said," Ayana replied. "I suggest you take him seriously. The city won't be the same for much longer."

"But where are we supposed to go?"

Given enough time, nowhere was safe, but she did not say that. "Anywhere."

Trey and Izzy exchanged a confused look. "Then come with Cass and me," the latter said to Ayana. "We'll find clothes for you and grab your stuff from the hotel, then head out. Cass has a car. We can go up north to Canada or south to... I don't know, wherever. It'll be a road trip."

"That's kind of you, Izzy, but I'm not going anywhere. Lancing is my home, and I belong here." Ayana handed Trey's parka back to him. "Go. You need this more than I do. I'll find my own clothes."

"Are you sure?" he asked, averting his gaze.

"I've never been more certain of anything in my life."

Izzy glanced at Jason, shuddered, then met Ayana's gaze and held it for a long moment. Though she looked like she wanted to say more, she just nodded. "Okay. Take care, Ayana."

When they were alone at last, Ayana turned to Jason. He lifted a hand and beckoned for her. She walked over until she stood before him, her fingers trailing along his halo of scintillating light. She watched with rapturous wonder as her hand warped and twisted, then reformed, unharmed, once it passed through the luminous veil. Instead of pain, she felt only a tingling warmth where the light touched.

But of course, that was expected. She was the Bride of the Cosmos.

She stepped through his aurora of light. The heat of a thousand suns enveloped her like an ocean wave, dragging her into him. His darkness caressed her body. The endless abyss stretched before her. She teetered on the brink of it, her heart full of delirious joy at the privilege of piercing its unfathomable expanse. Tears pricked her eyes.

"I love you, husband," she murmured.

"I love you too, wife," he said.

The resonance of the universe sang through her

blood and set her skin ablaze with longing. Cupping his face with both hands, she sought the place where his mouth should've been, her lips parted for a passionate kiss. Thick, wet warmth brushed against her tongue, tasting like iron and gold. His hands caressed her—so many hands, on her legs, her hips, and the small of her back. Teeth scraped along the vulnerable flesh of her throat and thighs at the same time. She arched into the touch as insatiable hunger swelled within her. Opening her eyes, she gasped. A dazzling kaleidoscope of color undulated back and forth around her in mesmerizing whorls.

A presence entered her, transcendent and supreme. Her eyes fluttered closed again at the explosion of euphoria. It rolled through her as heat, as light, suffusing every part of her. Eons passed in that state of sublime bliss, the sensation intensifying to exultant heights as the touch of the infinite roamed over her body. She drank of divine ambrosia. Stars formed and expanded and died within her, a detonation of energy and life. The center of the universe split open, and she gazed upon its true face.

THE END

Acknowledgements

This book was both a labor of love and an absolute shot in the dark. It would not have been possible without the following amazing people:

My husband Dan Shilling, who encouraged me at every step of the way, brainstormed ideas with me, and boasted about my project to everyone who would listen. Without him, an eldritch god would not have a name.

Brendan Ha, who imagined the world that inspired my own. His boundless creativity and dedication to his craft are truly aspirational.

Elizabeth Tillery and Brooke Kelly, whose creative expressions inspired the characters Ayana and Connor.

My online writing group, CWSG. They lifted me up during difficult periods of this journey, taught me important lessons on writing and being a human who writes, and provided valuable feedback and ideas to make the story the best it could be.

T. D. González, who came up with the idea for the cover.

My alpha and beta readers: Eliwood S. Gheist, T. D. González, Emily, Austin, M. K. Lollar, Nip, Megan Schlichting, Doug Bailey, Brooke Kelly, Hiria Dunning, Jae Koyanagi, and Kelsey Ann. They read the rougher versions of the story and saw the potential nestled in its lines.

The Bluesky crowd. You're all hilarious.

And all my friends and family who cheered me on and believed in me.

A. M. Shilling is an avid storyteller and artist interested in morally questionable people, their terrible circumstances, and how they manage to love one another despite it all. When she's not contemplating her favorite villains like a sommelier appreciating fine wine, she enjoys roleplaying games and watching cooking shows with her husband.

Visit her website at amshilling.com.

www.ingramcontent.com/pod-product-compliance
Lightning Source LLC
LaVergne TN
LVHW091658070526
838199LV00050B/2200